GARDEN OF THORNS AND LIGHT

Shylah Addante

Month9Books

Trade Paperback ISBN: 978-1-951710-36-1
ePub ISBN: 978-1-951710-43-9
Mobipocket ISBN: 978-1-951710-44-6

Published by Month9Books, Raleigh, NC 27609
Cover by Parker Book Design

Month9Books

For David, Hazel, and Holly who fill my world with light and magic.

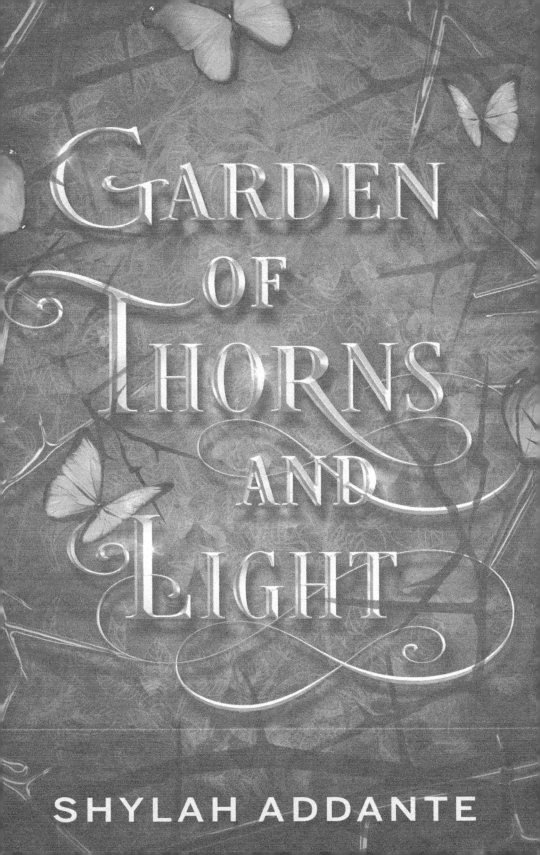

Garden of Thorns and Light

Shylah Addante

M y bedroom is almost completely dark, the only source of light a sliver
of moonbeam shining through the small opening where the curtains
meet. It casts the normally vibrant colors of the room into varying shades of
gray. It's also uncharacteristically quiet for a summer night on the outskirts
of Philadelphia. The absence of passing cars and distant sirens is somehow
made more conspicuous by the periodic chirp of a lone cricket and the soft
whisper of the ceiling fan.

Then the music box begins to play.

The song is slow and disjointed at first, rust-covered and tinny from years
of disuse. As the gears within find a rhythm, a melody emerges, soft and sad
against the otherwise silent night. It's a tune that is somehow both foreign
and familiar—some kind of long-forgotten lullaby that evades my attempts
to pin it to a specific memory. The only things that come to mind are hazy
impressions: the warmth of sun on skin, the earthy scent of deep woods, the
sharp sweetness of sap. And permeating all of them, the color green.

The images are so elusive, so distractingly tantalizing, that it takes a few
moments for me to realize that something is very, very wrong.

The box, a birthday gift from my mom, didn't work, hadn't worked, in years. It was a family heirloom, a beautiful but broken antique that had been rendered useless when the winding key was lost years and years ago. She had made all of that clear earlier, when she placed it on my nightstand, even going so far as to show me the little octagonal hole in the side of the box where a key *would* have gone, if there had been one.

The box couldn't work, but that isn't stopping it from playing now.

"*Amethyst,*" a voice whispers in the dark, seeming so close that I can almost feel a breath tickle my ear.

I react as any sensible six-year-old would when faced with an inexplicable situation in the dead of night and pull the blankets up over my head. I call out for my mom, but my words come out in a hoarse croak, held hostage by the fear beginning to clutch tightly around my chest and throat. I take a breath and try again. While the new sound that comes out is little more than a squeak, it must resonate with whatever is in the room, because the music stops.

I wait, breath held, listening hard for any sign of movement, but there is nothing except for the soft swish of the fan. Even the cricket has gone silent. A lamp sits on the nightstand only a foot away from where I lie huddled underneath my *Powerpuff Girls* comforter. It's a risky move to reach out beyond the safety of my sheets, but if movies and TV have taught me anything, it's that things that dwell in the dark lose their power when the lights come on. I take another breath to steady myself before throwing the blanket off my head and reaching for the lamp, but before I can flip the switch, the room illuminates on its own.

Dozens of little lights brighten my bedroom, floating lazily in the space above my bed. At first, I think they're fireflies, but they're brighter than any I've ever seen before, tiny white lights that glow like little stars, and as far as I can tell, there are no insects attached to them. I follow one as it drifts down next to me and lands on the nightstand. It bobs its way to where the music box sits and enters the keyhole. As soon as the light disappears into the tiny cherry box, the music begins to play again.

As if cued by the song, the other lights start to dance, twirling with each other as they circle the room. This can't be real. I must have been transported into another world, my bedroom carried off like Dorothy's house and dropped into some other place. Magic like this doesn't exist on Earth, and certainly not in Philadelphia. All of a sudden, it's not enough for me to sit back and watch the lights. I have the urge to touch them, to dance with them, to be a part of them.

I stand on my bed, wobbling slightly as the mattress sinks beneath my feet, and reach out for the nearest floating light. But as my fingers are about to make contact, it bobs away, just far enough to be out of my reach. I take a step forward, my hand still grasping at air, but the light evades me for a second time. And then a third. Again and again, until I find myself leaning over the foot of the bed, one hand clutching a wooden post for balance while the other stretches out toward the light.

I can feel its warmth on the tips of my fingers when the music box's song ends. Distracted by the sudden silence, I miss my chance, and the light dances away. It joins the others as they form into a soundless procession toward the open window and slide, one by one, through the space between the curtains.

"Wait!" There's desperation in my voice as the last light disappears through the gap. I jump out of bed, cross the room, and stick my head out of the open window.

The backyard looks like a wonderland with the dozens of lights swirling in midair toward where our lawn meets the edge of the woods. I watch them for a moment, transfixed, before pulling one leg up onto the windowsill. But before I let myself drop onto the grass on the other side, I look back at my bedroom door and think of my parents sleeping in the room down the hall.

A heavy ball of guilt settles in my stomach, and I can feel it weighing me down, anchoring me to my bedroom floor. I swallow hard, trying to bury the feeling and turn away from the door. As soon as my eyes find the lights again, now dancing at the very edge of the tree line, the invisible chain tying me to the room breaks, and I push myself out into the cool night air.

The grass is cold and slick with dew. Halfway to the woods, I slip and fall on my backside, coloring my pajama bottoms brown and green. But there's no time to worry about what my mom might say about the grass stains in the morning. With each step I take, the lights move farther and farther beyond the trees, some fading away completely, concealed by dark branches.

If I hesitate now, they might all disappear.

By the time I reach the edge of the woods, only one light remains. It hovers at eye level, just inside the first line of trees, and its brightness seems to make the forest behind it even darker in contrast. I shuffle my feet as close as I can to the place where the grass meets the dense forest, my toes clinging to the very edge of the lawn, and reach out for the light.

It moves away.

Without moving my feet into the woods, I lean forward, stretching out my arm and my fingers as far as I can, but it's not enough. I lean so far that my legs shake, and I can feel myself losing my balance, but my fingers are just an inch away and closing. My face is hard with concentration as I push farther, with only centimeters to go now. I can feel the heat of the light, like a tiny sun on my skin, millimeters away.

But then, from the darkness, something cold closes around my wrist.

There is a moment when the light illuminates the scene fully, and I can see a pale hand covered in large green thorns. The scream that escapes from my mouth is so high-pitched that I'm sure it can be heard for miles. My feet leave the grass as the hand pulls me into the forest, my body dragging against the muddy ground. In the distance, I think I hear someone—my mother, maybe—calling my name, but before I can respond, my head explodes with pain as it connects hard with a tree.

The world goes black, my shriek of terror echoing through the otherwise silent night.

Ten years later, it is the sound of my scream that wakes me up. My heart is pumping like I've just jumped off a treadmill, a feeling exacerbated by the trickle of sweat running down the back of my neck. I am still trying to shake my wrist free from the monster in the woods when I realize that my face is not resting on the dirt of the forest floor but against a hard wooden surface. I lift my head from the desk and see eighteen pairs of eyes belonging to the other students in seventh-period English all staring back at me.

"Is everything all right, Amethyst?"

Mrs. Cannel's voice, to anyone else, would sound unconcerned, but even though her tone is flat, and she doesn't stop flipping the pages of the notes in front of her, I know she's anxiously waiting for my signal. If I need to go, I itch my left arm. If I'm okay, I itch my right. It's a system we worked out after Mrs. Cannel's classroom became my place of refuge, a quiet room where I could hide out during the unstructured times of the day when targets emerge on the backs of all of us who find ourselves on the margins of high school society. So, instead of study halls or lunch, I spend my free time in Room 314, mostly just reading or doing homework. Or, sometimes, devising elaborate ways for Mrs. Cannel and me to communicate wordlessly when I have one of my nightmares in class.

I take stock of myself, and while my heart is still racing, I've stopped screaming—so that's a plus. I take one calming breath to make sure my lungs are still functioning and then lift my shaking left hand and scratch my right elbow. No one but Mrs. Cannel seems to notice. The rest of the class has broken into a dozen whispered conversations in the few-seconds' pause in the lesson. While I can't quite make out what they're saying over the pounding of the blood in my ears, I get the gist of it. They're the same words that have followed me for the last ten years.

Freak. Loser. Crazy.

Insults born from the rumors that started almost immediately after the almost-abduction. Stories spread at PTA meetings and playgrounds that I was "unbalanced" and "detached from reality" and "dangerous to other children." That was when I stopped getting invitations to birthday parties and sleepovers and started having appointments with the school psychologist and going to bed with my window nailed shut.

I look down into my hands and allow my hair to fall over my face, forming a shield. Whispers I can handle. All I have to do is wait. Wait until they get bored and move on to Hannah Snapps's acne or Jeff Vance's unibrow. Wait until someone else does something stupid to distract them. I learned that whispers only last as long as you're the most interesting thing in the room. I learned to wait, to stay silent, to disappear into the background. Sooner or later, something comes along to take the attention away.

"Mouths closed and eyes up front!" Mrs. Cannel's voice cuts through the conversation, leaving a heartbeat's silence in its wake. Then comes the sound of chairs scraping across the tiled floor. I brush my hair away tentatively and see that my classmates are once again copying down the notes Mrs. Cannel has written across the whiteboard. For a moment, I catch her gaze, and I give her a grateful half smile.

She nods a "you're welcome" back at me before returning to her lecture.

"Robert Frost is probably best known for the poem 'The Road Not

Taken,' which explores humanity's free will and our tendency to dwell on, and sometimes regret, the choices we make."

She underlines the name of the poem before flipping the switch of the ancient overhead projector. It whirs into life with a blast of heat that I can feel even in the back of the room, and the first stanza of the poem appears on the board.

> *Two roads diverged in a yellow wood,*
> *And sorry I could not travel both*
> *And be one traveler, long I stood*
> *And looked down one as far as I could*
> *To where it bent in the undergrowth*

"Before we get into the actual analysis of the poem, it's important to know a bit about Frost's early life, because, as we have seen with Dickinson, Plath, and even Cummings, poetry is extremely personal and flavored by the author's experiences."

She turns back to the board, her red marker squeaking against the white surface as a new series of bullet points takes shape.

"Robert Frost was a troubled child who, from a young age, claimed to hear voices when he was alone."

As soon as she says it, I know I'm in trouble. Anna Reynes, head of the varsity volleyball team, turns in her chair, and for a split second, our eyes meet.

"A phenomenon that, coupled with a less-than-supportive family, resulted in a childhood rife with anxiety and erratic behavior in school."

I look away, down onto my notebook, but I know it's too late. Anna is smiling. Not the toothy, apologetic smile that she gives to teachers when she's late for class. Nor the pouty-lipped simper that she'll use on whoever her boyfriend is this week. This is a special smile. The kind of smile a snake would wear before sinking its long, venom-tipped fangs into a mouse. A smile she reserves only for me.

"Though creativity is often born out of early trauma, it is—"

"Mrs. Cannel?" Anna's voice is high and sweet and full of danger. I pick up my pen and feign more note-taking, shrinking down into my seat. She might only be asking a question. She could still change her target. *Invisible,*

I think as I will myself to disappear from her line of sight, but it's too late.

"Are you saying that we should *encourage* people with psychotic tendencies? I mean, not everyone with delusions is going to be Robert Frost. Some of them wind up as *serial killers*."

Then *it* starts.

First, it's only a giggle from Anna's boyfriend, Marc, but like a contagious strain of the flu, as soon as it's airborne, it spreads. It leaps from person to person, great big guffaws from a burly football player and a semi-suppressed chuckle of relief from Hannah Snapps.

Whispers I can handle, but this—the laughter—it cuts through my shield. I can feel it, like a finely sharpened knife, slicing its way through my defenses until it finds its way to my heart. My face is warm again as, unbidden, tears form at the corners of my eyes. When I was little, I used to think that they would stop at the sight of tears. That they would feel so badly about making me cry that they would retreat and maybe even apologize. But I learned soon enough that hoping tears will quash laughter is like hoping jet fuel will extinguish fire.

Before anyone has the chance to see, I grab my notebook and backpack and walk out of the room as fast as I can without breaking into a sprint. Somewhere beyond the laughter, I hear Mrs. Cannel calling out for me, pleading with me to wait. It's too late, though. Just as I turn down another hallway adorned with a banner conratulating the Class of 2012, the first tears spill over and run hot down my cheeks.

I make my way to the science wing, which is mercifully quiet thanks to the end-of-year lab exams taking place. I pass by a room full of freshmen, each one either squinting into a microscope or bent over a Scantron sheet, meticulously coloring in bubbles with number-two pencils. None of them notice as I slip into the girls' bathroom across the hall.

As soon as the door closes behind me, more tears fall in earnest. I lean back against the metal frame and squeeze my eyes shut, trying to choke down the sobs punching their way out of my chest.

Reflexively, I bite down on my lip, a trick I learned from my father a long time ago as he drove me to the emergency room after a nasty spill on my bike. It was probably the best, and quite possibly the only useful, piece of advice he has ever given me: that focusing on pain you create helps to distract the mind from any pain inflicted on you.

It only takes a minute or so to calm down after that. As soon as I'm sure that the tears won't resurface, I walk over to the row of sinks on the wall opposite the windows to assess the damage.

A small sixteen-year-old girl stares back out of the mirror at me. Her wheat-colored hair falls in soft waves down past her shoulders, and her eyes are violet, the same shade of the gemstone for which she was named. In some other place with some other past, she would be pretty, the splotches of red on her cheeks and the swollen areas around her eyes left over from the crying jag notwithstanding.

But not here.

Here it wouldn't matter if I had the face of a supermodel and the body and paycheck to match. I'm damaged goods. Someone's old used car that crashed and got repaired. Sure, it looks fine, and maybe even runs okay, but you never know what's lurking under the hood, so you're better off not to take a chance on driving it.

Shaking my head, I look away from my reflection and turn on the water. While I wait for it to warm, I roll up the sleeves of my shirt. The skin underneath is covered in dozens of scars, some white with age while others are red, raw, and still healing.

Damaged goods, I think again.

Frowning, I run a finger over one of the older marks. It's an inch or so long, and the pale line of healed skin feels hard and out of place beneath my touch. I press down on it, and a spasm of pain shoots up my arm. When I look down to investigate, however, everything appears fine.

False alarm.

Sighing, I bend down over the sink and splash the water onto my face. It's still only lukewarm, but it feels good against my puffy skin. With my eyes still closed against the water, I reach out for the towel dispenser to the right of the sink. It takes a few seconds of blind grasping before I find the handle, crank out a long sheet of rough brown paper, and use it to wipe my face dry. Most of the water runs off the thin paper and down my arms, soaking the shirt sleeves that I had so carefully rolled up to protect.

Great.

I pull the sleeves back down over my scarred arms, the wet cloth cold and clingy against my skin. When I finally get my wrists covered, I try to wring some of the water out, but I only end up stretching out my cuffs so that I look like I'm wearing a soppy costume reject from the *Lord of the Rings* set.

All I need now is a pair of stupid pointy ears, I think, returning my gaze to the mirror.

The red has drained away from my cheeks but not from my eyes. Unless I want to walk the halls Sia-style, there's no way to hide that. I try to use my fingers to brush my hair over my face in a way that doesn't look dumb or obvious, and that's when I see it:

A thorn, jutting out from the soft area just above my wrist, long, green, and razor-sharp.

I almost feel a little guilty as I pinch the thorn between my left thumb and forefinger. The little guy isn't doing anything wrong, after all. Maybe he deserves to be left alone. But then my thumb slips on the thorn's smooth surface, and a sharp sting of pain surges through my hand as the point embeds itself deep into the pad of my thumb.

Yup. Okay, it's time for you to go, I think as I suck on the tip of my thumb in an attempt to stanch the bleeding.

This time, I bunch up the damp fabric of my shirt and wrap it around the thorn before I take it between my fingers again. I hold it as tightly as I dare and twist, wiggling it back and forth like a child trying to wrench free a loose tooth. It only takes a few seconds of work before there is a loud snap that coincides with fresh pain in my right wrist. I bite hard on my lip to hold the scream in, but I can't stop my eyes from watering as the throbbing radiates up my arm. At least I can comfort myself with the knowledge that it will only hurt for a few hours. After that, it will scab over and scar just like the rest of them have done for the last five months.

The day I found the first thorn, I panicked. I had been brushing my teeth, still in the tank top and pajama bottoms I wore to bed, when I looked in the mirror and saw a strange bump on the back of my elbow. At first, I thought it was a giant pimple, but when I squeezed it, I quickly realized that it was not even close to normal.

Instead of pus, something small and green emerged from beneath my skin. I knew from first sight what I *thought* it looked like, but it took me three hours bouncing from WebMD to various horticultural websites before I was able to convince myself that I had a thorn growing out of my arm. I remember vividly the feeling of relief when I realized that this was what I had been waiting for: tangible proof of my almost-abduction at the hands of a monster.

Monster. That word had stopped me dead in my tracks, just a few feet from my father's bedroom door. I clutched the place on my elbow where the thorn poked through, as my relief dissipated into revulsion. If this thorn was enough to prove that creature had been real ... didn't it also prove that I was a monster, too?

And what would my father, not to mention everyone else, think then?

I turned away from the door and instead took a pair of sturdy-looking shears from the kitchen and cut the thorn off as close to my skin as I dared. It hadn't hurt, but a strange green liquid oozed out of the wound, soaking through each bandage I applied in a matter of minutes. I had to wear one of my dad's giant sweatshirts around that day to conceal the puffy wad of tissues that I duct-taped to my elbow when the Band-Aids ran out.

Everything seemed fine until I tried to change the tissues that night and found that not only had the thorn grown back, but it had also sliced its way through both the soft paper and the layer of duct tape. I was so scared that I even entertained the thought of asking my dad about it.

In the end, though, I found a pair of pliers in the garage and used them to pry the thorn out. That time it *had* hurt, and it only took one look at the thorn to know why. The green part that I'd cut off earlier was only half of the stupid thing. Beneath the skin, the thorn had a series of white roots that must have entangled with my nerves and blood vessels. I fell asleep that night with my arm still throbbing, wondering what was wrong with me.

I still haven't figured out the second part, but I *have* learned that the pain fades over time. I also learned pretty quickly that while the thorns do eventually grow back, it will take days, even weeks, if I clean out most of the root system when removing them.

The only problem I haven't been able to solve is the scarring. Long-sleeved shirts were easy to use during the winter, but now that it's the end of June, they're starting to draw their own brand of attention. Dr. Zahn hasn't said anything about them yet, but I've seen her staring at my arms. It'll only be a matter of time before she starts asking questions about my wardrobe.

Not that she'd believe the truth if I told her.

I wait for half a minute, putting pressure on my wrist with my other hand, before pulling my sleeve back up to check my wound. The paper towel itself is still brown and dry for the most part, a good sign that the bleeding has stopped—at least temporarily. As quickly as I can, I fish my Neosporin and three Band-Aids out of my backpack and do my best to draw the skin of my wrist back together. It's not my best work, but the flush of one of the toilets behind me means it will have to be good enough.

The hallway is starting to empty out as students rush to eighth period. Most days I would be rushing, too, trying to beat the buzzer to PE; but not today. Today, like every Thursday, I walk past the hallway that will take me to the gym and make my way to Dr. Zahn's office. It's a short walk, but I wind up running the last few yards as the buzzer sounds again for the start of class.

"Sorry I'm—" I begin, pushing the office door open, but I stop when I realize I am only talking to myself: the squashy leather armchair where Dr. Zahn usually sits is empty. It's strange but not unheard of. Sometimes when a student is in crisis, she has to cancel our appointment to attend to the emergency. Usually on those days, though, someone from the office calls in to my seventh period class to let me know about it.

Only maybe I wasn't in class to get the message.

I waffle in the doorway for a minute, trying to decide whether I should double back to Mrs. Cannel to see if she has a message for me or maybe assume Dr. Zahn canceled and head directly to gym. Then I remember that Coach Draper has been on a dodgeball kick lately and decide to see how long I can hide out here before someone comes looking for me.

I take my usual place on the couch and scan the crowded bookshelf next to me for something to flip through while I wait. Shoved, seemingly forgotten, among the dozens of psychology and self-help books is a single spider plant, shriveled and brown. I reach out to poke the soil, expecting it to be hard and parched, but it's not. My finger sinks through the swampy dirt, and when I pull it back out, the rotten brown remains of the plant's roots come with it.

"She drowned you," I say to the plant, stroking one of its wilted leaves. I can almost imagine it shuddering at my touch, relieved that someone is here to console it in its final moments.

No, you're not done yet.

I move some of the waterlogged branches around, pulling them up at their bases in search of a part that might be salvageable. Near the very center of the dead plant, I find what I'm looking for: the tiniest of green shoots with healthy white roots attached. Smiling, I pull my travel mug out of my backpack and then open the window on the far wall. As I lean out to make sure no one is below so that I can safely empty the dregs of my coffee onto the alley below, something sharp digs into my thigh.

"Ouch!" I gasp, reaching into my pocket and retrieving the thorn I pulled from my wrist earlier. I must have pocketed it in my rush to hide it from the girls in the bathroom. Rolling my eyes at the little troublemaker, I toss it and the coffee out of the window and then carefully extract the little plant from its swampy death trap of a pot and rehome it in the mug.

Behind me, the door creaks open. I turn around, ready to admonish Dr. Zahn for her woefully inadequate plant-care abilities, but when I see who stands the doorway, I stop dead, a fresh panic crushing my heart and lungs.

"Please sit down, Amethyst," Dr. Zahn says in the soft voice she uses during our sessions. "Your father and I have something to discuss with you."

Dr. Zahn, barely taller than I am, only comes up to my father's shoulders, though that doesn't stop him from cowering behind her, guilt etched across his face as plainly as the gray-brown mustache on his upper lip. It's a look I've seen before—one that always coincides with new and unpleasant treatment ideas that he and my doctor have come up with: medications that make me feel like a zombie and only make the nightmares more vivid, a weekend excursion into the woods for a hellish and ineffective three days of exposure therapy, switching schools again and again and again ...

I don't know what else there is left to try, but it can't be good.

"Please?" Dr. Zahn asks, gesturing for me to sit down on the couch. I respond robotically, my knees giving way so that I hit the couch with enough force to elicit a *hiss* of protest from the leather cushion. I clutch my makeshift flower pot in my lap as if it were a talisman against whatever my dad and Dr. Zahn, now both seated in the squashy leather armchairs across from me, have planned.

"Before we get started," she continues, looking over to my father, "I want to spend just a few minutes unpacking what happened in Mrs. Cannel's class last period. Do you mind stepping out—"

"It's fine," I sigh, waving for him to stay seated. "It'll save me the trouble of having to tell him later."

Dr. Zahn nods in agreement and reaches behind her to pull a clipboard from her desk.

"Amethyst, she said that you caused a … disturbance." Dr. Zahn fumbles over the last word, her unease causing both my father and me to recoil. It's been two schools and three therapists since I was labeled "disturbed," and the word brings us both back to what I'm sure is the same chalky white room with the slight odor of singed flesh and the echoes of my preteen screams.

"It was just a nightmare," I say, shaking the memory away and trying to sound casually unconcerned. "I was up late studying."

I look up and see the doctor scrawling another series of words across the clipboard. My dad tries to not-so-subtly read her notes until he glances back to me and sees me watching. His face reddens just slightly at being caught, but there is something else, too. Apprehension? Anxiety?

Whatever it is, it causes dread, cold and heavy, to seep into my chest.

"The sleeping in class, the outbursts, the anxiety—your teachers are worried about you, Amethyst. *I'm* worried about you." She pauses, looking at my dad sitting beside her, waiting for him to speak. When he continues mutely staring at his hands, she continues. "Your *father* is worried about you. I—we think it might be time to consider different treatment options."

Called it, I think morosely, the memory of the metallic taste of electricity on my tongue.

"You said it was natural for someone like me to have nightmares, after … " I pause, trying to find the words I need to defuse the situation. "After what happened."

It's a lame finish, but bringing up monsters and mysterious lights right now probably won't get me a pass off the crazy train.

"*Occasional* nightmares. And not lasting this long. You were six years old when"—she wiggles her fingers to make quotation marks in the air—"*it* happened. It's been ten years. You shouldn't still—"

"Shouldn't still *what?*" I don't shout, but the words echo loudly off the office's cinder block walls, causing all three of us to wince. "Remember that

that *thing* in the woods was never found? Be angry that it took off with my mom and no one cared? Or is it that I shouldn't still be terrified that it's still out there, waiting for me?"

My dad buries his face in his hands at my words, as if he's trying to hide from the accusation in my voice.

"That's paranoia, Amethyst," Dr. Zahn begins, "and that's what I'm talking about. You're not getting better because you're not allowing yourself to." There's an edge of something in her usually calm voice—almost as if she's pleading with me. "Your mother left you both of her own free will. And yes, you were taken from your bedroom, and that was a very intense and traumatic event for such a young child, but you've been safe now for *ten whole years.*"

She's wrong, and I have to bite my tongue to keep myself quiet. It's actually been nine years, eleven months, and fifteen days since that night. And nine years, eleven months, and fourteen days since I woke up in the hospital and was told that my mother was gone. Not *dead* gone. That would have been easy. No, she was the gone that involves a note on the kitchen table and a lot of unanswered questions.

Gone gone.

That wasn't her, though. She wouldn't have left me like that. She wouldn't have left me at all, not unless she'd been forced to. It was obvious to me even then, from that hospital bed, what really happened:

Whatever tried to take me had taken her instead.

There had been a four-week grace period after that night, a month where my father indulged my theories. But weeks later, when I still refused to stop talking about the lights in my bedroom and the thing in the woods, that's when things went bad and doctors got involved.

My story just didn't fit with the police narrative that wanted to connect my attempted abduction to my mom's disappearance. A jilted parent wanting to run off with her only daughter made a lot more sense to them than some fairy tale a six-year-old kid concocted—especially when child psychologists started throwing around terms like post-traumatic stress disorder.

For a moment, the memory of an otherworldly face pressed up against the bathroom window swims before me. I shudder involuntarily and look sideways out the tiny window in Dr. Zahn's office, half expecting to see the creature, but there's nothing but my reflection staring back at me.

"I think what you need is—" she pauses to draw a breath—"a break."

"Summer vacation starts in a week," I begin, turning away from the window. "I'll have two months' worth of ... "

I trail off when I notice something in her hand. At first, I think it's just a piece of paper, but then the light catches it, and I can tell from the glossy cover that it's a brochure. Dr. Zahn follows my path of vision and extends the pamphlet toward me as she speaks.

"I think you might benefit from spending them up at Hillbrooke."

I take the brochure from her. The front of the pamphlet is covered with pictures of smiling people amid spacious grounds filled with lush lawns and huge elm trees. Written across the top in a fancy, loopy font is:

Hillbrooke Heights
Adolescent Inpatient Treatment Center

I'm so shocked that my mouth drops open, something which, until this very moment, I thought only happened in the movies.

Upon closer inspection, I can see that half of the smiling people on the cover wear long white coats. In the distance, the green campus is surrounded by a high metal fence. Panicking, I shove the brochure back at Dr. Zahn, as if we are playing a game of hot potato, and the last person with the paper is the one who has to go.

"I am *not* crazy!" I object, my voice cracking midway through so that the word "crazy" comes out all shrill sounding.

"Amethyst, no one said you were. There is absolutely nothing wrong with inpatient treatment." Dr. Zahn's voice is low and slow, a trick she likes to use to calm me down. But it doesn't work now. "Many people find it—"

"Did *he* put you up to this?" I spit, hoping that the glare I give my father is as acidic as my tone.

"He did not," she says calmly. "When I brought it up to him, he came up with an alternative, didn't you, Dave?"

Dr. Zahn smiles at my father and places a steadying hand on his shoulder as a panic-stricken look crosses his face.

Dad and I haven't had a real conversation together since my mom disappeared, seemingly taking with her the magical connection that is supposed to tether parents to their children. On average, we see each other twice a day: once in the morning when he drops me off at school and again in the afternoon when he picks me up. Both events are silent affairs as Dad listens to sports talk radio while I try to drown it out by turning my music as loud as I can without causing irreversible hearing damage. The rest of the time, I'm in my room, and he's on the couch.

Most days we exist less like a family and more like a pair of cordial roommates.

Now that I'm forced to face him directly, I can't help but be surprised at the small differences I notice in his appearance. His hair, which I remember being a rich, chocolaty brown, is thinning and flecked with gray. There are more lines on his face and dark circles under his brown eyes.

He looks old.

"This came for you yesterday." He grunts, pulling a small brown something out of his pocket and sliding it across Dr. Zahn's small coffee table to me. The action is so reminiscent of one of those old gangster movies that I almost expect him to say it contains an offer I can't refuse.

He doesn't, though. He sits and stares down at the package sitting between us. I pick it up to look it over. It's nothing special, just what feels like a book wrapped in brown paper with a letter taped to the top from—

For the second time today, my mouth drops open.

"*Gran* sent me something?" I ask when I recover from the shock of the return address.

"I know it's been a ... a while," he says, avoiding my eyes.

Well, that's pretty much the understatement of the century.

"My grandmother, who hasn't sent me so much as a birthday card in a decade? When did she suddenly decide I was worth her time?" I mean for it to come off as blithely indifferent, but instead my words are laced with the pain of rejection.

"Amethyst," he starts, his voice low and oddly soft. He glances sideways at Dr. Zahn, who nods encouragingly, before reaching out and placing his hand over mine. It's a gesture of comfort so out of character for my father that I am momentarily rendered speechless. "She went through a rough time—we all did—after your mother ... " He stops, the pain of her memory constricting his throat.

I know this because the same thing is happening to me. Talking about Mom is still hard for both of us. That's one of the reasons we stopped.

"After she left us. And then with your grandfather passing away right after … " He squeezes my hand before continuing. "She lost her whole family in just a couple of days."

Incredulity and hurt burn away the small sentiment of connection I momentarily felt between us, and I rip my hand away from his.

"You're seriously going to defend her? She still had a family, but she didn't want us!" I say, my voice cracking.

I turn back toward the window in a pitiful attempt to hide the tears, unbidden and unwanted, filling my eyes.

"Well," I continue, my voice now a watery whisper as I give up the pretense and wipe my face with the still-damp hem of my sleeve, "I don't want her, either."

I throw the package back down onto the table and watch it slide along the smooth wood before coming to a rest against my father's hands. He picks it up, holding it gingerly like it's laced with anthrax or an explosive.

"Just give her a chance," he says, pulling the letter from the package and offering it to me. He holds it out for a few seconds before sighing and opening it himself. He extracts a folded-up piece of stationery and something else—a second, smaller envelope—before laying both in the center of the coffee table.

I have no interest in the letter, but the envelope tugs at my curiosity. Did she send me money? A weird inheritance? Or maybe it's something else entirely …

Maybe it's something that has to do with Mom.

It's that thought that pushes my hand out to grab the envelope. I flip it around and use my pinky to tear through the thin paper. When I have a rip large enough to wedge my hand into, I feel around for its contents and pull out a long smooth piece of paper.

It's a bus ticket to Morgan Springs. To my grandmother's house.

"Is this supposed to be a joke?" I ask, unable to keep my voice steady.

"No, it's supposed to be an invitation. She called about it last week, and I thought it sounded like a nice place to spend your summer."

"You thought it sounded *nice* to ship me off for two months to live with her? A woman I don't even know?" Hysteria creeps into my voice, and it seems to rise an octave with each word.

"Amethyst—" He tries the soothing tone again, looking at Dr. Zahn for some indication of what to do next.

"And *you*," I say, directing my accusations at the doctor, "want to send me off to some institution?" My voice is rapidly approaching a pitch only audible to dogs.

"Amethyst, I—" Dr. Zahn begins, one hand pressing up against her temple.

"Did either of you even *stop* to consider what *I* wanted? That what I might need is a break from—"

"AMETHYST!"

My father's voice booms off the walls, and I hear it echo down the silent hallway. I haven't seen him this angry ever, and I guess, from her mouth open into a surprised "o," neither has Dr. Zahn. Both of us stare at him in stunned silence, and he doesn't yell again, though his hands and jaw remain clenched, and a vein in his forehead continues to throb.

"Did *you* ever stop to consider that maybe you're not the only one who needs a break?"

His words come as hard and fast as a slap, and with just as much pain. I press myself back into the sofa, physically recoiling from the emotional impact of his words. The hurt must reflect on my face because he starts backpedaling.

"Look, I didn't mean it like that," he says, swallowing hard. "It's just ... I think—and Dr. Zahn agrees—that some time away would be good. For both of us."

"Then why don't the both of you go spend the summer in Morgan Springs?" It's a childish thing to say, but if I'm not treated like an adult, then I'm sure as hell not going to act like one.

"This isn't up for discussion, Amethyst!" he says, collecting the letter and package and placing them on the left side of the table before pulling the brochure from Dr. Zahn's lap and laying it on the right. "You're going to your grandmother's, or you're going to Hillbrooke."

The walls come crashing in around me, and I finally see the trap they've set. Dr. Zahn was the setup with Hillbrooke, the option so bad they knew I'd never take it. Then Dad swooped in with the alternative that's marginally less awful—my grandmother's. They're trying to trick me by giving me the illusion of choice, because no matter which I pick, they win.

They win, and I lose.

19

Eight days later, I'm crammed up against a dingy bus window because the man next to me never learned about the concept of personal space. Or, for that matter, personal hygiene. I pull the cowl of my turtleneck up over my nose and check my phone. It's 4:49 p.m., which means I've been on the road for almost six hours.

I press my forehead up against the glass and close my eyes in an attempt to block out the unending stream of green flying by. The scenery hasn't changed in the three hours since we entered the Allegheny National Forest—eight hundred square miles of trees, trees, and more trees. Still, I'd rather be trapped on this bus in the middle of nowhere than with Dad on the way to Hillbrooke, something that was still a very real possibility earlier today.

I did my best to stonewall over the last week, but even after seven days of silence, four days without eating, and a morning of hysterical begging, they hadn't budged. I made a last-ditch attempt to lock my dad out of the car but was defeated within seconds by his Chevy Volt's keyless entry.

Even then, though, I didn't admit defeat.

It took the car pulling up to the intersection that divided our route. Dad pulled into the left lane that would take us to the highway and, eventually,

Hillbrooke. When the arrow turned green, and he started to accelerate forward, I finally conceded. He swerved across two lanes of traffic and almost hit a junked-up van to make the right that would deliver me to the bus station instead.

So, to Grandmother's house I go.

Sighing, I open my eyes just in time to see a large rustic-looking sign fly past. Its green lettering is faded and reads:

Historic Morgan Springs
Est. 1800
Population 790

Fabulous.

It's another ten minutes of driving before the trees begin to thin out, and another five after that before I see the first signs of an actual town in the form of a few small houses scattered amid the woods. One more minute and the bus turns down another road, and Morgan Springs proper comes into view—a single main street dotted on either side by a half dozen mom-and-pop shops.

There isn't even a traffic light.

The bus pulls into a parking lot made of hard-packed dirt, kicking up so much dust that, for a few seconds, it's impossible to see anything out of the window. When the air clears, I see that we've arrived at what must pass for a bus station in this town—a small glass enclosure at the far edge of the lot. There is one person waiting in it. A tall woman in her sixties with tightly curled gray hair that fans her face as the dust swirls around her.

I squeeze myself through the five inches of space between my neighbor and the seat ahead of him and pull my suitcase down from the overhead rack. As the bus idles, I contemplate whether I should sit back down and ride it all the way to Buffalo. Then my seat buddy lets out a long, loud belch that the fills the air around me with the stench of half-digested Cool Ranch Doritos.

I decide to take my chances with my grandmother.

Not surprisingly, I'm the only passenger disembarking, and the driver seems annoyed that she has to get up to open the bus's side compartment to retrieve my single shabby suitcase. She passes it over to me, then waits, her hand outstretched, her eyebrows raised.

"Oh ... " I mumble, my face turning red as my free hand flies uselessly to my empty pocket. "Sorry, I don't have any cash."

The bus driver sighs and rolls her eyes before slamming the compartment shut and returning to the bus. It rumbles into life and throws up another choking cloud of dust as it pulls out of the lot.

I'm still coughing when I reach the enclosure where my grandmother waits, her hands clutched stiffly around a leather purse almost as large as my suitcase. A thrill of fear grips me as the reality of my situation finally sinks in, and I realize there is no escape. This is my home for the next two months, and this stranger is my new, albeit temporary, guardian.

I stop, awkwardly, a foot away from her, unsure of how to reintroduce myself to someone I haven't seen in ten years. Across from me, Gran's eyes are narrow, scrutinizing, as she takes me in. They linger for a moment on the sleeves of my shirt, their length out of place for a day in late June, before meeting my eyes.

"Amethyst," she says plainly with a smile that comes just a second too late to be natural. "It's good to see you."

She falters for a moment, and I assume that, like me, she is trying to navigate her way through the awkwardness of this conversation. So, in the spirit of shared unease, I offer up my mediocre attempt at a greeting.

"Hey, Gran." I try to say it with a smile of my own, but the muscles in my face don't cooperate, and I feel a grimace forming instead. "You, too," I finish, giving up on smiling and settling for simply polite chagrin.

Another long moment passes in silence, Gran's blue eyes not moving from my own, before she speaks again.

"You must be hungry." It's an assumption, not a question, but one made presumably with my best interests in mind, so I try my best not to sound rude when I respond.

"Not really," I say, my voice as tired as I feel after a long day of traveling.

"Well, I'm sure you will be by the time we get there," she says, turning to walk toward the only car in the lot. I follow, my suitcase carving deep grooves into the hard-packed dirt. I throw it and my backpack into the open trunk before pulling myself into the passenger seat.

"I thought it would be nice to have dinner out tonight," she continues, trying the smiling again with more success. "Let you see a little bit of the town."

"I thought I *did* see the town," I say, looking out of my window at the shabby bait and tackle shop bordering the parking lot. "There's more?"

"No, not really," she says, turning the key and reversing out of the spot.

I take one longing look at the bus stop and sigh, wondering if I made the right decision in coming here.

Barely two minutes later, we pull into the parking lot of the Burnt Biscuit, a building that looks more like a log cabin than a restaurant. Outside, the lot is full, and muffled conversations float out through the screen door that must be the entrance.

I suppose it must be easy to fill a restaurant when you're the only game in town.

"Hey, Bea!" a red-faced hostess calls to my grandmother as we enter. "Sit anywhere you like. I'll send someone over in a minute with a couple of menus."

Gran waves in understanding, and we begin to make our way to the only open table in sight: a small booth in a back corner of the dining room. With no other option, we're forced to sit almost knee to knee, facing each other for the first time in ten years. I look down and begin to tear the edges of my napkin to distract myself from Gran's gaze, now sweeping across my hairline. She doesn't speak, and it occurs to me as she begins to drum her fingers anxiously on the table that she's just as uncomfortable as I am.

"Hey, Mrs. F and ... "

I look up and see a boy not much older than me standing over our table, two plastic-covered menus under his arm. He's looking back at me, a surprised smile on his face.

"Hello, Benjamin," she says with the authentic warmth that she failed to muster for me earlier.

Irrationally, I feel a pang of jealousy toward the waiter—that his tertiary relationship to my grandmother could elicit a response that her own granddaughter could not. Rejection begins to rise in my chest like an incoming tide—, slow but unyielding, and threatening to drown me if I fail to take action. Instinctively, I bit my lip, trying not to focus on the way her easy smile changes the shape of her face so that I can almost see my mother in her weathered features.

"This is Amethyst, my granddaughter. She's going to be staying with me for the summer," she explains to the waiter before turning her attention to me. "Amethyst, this is Ben Taylor."

I nod in acknowledgment of his existence, not trusting myself to speak through my suddenly tight throat.

"Well," he says, "welcome to Morgan Springs, Amethyst."

"Thanks," I say, my voice thick and wet and miserable sounding.

Ben flinches and turns to Gran with a look that asks whether he's said something offensive. She shakes her head dismissively.

"Okay, then," he says, his tone uncertain. "What can I get you ladies to drink?"

Gran orders an iced tea, but I can't find it in me to even look at the menu. I try to shake my head to indicate that I don't want anything, but the action dislodges a tear that falls into the pile of napkins in front of me, so I wind up just staring down in silence. I expect him to walk away when I don't respond, but instead Ben gives me an odd, searching look.

"How 'bout I start you off with water until you decide?" he asks.

I nod, and the action frees another traitor tear, which rolls down my nose before splashing onto the table.

"All right ... " Ben says after a moment of hesitation. "I'll, uh, be right back with those."

I wait until I hear his footsteps fade into the general din of the busy restaurant before I wipe my sleeve across my eyes and force myself to look at the array of antique cast-iron skillets arranged next to me on the wall.

"Ben's a nice boy," she says, and from the corner of my eye, I see her still watching Ben, apparently oblivious to my tears. "He cuts the grass for me once a week—hasn't raised his price in ten years."

She chuckles at the thought, but her laughter fizzles out quickly when I don't join in. We lapse back into silence, and, as soon as I'm sure I've reined in the waterworks, I return to shredding my napkin. I don't look up again until Ben returns with the drinks.

"Are you all set to order?" he asks after placing the tall plastic cups on the table and pulling a notepad out of the apron tied around his waist.

"I think we are," Gran says, even though I haven't so much as looked at the menu in front of me. "I'll have the turkey club with—"

"Sweet potato fries," Ben finishes for her, not even bothering to write her order down. "I don't know why I even bother asking anymore."

Both he and Gran laugh, and that's all it takes to upend the little control I've been able to reclaim. Here or home—it doesn't seem to matter where I am—I'm a chronic outcast.

An outsider. An "other."

"And for Amethyst?" he says, the laughter still playing on his face.

"Nothing. I'm not hungry." I push the water and menu back toward him, feeling the first shudder of a sob try to shake itself loose from deep inside my chest. Ben looks uncertainly at Gran, whose gaze is once again on me, her eyes now wide in shock as she takes in my face. Fleetingly, I wonder what my expression is giving away, but then a second sob makes a bid for freedom, and I redouble my efforts to contain them.

"Could you give us a minute, Ben?" she says, her brow furrowed as she stares at me from across the table.

"Yeah, sure," he says. But before he leaves, he gives me one last look, his brown eyes surveying my face with a look I'm all too familiar with: pity.

"This is going to be a very long summer if we don't figure out how to talk to each other, Amethyst." Gran sighs. "I want you to be happy here."

It's the word "happy" that pushes me over the edge, rendering me unable to withhold the flood that has been threatening to consume me since we sat down. The mixture of exhaustion, rejection, and abject unfairness of my situation finally wins out over my fear of embarrassment, and I break down, full-on ugly crying, in the middle of the Burnt Biscuit.

To her credit, Gran doesn't try to quiet me—or maybe she does, and I'm just too far gone to notice—and lets me get the worst of it out of my system. When I'm finally able to draw a few shaky breaths, I realize that the restaurant has gone eerily quiet as a half dozen faces turn toward our table. A woman has a hand pressed over her open mouth, and another man shakes his head. Behind them all, framed in the door of the kitchen, I see Ben, his arms crossed and his brow wrinkled in concern.

"Look, Amethyst," my grandmother begins. Her voice is softer even if it's not quite gentle, and her face shows no sign of anger or frustration over my outburst. "I know that I made a mistake. I thought ... Well, I thought it would be better if ... "

I can see shame written in the creases between her eyebrows. Deep down, somewhere past my self-pity and resentment, I feel a twinge. It's hard to peg down the feeling, but it's heavy and pulls at the edges of my foul mood, diluting it with guilt.

"I just want to make things right between us," she says in a tired voice.

When I don't respond, Gran reaches out and takes one of my hands in hers. She angles herself so that her body blocks the onlookers from watching our conversation.

"I think that you need help, Amethyst," she says, quietly, so that no one around us can hear. "But not the kind you'd get at Hillbrooke. That's why I brought you here, Amethyst. I think that I might be the only one who *can* help you." She finishes speaking, and her thumb traces a deliberate line over my wrist, causing me to gasp and flinch away as the pressure crosses over my semihealed thorn removal from last week.

I pull my hands quickly under the table, trying to hide them from the appraising look that has returned to Gran's eyes, but she refocuses it on my face instead.

"I won't push you, dear. I want you to know that when you're ready to talk, I'm here," she says, before calling for Ben to bring the check.

A few minutes later, we're back outside of town and driving down a winding, tree-lined road. Every so often, Gran clears her throat or looks at me out of the corner of her eye, as if she wants to say something. She doesn't, though, and I can feel ten years of silence stretching between us.

The car is getting too warm, and when I try to swallow, my throat feels tight and dry. And the constant line of trees, branches stretched over the road like hundreds of arms beckoning me to the dark within, isn't helping.

Roughly ten seconds before I'm about to lose it, there's a welcome distraction as the trees abruptly give way to an open space. At first, I think it's just a field, but then I see the large structure in the middle—iron and brick and wildly overgrown. It looks like an ancient ruin.

"What's that?" I ask my grandmother, pointing.

She must know what I mean, because she doesn't look over when she answers. "Just some abandoned property."

I wait for some elaboration or explanation, but she doesn't seem to want to talk now that I'm actually a little interested in what she might have to say. Rolling my eyes, I turn back and stare at the ruins until they disappear behind a fresh resurgence of trees. I close my eyes to block them out.

A few minutes later, she turns, slows, turns again, and then stops completely.

"Well, here we are, Amethyst. Home sweet home."

I open my eyes and am greeted by the sight of my grandmother's house. I know right away it's an old Victorian from its high-pitched roofs, wraparound porch, and rounded turret. It's painted a slightly more mellow shade of green than Gran's car, and the accents on the shutters, railings, and shingles are all a pale yellow. The coloring is way too contemporary to be original, but everything else, from the iron weather vane to the elaborately shaped wooden details of the porch, hearken back to the 1800s.

The house is surrounded by the forest, but the trees are held at bay by large lawns spreading out fifty yards in every direction. The only break in the grass is a single willow tree in the center of the right side of the yard, an old rope-and-wood swing partially concealed behind its leafy curtains. Even though I don't want to be here, I have to admit that I couldn't ask for a more beautiful summer home.

"Come on, let's get your stuff inside."

She opens the front door, and I feel like I've traveled back in time as I step into Gran's parlor. It's a room right out of the past, filled with antique furniture; long, heavy window hangings; and even a baby grand piano. I'm definitely not in Philly anymore, Toto.

Philly.

"I should let Dad know I got here okay," I say as I rummage in my backpack for my cell phone.

"The phone's in the kitchen, dear. Let me show you."

My hand closes around the phone, and I pull it out of the bag.

"It's fine, I've got—" I stop, looking down at the tiny red *X* in the right corner of the screen. "No service."

"No, I'm afraid not. We don't have any service this far out in the country. The closest tower to us is just outside of Greenport, I think. That's almost fifty miles from here."

This place is getting a lot less pretty by the minute.

"Fine. That's fine," I say. "I don't have to call right now. I'll send Dad an email or something later."

My grandmother gives me an apologetic look.

"You don't have internet, either." It's not so much a question as it is an accusation.

"Don't even own a computer," she says with something that sounds like pride. There must be horror on my face, because she adds quickly, "But the library in town does. I can take you down there if you want."

I can literally feel the bonds connecting me to the outside world severing. No phone. No internet.

"Do you have a TV?" I ask, desperation creeping into my voice.

My grandmother smiles.

"Of course I do, Amethyst," she says, and relief floods through me until she finishes with, "but no cable, though."

Even Hillbrooke has cable, I think, remembering the stupid brochure Dr. Zahn made me read. But I can't let myself go down that path. I don't need their cable, and I don't need their treatment. I'll stick it out in the middle of nowhere as long as it means no doctors.

"Where do you want me to put my stuff?" I ask, hoping that I'll be sleeping on a bed and not a straw mattress.

"Are you sure you don't want me to make you something to eat?" Gran asks, stopping with one foot on the bottom step of the staircase.

I shake my head. My stomach is in knots, and right now all I want to do is lie down.

"All right, then. The kitchen's down that way if you change your mind." She gestures down a hallway that leads to the back of the house.

"Okay," I mumble, and she turns to lead the way up the stairs. I follow, my suitcase thumping behind me as we go.

Much like the parlor, the staircase is awash in antiquity. Large oil paintings in heavy, ornate frames hang from the walls on either side, so expertly maintained that I feel like I'm in a museum. There're a lot of landscapes and a few still lifes of fruits and vases of flowers, but about halfway up, another painting catches my eye. It's tiny, barely the size of a magazine, but the colors are so vibrant that it seems to almost leap off the wall at me.

In the center of the painting, a beautiful young woman stands wrapped in a gauzy white gown while her long golden curls swirl behind her. All around her, the trees have bloomed to life, the petals of a thousand tiny flowers opening just for her. But it's her face that draws me in. Her wide blue eyes stare upward at something just off the edge of the canvas, while her mouth is slightly open in amazement. As I lean in close, I notice that her skin is tinted with the faintest hint of purple, a touch that gives her an almost luminescent quality. The longer I look, the more I am certain that she is not human. She's ethereal. Unearthly.

It's like nothing I've ever seen before, but as I study it, tracing the smooth, pale lines of her face with my own eyes, I get a strange sensation of déjà vu.

Ahead of me, Gran is still talking as she ascends.

"I work down at the Community Gardens a few hours every day, so you'll be on your own some of the time," she says.

"Uh-huh," I mumble absently, only half listening as I narrow my eyes at the painting.

Around the edge of the girl's face, the lilac tint of her skin turns darker, almost plum colored in some places. The size of the painting makes the spots slightly bigger than the head of a pin, but they aren't round, they're triangular. Triangular and accented at their minuscule apexes with a fleck of white. It gives them the illusion of being shiny.

Or sharp.

"I know that the house is rather technologically challenged, but you're welcome to any of the books in the reading room and to the television, of course. And to anything you want in the kitchen. If I don't have what you like, just let me know," Gran continues, unaware that I'm only catching about every third word she says.

I reach out for the painting. I need to touch it, to run my fingers over the woman's face, to explore the brushstrokes and confirm with my hands what my eyes are telling me I see.

The tip of my index finger is just a centimeter away when a hand closes around my wrist. I jump so violently that I release my suitcase, and it bounces back down the stairs before upending a tiny table that's probably ten times as old as I am.

I follow the arm up to find my grandmother's face staring down at me from three stairs up.

"As I was saying," she continues, looking from me to the painting and then down at the broken table at the bottom of the stairs, "the only thing that I ask is that you be careful around the antiques."

I nod, and she releases me. I scurry down the stairs to retrieve my suitcase, trying to right the table, but one of the legs has broken clean off. Instead, I prop it up against the heavy railing and turn to see my grandmother staring intently at the painting of the woman I was just looking at. She doesn't break away until I've caught back up to her, and when she does, she looks at me with narrowed eyes, searching my face for a few seconds before continuing up to the second floor.

My new bedroom is at the end of the hallway, in the back of the house. When Gran opens the door, the air that pours out into the hallway is stale and smells distinctly of mothballs. While the bedroom itself looks pristine, there is a sense of neglect, as if no one has entered it in years.

The bed against the left wall of the room is made of ash, and the headboard, baseboard, and posts are all covered with leaves intricately carved into the wood. The tall chest of drawers and desk against the right wall bear the same pattern carved into their various knobs and handles. The room has a single window, and when I cross to open it in the hopes of driving the mothball stench from the room, I find that it overlooks the backyard and the woods beyond it.

Behind me, my grandmother clears her throat. "This was your mother's room," she says.

I probably should have guessed as much, but somehow the thought never occurred to me. I'll be sleeping in the same bed where she slept and sitting at the desk where she sat. It feels strange to be this close to her even if we remain separated by a decade of time and space.

Strange and sad.

"My ... mother's?" I choke out before the emotion can cut off my ability to speak. To distract myself, I fiddle with the curtains, heavy purple things that kick up a cloud of dust when I disturb them. The coughing fit that follows gives me a good cover for the moisture in my eyes.

"Yes, but it's yours now for the summer," Gran says, and I can tell from her voice she's standing right behind me. "Or for however long you need."

I take a step back from the window and find that Gran's not looking at me. She's looking past me, out into the woods, her eyes sweeping from left to right as she scans the tree line.

"One more thing, Amethyst." Her eyes move back to me as she speaks. "Under no circumstances do you go into the forest. I want you to promise me that."

I almost laugh at the request.

"Trust me, that won't be a problem."

"Good," Gran says, smiling and reaching out past me to pull the window shut. Then there's another puff of dust as she releases the curtains from where they're tied back so that they close together, blocking out any view of the outside world.

She gives my upper arm a little squeeze and moves toward the door. Before she leaves, she pauses to turn and face me again.

"Amethyst," she says, her voice wavering, "I *am* glad that you're here."

And then, without giving me even a fraction of a second to respond, she sweeps out of the room, closing the door behind her.

As soon as the door clicks into place, the wave of exhaustion that I had been holding at bay washes over me. Not bothering to take off my sneakers or turn off the lights, I let out a long sigh as I flop back down onto the bed.

Hours later, I wake up shivering, the night air cold against my skin and no blanket to shield me from the breeze blowing in.

But Gran shut the window.

It's that thought and not the chill of the air that sends a new shiver down my spine. With my heart accelerating exponentially, I open my eyes. The room is dark, another sign that something is wrong. As my eyes adjust, I scan the room. The door is shut, my suitcase on the floor where I left it, and both the desk and dresser are unchanged. The only hint of something amiss is the slow flutter of the curtains as the wind blows in.

I exhale a breath that I didn't realize I was holding as I decide to subscribe to the perfectly rational assumption that Gran came back in and opened the window. Obviously I didn't notice because I was asleep, and she was careful to be quiet. Nodding to myself, I pry my sneakers off with my feet, pull the blanket up over me, and roll over to face the wall.

Just go back to sleep, I tell myself. *Everything is fine.*

"*Amethyst ...*"

My eyes snap back open at the sound of the voice.

Her voice.

I freeze, not daring to even breathe, lest she hear me, and I stare at the smooth, dark wall. To my horror, I watch as the gray of the wall warms to the color of cream as some source of light illuminates the room from behind me.

No. Not here, too.

I roll over and see them: half a hundred twinkling lights bobbing and weaving around my tiny bedroom. And even knowing that they are evil—monstrous, even—I physically can't stop myself from reaching out for them.

Stop! I scream inside my head as my legs, no longer under my control, throw themselves over the side of the bed.

Please! I beg as my feet shuffle against my will, following the lights as they swirl in the air and then out the open window, one by one.

Don't! But my hands are already closing around the purple curtains, pulling them apart so that I can once again see out into the backyard. It's empty—just an endless swath of darkness stretching out before me. For a fraction of a second, relief floods through my body, until I hear it again.

"*Amethyst ...* " her voice hisses from directly below me.

I should shut the window, lock it, and close the curtains. I should turn and run screaming from the room. But instead, I lean forward out of the open window and look down.

She stands on the grass below me, illuminated by the soft glow of the lights, and the scene almost resembles the woman from the painting on the staircase. Her hair dances around her, and her pale face is alight with a childlike look of wonder. The only difference is that her skin is tinted green instead of lavender.

She smiles up at me, and as she does, I see long fangs slip over the flesh of her lips. Then she opens her mouth, and I expect to hear her call out for me again, but instead of words, a long, inhuman growl roars up. It's so loud that I cover my ears, using my hands to shield against the sound.

My arms fall limply, however, when I see what is happening below me.

The creature—no, *monster*—is transforming. Her mossy green eyes are now a bright red, the color of fresh blood. Thick green-and-gold thorns rise, like hackles on a dog, on her arms and around her face as her fingernails grow into long, sharp claws. As she changes, the guttural growl still echoes all around me, so all-consuming that I can barely hear my scream as it erupts from my throat.

I wake up, for real this time, with the roar of a lawn mower drowning out my scream as I sit straight up in bed. As my eyes give out their own shrieks of pain, I realize that, to my immense relief, the overhead light is on. Rubbing my eyes, I slide out of bed and almost fall face-first onto the floor as both of my feet cramp in response to a night spent crammed into my sneakers. I ignore the throbbing in them and hobble over to the window, pausing for just a second to take a deep breath before flinging the curtains apart.

The window behind them is shut, and even after I push it open, I can see nothing below me but the roof of the wraparound porch and the green summer grass beyond.

It was just a dream, I tell myself with a small laugh of relief. Still smiling, I push myself back inside my room, shut the window, and set myself to the task of locating my toiletry bag.

Twenty minutes later, I'm showered and dressed for the day in a pair of jeans and another long-sleeved T-shirt. It's not even 10:00 a.m. yet, and already I can feel the light cotton beginning to cling to me. For a moment I consider changing into a tank top. I didn't find any new thorns today, and I could probably figure out a lie to explain the scars crisscrossing up and down my arms to Gran.

She hasn't heard anything about me in ten years, I think as I run a brush through my hair, collecting it in one hand to pull it back into a ponytail. *I could tell her it was a bike accident or that I fell out of a tree or …*

My train of thought derails as I see the beginnings of a small thorn on the side of my face, just above my right temple.

"You've *got* to be kidding me," I say, reaching up to run my finger over the dime-sized bump. It's still smooth, so at least I don't have to go through the pain of extracting it just yet. Frowning, I abandon both the ponytail and the tank top. Instead, I part my hair on the side, taking care to make sure that it amply covers my temple, pinning it in place so it stays put.

So much for staying cool today.

Sighing, I turn away from my reflection and head out in search of breakfast. The sound of the lawn mower grows louder as I reach the bottom of the stairs.

"Gran?" I call out, shouting to be heard over the noise, but there's no response.

I walk down past the empty parlor, then through the empty dining room, and finally wind up in the empty kitchen.

"Gran?" I call again. As if in answer to my question, the breeze blowing through the open kitchen window ruffles a paper on the counter. It's written in my grandmother's neat, tiny handwriting and is addressed to me:

Amethyst,
I didn't want to wake you, but I will be out at the Gardens until five or so. There's stuff for breakfast in the fridge, and I got some cold cuts for you for lunch.
Benjamin will be by sometime today to cut the grass. I've left his check in the mailbox on the front porch. He'll know to pick it up there.
The number for my office is next to the phone. Give me a call if you need anything.
—G

So I've got the house to myself for the day, I think, folding up the letter and placing it in the back pocket of my jeans. *Maybe this won't be so bad after all.*

I find a box of cereal in one of the cupboards and settle down at the gigantic dining room table to eat. From my chair, I have a full view of the side yard through one of the large bay windows. Halfway through my bowl of Apple Jacks, Ben makes his appearance, pushing the lawn mower across my field of vision before disappearing again at the window's edge.

I abandon my cereal and walk over for a closer look. Even though it's only late morning, the temperature is already hot enough to have turned the back of his shirt dark with sweat. As I watch, he stops, the mower idling, and pulls the shirt up over his head, using it to mop his brow before tossing it down beside him. His sudden loss of shirt sends heat flooding into my face. I feel like I'm encroaching on his privacy, but I can't make myself look away from the way his back muscles move as he pushes the mower back into action.

"Ouch!" I gasp, rubbing my hand across the place where my forehead just connected with the glass of the window. Then I erupt into a fit of laughter.

No, not laughter, *giggling.*

I try to remember the last time I giggled and can't. Somehow that only makes me giggle harder. Soon I'm in an all-out fit—the kind that gets worse the more you try to stop yourself. Tears stream down my face as I submit, doubled over, to the laughter.

It's a few minutes before I'm finally able to recover myself.

Wiping my eyes, I try to catch my breath as the last remaining giggles continue to trickle out every few seconds. Using the window to steady myself, I push up into a standing position.

Ben stands just a few yards away, leaning up against the idling lawn mower, staring directly at me.

His eyebrows are raised in that same surprised look he wore during my tirade in the restaurant, the only difference being that there is laughter playing on his face now instead of pity.

For a moment, our eyes lock, and I feel electricity spark between us, as unexpected as a flash of lightning on a cloudless day. He must feel it, too, because the crooked smile on his face is replaced by a question mark, and his hand, half-raised in greeting, freezes in midair. He cocks his head sideways, examining me again.

I should smile, shrug, wave, or do anything but continue to stand framed in the window with my mouth hanging open. All systems are jammed, though, and the only message my brain can get through to my body is a singular nonspecific directive to *Move*.

My body's response is to fling itself, in the most ungraceful way ever, sideways out of his range of vision. I collide with the dining room wall and send one of Gran's framed pictures crashing to the floor next to me. The glass doesn't shatter, but a large crack is now working its way across at least seven inches of it. My face is hot with fresh embarrassment, and I don't move again until I hear the sound of the lawn mower fading to the other side of the house.

Smooth, I think, pulling myself up from the floor. I almost fall again when I put weight on my left foot and feel the weird pins-and-needles sensation that comes from sitting on it for the better part of fifteen minutes. Steadying myself on the back of one of Gran's dining room chairs, I shake it briskly until the blood flows back in a painful tide.

When I trust my foot enough to walk on it, I cross back to where the picture sits on the floor, bend down, and scoop it up. I run my hand across the long crack, trying to think of a way to repair the damage before Gran gets home, but as this is probably the only thing duct tape can't repair, I'm out of luck. Sighing, I turn the frame over and work the cardboard backing off with the hope of at least salvaging the picture.

I pull too hard, and the backing separates violently from the frame, sending both it and the glossy picture within crashing to the floor again. This time the glass does shatter, sending a shower of shards across the hardwood floor.

Ugh.

Stepping lightly to avoid the biggest pieces of glass, I chase the picture across the room, where it's landed in one of Gran's fake-flower arrangements. It's not until I free the photo from the dusty clutches of a plastic hydrangea that I take my first look at it.

I almost drop the picture in shock.

Staring back at me from the grainy color portrait is my mom.

Her face is younger than I remember, and her hair hangs down past her shoulders. She must be about my age, judging by her height and the copious amount of neon colors saturating every inch of her wardrobe. Next to her, I recognize a younger Gran, her hair light brown instead of gray, her eyes not on the camera, but on the man to her left.

I don't remember my grandfather, not in any specific capacity, anyway. When I've tried to call his face to memory in the past, all I've gotten is a vague sense of sickness and old age. The man in this picture is nothing like that. This man is tall, at least a head taller than Gran, with fine hair so blond that the brightness of the day washes it into white. Aside from a slight stoop to his shoulders and the faintest hint of shadows under his eyes, there's no sign at all that he's ill.

For the second time today, I feel like I'm intruding on some secret moment.

My eyes travel back to my mother, and I find myself tracing every millimeter of her image, trying to scan it directly into my brain. Her cheeks are flushed pink, and no wonder—she and my grandparents are standing outside. I can see the outline of a brick wall behind them, the white-hot sun burning against a clear blue sky. She must be broiling in that turquoise sweater, even if one of her shoulders is hanging out of the oversized neck hole.

Wait a minute.

The pieces lock into place as I look from my mom's modest attire to my own. No one would wear a sweater in the middle of a Pennsylvania summer unless they were trying to hide something. I scan the edges of my mom's face, but the photo is so pixilated that I can't make out anything that might be a thorn. My eyes go down to her right hand, which is invisible, hidden behind Gran's back.

My last option is her left hand, but when I cut across to look at it, there's nothing there; the picture stops just below my mom's left elbow.

I squint down at the wavy right edge of the photo and realize that it doesn't just end—someone has physically removed a part of it. I hold the picture up so that my nose is almost touching its glossy surface, examining the place my mom's arm extends beyond its border. She must be holding on to something with her left hand.

Or someone.

I flip the picture over, and scrawled across the back in a handwriting I don't recognize is:

Spring Opening, 1980
Arthur, Beatrice, Annabell & Ab

The final name is cut off with the rest of the picture. My only hint toward the identity of the photo's fourth occupant being the tantalizing "Ab" and the year, and with no Sherlock Holmes (or even a Google search) to help me, both are essentially meaningless. Deflated, I turn the photo back over and give it a shake as if that will make the mystery person topple suddenly into the frame.

Unsurprisingly, it doesn't work.

From behind me, the call of an obnoxious bird pulls at my attention. It takes me a moment to figure out why the long, low whooping sound is bothering me, but then it dawns on me that the only reason I can hear the bird is that the lawn mower engine has gone silent. Placing the photo on the table, I creep over the broken glass to peer out the bay window.

Nothing.

I'm just coming to the conclusion that Ben's packed it up and gone home—a realization that makes me feel oddly disappointed—when I remember Gran's note. He'll want his paycheck, and that's on the front porch.

I sprint to the parlor and open the curtain of the window overlooking the front porch. I'm not going to let him catch me off guard this time. All I can see through the centimeter of open space is a sliver of empty porch.

Frowning, I open it a little wider, and then a little wider, until my entire face is peeking through, my heart sinking with every inch. From my vantage point, I can see the mailbox affixed to one of the supports of the porch, and there is no sign of Ben anywhere.

A loud knock at the front door sends me reeling backward, and I collide with the table I broke yesterday, sending me and the table crashing to the floor. I land hard on my elbow, a little yelp of pain escaping before I can get my hand up to my mouth to smother it.

"Hello? Mrs. Faye?" Ben's voice calls from the other side of the door. There's a moment where I entertain the thought of just pretending no one is home, but then he continues, "Is everything all right in there? I heard a crash."

So much for that plan.

Rubbing my elbow, I step over the remains of the end table, which now looks like it might never stand again, and walk over to the door. I have to stand up on my tiptoes to look through the peephole, and when I do, I see the top of Ben's head, his wavy brown hair pulled and magnified by the glass so that it looks distorted.

Just as he raises his hand to knock again, I open the door just enough to see a sliver of his face. I catch a glimpse of his smile pulling up the side of his sun-kissed cheek and take a fraction of a second to notice the flecks of green around the pupils of his brown eyes; then I look down at my feet. I can feel the memories of our first two encounters hanging between us, a mixture of shame and embarrassment boiling in the pit of my stomach as I speak.

"Can I help you?" It comes out in a whisper, shy and uncertain.

"Hi, yeah, Amethyst, right?" he asks, and as I nod, he angles himself to get a better look at me through the crack in the door. I smell the sweet scent of freshly cut grass as he moves closer. "It's Ben. From last night. I'm here to—"

"Mow the lawn, I know." I study a stain on my right sneaker. "Your check is in the mailbox."

I try to shut the door in a preemptive strike against having to answer any awkward questions about my giggle fit today or my rage fest last night, but before I get the chance, Ben's fingers curl around the doorjamb, blocking my attempt.

"Do you think it would be possible for me to get a glass of water?" he asks. "It's got to be at least a hundred degrees out here."

I look up and see him smiling at me through the crack in the door. A kind of static buzzing fills the space between my ears the longer I look at him, drowning out any kind of cognitive thought that should be happening.

Distraction, a voice calls from somewhere deep inside my brain, and I look down again, but not down far enough. My eyes land on his chest, tan and gleaming slightly from a long morning of yard work. And just as I'm learning that people outside of Hollywood actually can have six-pack abs, the static in my head completely overtakes the tiny voice calling out reasons for me to just shut the door and hide until he goes away.

"Yeah, um, sure. Be right back," I hear myself say, and then suddenly I'm on my way to the kitchen, grinning like a fool.

I fill a glass halfway with ice and then take out a cube for myself and rub it against my forehead. It seems to have gotten very warm all of a sudden.

After drying my face with one of the hand towels next to the sink, I top the glass off with water and head back to where Ben waits. To his credit, he hasn't invited himself into Gran's house, though the door is open a little wider than I remember.

As I pass the water through the crack in the door, his hand touches mine, and again I feel a jolt of electricity spark between us. I pull my hand back into the safety of the doorway and watch as Ben makes a cheers motion with the glass before taking a long drink.

"Well," he begins, wiping his mouth with the back of his arm, "thanks for saving me from a slow, painful death by dehydration."

I don't know what to say to that, so I shrug and make a noncommittal squeak. Ben takes another drink, his eyes moving from my own up to a spot on my forehead. A surge of panic pushes my hand up to my right temple, but as far as I can tell with my fingers, the thorn is still safely concealed.

"You did something different with your hair," Ben says, nodding at the place where my hand covers my temple. "It wasn't like that yesterday."

"Oh … yeah," I say, clearing my throat and smoothing my hair down one more time.

"It looks nice," he says.

The compliment catches me off guard, and that's when it hits me that he's *flirting.* This whole conversation is hurtling into a place beyond my area of expertise. I have no idea how to respond, so I give his right shoulder an uncertain smile of thanks. Ben's eyes dart back down to mine, and out of nowhere, I realize how close he is to me. Our faces are only about a couple of feet apart, and that is enough to make me feel slightly light-headed.

"So you're just here for the summer, then?" he asks, shifting his weight to lean against the doorjamb.

"Yeah." I have nothing more eloquent than that. One word punctuated by a cough to fill in space where more words should go.

"Hmm … That's going to be a problem," he says with a sigh. His brow is wrinkled in concern, and he's looking so intently at my face that I suddenly feel like I must have morphed into a particularly difficult math equation.

"What's a problem?" I ask, not quite sure what he's playing at.

Ben shakes his head and raises the hand not holding the glass of water to pinch the bridge of his nose.

"I just don't know if I'll be able to do it," he says, his voice edged with worry.

Now I'm completely lost. Did I black out and miss part of this conversation or something?

"Do what?"

"I don't know if I'm going to be able to make up enough lawn-related emergencies to get me over here for a whole summer … "

He pulls his hand away from his face, and I'm hit with the full force of his brown eyes. There's a spark of playfulness twinkling in them, and I realize that I haven't missed anything at all.

"Of course," he continues, a hopeful smile lighting his face, "I wouldn't have to keep breaking my back trimming hedges if you'd, say, want to go out sometime."

"Um … "

In my moment of hesitation, two warring factions fight the first skirmish of what will probably be a long and drawn-out conflict between my common sense and whatever mysterious force is spiking my thoughts with mental nerve gas.

On the side of common sense is sixteen years' worth of experience with the human race. Ben Taylor, surprisingly, isn't the first boy to ask me out. I'm not ugly, so it happens from time to time. Boys from other schools who come across me at the mall or in the bookstore, who don't connect my name with the girl on news reports ten years ago. I went out with a few of them, and I even had fun with a couple of them. But eventually, even the guys from different schools found out through a friend of a friend about me, resulting in more than my fair share of "it's not you, it's me" texts.

And all that was before the thorns. There's no use in even saying yes now, when I'd have to keep my distance the whole night, making sure that I don't accidentally slice my date open while he's trying to hold my hand. That would bring up a lot of unnecessary questions and, depending on how badly I injure him, potentially a lawsuit.

Better to stay at home with a book.

But the other side is unrelenting, pointing out things like the way Ben's nose crinkles when he smiles or the fact that we're six hundred miles from Philadelphia in a land with no cell-phone reception. It detonates a bomb filled with a chemical agent that is almost always deadly to the common sense of any teenager: hormones.

I only have a few seconds before my better judgment is drowned in a sea of emotion set to the tune of a thousand Taylor Swift songs. I have to act fast.

"What, am I the only teenage girl in town or something?" I ask, allowing skepticism to flavor the question so that it comes out as aloof, almost cool. A small miracle, considering the alarm sounding in my brain as the last few soldiers of common sense band together, huddling against the increasingly frantic beating of my heart and hoping against hope that my dig is enough to send him packing.

"No," Ben says. And inside me, both sides pause, breath held, waiting in strained silence to see which way the battle will go. "Just the most interesting."

In a fit of valor that will forever be remembered, my last shred of common sense grasps hold of my mouth and pushes out one final command before he is swept away into oblivion.

"I'll … think about it," I say, the rush of hormones bringing a fresh tinge of pink to my cheeks even as I give the lukewarm answer.

Ben doesn't seem at all surprised. Instead, he shrugs, the smile on his face unwavering.

"Hard labor it is, then," he says, shaking his head in mock disappointment. "Do you think it's too early to start raking leaves?"

With no cynicism to weigh me down, the laughter comes all too easy. I'm floating away, adrift at sea. Sure, I have no provisions, no plan of survival, but those are problems for another time. Right now, I'm just going to enjoy the sun.

"What's so funny?" Ben asks.

Everything is what I think. Everything about this moment, this place, this boy in front of me is funny.

"Just the idea that I've only been here a day and I've already got Gran free lawn care for the summer," I say instead.

"I didn't say anything about *free*."

Ben almost seems genuinely concerned, so I throw him a sly smile before I close the door.

A s soon as the door clicks into place, I lean back against it, half-exhausted and half-exhilarated from the exchange. My legs feel shaky, so I slide down into a sitting position and listen for the retreating sound of Ben's footsteps as he thumps down the porch steps. A minute later, I hear an engine roar to life followed by the crunch of gravel as the car rolls out of the driveway.

It's a few more minutes before I pull myself to my feet and look out of the peephole. The porch and the driveway beyond it are empty, and thank goodness for that. If I had spent much more time in his presence, I might have done something stupid—like agree to go out with him. Time and distance seem to have cleared my head, and I feel slightly relieved.

Carefully, just in case I've missed something through the peephole, I open the door and look up and down the porch. No sign of Ben, but sitting in the center of the porch is his glass. It's still half full of water, and propped up between the few remaining ice cubes is a single daisy.

Oh, he's good, I think as I pluck the flower from the glass and twirl it between my fingers. I *should* toss it, but my common sense must still be in recovery, because instead I hold it up to my nose and inhale its sweet scent before tucking it gently behind my ear. The smile that blooms on my face is unbidden and easy.

It feels good to smile again.

I practically skip all the way to the kitchen as a resurgence of squee continues to flood through me. As I wash the glass and my cereal bowl out in the sink, flashes of the conversation rush through my mind—my very own highlight reel. Some of the snippets, like when Ben said my hair looked nice, I replay a few times, analyzing the tone and inflection of each syllable. While others, like the few glimpses I snuck of his chest or arms or stomach, I watch in slow motion, heat rising in my face.

I'm being silly and stupid, but since no one is around to see me, I don't care. It feels like it's been a thousand years since I've had a conversation with someone who isn't either a family member or a therapist, and I'm going to let myself enjoy Ben while he lasts.

Plus, he's not too bad on the eyes, I think, which sends me into another fit of giggles.

I finish the dishes and the laughing at the same time and lean up against the sink to catch my breath. I stare out of the little window above the sink at the back lawn, where Ben has cut the grass into that green checkerboard pattern you see on baseball fields. I nod in approval.

The boy does good work. I make a mental note that the azalea bushes could do with a trim; they're growing a little out of control.

I look from the bushes across the yard, scanning for more chores I can add to Ben's list. I was only half kidding about getting him to do some extra work for Gran. As long as he's hanging around, he might as well help out. As my eyes sweep the farthest reaches of the lawn, the woods come into focus, a tangle of trees, dark even now in the middle of the day.

Just looking at them is enough to send a wave of unease through me.

I try not to linger on the trees, but a flurry of movement draws my eye, and that's when I see her framed in the gap between two trees: the creature from my nightmares.

I take three steps backward, my eyes still on the monster, before my back is up against the kitchen's island. She doesn't move from the forest's shadow, even as I slide my way around the edge of the counter. For the briefest of moments, I look away from her to the back door to confirm that it's locked.

It is, but in the half second it took to check, the monster has disappeared from the tree line. There is a single, sweet moment of relief before I hear the soft rattle of something trying to turn the handle of the back door. Ice starts to pour into my bloodstream, threatening to freeze me where I stand.

Move, I plead with myself, but I can't seem to look away from the doorknob. I watch as it slowly turns, twisting until it comes up against the lock. There is a heartbeat of silence and then …

WHAM!

Something collides so hard with the heavy wood of the door that the windows rattle. The sound is so loud and violent that it shakes me out of my terror and sends me sprinting out of the kitchen. For a split second, I think about breaking for the safety of the upstairs, but then I remember that the front door is unlocked.

And I am one hundred thousand percent certain that it won't matter where I am if that thing gets in the house.

I crash into the dining room, knocking a chair over in my haste. I can see the front door on the other side of the adjacent hallway and barrel on toward it. My sprint is all-consuming, and every fiber of my body from my legs to my lungs to my brain is locked on the target. I'm so focused that I forget about the minefield of broken glass still covering the hardwood floor until one of the larger shards embeds itself in my foot.

I bite back the scream that the pain sends up my throat and slow my pace from a run to a shambling speed walk, treading on the ball of my right foot in an attempt to prevent the glass from cutting deeper into my flesh. Every other step is a fresh agony, but I don't stop.

I *can't* stop.

The span of space from the dining room to the front door can't be more than thirty feet, but by the time I place a shaking hand up against the smooth hardwood, I'm sweating and out of breath. Fear and pain cover my fingers like a pair of thick wool mittens, and it takes me a few breathless seconds to slide the chain lock into place.

Biting my lip against the pain in my foot, I push myself up to look through the peephole. There's nothing to see except for the air shimmering slightly in the summer heat.

I'm just about to sigh in relief when the door opens so violently that the impact of it knocks me to the ground, my forehead now dueling with my foot for the title of most pain-filled part of my body. My vision blurs so badly from the impact at first that I see two of everything: two doors, two slivers of blue sky, but it's the two clawed hands that catapult me into action.

Leaning back on the palms of my hands, I kick both feet out against the door. I *do* scream this time, as the wedge of glass drives itself another half-inch into my heel, but so does the thing on the other side of the door as it slams against her arm.

The door pushes back against my feet, and I catch a glimpse of a green-purple bruise forming on the thing's forearm before it completely retracts.

I jump on the opportunity, literally, leaping up to turn the dead bolt into the locked position. I press my ear up against the door and hear a low hiss, like the sound of an angry snake, followed by a buzz that reminds me of the frantic flutter of insect wings.

Then, nothing.

I count to ten and then to twenty before daring to peek through the peephole again. The porch and front yard are both quiet, empty, and this time no creature blasts me backward in an attempt to get into the house. As soon as I realize that I'm safe, my legs go out from underneath me and I half slide, half fall down the door to the floor.

I feel my throat tighten as my terror begins to ebb away, but I can't give in to tears, not yet, anyway. There's the small matter of the three inches of glass protruding from my heel. I should probably grab a towel or something, but I don't think I could walk to the kitchen now even if I wanted to. Instead, I take off my T-shirt, wrap it around my hand, and do my best to prepare mentally for a lot of blood.

Just touching the shard jostles it enough to make me shriek. I close my eyes and bite my lip, willing the pain away. I can taste copper in my mouth, but it barely puts a dent in what my foot is feeling.

This isn't going to be fun, I think before tugging on the shard with both hands. It slides out in a surge of pain that, as soon as it clears my foot, subsides considerably. I let the shard fall to the floor and immediately apply the shirt back down onto my heel. Even through the wad of fabric, I can feel the warmth of my blood spilling out with each throbbing beat of my heart. I start to feel dizzy and, needing a distraction, I pick up the shard of glass. It's almost the size of the palm of my hand and streaked with bright red.

And green.

It's not the greenish yellow that you'd see with an infection. It's a deep, earthy green, like the needles of a pine tree. Bile burns up the back of my throat as my stomach turns over in revulsion. I slowly lift the shirt from my foot. While the purple fabric is overwhelmingly awash with red, the point where the shirt was in direct contact with the cut is a dark, undeniable green.

I turn my gaze to the gash on my heel. It's still leaking a steady stream of blood down my foot and onto Gran's floor. Bracing for what I'm about to inflict upon myself, I clench my left fist while I reach out with my right and bury my index finger in the cut. The pain is so sharp and sudden that bright-white lights pop in front of my eyes, and the first gray tendrils of unconsciousness grasp at the edges of my vision. I push past it, tears rolling down my face until my fingertip connects with bone. Then, with a scream that claws its way painfully out of my throat, I rip my finger back out.

A thin green film encases my finger all the way up to the first knuckle. I rub my coated finger with my thumb and discover it's sticky.

"It can't be," I whisper, raising the finger up to my face for a better look. But even just an inch away from my eye, I can't be certain. Swallowing hard, I stick out my tongue and taste it.

The sweetness of the sap is enough to make me vomit.

It takes an hour for me to move away from the front door, afraid that if I take my eyes away from the smooth wood, the creature will return. When I finally convince myself that it's gone—at least for the time being—I pull myself shakily to my feet and begin to clean up the damage I did to both myself and Gran's first floor. It takes another hour to sweep up the broken glass and then mop away the mixture of blood, vomit, and sap I've trailed across the hallway and dining room. I try, unsuccessfully, to repair the damage to the end table before giving up and shoving it into one of the downstairs closets in hopes that Gran won't notice its absence until I'm back in Philadelphia.

Then I pick up the photo from the table and head upstairs to shower and take care of my foot the best I can. Balanced on my good foot, I examine the cut in the mirror and realize that it probably needs stitches. Unfortunately, without going to the hospital, the best I can do is a handful of extra-large Band-Aids and a few feet of gauze to hold things in place. It's not perfect, but it seems to do the job—just as long as no one looks too closely at my bulging sock.

I hobble back to my bedroom and unzip my suitcase for a fresh change of clothes. As I dig down through the shirts and jeans in search of a pair of sweats, my hands come across something hard and square. I pull it out and find the small package Gran sent along with her invitation.

Dad must have slipped it in here, because the last time I touched it was to toss it, unopened, into my bedroom trash can. I contemplate doing the same here, but I don't want Gran to find her gift mixed in with the week's garbage, so, instead, I slip my finger in between the folds of brown paper and tug.

The book inside is an old leather-bound thing, so grimy with age that I can barely make out that the front cover appears to be a faded copy of the painting of the woman hanging in the stairwell. Printed in flaking gold lettering in the flowers above her golden head is the title:

Fairy Stories

Curious, I give up the search for my sweats and pull on a pair of pajamas from the top of the suitcase and flop down on my bed with the book. After I pull the covers up to my chin, I flip to the contents, scanning for "Cinderella" or "Snow White," something familiar enough to distract me from the pain in my foot and the specter of the creature lurking somewhere beyond the trees, but they are nowhere in sight. In fact, upon a second look, I realize that I don't recognize any of the stories listed. Intrigued, I turn the page to the first story, "Ithir," and begin reading.

> Long ago, before the existence of either men or fae, there was only Ithir, the earth goddess. Her breath was the magic of creation, warm and soft as it brought life to everything it touched. Fish leaped from her rivers, and birds soared above her grassy plains. And, in the warmest place beside her earthen heart, the first men emerged, and Ithir loved them best of all.
>
> Ithir's creation wind blew over their flocks and their crops, and her human children flourished, spreading out farther and farther as they grew in number. Soon, they had moved so far away from her heart that Ithir began to struggle to reach them.
>
> She was growing tired after giving so much of herself for so long.
>
> For just a moment, she paused to draw a breath, and in

that instant, destruction fell upon her children. Ice choked their rivers, and their crops withered into the frozen ground. Darkness and death danced upon her creation and claimed the lives of thousands of her beloved humans.

So powerful was Ithir's grief that it wrenched her apart, creating a great chasm which filled with her tears for her lost children. So great was her pain that her very heart broke open, releasing her life's breath upon those humans who had remained closest to her earthen heart. It wound itself into their very souls, and thus were the first fae born.

Not "Snow White," I think, but it did the trick. The combination of the story and the warmth of the blanket and the downy softness of the bed have brought me right where I wanted: to the edge of unconsciousness.

But before allowing myself to sink into what I hope will be a long, dreamless sleep, I reach under my pillow and pull out the picture of my mom and grandparents that I rescued from the sea of shattered glass. I put the photo in the book to save my place, running one finger over the right side of the image—along the false edge where another inch of the picture should be.

My last conscious thought is to wonder who it was that got cut out—and more importantly, *why.*

The question is still on my mind when I wake up the next morning, and I realize that the only answers I'm going to get are likely to come from my grandmother. So after a quick detour to the bathroom to brush my teeth and do a thorn check, I follow the smell of sizzling bacon to the dining room, where she's laid out a huge breakfast spread.

"Goodness, I'd forgotten how much teenagers sleep," she says when I walk in. "You were out like a light when I got home yesterday." She places a couple of slices of toast on her plate. I follow her lead and load up on eggs, bacon, and a slice of cantaloupe before taking the seat opposite her. We eat in silence for a few minutes, and I try to think up the best way to broach the topic of the photograph. But just as I'm about to speak, Gran breaks the ice instead.

"I peeked in, you know, just to make sure you were still breathing and saw you received my gift." She pauses, waiting for me to respond, and then clarifies: "The book I sent. Have you had a chance to read it?"

"A little," I reply before pivoting to what I really want to talk about. "I was wondering … it's probably going to sound random … "

Gran's face lights up with the kind of smile a teacher wears when you puzzle out the answer to one of their trick questions.

"You can ask me *anything*, Amethyst," she says, putting her fork down to give me her undivided attention.

"Well, I was wondering if my mom—if she had many friends when she was my age. Any close friends?" I decide to ask the question in the most generic way I can, just in case.

Gran's face falls. Apparently that question wasn't the one she had been expecting.

"Annabell—your mother—had a lot of friends from school, and of course, a few of them I think she considered close."

A generic answer for my generic question, but I'm not going to let it go that easy.

"Do you remember any of their names?" I ask, hoping to get a hit on the mysterious "Ab" from the back of the photo.

Gran gives me an uncomfortable look. I can see suspicion growing in her eyes, and I'm thankful I was smart enough not to mention the picture.

"There was Shelby Hooper from down the road. Your mother knew her from elementary school right on up through their senior year," Gran says. "And Katrina Blake and Crystal Graves from her dance class, if I remember correctly."

Now it's my turn to be disappointed.

"No one else?" I ask.

"No, not anyone who stands out. Why?" says Gran, her eyes narrowing.

I know for sure not to mention the picture now, so I go with my second option: play to her sensibilities.

"No reason. I just"—I look down at my eggs—"I just don't know much about her, and I was wondering last night if she was popular or if she was like … "

Pause for dramatic effect.

"If she was like me," I finish, looking back up just in time to see the suspicion replaced by concern on Gran's face. She opens her mouth, and I can feel her teetering on the edge of spilling something. What it is I never find out, as the sound of a Weedwacker roaring to life outside distracts us both, and the moment slips away entirely.

Gran leans back in her chair to look out of the bay window.

"Is that Benjamin?" she asks, craning her neck in an attempt to see around to the front yard. "What in the world is he doing back here already?"

I drop my face into my hands to conceal the pink flooding into my cheeks, sighing loudly.

"I can't believe he was serious," I say into my fingers.

"Serious about what?" Gran asks, turning away from the window to look at me.

"Nothing," I say, waving her off. "I'll take care of it."

I push my chair away from the table and catch a glimpse of Gran's face before I turn toward the entryway. She's trying very hard not to smile and failing *miserably.*

Ben doesn't notice me until I lean over the porch railing and knock my knuckles against his thick skull. He shuts the machine off and pulls the thick goggles away from his face, but he's not fooling me. He's wearing a polo shirt and a pair of nice khaki shorts—definitely not landscaping attire. I consider telling him he missed a spot and walking back inside, but then he smiles, and that train of thought departs without me.

"You know," I begin, feigning annoyance, even though I have a grin on my own face, "I'm seriously starting to consider a restraining order."

He laughs at that, and I feel it rush through me like a mood-enhancing drug.

"Hey, I tried to warn you yesterday. I had all night to think of a million things to keep myself busy *all summer long.*" He emphasizes the last three words, and I feel another wave of giddy pleasure.

I'm seriously getting high off this boy. The thought makes me laugh, and my laughter seems to encourage Ben.

"Unless, of course, you've changed your mind and want to—"

"Do something. Yeah, I know," I finish for him. "Are you always this persistent?"

"One of my better qualities," he says, not missing a beat. "So?"

I'm about to politely decline when the idea hits me.

"It must be your lucky day, Ben, because I *do* want to do something," I say, a sly grin curling the edges of my mouth.

Ben almost drops the Weedwacker in surprise.

"Really?" he asks, not waiting for me to answer the question before he plows ahead with a plan way too well thought out to be impromptu. "I thought we could hit up a movie, or maybe grab a bite—"

I stop him before he gets too ahead of himself.

"I was thinking something a little more … low key," I say, crossing back to the open front door.

"Gran, I'll be back later! Ben and I are going to the library!" I yell in the general direction of the kitchen before turning to find a look of confusion on Ben's face.

"The library?" he says as I jump down the last few stairs and land next to him.

"My trip, my rules," I say as I lead the way to his car. "Unless you want to stay and trim the hedges or something."

Ben doesn't answer except to shake his head in disbelief, and I almost feel bad for using him as a glorified taxi downtown.

Almost.

The ten-minute ride into town passes surprisingly quickly, with Ben and I filling the time with idle chitchat about movies and music. He carries the brunt of the conversation in the beginning, but soon I find that it's a lot easier to talk to him, something I attribute to the fact that he's not sweaty and shirtless. My guard drops so low that I almost talk myself into trouble as we make the turn onto Main Street.

"Yeah, I'm thinking about agricultural studies," Ben says. "Cornell's the dream, but it might be too far from home."

"I don't think I could ever get far enough away," I say wistfully, imagining the glorious day I ride—or better yet, fly—off to some distant college.

"Why's that?" he asks as he puts his blinker on to make the left into the library parking lot.

It's an innocent question, but the answer, the true answer, is information that I only dispense on a need-to-know basis, and Ben Taylor most definitely does not have clearance for that kind of access.

"Just want to see the world, I guess."

Thankfully, we park just as the lie passes my lips, and Ben doesn't have time to follow up before I'm unbuckled, up, and out of the passenger's side door.

The Morgan Springs Public Library is housed inside another old Victorian-style building. Unlike Gran's, however, the space has been completely gutted to create a single gigantic room. The first floor is dedicated to a large reception desk, a brightly decorated children's section, and a row of ancient-looking computers opposite a few scattered study tables.

A bell tinkles as Ben and I enter, and the librarian, a middle-aged and tired-looking woman, glances up from behind the mahogany desk. She doesn't speak, though her eyes say very clearly that she isn't happy that we've interrupted her quiet morning. Her gaze follows us as we continue toward the study area, so I make a beeline for the children's section instead. When we're out of earshot, I pull Ben down to one of the minuscule tables meant for six-year-olds, and both of us sit awkwardly across from each other with our knees up to our shoulders.

"This is a … cozy place for a date," Ben says, shifting uncomfortably on the hard plastic chair. "What are we having, invisible tea?"

I fight to not roll my eyes at the joke. I still need a ride home, after all.

"We're not on a date," I correct him, and his face falls.

Oops.

"We're on a … " I search for a word that's relationship-neutral without being lame. "A mission."

"Mission, huh?" Ben muses, seeming to recover a little bit of his lost steam. "What kind of mission?"

"The secret kind," I say as I reach into my pocket and pull out the photo of my mom and smooth it out on the table between us. Ben pulls it toward himself and bends down to examine it.

"This is my mom," I say, pointing to her image. "According to the date on the back, she was right around my age when this was taken."

"Okay," Ben says, following my finger. "So what's the mission, then?"

"To find out who this is," I respond, moving my index finger to the area where the picture cuts off abruptly. "My mom has to be holding on to someone. Someone who got removed from the picture."

Ben looks up from the photograph, and I can see that he's confused.

"You can tell by the angle of her arm," I say, trying to explain it better. "See? She's—"

"I see it," Ben says. "But why do we care? Why does it matter who it was?"

His question catches me off guard. If this were Philly, no one would need to ask me why I was interested in a twenty-year-old photo of my mom. They all had a decade's worth of context to color their conclusions and could affix whatever label applied to their opinion of me: a cry for attention, an obsession, a delusion, or just plain old paranoia. Actually, who am I kidding? No one back home would ask because no one talked to me there. Except for Dr. Zahn, and that was only because the state of Pennsylvania paid her to pretend to care.

But they would all be wrong. I need to know who this person is not because of what happened in my past but because I'm growing increasingly scared about my future. If I know who it is, then maybe I can find them and ask them if she ever shared a secret at a sleepover about growing thorns. It might be a long shot, but finding out you bleed sap is enough to make any person a little desperate.

Of course, I can't tell Ben any of that without sending him screaming for the hills.

I look up from the picture and find him staring at me, his warm brown eyes full of concern, and I realize I can't lie to him, either.

"I—" My voice catches in my throat like it always does when I try to talk about her. I cough and push through it. "I haven't seen her, my mom, since I was six … "

I mean to say more, but I can't. The wall I built up around the pain of her disappearance is too high and has been up too long to break through in the course of a single conversation. Plus, I don't know what would happen to me if I did, and I don't want to find out sitting in the kids' section of a library with a boy I just met. I look down at my mom's face so that Ben can't see the moisture stinging the corners of my eyes.

"All right, then. Do we have anything to go on?" Ben says. There's no demand for further explanation in his voice, just complete acceptance.

"Um, yeah," I say, flipping the photo over. "We've got a year, 1980, and a partial on the name: Ab."

"Okay," Ben says, grimacing a little as he gets up out of the tiny chair. "Then let's get to work."

"Again? *Seriously?*"

I don't yell, but my voice is loud enough to attract the librarian's attention. She scowls and shushes me before burying her nose back in a bodice ripper with a front cover that would make Gran blush. Rolling my eyes, I take a quieter approach to express my frustration with the library's ancient computers and click the mouse frantically, attempting to prod the frozen screen back to life.

"Hey, careful with that!" Ben's voice is a whisper, but I can still hear an undercurrent of laughter in his words. "It's probably an antique!"

I swivel around in my chair to see Ben emerging from the basement with another armful of books. He opted to take the low-tech approach after we discovered that only one of the library's three computers was able to connect to the internet. At first, I thought I got the better end of the deal with not having to access the dusty corner of my brain that remembers how to use the Dewey decimal system. But now that I'm restarting my computer for the twelfth time in an hour, I'm beginning to have my doubts.

"I can't find *anything!*" I whisper back at him, pushing my chair backward to roll up next to him at one of the study tables. "Half the time I can't load the browser, and the other half, the stupid thing freezes when I finally find something halfway interesting."

"I still think you're in the wrong mind-set. The picture is from 1980, right?"

"Yeah," I agree, not quite sure where he's going with this line of thought.

"Well, the eighties were a dark and strange time," he says. "Back then, before the internet, people used these."

He holds a book up to me as if it's some kind of primitive artifact.

"They're called books," Ben continues as if he's explaining astrophysics to a kindergartener. "*Boooooks.*"

I pull the book out of his hand and whack his arm hard enough to shut him up.

"Yeah, well, so far you've had as much luck as I have," I say, pushing back toward the computers before he can retaliate.

"I've got a good feeling about these," he says, patting the top of the nearest stack. I roll my eyes and return my focus to the monitor, now freshly booted up and ready for my thirteenth attempt. I click the browser icon, and after a few seconds of loud moaning from the computer, it opens.

Excellent, I think. *Off to a good start this time around.*

I watch the cursor blink slowly in the little search box as I contemplate what to enter. I might only get one shot before I have to reboot again, so I have to make it count. However, I'm running out of combinations of search terms to try with not much to show for any of them.

The only thing I've confirmed from my search so far is that Googling "Ab" without any other kind of qualifying terms will get you about seven million pages dedicated to half-naked men. Unfortunately, adding "Ab" in with "Morgan Springs" only gave me links to the local hobby shop and the four nearest American Baptists churches. "Ab" in with "1980" showed me that lots of well-cut dudes in the eighties made some terrible decisions concerning their choices in athletic wear.

A few of those neon leotards I will *never* be able to unsee.

In the reflection of the monitor, I see Ben pull another book from his pile and start to leaf through it. Suddenly I realize that the problem might not be with my search terms; something might have happened to Google's algorithms to make it not function properly anymore. I figure I should probably test it out with a term I know will bring up results—you know, to make sure it's working right. With a quick glance behind me to make sure that Ben is still engrossed in his books, I raise my fingers to the keyboard and type:

"Benjamin Taylor" and "Morgan Springs"

The computer makes a noise that sounds like the electronic equivalent of a death rattle, and there's almost a full minute where my mouse's cursor is transformed into an hourglass. But the page finally loads up the results to my query, and I'm staring at the electronic record of Ben's life thus far.

It's not pretty.

The first page of results looks like a dozen articles from the same local newspaper, the *Morgan Springs Journal.* A quick scan down the headlines reveals that my new friend Ben is very well known in the local area, and not for being a particularly upstanding citizen. I click on the first article, titled "Area Teen Arrested for Trespassing," and skim through the first paragraph.

`Local teen Benjamin Taylor was arrested`
`last night after breaking into the`

recently closed Morgan Springs Community
Gardens. Authorities were tipped off to
the break-in by Hazelle Jenkins, who
lives about a half mile past the Gardens
located on Route 144. While police did
not observe any immediate damage to the
property, Taylor was held overnight until
the gardens, and surrounding area, could
be fully inspected during the daylight
hours.

Well, that's not so bad, I think, clicking the back button to return to my
search results. There was no damage done, and really, what kid hasn't done a
little trespassing? It was probably a stupid bet or something, and he was the
last one out.

The page loads, and I move down to the second headline. Immediately, I
know that this one won't be as easy to explain away.

Morgan Springs Student Arrested
After School Brawl

MSPD responded to Lincoln Central
High School today after school officials
reported an altercation happening in the
school's student parking lot. The police
report indicates that when officers
arrived at the scene, they discovered
18-year-old Benjamin Taylor sitting on
top of the chest of local football star
Jared Barnes, punching him repeatedly in
the face.

Captain George Lawrence of the MSPD
was able to pull Taylor away from Barnes,
suffering a few minor lacerations in the
process. Barnes, on the other hand, was
transported to Forest County Medical

Center and treated for a broken nose
and fractured collarbone. His teammate
Ryan Wilson, who has spoken with
Barnes, reports that the Morgan Springs
quarterback will miss the last four games
of his senior season.

"Taylor just went off," Wilson said in
a phone conversation with the *Journal*.
"We were walking home after practice and
just happened to cross his path in the
parking lot, and he went after Adam.
Completely unprovoked."

Taylor is scheduled to be arraigned
this Friday and is facing charges of
aggravated assault and assault on a
police officer.

Holy. Crap.

My mind racing, I click back to the previous page. As I wait for it to load, I realize my heart is pounding. Ben kicked a kid's butt so hard he *sent him to the hospital*. No, wait, not a kid. He sent a *high school football player* to the emergency room. The boy's got some serious anger issues, which I have no intention of exploring in any way, shape, or form. Especially not on a ten-minute ride back to Gran's house.

I need to get out of here like *now*.

"Hey, Amethyst, I was just thinking—" Ben's voice is right behind me, so close that it makes me jump. I spin around, trying to block the screen with my head, but I can tell from the look on his face that he's already seen.

I watch, horror-struck, as the muscles at his jaw clench and the book in his hand falls forgotten to his side.

"Ben, I can—" I begin, but he waves me off.

"Did you get to the sixth one?" he asks, his voice deadpan and his eyes staring over my shoulder to the computer screen.

"The what?" I say, confused.

"The sixth article. Did you read that one yet?"

"No," I say, looking out of the corner of my eye to where the librarian still sits with her face buried in *Pirates of Passion.* "I-I just read the first two."

Ben reaches around me, placing his hand over my own on the mouse, and begins to scroll down to the article in question. This time there is no spark of electricity between us, just a fresh wave of fear. He uses my finger to click on the sixth search result, another newspaper article, with the headline: "Morgan Springs Woman Recovering After Rescue from Woods; Husband Still Missing."

Ben removes his hand from mine as the page loads, but he remains just behind me, so close that I can feel his breath on the back of my neck. I bite my lip out of instinct, but it doesn't work as well on fear as it does on pain. Finally, the article loads, and the first thing I see underneath the headline is a photo of a man, a woman, and their young son smiling up at the camera. The caption under the picture is dated 2002 and describes its subjects as Adam and Savanna Taylor with their eight-year-old son, Benjamin.

"Read it," he says.

"No, Ben, I—" I start, but he cuts me off, his voice cold.

"Just read it. And then ... and then I'll explain to you about the other stuff."

I don't want to make him angry, so I do as he says.

> One of two Morgan Springs residents reported missing in the Allegheny National Forest late last night was found unconscious this morning on the side of Route 22. Savanna Taylor, 34, was found by truck driver Randall Stephens at approximately 5:45 a.m. Mrs. Taylor was transported to Forest County Medical Center, where she is being treated for exposure and dehydration.
>
> Authorities continue to search for Mrs. Taylor's husband, Adam, who was last seen entering the national forest with his wife early yesterday morning. He is described as being 35 years old and 5 11 with dark-brown hair and green eyes. Taylor was last seen in a green-

and-black checkered shirt and blue jeans.

Anyone with any information on the whereabouts of Adam Taylor should contact the Morgan Springs Police Department or the Allegheny National Forest Ranger Station.

"Finished," is all I can make myself say as I scroll back up to the picture of Ben's family. There's a dull ache in my chest as I look at the smile on his chubby childhood face.

I hear the sound of a chair scraping across the floor behind me, and I turn around to find Ben slouched in it, his head in his hands. When he finally speaks, he talks to the floor.

"About ten years ago, my parents went out hiking. They'd gone a hundred times before." He pauses, and at that moment I know that his throat is tightening the same way mine does when I try to talk about my mom. He clears it, and I hear the emotion flooding into his voice when he continues.

"Your grandmother used to babysit me when they went out, and I was at her place the day they went missing. My mom and dad were supposed to be back before dark, but they didn't show, so Mrs. Faye called the cops."

I can see it playing out as clear as if I were there. Little Ben is sitting in the living room watching cartoons on Gran's gigantic old television while she uses the phone in the kitchen to make the call. A few dozen police officers and volunteers are combing through the forest with flashlights as the darkness falls around them, calling out "Adam!" or "Savanna!" every few seconds.

"A guy in a pickup truck found my mom on the side of the road the next morning and brought her to the hospital. She was unconscious, and I remember sitting there next to her while the doctors talked to your grandmother. I remember them saying that she might never wake up." Ben's voice cracks, and he breaks off abruptly.

"What about your dad?" I ask, trying not to notice as he wipes his eyes with the back of his hand. It's a minute before he answers.

"They went out looking for him again, but they—they never found him," he says, his voice tight.

"And your mom?"

"Mom was in the hospital for almost three days before she woke up.

Screaming. At first, it was just these high-pitched shrieks, but then she started to yell words. She screamed for my father to run or pleaded for her life." Ben runs his hands through his hair and cradles the back of his head with his hands.

"One time, she woke up yelling about lights. Lights in the trees," he continues, exhaustion creeping into his voice. "I was the only one in the room for that one, though."

My breath catches in my throat as the memory of a dozen dancing lights twinkling in my bedroom swims before me.

The creature is here, and so are the lights. Two missing parents and dangers are lurking in the woods. I can see all of the pieces stretching out before me—a gigantic jigsaw puzzle that I won't know how to complete until I get a glimpse of the final picture.

"Did … " I begin, my voice trembling. "Did she say what happened to her?"

Ben shakes his head.

"The paramedics said exposure. The ER doc said shock. Later, the therapist said she had a break with reality." I can tell from his voice that he doesn't believe any of it.

"But what do you think it was?" I ask, slowly, carefully.

"I don't know," he says to the floor. "But something happened out there in the woods, and it took everything she was. Once she got home, that was it. No more hiking. No more gardening. No more anything. She hasn't left the house in ten years."

I look at Ben, at his sadness and confusion, and I want to reach out and tell him that I know what he's going through, probably more than anyone else in the universe. I can see the parallels of our stories, and I now don't need him to explain the fights or the arrests. I know how it feels to be labeled, to have a hundred pairs of eyes on you every day, a hundred different mouths spreading a thousand different rumors.

When they targeted me, I turned inside, built my wall, and bit my lip to keep them out. I guess that's the difference between us. While I hid, he fought, and while I was getting a psychiatric record, he was getting a rap sheet.

Both of us exist in a world that wants to shut us away because the things we saw, the things we believe, don't fit in with their idea of normal.

I want to tell him all of that, but my walls are still up, and I'm not sure if I'll ever be able to tear them down. So instead, I reach out and place my hand on his.

"I'm so sorry, Ben."

And I am.

I'm sorry for doing the stupid search. I'm sorry for making him have to relive this for me in the middle of the Morgan Springs Library. But mostly I'm sorry for not being able to say more than that I'm sorry, for keeping all of the things I know about lights and monsters locked away inside me.

I'm sorry I can't make myself trust him.

Ben shrugs his shoulders and lifts his head up to look at me for the first time since he began speaking. His eyes are red, but there's no trace of tears on his face.

"It's fine," he says. "You probably would have found out eventually—it's not exactly a secret around here." He gives me a sad sort of half smile. "It was just … "

He shakes his head dismissively.

"Just what?" I ask, giving his hand a small squeeze. The action seems to restart the connection between us, a biological set of jumper cables sending a new spark from me to him.

For the first time since I've met him, Ben looks embarrassed. I can see his ears turning pink beneath his hair.

"It's just, well, it felt like you were a clean slate. Someone who could finally see me for who I am instead of for what happened to me—or what I'd done in return." He shakes his head again. "I don't know if that makes any sense."

I can't help but smile, even though there's a burning lump of guilt eating away at my stomach. I *should* say something. Tell him he's not crazy. Tell him that he's not alone.

"It makes perfect sense to me," I say instead, trying to put all of those things I can't say into another prolonged squeeze of his hand.

A few moments pass in silence, both of us looking down at where my hand covers his. With each passing second, the temperature of the room seems to increase by ten degrees, until finally, I use the excuse of an itch on my arm to extract my sweaty palm from his. The room all around us is charged, palpable energy pulsing in the air between us.

"What's that book?" I ask, searching for something to distract me from the way Ben's eyes are boring into mine.

"Huh?" He follows my pointed finger down to where the brightly colored book sits in his lap, forgotten. Then his eyes widen. "Oh!"

He grabs the seat of my chair and rolls me closer to him until we're shoulder to shoulder with the book in between us. The bright colors are a design, a crisscross of geometric neon lines, and below it is an inscription that reads: "Class of 1980."

"A yearbook! *Of course!*" I yell, and the librarian slams her book down on the reference desk in annoyance.

"Sorry!" Ben calls to her with an apologetic look, but I ignore her, fumbling to peel the glossy pages apart.

Nineteen eighty. That would mean my mom was sixteen, and with her fall birthday, she'd be a junior. There can't be more than a couple of hundred kids total in the entire school, which means that as long as "Ab" was a local, it shouldn't be hard to figure it out.

I flip through to the center of the book to the start of the junior class. I figure that's the most likely place to find my mom's old BFF.

"I'll start on this page. You take the right," I say as Ben leans over the book. Together we begin to scan through the rows of big hair and bad wardrobes.

Leanna Applegate. Jeffrey Bigelow. Sandra Bruce. Christopher Chambers. Leonard ...

"Amethyst." Ben's voice is strange, a question. "I think I've got her."

My heart racing, I look down at where he's pointing. There's no picture, just one of those PHOTO UNAVAILABLE boxes with the silhouette of a girl. Printed underneath it is the name: Absynth Faye.

I look at the picture to the right of her and see my mom's sixteen-year-old face smiling sadly up at me from above her caption: Annabell Faye.

"Do you know her?" Ben asks. "Is she related to you?"

I shake my head. "No, I-I've never heard that name before in my life." I stare down at it again.

Absynth.

If she knew my mom, then Gran would have said so. I mean, if it were a cousin or something, my mom would have known her, would have been friends with her, and Gran would have mentioned her.

Unless she didn't want me to know.

I pull the picture out of my pocket and run my finger down the edge where the mystery person was cut away, removed from memory. If someone went to enough trouble to take her out of this picture, of course they would omit her from a recounting of my mom's old friends. Something happened with Absynth, and it's something my grandmother doesn't want me to know about.

"I wish I knew where this was taken," I muse aloud. That could be another clue.

"Those are the old Morgan Springs Gardens," Ben says without a moment of hesitation.

"How do you know that?" I ask, searching the picture for a sign or placard or something.

"I used to go there all the time with my mom." He points to an area just behind my grandmother. "That's the reflecting pool."

"Can we go?" I ask, sure that the answer will be yes, but instead Ben wrinkles his brow in concern.

"That depends," he says cryptically.

"Depends on what?"

"On your feelings on a little late-night trespassing," he says, a mischievous smile playing on his face.

"With you? I don't know … "

That wipes the smile off his face. I let him deflate a little further before I continue. "According to my research, you're not very good at it."

Ben laughs at that.

"That was like six years ago. I've gotten way better since then."

"It's good to know I'm in the company of a career criminal," I say, looking over my shoulder to make sure the librarian isn't looking our way before slipping the old yearbook into my bag.

Ben raises an eyebrow at this.

"This is a library, you know. You could just check that out."

"But that would imply that I plan on giving it back," I say as I give him a small smile and sling the bag over my shoulder.

"And I'm the criminal," Ben says, shaking his head as he follows me out of the library.

Because daylight is not super conducive to breaking and entering, and also because Ben has an afternoon shift at the diner, he drops me back off at Gran's. We use the return trip to discuss our plan for the evening. He'll pick me up after his shift ends, sometime around eleven tonight, and together we'll head out to the Gardens. My only job in all of this is to make it out of the house without raising any suspicion in Gran.

"Easy as pie," I say, my hand on the door handle. "Where should I meet you?"

Ben scans the yard around us, zeroing in on something just to the right of the house.

"I'll park down the road and wait for you under that tree."

I follow his gaze and see that he's talking about the old willow tree in the side yard. I feel a pang of anxiety in my chest at the thought of being outside and so close to the woods after dark, and suddenly I realize what a terrible idea this is. Not just because of the possibility of being mangled by a real-life monster but also because I can feel myself teetering close, very close, to crossing an invisible line with Ben: the line that divides acquaintances from friends and, my stomach flips over when I even consider it, friends from, well, more than friends. And while it's nice to have any one of those, each level comes with new problems and, especially for me, more pain when the truth eventually comes out.

And if I've learned anything in life so far, it's that physical pain—like getting ripped apart by a monster from your nightmares—is nothing compared to the pain of being set aside or, worse, abandoned by someone you care about. The former has a definite end—the pain will cease when your heart stops beating or when your lungs stop breathing. The latter, though, that's a nonfatal wound, a gaping hole carved into your chest that festers and spreads like an infection through your body. The kind of pain that isn't kind enough to kill you. The kind of pain that takes up residence in every cell of your body and never, ever ends.

"Amethyst?"

Ben's voice brings me back to the car, and I look over to find him staring at me. He's smiling, but I can see a question in his eyes.

"Are you sure you want to do this? We don't have to," he says, but I shake my head and wave his question away.

I take a deep breath and use it to push my fear back down deep inside of me. There's nothing to be scared of, not with Ben, anyway. We're two people going on an adventure. We're Frodo and Sam, only taller and with less foot hair. This doesn't have to be anything more than that, and we don't have to be anything more than friends.

"No, that's fine. I'll see you tonight."

I give Ben one more smile before I open the car door and make a run for the house before I do anything stupid.

The rest of the afternoon feels like I'm living in a weird time warp that's simultaneously moving at a thousand miles an hour and not moving at all. This is probably because although I've made a philosophical stand against my anxieties, they seem yet to have gotten the memo. One minute I'm excited at the prospect of visiting the Gardens, where my mother—and possibly this "Absynth"—took a photo together one long-ago summer's day, and the clock slows to a stop. The next I'm terrified about being so close to the woods after dark, and time jumps ahead an entire hour. Intermingling with both extremes are thoughts of Ben, which are either wholly exciting or wholly terrifying, depending on my mood.

The anxiety becomes so strong that my stomach is in knots by the time dinner rolls around. Even though the pot roast Gran made looks incredible, just the smell of it is enough to make my insides churn unpleasantly. She must know something's up, because she puts her knife and fork down and folds her hands underneath her chin to stare at me.

"Is everything okay, Amethyst?"

"Yeah, fine," I say, spearing a carrot with my fork and popping it into my mouth. It sinks like a lump of lead all the way down my throat and into my stomach.

Gran seems unconvinced, but she resumes cutting her piece of roast anyway.

"How was the library?" she asks a little too casually so that I can almost hear the question she wants to ask underneath.

I feign ignorance.

"Fine," I say again before adding, "It was nice to have access to the internet. I think I was starting to go through withdrawal."

Gran nods, but it seems I'm not off the hook yet.

"And how's Benjamin?"

There's only a hint of a smile on her face when she says his name, but it's enough to make me blush.

"He's good," I say, trying to downplay the moment, but that makes her smile all the wider. She's got the wrong idea completely.

"He's a good buddy," I say. "I mean, it's nice to know someone my age in town."

Gran gives me a searching look, but she doesn't ask any more questions about the library or Ben after that.

After dinner, Gran and I spend the next few hours watching TV, something that should provide an easy distraction, but tonight everything seems to be set on agitating me. First, we watch the local news, and I find myself wondering if Ben's arrest was the leading story a few months ago. Then I find myself wondering if they showed his mug shot, and then how he looked in his mug shot.

Probably pretty good, I conclude after a few minutes of silent consideration.

Then the game shows come on. It's a doubleheader of *Wheel of Fortune* and *Jeopardy,* and every other answer to a puzzle or question sends another surge of adrenaline through me. A hyperactive mother of three wins $35,000 when she solves the bonus puzzle correctly by guessing "What is a willow tree?" An elderly man doubles his money with the answer "What is absinthe, Alex?"

When the evening movie turns out to be *The Secret Garden*, I give up on distractions and tell Gran that I'm going to bed. She doesn't say anything more than a quick "good night," but I can feel her eyes following me all the way up the stairs. Some small, anxiety-ridden part of my mind voices a concern that she knows, or at least *suspects*, that something is up. I can feel the first tiny fingers of worry beginning to clutch at my heart, my lungs, but I don't let them take hold.

Gran doesn't know anything, can't know anything.

Unfortunately, being in my bedroom alone with no distractions is just as bad as being downstairs with Gran. I try to make myself busy by finally putting the contents of my suitcase away in one of the antique dressers. When that's done, I spend a half hour cleaning and re-dressing my foot and then another fifteen minutes rearranging the contents of my toiletry bag.

After replacing my toothpaste at the top of the bag, I turn to the last undone task: my rat's nest of a bed. I shake the blanket free from the sheet it's tangled in, sending something heavy thudding to the floor on the other side of the bed. Confused, I bend down to look under the frame and see the book of fairy stories lying amid the colony of dust bunnies.

Yes, I think as I abandon making the bed and grab the book instead, turning the pages until I find the place where I left off.

> *Uaine and Liathe*
> The creation of the fae allowed Ithir the chance to teach others how to use her magic. She instructed in them both how to create and how to destroy, though in smaller, less catastrophic ways than her own, so that the fae could act as protectors of her human children and ensure that they never experience such devastation again.
>
> However, as the centuries passed, the fae began to abuse their power: some seeking to rule over the humans, others wanting to destroy them entirely. They did not hide their intentions well, and soon Ithir became aware of their plans. Angry, she was tempted to destroy the fae, but, as they too were her children, she found herself unable to hurt them.
>
> Instead, she used her magic to bind the fates of both together,

and from that day on, the belief of humans in the fae became the source of their power.

The fae were divided on how best to curry the now necessary favor of the humans. The Uaine believed that creation magic used to help the humans would ensure their power, while the Liathe believed destruction and fear were more certain ways of keeping the humans in line. The divisions became so entrenched that soon each side had forgotten how to use the magic of the other, and they fell into war—harming not only each other but, even more, the humans they were created to protect.

Ithir, her own magic now waning, saw only one option.

She gathered her remaining strength and used it to cast a veil between the Liathe and the Uaine so that, while they shared the same earth, never again would they be able to touch. Forever, the Uaine would give life only to have the Liathe, in their wake, take it away. A cycle of endless creation and destruction that the humans learned to call nature.

A gale of laughter cuts through the silence, and I drop the book in surprise. It bounces off my foot, sending a spasm of pain up my leg. Swearing, I kick it back under the bed and check the clock on my phone.

It's just after ten.

I thought old people ate mushy pasta at early-bird discount diners and went to bed right after the evening news. Either my grandmother is younger than she looks or a lifetime of television stereotypes have misled me. Whatever the reason, if she decides to stay up to see how the end of the movie plays out, I'm screwed. There's no way to get to either door without passing by the living room.

Again, anxiety tugs at the inside of my chest, squeezing my lungs so tightly that I have to sit down, take a deep breath, and forcefully remind myself that she does not, *cannot,* suspect anything.

Clinging to that idea, I stand up and start rummaging through my dresser until I find a black hoodie. I exchange it with my long-sleeved T-shirt, pull the hood up over my head, and secure it snugly so that only my eyes and nose can be seen through the hole. I turn to look at myself in the mirror, but instead of seeing the sexy cat burglar I've concocted in my head, I'm staring at that kid from *A Christmas Story.* You know, the one whose mom encases him so tightly in a snowsuit that he can't put his arms down. Rolling my eyes, I undo the hood and grab a baseball cap instead.

I'm still not Catwoman, but it's going to have to do.

I spend the rest of the time sitting on the edge of my bed, listening hard for the sound of Gran's footsteps coming up the stairs, holding out hope that she'll tire before it's time for me to go.

When 10:55 rolls around, however, I finally have to accept that, with Gran blocking both of my exits, there's no way I'm seeing Ben tonight. My heart drops into my stomach as I imagine him standing, shivering slightly in the cool night air, under the willow tree in the yard. Waiting for someone who won't be coming.

I wonder how long he'll stand there. Fifteen minutes? An hour? Against my will, I find myself smiling at the thought of walking out in the morning and finding him curled up and asleep at the base of the trunk.

But that won't happen.

Most people would wait about ten minutes and then leave. So naturally, Ben would …

I slap my forehead.

As he's proved multiple times since I met him two days ago, Ben is not most people. Ben will not leave quietly.

Ben might *actually* wait outside all night, or worse, he might do something completely crazy like knock on the door. A surge of panicky adrenaline kicks my heart into high gear.

It's this thought that pushes me to my feet, and I walk automatically to the only exit available to me: my bedroom window. It opens silently, but even when I'm leaning so far over the ledge that half of my body is enveloped by the night, I still can't see around the side of the house to where Ben should be waiting.

That's it, then. I'll have to wait and hope that the worst that happens tonight is Ben catching pneumonia. But just as I'm withdrawing in defeat, I catch a glimpse of the roof of the wraparound porch looming tantalizingly about ten feet below my window. In that instant, my heart, fueled by a mingling sense of panic and reckless abandon, makes a decision with little consultation with my brain.

Instead of retreating into the safety of my bedroom, I throw my legs, left and then right, over the sill and slowly lower myself down until I'm hanging straight out below the window. The only thing that separates me from a long, hard fall is the ten points of connection between my fingertips and the wooden sill, and I can already feel them beginning to slip under the weight of my body. I stretch my feet out as far as they'll go, but the few centimeters don't change the fact that the gap is at least ten feet, and at my tallest, I'm barely over five.

I'm going to have to let myself fall.

Okay, I think, steeling myself, *I can do this.*

Three.

I take a breath so deep that my lungs are stretched to the point of pain.

Two.

I close my eyes with the wild hope that not being able to see myself fall will somehow make this easier.

One.

My brain gives the order to release, but even though my arms are now shaking from the effort of holding me in place, my fingers refuse to let go. They seem content to continue hanging on indefinitely—or perhaps just until gravity rips my body away from my arms, freeing them to escape back into the safety of the bedroom above.

With no way to pull myself up, and an apparent inability to let myself drop, I resign myself to my new reality. Maybe tomorrow Gran will notice me, suspended from my bedroom window, and the local fire department will come and extract me. Or maybe it will be Ben who finds me, and I'll finally drop from where I cling, having died from embarrassment. Or maybe I'll just hang here forever, living off rainwater, growing old on this ledge, my body fusing with the wooden shingles of the house until I disappear completely.

Someplace inside me knows I'm acting ridiculous and *slightly* melodramatic. But this entire situation is ridiculous and slightly melodramatic, so a certain amount of hyperbole seems appropriate.

I open my eyes and press the side of my head against the house so that I can peer down at the roof below.

Despite my silent pleas, it hasn't moved. If anything, the gap between where my feet end and the roof begins seems to have somehow increased in the minute since I first lowered myself out of the window.

I give the roof a nasty look before craning my neck up to where my hands still resolutely cling to the sill, and that's when I see the spider, brown and hairy, clinging to the wall about six inches away from my outstretched arms.

Every hair on my body stands on end as it and I look at each other, engaged in a game of chicken one and a half stories above the ground. I stare at it, not daring to look away or even breathe, but in a moment of weakness, muscles around my watering eyes overpower my brain, and I blink.

In that space of less than half a second, the spider must sense his moment is at hand, because he begins his slow, skittering victory march toward my right arm. Suddenly the shrinking distance between it and me seems a lot more terrifying than the drop down to the roof, and the jolt of fear that shoots up through my arms as the first of the spider's hairy legs grazes my skin is enough to finally unfreeze my fingers and send me into freefall.

Less than a second later, my feet hit the roof with a muffled thud as I land in a crouch. I hadn't anticipated the sound, and my entire body tenses as I listen for any sign that my grandmother heard. After a few seconds of silence, I take one last look up at the spider, who is now crawling triumphantly up toward my open window, before shimmying myself over the edge of something for the second time in five minutes.

The second part of the descent is easier than the first. I want to chalk that up to my having conquered my fear of hanging from ledges, but it's probably more because the roof of the porch is significantly closer to the ground, combined with the fact that there's a lot less dangling and a lot more standing on the railing four feet below me. It only takes ten seconds for my sneakers to land on the freshly cut summer grass.

Hunched over so that I stay below the window line, I creep slowly toward the side of the house where Ben should be waiting beneath the tree. Just as I reach the corner, something moves in the periphery of my vision. I don't want to look, but my head seems to turn automatically toward the dark edge of trees that encompasses the backyard. There's just the hint of a breeze brushing up against the black branches, but it's negligible. For a moment I think I catch sight of a pale face, illuminated in the dark by the moon, but it's gone before I can focus on it.

It's enough to send me sprinting for the safety of the willow.

I cross the side lawn in less than a minute before stopping just short of the tree to make sure that my hair is still securely covering the bump on my forehead, then I walk slowly through the drooping branches.

The moonlight cuts through the leaves at odd intervals, making it hard to see anything more than a few inches in front of me.

"Hey, you made it."

Even though I know it's Ben, I still let out a little squeak of surprise at the sound of his voice. I turn toward the left and squint into the shadows as he takes a step forward into a shaft of moonlight. He looks down at his watch and smiles. "And right on time, too."

"Yeah, well, it's amazing how much time you save by skipping the stairs and rappelling out of the window without a rope instead." My heart is still beating fast from my sprint, so although I want to sound cool, my words come out breathless and warbling.

Ben raises his eyebrows.

"Seriously?"

"Yeah," I say, gaining control over my breathing. "Gran's still awake. Apparently, she's super into late-night movies."

"Impressive," Ben says sagely, and I'm not sure whether he's talking about my stunt work or Gran's taste in cinema.

I blush in the semidarkness anyway, and there are a few heartbeats where I stand and listen to the slow rhythm of his breathing. When I realize that he must be doing the same, I clear my throat and throw us back into conversation.

"So, what did I nearly plummet to my death for? It'd better be good." I can almost physically see my voice slicing through the moment.

"Oh," Ben says, slowly shaking his head as if he's waking from a dream. He clears his throat, and I can hear an undercurrent of excitement flowing through his words. "Oh, it's good, all right. You ready to go?"

He holds his hand out to me, an invitation, sure, but to what? To the Gardens or something else? Something that I can feel us both teetering on the edge of? There's a moment of hesitation where I look backward, toward the place beyond the branches of the willow, where the lights of my grandmother's house burn brightly against the darkness.

I can feel it tugging at me, pulling me back away from the ledge I'm now standing on. And from somewhere in the depths of unknown things beyond the edge, Ben's hand is reaching for me. The parts of me scarred from years of pain and anger and silence bind me and hold me where I am. Thick coils of fear paralyze, preventing me from jumping into the unknown. But as I turn away from the house and find Ben's face, I know there is another way.

"I've already come this far, so sure, why not?" I reply, taking a step forward and allowing Ben's hand to envelop my own. There's that electric feeling again, but not the shock of a spark. Instead, a warmth spreads up my arm as if I've been plugged into an outlet and am only now realizing how depleted my battery had been.

No, I may not be able to jump.

But I can let myself fall.

The walk out of Gran's yard and down the dark road to where Ben's car is clandestinely parked feels remarkably quick, and all too soon he releases my hand so that he can hold the car door open for me.

"Thanks," I say as he shuts me in. A few seconds later, he's buckled into the driver's seat, and we're off.

"How far do we have to go?" I ask, narrowing my eyes as I try to discern any familiar landmarks flashing into brief illumination from Ben's headlights.

"We should be there in about a minute. Actually"—he looks away from the road and gives me a sheepish smile—"would you mind closing your eyes?"

I raise my eyebrows at him.

"*Please?*" he asks, and I am incapable of resistance.

I close my eyes, and just a few seconds later, I feel the car slow, turn, and roll to a gentle stop. Ben cuts the engine, and I listen to the click of his seat belt unlocking, then to the quick succession of his door opening and closing. Finally, after a second or two of quiet, my door opens.

I unclick my seat belt, and then Ben's hand is holding my own, guiding me first out of the car and then down a path. I can't tell if it's just hard-packed dirt, or maybe brick or concrete, but it's not the soft squish of grass I feel under my feet as we walk. Something tickles the hand not in Ben's, and I recoil, pushing myself into him with such force that we both almost go crashing to the ground. At the last second, he catches his balance and rights both of us.

"Sorry!" I say, my face burning with embarrassment. I'm suddenly quite thankful that I have my eyes closed—it means I don't have to see his reaction.

"What happened?" he asks, and there's no laughter in his voice. If anything, he sounds on edge.

"Something ... something touched my hand," I reply, gesturing vaguely to my left.

I hear him sigh in relief.

"Just long grass," he says, giving the hand he still holds a quick squeeze and sending a pulse back through me. "I thought maybe ... "

His voice trails off. I wait a few seconds, and when he doesn't finish, I prompt him. "Thought what?"

"Nothing," he says lightly. "Eighteen years old, and sometimes I still get a little freaked out by the dark."

I know the feeling. The image of clawed fingers curling around Gran's front door floats to the surface of my memory, and I feel the hairs on the back of my neck stand on end.

Suddenly it occurs to me just how stupid I'm being. That creature could be here, now, watching us and waiting. Not only have I put myself in danger, worse, I've brought Ben along with me.

"Just a second, okay?" he says, stopping and letting go of my hand. Before I can respond, I hear the sounds of him walking a few feet away and then a long, low creak of metal on metal.

A few seconds later, Ben's back beside me. But this time instead of taking my outstretched hand, he walks behind me and puts his hands over my eyes. Any other time, I would probably be giddy to the point of stupid feeling his warm breath tickling the back of my ear. Here and now, however, the steady beat of fear my heart is pounding out grounds me firmly in my senses.

"Ben?" I ask, and I can hear the fear creeping into my voice. I open my eyes and stare at the dark created by his palms. "I think we should probably go. I—"

"Okay, Amethyst, you can look now," he says, and his hands fall away from my face.

All my protests fade away as I take in my new surroundings.

We're standing in the middle of a garden, but not the kind my grandmother has in her backyard, where she grows cucumbers and peppers.

No, this is the kind of garden you see in old movies set in windswept British countrysides, where rich members of noble families spend their summer holidays. Tall brick walls surround us, forming a barrier from the outside world. Inside the walls, hedges run every which way, forming secret pathways now wild and narrow from years without trimming. I can't see Ben's car, let alone the woods I know loom on either side of where we stand, and a little of the terror melts away.

Moonlight falls on old marble statues, thick with moss, and wrought-iron benches covered in ivy. In the little section that we're in, there must be a dozen different flower beds, their original tenants long ago choked out by black-eyed Susans and wild daisies. It has obviously been neglected for years, but there's still an undeniable sense of beauty in it.

"How old is this place, Ben?" I ask, walking a little way away from him to run my finger across the chubby arm of a mossy cherub.

"It's been here since the 1800s, I think," he says with a shrug. "They closed it down years ago when they built the new one closer to town. People said they wanted greenhouses so that they could use it all year round."

Something about that sends a flash of anger through me.

"They just *abandoned* this one?" It's a question, but it comes out more like an accusation.

"Kind of. I mean, people still care enough to call the cops if some twelve-year-old kid starts messing around with it."

I turn back to look at him, expecting to see a sheepish smile on his face. Instead, he looks solemn, almost sad.

"But no one wants to take the time to take care of it. So here we are," he finishes, gesturing to the overgrown mess surrounding us. His smile is back, but it doesn't quite reach his eyes, and I recognize the look. It's the same way I used to look at my mother's empty chair back when my dad and I were still sharing meals. It's grief and loneliness and a slightly desperate desire to make it right again. Neither of us wants to talk about our mothers, though, so instead, I walk back to Ben and place my arm through the crook of his.

"Come on," I say, pulling him away from whatever memories are holding him captive. "Give me the grand tour. I want to see everything."

It's almost incredible how well Ben still knows the Gardens. As we make our way through the twists of hedges, he points out every bed and can tell me which flowers used to be there. He knows the stories behind the statues and the reasons behind the different ways the bricks are patterned. I don't say much as he leads me from section to section. Instead I allow myself to get caught up in his words. The way he describes things, I can almost envision how wonderful this place must have been in its heyday.

I'm about to tell him as much when he stops short, his face lighting up in earnest.

"And this," he says, "is my favorite part."

I follow his gaze and see that we're standing at the entrance to a large rectangular space. High hedges surround us, but there are several other breaks in the hedge, other ways in. We must be in the very center of the Gardens—all of the paths must eventually wind up here.

Inside the hedge wall, there are no flower beds, only a sea of grass that is high enough to cover my waist as Ben draws me deeper in. It's completely different from any other part we've seen so far, but I don't understand how an overgrown lawn is better than the rose garden or the wishing well.

"The reflecting pool," Ben says as he pulls me to a stop.

And then I see it stretching out before us, dark and deep, concealed by the tall grass around it. A long rectangle filled with water so still and dark that it is a perfect reflection of the night sky above us. As I take it in, Ben kneels down on the flagstone edge of the pool and touches the water so that a wave of ripples turns the reflection into a Van Gogh painting.

"Some days my mom doesn't even remember her name," he says, his voice rough. "But this place, I *know* she'd remember it. It's special. She used to say that it was like looking into another world."

It occurs to me that, for us, it is another world, or at least an echo of one. For him, it's a touchpoint to his mom, a place in space and time where he can reclaim her if the stars are aligned in the right order. For me, it's where my mother wore a sweatshirt on a summer's day for reasons I can only guess at. A place that is my only connection to the mysterious Absynth, who might just hold the answers I'm so desperately seeking not just to my mom's past but to the very strange things happening to me now.

After another few heartbeats of silence, Ben stands and clears his throat.

"So what do you think?" His voice wavers almost nervously.

I take a moment to look around before I answer.

"It's beautiful, Ben," I say, and although I mean it with all my heart, I hear him scoff in disbelief beside me.

"Well, I don't know about beautiful just yet, but it's got potential. It just needs a little work."

"A little work?" I laugh, looking around again at the sea of grass we're standing in, noticing several small trees rooted in the far corner. "There's enough here to keep someone busy for a year."

"Or two people busy for a summer."

It takes a few seconds for the meaning of his words to sink in, and when they do, my breath catches in my throat. My hand reaches up to unconsciously sweep over my forehead, feeling to make sure my secret is still concealed. Flirting in doorways is one thing, but this, the idea of spending a summer side by side with Ben, is another thing entirely. Even tonight I was too careless. What if the next time Ben reaches out to hold my hand, he withdraws in pain, a thick thorn protruding from his palm? Or what will I say when he asks why I'm wearing jeans and a long shirt in the middle of July? How will I explain daydreams that turn into nightmares and leave me screaming in the middle of the day?

There are a thousand—no, ten thousand—reasons to tell him no, but then I look into his eyes, already burning with excitement, and they all blow away on the gentle night breeze.

I'm already falling, and unless I suddenly sprout wings, there's no escaping Ben's gravitational pull. I can only hope that the landing is soft when I finally hit bottom.

"That depends," I begin, turning to smile at him. "Do we have to do all the work in the dark?"

I wait for him to laugh, but instead, he shuffles uncomfortably from foot to foot.

"What?" I ask, confused. "Do we *really* have to do all the work in the dark?"

"No," he begins, staring down at his shoes. "Well, to *really* fix it up, we'd need to get permission from the owner, and I thought … well, I thought that you'd be best for that."

"Why? Because you've got a criminal record tied to this place?" I ask, because if that's the reason for him not asking directly, it's a bad one. "If anything, Ben, that only *proves* how dedicated you are! I'm not even from around here—no one would listen to me."

"Oh, I think the owner might," he says, flashing me the tiniest of half smiles.

"And why's that?" I can't think of anyone in the state that would take my advice, let alone in this town.

"Well, because you're her granddaughter," Ben says uncertainly.

A memory from the day I arrived in Morgan Springs flashes before me. I had been teetering on the verge of a panic attack as Gran drove me home for the first time when a break in the endless line of trees caught my attention. I'd seen the Gardens that day. I'd even *asked* her what they were.

Just some abandoned property, she'd said.

Not a lie, exactly, but not the whole truth, either. She'd done the same when I asked her about my mother's friends by giving me an incomplete list, by leaving out Absynth. And this place is connected to them both, my mother and Absynth, and Gran doesn't want me to know that she is as well.

"I'll do it," I say, and Ben's face breaks into a wide smile.

Ten minutes later, Ben is parked at the very edge of Gran's lawn. The house beyond is dark except for the little yellow porch light.

"Are you sure you don't want me to walk you up to the door?" Ben asks, looking beyond me at the stretch of dark grass between us and the house.

"No, it's fine," I say, looking at the clock on his dashboard, which reads 12:51. "She didn't *explicitly* set a curfew, but I don't want to test that just yet."

Ben laughs.

"Yeah, you're probably right about that," he says, turning his gaze back on me. "So I'll see you tomorrow?"

Suddenly I realize how small the car is and how little space there is between us and how much I like the way Ben is looking at me right now.

"Yeah," I say, my voice higher than normal. "I'll call you tomorrow, right after I ask her."

I mean to leave, but I can't seem to get my arms and legs to coordinate with my brain. Instead, the only thing my body seems to be responding to is Ben's face, which is slowly leaning closer to my own. And then I'm moving, too, the gap closing doubly fast as the magnetic force between us strengthens. The static is buzzing again in my ears, drowning out my pounding heart, my shallow breaths.

God, he smells good, I think as we draw within two inches of each other.

BAM!

The sound is so jarring in the stillness of the moment that I scream, and Ben swears loudly. A cat, who has landed on the hood of the car from who knows where, hisses at us as if we're the ones to disturb him, before running off again. As I watch him disappear into the darkness, I become uncomfortably aware of how close I am to Ben now that whatever magic of the moment has been shattered. As inconspicuously as I can, I draw away from him and open my door.

"Well, good night, Ben," I say, extending my hand.

"Night, Amethyst," he says, taking it. But instead of shaking it, he holds it between both of his own and gives it a gentle squeeze.

It takes all of my mental strength to pull my hand from his, get out of the car, and walk quickly for the safety of the porch. I give Ben one last smile and a wave when I reach the front door, to signal for him to go. A second later I hear the engine turn over and watch Ben pull away until the taillights disappear beyond the line of trees.

Turning away from the dark road, I reach for the doorknob and find, to my horror, that it refuses to turn.

"Oh, come *on*," I whisper to it, jiggling the handle a little harder, willing it to open, but it's no use. My heart pounding, I check the windows on the front side of the porch, trying, with increasing desperation, to wedge my fingers between the antique wooden panels and pry them open. None of them budge, but the last one gives me a nasty splinter for my trouble.

Swallowing hard, I leap down the side of the porch and make a run for the back of the house, hoping with every fiber of my being that Gran has left the kitchen door unlocked. The only other options are to either get bitten by a radioactive spider and scale the wall back to my window or wake Gran up and explain what I'm doing locked out of the house at one in the morning.

I creep up the stairs as quietly as I can and reach out for the screen door, my first test. Holding my breath, I push the latch down, and relief rushes through me as it swings open without a sound.

"*Please, please, please, please,*" I plead with the second door before turning the knob. It moves a quarter of an inch before freezing in place, locked.

Frustration rolls out of me in waves as I rest my head against the smooth oak of the door. But before I can try to figure a way out of this, a twig snaps somewhere behind me.

Somewhere close.

"Ben?" I whisper, even though I know that it can't be him.

There is no response except for the creak of a wooden stair behind me. Maybe if I don't turn around, don't look, it'll go away. Maybe if I just stay still …

"*Amethyst*," the familiar voice rasps, and I can feel the monster it belongs to drawing closer.

All systems are failing now. My heart is beating so fast that I can no longer make out the feeling of individual beats. Meanwhile, my lungs have forgotten their job entirely as I struggle, face still pressed against the door, to take a breath. Alarms blare, and lights flash behind my eyes, and my brain, in a last-ditch effort of bravery, orders my legs to turn around.

Whatever it is, I'm going to die facing it.

My muscles scream in protest, demanding oxygen in payment for the effort it takes to spin me around, but my lungs are done. Burnt out and useless.

The creature from my nightmares stands on the very top stair. Her eyes are green-and-yellow cat slits, and one of her thorny arms still bears the bruise from our fight at the front door. And her face, dark green patches like blush on the apples of her cheeks, highlights as it splits into a smile.

I feel my legs give way, feel myself sinking to the cold porch floor. I want to scream, know I should scream, but there is no air left in me, or perhaps in the universe at all. Black webs pull at my consciousness, and some part of me that still understands things like feelings is relieved that at least I won't be awake for it.

I should have kissed him, I think.

And then everything goes dark.

Death feels stranger than I imagined.

I'm lying down on a surface that's soft and spongy. For a fleeting moment, I think that all of those cartoon versions of Heaven must have been right after all, that I must be stretched out on some fluffy white cloud on my way to the pearly gates.

But then the mossy smell of earth and grass fills my nose, and reality comes crashing back down around me: I am still very much alive, and I am no longer on the back porch of my grandmother's house. My breathing quickens as adrenaline floods through my body, and I do my best to conceal the rapid rise and fall of my chest by taking short, shallow breaths.

I'm relieved to be alive. Somewhere deep inside of me, I know this. But right now a more vocal section of my conscious self is lamenting my situation, and I think of how much easier everything would be if the creature had simply killed me on the back porch, or in the bathroom, or, more preferably, all those years ago in the woods behind my parents' house. How I could have avoided a decade of whispers and therapists and the pain of losing my mom if only I'd had the foresight to let it kill me.

But isn't that what you did tonight? a voice inside me asks.

It's right. I had laid myself down at the monster's feet and offered myself up to it, knowing that I would die. But here I lie, alive, and I realize, after taking stock of my body, I am unharmed.

It doesn't make sense.

The curiosity that blooms because of that realization is so strong that it quashes every other emotion running through me, a single question taking up all the space, smothering out the panic and squashing down the fear: *Why?* It's that word that opens my eyes. I'm in the woods, staring up at the night sky through the intertwining branches of oak trees.

This should scare me, should send me into an anxiety attack so all-consuming that my heart will feel as if it is about to burst, but instead all I can think of is that it makes sense. Ten years ago, the creature tried to drag me into the woods. Why wouldn't it do the same now?

There is no fear in me. My fear was of dying, and from everything that I can tell, I am alive.

Lights burn against the inky black of the sky, but instinctively I know that they are not stars, though they twinkle just as brightly. The lights are not dancing now, I realize as I watch them sparkling in the highest reaches of the trees, because they do not need to lead me anywhere.

I am where they need me to be, which means she must be here, too.

I push myself up into a sitting position, my hands sinking into the mossy bed beneath me. The creature has brought me into the forest, that's for sure, because dark trees press around me from every side. However, the space I'm in now, a wide clearing surrounded by a ring of trees, is bright and feels, if that's even possible, almost safe.

Then I see movement out of the corner of my eye.

The monster crouches just across the clearing from me, perched delicately on the balls of her feet. I've never willingly been this close to her, and with no desire to run beating through my body, I finally get a chance to look at the creature.

From a distance, she would probably pass for human: two arms, two legs, a head with long, albeit wild, blond hair. But up this close, the things that are not right stand out. Her skin has a luminescence that can only stem from the fact that it is tinted with the palest hint of green. Her ears, which should be hidden underneath her tangle of hair, are just barely visible as their pointed tips peek out. And then there's her face, which I know best from its presence in my nightmares. A face with cat's eyes and pointed teeth and a menacing smile.

But that's not the face I see now.

The eyes of the creature staring back at me are wide, the pupils black and round instead of slits, her teeth hidden by a tight-lipped grimace. She's young, I realize, tracing the curve of her face with my eyes; too young. It's been a decade since my near abduction, and she looks like she hasn't aged a day, let alone ten years.

I search her face for any signs of her age, and I find something that causes my breath to catch in my throat. Barely visible along her hairline is a series of small bumps, rising and falling so minimally that they're almost undetectable against the rest of her skin. My hand jerks up to touch the lump on my forehead, still concealed beneath my hair, the very beginnings of understanding beginning to trickle slowly out into my brain.

For a few seconds, neither of us moves or even breathes. We sit, staring at each other, while somewhere, outside of this tiny thicket, the world continues to turn around us. The seconds stretch on and on in silence until finally the question comes bubbling out of me.

"What do you want with me?" I ask, unable to hold my curiosity at bay any longer.

The creature across from me cocks her head to one side, considering. Then she creeps closer to me, still crouched, skittering like a spider across the ground. She stops just a foot from where I sit, and when she speaks, her voice is as soft and soothing as a lullaby.

"To talk. That's all I've ever wanted to do, Amethyst."

Is it? I think back to the night she lured me, a child, out into the dark forest behind my house. To the bathroom where she scratched and clawed her way in through the window. To the front door where she tried to force her way into my grandmother's house.

"If that's true, why didn't you just say so?"

The creature gives me a pitying look, the kind a parent gives a child who doesn't quite grasp what they see as a simple answer.

"Would you have listened if I had?" she asks.

And as I look at her, wild and green and otherworldly, I know the answer.

"No," I say, looking down at my hands, a twinge of guilt pulling at me. "I don't think that I would have."

I look up again, expecting her to be disappointed or angry or even smug, but instead, she is smiling in a way that says, as soft as a whisper, *I understand.* And at that moment, my eyes once again find the bumps along her hairline, and I think that she does understand, maybe even more than I realize.

She might understand everything.

"Who are you?" I ask, unable to keep the question from popping out the moment it enters my mind.

"Who do you think I am?" she asks, her head tilting to the side again, one of her eyebrows raised.

I'm about to tell her that I have no idea who she is when my brain finally catches on, a highlight reel of images playing in fast motion before my mind's eye: a creature at the edge of the woods, a murky figure in a bathroom window, a thorny hand closing around my wrist, and then a photo of my mother, her outstretched arm around someone who's been cut out of a picture.

"Your name is Absynth." My throat feels like it's closing around the words, trying to prevent me from speaking them. "You … you knew my mother."

I look away again as tears threaten at the corners of my eyes. For some reason, I don't want her to see me cry.

"Yes," she says, and there's something far away in her voice that causes me to turn back to her. She's not crying, but her eyes have the glassy look that precedes tears. I wait, my skin prickling with the electricity of her answer, for her to explain, but instead, she shakes her head and clears her throat. When she speaks again, her face is still serious, but the sadness has left her eyes.

"But there's something else I need you to know, and it can't wait, not even to talk about her." There's a warning in her voice that sends a shiver down my back. "Amethyst, there are people out there who know—or at least suspect—what you are. *Dangerous* people."

"What do you mean? *What I am?* I'm—I'm just … " But my voice trails off as I realize that there's no point in denial. Not here, not with her. Again, my hand finds its way to my forehead, still trying, unconsciously, to conceal my secret.

"Different," Absynth finishes for me, pulling my hand away from my forehead and taking it gently in her own.

I want to turn away from her, because that word stings with rejection, but Absynth reaches out and uses her free hand to hold my face in place. She locks her eyes with mine, and though I want to look anywhere but into them, I find that I can't.

"It is *nothing* to be ashamed of, Amethyst. Your mother was different, too. And so am I." She pauses, allowing a smile to bloom in earnest before she continues. "It runs in our family."

My brain crunches and strains like the old computers in the Morgan Springs Library, desperately trying to process the information it has just received. All circuits are overloaded, and somewhere inside my frontal lobe, my CPU is on fire. Before I go into complete system failure, my brain pushes out something that almost constitutes a question.

"*Our?* You're my… "

But Absynth seems to be prepared for this. Seems to understand what exactly is happening to me as my brain struggles to rewire itself to this new reality.

"Aunt," she finishes. "Annabell, your mother, she was my sister. My twin sister."

As my brain reboots back into function, it grasps for something familiar in Absynth's words. The only solid thing it can find to grab on to in the shifting world around me is the past tense.

"Was?"

A shadow passes over Absynth's face as she nods, and this time I can't stop the tears from coming. I thought it would be better knowing she was dead, better than the anxiety and pain that came with the uncertainty of her disappearance. But I didn't realize how deeply I had been clinging to that sliver of hope, that belief that my mother was out there, somewhere, waiting for me to find her—at least not until now, after it's been ripped away from me—and I realize that tiny sliver was the only thing holding back a tidal wave of longing and loss.

All of which now crashes over me, and I lose myself to the decade's worth of grief I've repressed. To her credit, Absynth doesn't try to patronize me by offering any of the weak words typically handed out during times of mourning. Instead, she lets me cry, unbothered. After what feels like hours, there's nothing left in me but a question.

"How?" I ask, my voice heavy.

Absynth looks beyond me when she answers, focusing on something I can't see, something from her past, and when she speaks, she sounds as if she's far from where we are now.

"As I told you, Amethyst, there are dangerous people out there. And

Annabell, well, she was always too trusting. I tried to tell her, to warn her, but … " She doesn't speak again until after she shakes the memory of whatever she's looking at away.

"But," she begins again, her voice light and airy again and her eyes back on me, "that's a long story for another time. It's *you* we need to talk about right now."

I want to argue, to make her tell me everything about my mother and how she died right now so that I can get it over with while I'm numb inside. But before I can protest, she reaches out to brush the hair away from my face.

"First things first, how long have you had thorns?" she asks, her eyes on the bump near my temple.

If anyone had asked me this question yesterday, I would have felt panic and tried to lie my way out of answering. Now, however, after everything I've learned in the last few minutes, I feel only a vague sense of relief at having one less secret to carry inside of me.

"A few months now … but how did you know?"

"You mean besides the fact that it's literally written all over your face?" Absynth laughs, and it's so genuine that I feel myself smile, just slightly, in return. Then she pulls something from her dress and holds it out between us. Sitting on her outstretched palm is a thorn, *my* thorn.

"You dropped this on a street in Philadelphia," she continues, looking down at the thorn in her hand. "I had suspected since you were young, of course, but when I found this, I knew for sure."

And just like that, I am two words away from finding out the truth of what has been happening to me. Why I'm growing thorns and bleeding sap. But as much as I want to know, there's a part of me that fears what Absynth's answer will be. Because as human and gentle as she is now, I've seen her, in life and dreams, become terrifying, no matter what her intentions may have been.

If that is a part of her, then it must be a part of me, too.

"Knew what?" I ask, quashing the fear before it can steal the question from my lips.

"That you're a *fairy*, Amethyst."

Everything stops.

The sheer impossibility of her statement is too much. My brain, already straining to grasp so much about tonight's events, gives up completely. There's no point in trying to make sense of something so ridiculous, so untrue, like this.

Instead, the only reaction I seem to be capable of producing is an uncontrollable giggle that threatens to bubble up out of me.

But then Absynth rises, and my laughter dies before it can reach my lips.

The hundreds of lights stationed in the canopy of the clearing dance down to meet my aunt as she stands, arms outstretched upward to meet them. In seconds, she's enveloped in their warm glow, a pale moon reflecting the light of a hundred tiny suns. And that's when, slowly, she begins to change.

Thick green thorns tipped with gold bloom from the bumps on her skin, running down her arms and the backs of her legs like hackles, with smaller ones forming a wreath around her face. Her skin is awash in color—rich green, pale silver, and deep dark black, painting her into more plant than person. Then, from behind her, a pair of translucent wings unfolds, stretching out in a six-foot wingspan before beginning to flutter so quickly that they become nothing more than a pale blur.

As she rises to hover a few inches above the mossy ground, I feel tears running down my cheeks. Not because I am scared or sad or even shocked but because I have never seen anything more beautiful in my life. Because I've never wanted something so desperately before.

But mostly I'm crying because this isn't real, and when I wake, I'll realize that everything I've learned tonight was just a product of my overtired mind.

Absynth must see my tears, because she lowers herself back to the ground and kneels before me, her impossible face just inches from mine, brows knitted together in concern.

"What's wrong, Amethyst?" she asks, her voice soft and sweet. "Did I scare you?"

I shake my head and feel more tears flood down my face.

"It's—it's just ..." I clear my throat, trying to find the words. "It's just not possible. I can't be—"

Absynth doesn't let me finish. "But *you are*," she says, and she reaches up to brush a soft finger over the bump on my forehead. As if awakened by her touch, I feel my skin open wide as the thorn pushes itself out. I expect pain, but there is none. Instead, I feel as if I've finally relaxed a muscle I didn't know I was clenching.

"I've been watching you struggle for years, Amethyst," she says, looking away from the thorn and back into my eyes. "Alone and outcast even in your own home."

Her hands move away from my face and down to my arms, where they deftly push up the sleeves of my shirt. She frowns, and my face flushes with shame as she runs her fingers over the scars crisscrossing my skin.

"I've watched you suffer in silence as you tried to keep yourself hidden from people who could never understand."

Absynth's hands close around my own, and she pulls me to my feet with a strength that doesn't match her small frame. Her eyes find mine again, and there's a fire burning in them now when she speaks.

"*I* understand, though. Probably better than you do yourself. This is a part of you that you'll never be able to hide, Amethyst. You're different, and you don't belong in that world." She pauses just for a second to squeeze my hand. "You belong in mine."

She smiles gently, and as she does, vines shoot up, wrapping themselves around the trees, weaving themselves together to form a living net around the glen we stand in. The tiny lights in the canopy dance down through the vines, and as their light passes over the plants, hundreds of tiny purple flowers bloom and die in fast motion, showering us in a silent blizzard of sweet-smelling snow.

My breath catches in my throat as the flowers and the lights bob slowly around us, and I feel tears in the corners of my eyes. But these are different tears—not born out of fear or sadness, or the aching loneliness left when my mom disappeared, but out of a feeling of relief that seems to radiate from inside my very soul.

There is a wall deep in my chest, a vast concrete monstrosity a thousand miles high and a hundred feet thick. My creation, constructed over the last decade to protect me from the inattention of my father, from the cruelty of my classmates. But Absynth's words are a tsunami powered by an earthquake massive enough to throw the center of my world off-balance. And as they crest over the top of the wall, cool and refreshing over the cracked and damaged landscape I've been hiding in, I realize that the wall was little more than a prison of my own design.

Absynth squeezes my hand, and we stand in silence for a few minutes as the tears roll down my cheeks. When I finally find my voice, it is thick with emotion.

"Is this magic?"

Absynth ponders my question for a moment, her eyes not on me but turned up to watch the dozens of lights flickering in the highest branches of the trees.

"No, it's *power*," she says, her eyes back on mine. "And it's already inside of you, Amethyst. I can teach you how to use it if you're willing to learn."

She squeezes my hand again, and I can almost imagine something fragile and small, like one of her little lights, beginning to glow in the dark space inside my heart. The sensation sends goose bumps up my arms and causes the hair on the back of my neck to rise. It's all too much to take in, too good to be true, but then the fingers of my free hand find the thorn still protruding out of my forehead, and I realize that *something* strange is happening to me and has been happening for some time.

"I am. I want to," I say, and the words feel like I'm falling again, but then Absynth catches me in a tight hug, and my feet find solid ground.

Over her shoulder, I see the first pale lines of gray dawn breaking through the spaces between the trees. I've been awake for almost twenty-four hours, and for the first time since I climbed out of my bedroom window, I feel tired. I'm yawning when Absynth releases me.

"I forgot how easily humans tire," she says, a slight frown on her lips.

"You don't *slee-ee-eep*?" I ask, another yawn stretching the last word.

"We do, just not as often or as long as you do. We get most of our energy from other sources."

Again, her eyes flick up to the lights above us. They seem dimmer now against the lightening sky. I want to ask her what they are, what they do, but Absynth seems to anticipate my question.

"Another time," she says. "Right now we need to get you back home before your grandmother wakes up." Her voice takes on a flat affect when she mentions Gran, the way a person might speak of some forgotten acquaintance long dead and seldom thought of.

We walk through the woods in silence, and it's only about fifteen minutes before the trees thin enough for me to see the outline of Gran's house. The sun must be close to rising, because the sky is a light lavender color, closer to pink than blue.

When we reach the tree line, Absynth stops so abruptly that I almost walk into her. She scans the darkened windows of the house for what seems like a long time before turning back to me.

"Meet me here tonight after dark. Don't let yourself be seen, and *don't* tell *anyone*. You're not safe until I can teach you how to protect yourself."

I nod, but now that we're away from the hollow in the woods and Absynth is back in her human form, it's hard to convince myself the last few hours were real, let alone someone else.

"I doubt anyone would believe me even if I did," I say with a smile that Absynth does not return.

Instead, her eyes narrow at the house over my shoulder, searching it again as she answers.

"You'd be surprised," she says, turning her eyes back on me, and I can tell that she's not joking about me needing to learn to defend myself. It sends a tremor down my spine.

"Right. Not a word," I say, trying to sound braver than I feel and turning to face the house. I'm about to make a break for the back porch when I remember.

"Crap," I say, turning back to Absynth. "The doors are locked. I can't get back inside."

She gives me a half smile. "Not a problem."

Absynth raises her hands, and as she does, I see thick vines sprout from the earth beneath my bedroom window. They grow, twisting around each other until they've formed a natural ladder from the ground to my bedroom.

"Thanks," I say, unable to suppress a grin. There's a moment of awkward silence before Absynth pulls me into another hug.

"Remember, tell *no one*," she whispers, and I nod into her hair.

"I'll see you later tonight," I say as we break apart, and Absynth nods, her eyes flicking back to the house.

I turn and sprint across the grass, my feet slipping on the dewy ground, not slowing until my hand reaches out to grasp the thick vines now clinging to the wooden wall of the house.

I turn back to the woods, which seem only to be getting darker as the sun rises behind me. I search the tree line for the outline of Absynth, but I can't seem to separate her shadow from the rest. I squint, trying to focus in on the spot where I left her, but then I hear the radio click on in the kitchen, and a shock of panic shoots through me.

I climb the natural ladder as quickly as I can and throw myself through the open window. I try to land quietly, but the ancient wooden floor betrays me. The creak cuts through the silence, and below my window, I can hear the squeak of the porch door opening. The voice of the morning DJ drifts out over the lawn, followed by the soft steps of someone in slippers moving across the porch.

My heart is hammering so loudly that I'm sure Gran must hear it. I sit, bracing myself for the moment she sees the vine ladder, but instead, I hear the steps retreat across the wood, followed by the screen door opening and closing for second time.

I slowly raise my head to the window ledge and peer down. Below me there is nothing but the wooden shingles nailed to the side of the house, leading down to a flat patch of green summer grass. No vines to be seen.

The relief is so complete that it wraps around me like a blanket, a sensation that only magnifies the exhaustion that is finally catching up with me. I kick off my shoes and stagger to the bed that used to be my mother's.

There are a million things running through my mind, but all of them are smothered out by the fatigue flowing through my mind like anesthesia. Hazy images of Ben and gardens and flowers and Absynth swirl into the black mist and then into nothing at all.

I am asleep before my head hits the pillow.

*K*nock. Knock. Knock.

My eyes open, and I am nearly blinded by the bright June sunlight filtering in through the open window. The curtains flutter slightly as a warm breath of summer air flows into the room. I push my hair back from my face and feel my forehead slick with sweat. It's got to be almost ninety degrees in my bedroom, and my long-sleeved shirt and jeans make it feel closer to a hundred.

Knock. Knock. Knock.

"Amethyst?" Gran's voice calls from the other side of the bedroom door.

My evening with Gran feels like it happened a lifetime ago, and in a way, I guess it did. The girl who climbed out of her bedroom window isn't the same one who walked out of the woods this morning.

They're not even the same species, I think as my finger touches the bump on my forehead. I left last night as a human, but I came back as something different, something else.

A fairy.

The word sounds silly and strange in my mind, even after the things Absynth showed me. Fleetingly, I wonder what Dr. Zahn's response would be if I told her that I'd discovered the monster in the woods, that she was actually my aunt and had been following me around for the last ten years to keep me safe because I'm a mythical creature with superpowers.

I envision her mouth hanging open as she tries to process my words, but then I realize how incredible it all does sound. I look at the open window for some kind of sign, but the bright light of day seems to cast everything about last night into doubt. Suddenly I'm not wholly sure I didn't dream the whole encounter up.

"*Amethyst?*" Gran's voice cuts through my unease. "Are you awake? Benjamin is on the phone for you!"

Benjamin? I think, my brain still clinging to thoughts of lights and flowers and the deep dark of the woods. But then something snaps into place, and I realize that she is talking about Ben. Ben, who I met last night in the space under the willow tree. Ben, who took me to his magical place at the center of the old Gardens. Ben, whose face had been inches from mine in the dark front seat of his car.

"I'm up!" I call back to my grandmother, practically leaping from the bed, my face hot from memory. Even though it's a million degrees in my stuffy bedroom, I wrap the comforter around me to conceal the fact that I'm still wearing my clothes from last night before unlocking and opening my door.

Gran is standing just outside, a gigantic cordless phone in her hand. I expect her to say something about my appearance—I'm sure that my face is beet red—but she doesn't speak as she passes the phone to me. She gives me a small smile, like she knows something that I don't, before turning to walk back down the stairs.

"Hello? Ben?" I say, my voice coming out more breathless than I would have liked, as if I'd run half a mile to get the phone from Gran.

"Hey." His voice is warm even through the phone's staticky speakers. "Are we a go for the Gardens?"

"Oh, uh," I stammer, glancing down the stairs to where my grandmother just disappeared around the corner, before retreating into my bedroom and closing the door. "I, uh, haven't asked her about that yet. I'm just getting up."

"What? You mean like getting out of *bed*? Seriously?" I hear him laugh on the other end.

"Why? What time is it?" I look at the open window, where the sun is now visible in the western part of the sky. Ben laughs again.

"Almost two," he says. "I've already done a shift at the diner. That's why I called!"

"Oh crap, really?" I walk over to my nightstand and check the alarm clock to confirm; it flashes 1:57 at me in large square numbers. I have no idea when I got in, but the dawning sun meant it must have been around five or six. I've had a normal eight hours of sleep, but of course neither Ben nor Gran knows what time I went to bed. Ben thinks I've been asleep since one in the morning. Gran since eight last night.

"I'm sorry, Ben, I overslept."

"Late night?" he asks, and even though his voice is light, there's something in his tone that weighs the question down with unspoken meaning. I know he can't have any idea what happened to keep me up so late, which makes me wonder what he thinks happened. Does he assume I was up late thinking about him and the Gardens and what almost happened in the car? And if he does, is it because he was up late doing the same?

My face gets hot again, and I'm grateful that Ben can't see me get flustered over the phone.

"Yeah." I hesitate, clearing my throat to give my brain time to concoct a believable fib. "I-I had some weird dreams."

"Dreams, huh?" His voice sounds serious, concerned. "Was one of them about spending the evening breaking and entering with a devilishly handsome landscaper? Because that wasn't a dream, Amethyst."

I grin like a fool into the phone, and I can't keep the laughter from escaping.

"Right," I say, trying to imitate his serious tone and failing as the laughter continues to bubble through. "That one was more like a nightmare."

"Ouch," he says, trying to sound hurt even though I can hear his smile through the phone. "You know, you're cranky when you wake up."

I roll my eyes, but my smile widens.

"I'll go talk to Gran now, and then I'll call you right back. Give me a half hour, tops."

"Well, hurry up, Sleeping Beauty, we're burning daylight here!" He's trying to sound exasperated and annoyed and failing miserably.

"*Bye*, Ben," I answer, my excitement at seeing him again creeping into the words. I hang up before I say something embarrassing—or worse, giggle again.

I've never had this kind of effortless connection with someone before, but something about talking to Ben is just so easy. I look up in the mirror and see my own reflection staring back at me. The smile makes my face look completely different, brighter and more alive than it ever looked in Philly. I may not be the same girl who climbed out of the window last night, but even that girl was not the same one who stepped off the bus and into Morgan Springs a few days ago.

I would have never had a conversation like that with anyone back home, not even close, but with Ben, he's just so open, so *honest*. I feel like if we kept talking, all of those things that Dr. Zahn and the half dozen other therapists had been trying to chisel out of me for years would just come tumbling out of my mouth. How much I miss my mom. How lonely I was living with my dad. How much those kids at school really did get to me.

How I've been growing thorns and bleeding sap for the last few months.

But I couldn't tell him that last bit, even if I had been tempted to. Absynth has forbidden it—the one rule she has given in exchange for teaching me more about what is happening to me. As my mind turns to my time with her, my hand travels to my forehead. Last night she had painlessly drawn a thorn out with the touch of a finger, but this morning there is no sign of a scab or even a scar from where the skin was broken. The bump is still a smooth ridge of healthy skin set just below my hairline.

And again the idea that it was all just a dream creeps in and takes hold of my mind. I walk over to the open window and look down, but there is nothing but the shingled walls of the house, the low slope of the porch roof, and green grass below. No vines and no indication that there ever were. I don't know what I was expecting, but normalcy below my window is not it.

I turn away from the summer afternoon because with every bird singing, every stretch of sunlit grass, I can feel the magic of last night slipping further and further away. Trying to distract myself, I shift my attention to getting ready for the day, and the weight lifts some when I think of the promise of an afternoon with Ben. I start to gather up my toiletries for a quick trip to the bathroom, but when I reach for my hairbrush, my hand freezes in its awkward outstretched position and my breath catches in my throat.

Balanced delicately on its black plastic bristles is a single purple flower.

Ten minutes later, I'm on my way down to the dining room, the smell of grilled cheese and tomato soup making my stomach growl so loudly that it sounds like I'm concealing a small dog underneath my shirt. I barely say good morning to Gran before I wolf down my first sandwich and half a bowl of soup. She smiles and waits for me to come up for air before she speaks.

"That's a new look," she says, her eyes traveling to a point on the right side of my head. Normally I would have a thorn panic, but today I know exactly what she's looking at: I've tucked Absynth's gift behind my ear.

"I just thought it looked pretty," I say in between spoonfuls of soup. It's mostly true. The flower is pretty, but wearing it, well, it reminds me of the beauty I saw last night—and the promise that that kind of beauty could live inside me, too.

"So," Gran begins, a twinkle in her eye that makes me blush, "what did Benjamin want?"

"Well," I say as I struggle to think of how to broach the topic of the Gardens. I decide that honesty is probably the best way to go. "He, uh, we, I mean, he wanted me to ask you something."

Gran's eyebrows pull together, and I can tell this question surprises her.

"About ... about the old Gardens down the road," I add, trying to clarify.

The confusion leaves her face and is replaced by a hard look that I can't read. When she speaks next, there's an iciness in her voice that I haven't heard before.

"What about the Gardens?"

I swallow the gush of anxiety starting to bubble up from my chest before continuing. "Well," I say, trying to adopt a light, casual tone to offset the frostiness emanating from across the dining room table, "we were wondering if it would be okay if we cleaned them up. You know, got them looking like they used to ... "

My voice trails off as anger, *real* anger, flashes like a warning light behind Gran's eyes.

"And he thought that *you* asking this time would change my answer?"

Now I'm the one caught off guard, and a surge of annoyance momentarily quashes my anxiety.

"Wait a minute. *This time*? You mean he's asked you before?"

Gran looks me over as if she doesn't quite believe my ignorance. Her eyes are narrow, but behind the anger, there's something else, something like sadness. But then she blinks, and it's gone.

"Once a year since the police pulled him in for trespassing when he was twelve," she says with a hint of exhaustion in her voice.

Having already met—and given in to—Ben's superhuman persistence myself, I can empathize with Gran. If I'm honest with myself, I'm a little impressed by her years of avoidance—Ben's charm is no joke. But that doesn't mean I'm going to give up without a fight.

"Well, why not let him do it, then?" I say, giving my grandmother what I hope is a winning smile. "I mean, the Gardens sure could use the work, and if he's willing—"

"Those Gardens are closed," she interrupts, and I feel my smile falter. "If Benjamin wants to do grounds keeping, then there's plenty of work around here."

She doesn't raise her voice, but there's still a warning buzzing through the undercurrent of her words. I know that I should drop it, that I should just leave well enough alone. But then an image of Ben's face, crumpled in disappointment, flashes across my mind, and my better judgment abandons me.

"But if we could just—"

Gran slams her spoon down against the wooden dining room table with a small *smack*. It's not a loud sound, but the action is so jarring, so out of character from the person I've come to know over the last few days, that she might as well have just shot off a cannon.

"The answer is no, Amethyst," she says, and it sounds like the formation of every syllable is causing her physical pain. "And that's final."

We sit in silence for a few heartbeats before Gran clears her throat and pushes herself away from the table. She stacks her still half-full bowl of soup on the plate containing the remnants of her sandwich and, without so much as another word, retreats into the kitchen. For a moment I entertain the thought of following her, but as I'm not sure if I want to apologize, argue, or cry, I decide it's too risky.

So instead I sit at the table and listen to the sound of running water as Gran washes her dishes in the sink, dreading the prospect of having to break the news of my failure to Ben.

Twenty minutes later, Ben and I sit across from each other at one of the library study tables. As tempted as I was to tell him the bad news over the phone to save me the trouble of seeing the heartbreak on his face, I couldn't do it. I owe him at least the opportunity to be disappointed with me in person.

He takes it better than I had hoped. He isn't happy, of course, but he also isn't blaming me, either.

"I was so sure she'd say yes to you," he says, and I nod.

The further removed I am from my conversation with Gran, the more confused I am by her reaction to our request. It's not like we're asking for a lot here—literally just her agreement to not sic the cops on us for doing a little gardening in our spare time. In fact, in light of how Ben and I are offering to do all of the heavy lifting ourselves, Gran's anger seems not only out of character but just plain bizarre.

Not that any of that matters now.

"I'm sorry, Ben," I say for the fiftieth time during our three-minute conversation. I know that there's probably nothing else that I could have said or done to change Gran's answer, but it doesn't make the failure hurt any less.

Suddenly, *embarrassingly*, I feel the sting of tears in my eyes.

My defenses flare up, and I bite down automatically into my bottom lip, looking down at my hands to avoid his gaze.

"Hey," he begins, his voice soft, "it's okay." I feel the warmth of his fingertips as he touches my chin, lifting my face to meet his. The gesture is so gentle, so *Ben*, that I can't help but smile, even if it is just weakly. He returns with his own grin, something that sends an increasingly familiar wave of pleasure through me.

"I just wish you could have seen it like it used to look," he says. "It was … "

His words trail off as his eyes lose focus. Then his hand is gone from my face, and the next thing I know, Ben is halfway across the room, walking away from me.

"Ben?" I ask, a little taken aback by his abrupt departure. "Are you—"

"Yeah," he says, flashing a smile back at me from over his shoulder. "Hold on. I'll be right back."

"But where—" I start to ask, but he's already halfway down the staircase before I can finish.

I'm just beginning to question Ben's definition of "right back" when I hear footsteps coming from the library's basement stairs. I catch a glimpse of the librarian overdramatically rolling her eyes over the rims of her glasses before he reappears.

"What's that?" I ask, pointing to the thick brown book Ben carries. I can tell from the dust smudges on his blue shirt that the book hasn't been moved from its underground home for a long time. My guess is confirmed when Ben sits down and opens it between us. The smell of mildew is so strong my eyes begin to water.

"*The Historian's Guide to Northwest Pennsylvania*," he says with excitement I don't understand. He begins to flip quickly through the moldy pages. "There's got to be *something* in here … "

I watch as he searches, my thumb and forefinger pinching my nose closed against the cloud of dust, or possibly black mold spores, that each turn of a page kicks up.

"Ah! Here we go!" he says finally.

Ben turns the book sideways between us so that we can both see the page. I crane my head slightly and read:

Morgan Springs Community Gardens

The Morgan Springs Community Gardens first opened on June 21, 1862, a gift to the town from Richard and Elizabeth Archer, longtime residents and benefactors of the area. The Gardens, built just down the small dirt road from the Archer estate, were the first municipal botanical gardens in western Pennsylvania and, unlike their eastern cousins, were constructed to resemble the Victorian gardens popular in England at the time.

Immensely popular from the date of their opening, the Gardens enjoyed a steady stream of visitors during the summer months until 1941, when the Archer family, now headed by Richard and Elizabeth's grandson, Dean, closed them for the season on October 1st. Little did he know that before the end of the year, the United States would become ensnared in the global conflict known as World War

II, a war that Dean himself, like so many
other young men, would not survive. His
loss left the Archer family devastated,
none more so than Dean's younger sister,
Christine, who left the estate to move
east to Boston.

Her departure left the Morgan Springs
Community   Gardens   leaderless   and
seemingly closed for good.

I look down the page to a black-and-white picture showing an unsmiling
man and woman standing in front of the same wrought-iron garden gates
Ben and I walked through last night. The caption under the photo identifies
them as Richard and Elizabeth Archer, but unfortunately, the image itself is
too old and grainy for me to make out the actual Gardens in any detail.

"Is there any more?" I ask, and in answer to my question, Ben reaches out
and turns the page.

Nineteen sixty marked the return of
Christine Archer, now Christine Darling,
to Morgan Springs. However, after nearly
twenty years of closure, both her family's
estate and the Community Gardens had
fallen into severe disrepair. Darling
set a timeline to restore both house
and Gardens to their former glory in two
years, an ambitious and, many thought,
impossible goal. But Christine wasn't
to be deterred, and on June 21, 1962,
one hundred years after their original
inception, the Morgan Springs Community
Gardens were once again open to the
public.

Below the continuation of the article is another black-and-white photo.
This one, however, features three people, an older couple who I can only

assume to be Christine and her husband and a girl who can't be much older than I am now. I look down below the picture for the caption, and my breath catches in my throat.

"Oh my God," I mumble, rereading the text to make sure that I'm not mistaken.

"What?" Ben asks, concerned. I point to the tiny print beneath the picture, and he reads it aloud:

"'Theodore and Christine Darling with their daughter, Beatrice, at the grand reopening of the Morgan Springs Community Gardens.'" He stops, his brow furrowed. "Wait, so, that girl is—"

"My grandmother," I finish, reaching out almost absentmindedly to touch the soft gray of her face. It's the same shape as my own.

I pull the book closer to me and continue to read the rest of the entry out loud.

"'The Gardens would continue their operation under the supervision of Christine's daughter, Beatrice, who married Arthur Faye on-site in June of 1964. Their leadership would oversee not only the biggest addition to the Gardens since initial construction but also their most successful years. The Fayes' tenure at the Community Gardens lasted for nearly four decades, until 2002, when the site was again closed in the wake of tragedy, following the death of Mr. Faye.'"

My throat feels tight as I finish the paragraph, driving my voice into a near whisper.

"I had no idea," Ben says, and I can hear remorse coloring his words. "No wonder she doesn't want anyone in there."

"She shut everyone out after he died," I say, remembering.

The day after my mother disappeared, my dad got called away from my bedside at the hospital by a nurse. There was a call for him at the central desk. It was Gran, telling him that my grandfather had passed away and that, considering everything else going on, there would be no services.

That was the last time she talked to either of us, until this summer. Even though Dad made an effort to invite her for Christmas dinner or to my school concerts, he never heard anything back. She could have just as well died along with my grandfather for all it mattered to me.

"I hadn't heard from her until a couple of weeks ago, when she asked me to come up here for the summer."

The memory of Gran's abandonment burns white hot in my chest for a moment, and then it's gone, replaced by a painful throbbing as I think about what those ten years must have been like for her. I realize that the avoidance was just a mechanism for her protection, that keeping me and my dad at a distance was to keep herself safe from any more heartache. I *know* this is true, because these are the same measures I've used for a decade.

Gran and I, it seems, are master masons, builders of walls that can be seen from space.

"Well," Ben begins, pulling the book away from me and beginning to close it, "I guess that's it. Game over."

"Wait," I say, reaching out and covering his hand with my own, stopping him. As our skin connects and I feel the warmth of him traveling through my fingertips, the idea begins to form. "We can't just give up."

"I don't see what else we can do, Amethyst." And when he says my name, a jolt of adrenaline accelerates the spread of his warmth up into my arm. "I don't think she's going to change her mind."

He looks up at me then, and even though his face is full of disappointment, he still smiles when our eyes meet. A smile of my own blooms as the warmth growing inside of me circumvents all of my defenses and works its way into the space that surrounds my heart.

Despite all of my efforts to keep people out, Ben has found his way in—and if this eighteen-year-old boy can break down my great wall, who's to say that we can't do the same for Gran.

"She did about me," I say, squeezing Ben's hand and smiling all the wider when the look of incredulity crosses his face.

"Okay," he says. "How do we get her to come around?"

I think for a moment, trying to isolate how exactly Ben had succeeded where so many efforts on the part of my dad and my doctors and my teachers had not. They had come at my defenses with ladders and trebuchets, with false peace banners and Trojan horses, all of them looking to conquer.

Ben had, on the other hand, knocked on the front door and left a flower behind in his wake. He had shown me his intentions and left the choice to me. He had been persistent, of course, but that's what it takes to enter a place that's been closed to the outside world for so long.

We don't open up for just anybody—you have to prove you mean well.

"We don't," I say to Ben, smiling at his confusion. "We're just going to fix up the Gardens anyway and hope for the best."

Ben opens his mouth, closes it, opens it again, and then starts to laugh. I can't help but join him, even though the librarian is shooting daggers at us from behind her desk. Not wanting to incur her wrath, I stand up from the table, and Ben follows me out into the June afternoon. I stop just outside the door and turn to face him.

"So?" I ask. "Are we doing this or not?"

"I, uh … " He reaches up and runs a hand through his hair, causing it to stick up in a million different directions.

It's kind of adorable.

"What?" I ask, looking away from his hair to see his forehead wrinkled in concern.

"It's just … I don't have the best track record with the police here. If we get caught … " Ben's cheeks flush slightly.

"Hey." I reach out and catch his hand as he goes to run it through his hair again and hold it between both of mine. "We're not going to get into any trouble."

I make myself look into his eyes as I finish. "I promise."

He seems to think about it for a minute and then lets out a long, overexaggerated sigh, and I know I've convinced him.

"All right, I'm in," Ben says. "But if we get thrown in jail for this, the bail money is on you. Deal?"

"Deal," I say.

And even though there's so much to do, a whole summer's worth of work to make the Gardens what they were—so that maybe we can help Gran and Ben's mom do the same for themselves—we just stand there on the back porch of the library, hand in hand, staring at each other and grinning like fools.

"My idea, my rules," I say, elbowing Ben's outstretched arm to the side and handing the bemused cashier my debit card.

"Don't take that," Ben says, ignoring my warning and trying again to pass a wad of crumpled-up bills across the counter.

I pull one of the paint stirrers from a nearby display and swat the back of his hand hard enough to make him retreat.

"Don't make me use this on you next," I say, brandishing the thin piece of wood at the cashier, who gives Ben an apologetic look before sliding my card.

"Chicken," Ben mumbles as the clerk hands me my receipt. I roll my eyes and reach out for the bags, but before I can grab them, Ben's hands snatch them away.

"I've got these, unless you're going to resort to violence again," Ben says, trying to sound afraid. I roll my eyes again, but neither of us can keep a straight face as we walk out of Top Hardware with $200 worth of brand-new gardening supplies.

As Ben loads the goods into the trunk of the Camry, I buckle myself into the front seat, carefully scanning for any familiar faces. Even though we opted to drive the extra fifteen miles to the sprawling metropolis of Bridgefield (population 2,500) instead of buying our supplies from Tom's Toolshed in Morgan Springs, there's still a decent chance someone might recognize us and report back to Gran.

Luckily the only people I see are a group of preteens skulking around outside the gas station—decidedly not members of Gran's circle of friends.

"We good?" Ben asks as he plops down in the driver's seat and slams his door.

"Coast is clear."

Ben replies by smiling and revving the engine so loudly that one of the gas station kids drops his slushie down his front.

"Sorry!" I yell out the open window as we speed by the kid, whose friends are doubled over in laughter.

Between the library and our tool excursion, it's already late in the afternoon, but Ben and I are too keyed up to wait another day to start our work in the Gardens. So before we leave town, he pulls into the parking lot of a roadside convenience store so I can use the pay phone to call Gran with our preestablished cover story of going to the mall in Greenport.

Ben's suggestion, of course, had been to tell Gran we were going to the movies together. An idea that had set my mind ablaze with what an actual evening with Ben in a dark theater would be like: the single shared armrest between our seats, the warmth radiating from his shoulder just inches from mine, the tickle of his breath on my ear as he leaned over to whisper to me. Even the fantasy of it filled me with a mixture of desire and anxiety so strong that I had to fake a bathroom emergency to escape Ben's hopeful gaze.

It took five minutes of deep breathing and cool water on my wrists before I was able to rejoin him in the garden-hose aisle of the hardware store, where I told him I didn't think the movie story would work.

"What if Gran asks me about the plot? I don't think I could lie well enough to convince her," I said.

"The mall it is, then," Ben said before winking and adding, "but we should probably plan to see a few movies, just to, you know, beef up your cover-story repertoire."

Having never experienced cardiac arrest before, I cannot say for certain that I experienced heart failure in the moments that followed his comment, but the way my heart stopped and then sputtered slowly back into a disjointed rhythm makes me think I was close.

I glance over at where Ben is pumping gas into the Camry. He catches me looking and smiles, which sends fresh heat into my face. Hastily, I turn back to the pay phone, pop my quarter into the slot, and dial Gran's number before Ben can notice the pink creeping into my cheeks.

It takes three rings before Gran answers.

"Hello?" The question is pronounced—she must be looking down at her caller ID and wondering what in the world the Bridgefield Snack N Save could want with her.

"Hey, Gran," I say, trying to sound as innocent and nonconspiratorial as possible.

"Oh, Amethyst!" she says, her voice brightening. "What are you doing all the way in Bridgefield? Is Benjamin with you?"

"Yeah, he's here," I say, sneaking another glance at the car, but Ben isn't there. He must have gone inside to pay. "Listen, I was wondering if it would be all right with you if I went to the mall with him over in Greenport. I—"

Before I can get out the rest of my well-rehearsed speech about how I need time in my natural teenage habitat of fluorescent lights and greasy food, Gran interrupts.

"Oh, Amethyst, that's *wonderful.*" And even through the phone, I can tell she's reading more into this outing than I am comfortable with.

"It's not like that, Gran," I say quickly, trying to counter whatever mental images of Ben and me she's conjuring. "He was already going, and I'm just tagging along. We won't even be together. He has to—"

"It's fine, Amethyst. Do you want me to save some supper for you, or—"

At that moment, Ben walks out of the store with two bottles of soda, a bag of chips, and four hot dogs, whose origins I'm not going to think about.

"No, I'll grab something there. Thanks, though," I say, my stomach rumbling.

"Okay, then, dear. You kids have fun."

And that's it. We say our goodbyes, and I walk back to the car, where Ben is waiting for my report. I fill him in on the brief conversation between bites of my chili cheese dog as he pulls the car out of the parking lot.

"That was easy," he says when I finish, and I nod, taking a long swig of my soda.

"I know. She didn't even ask what time I'd be home," I say, shaking my head. "I probably could have said I was going on a three-county crime spree as long as it was with you."

As soon as the words are out of my mouth, I know I'm about to regret them. Ben's eyebrows have disappeared beneath his brown hair, and there's a smirk playing at his mouth that means he's about to say something completely asinine.

"I guess I'm just irresistible to you Faye ladies," he says, flipping a potato chip into the air in an attempt to catch it in his mouth.

It bounces off his nose instead.

"Oh, yeah," I reply, trying to sound completely unimpressed as I mock-fan my face. "Totally enchanting."

But then Ben's face splits into a wide grin, and my heart starts to thud erratically.

"So," I begin, trying to change the subject to anything but his irresistibility, "I've been wondering, how are we going to get into the Gardens without being seen, especially with"—I gesture to the bags of gardening supplies piled onto Ben's back seat—"all this stuff?"

"I've been thinking about that, too," he says, not taking his eyes off the road when he answers. I notice his playful smile is gone now, too, and suddenly I feel like I've said something wrong.

"What?" I ask, trying to angle myself to get a better read of his face.

"Nothing. I mean, I know a way. There's a trail. But … " He surprises me by pulling over to the side of the road and putting the car into park. He turns to look at me, his open mouth searching for the right words, and his brows knit tight together in concern. He takes a breath, closing his eyes. He does not open them when he speaks.

"But we'll need to go to my house first, and … " He finally opens his eyes but is pointedly looking down at the steering wheel instead of at me, and I know immediately what's wrong.

"And you don't know if you're ready for me to meet her. Your mom, I mean," I finish for him.

Ben nods, but he still doesn't look up.

"No one's been to my house since the accident—except for a social worker, you know, to make sure I was eating and everything. And she's … well, I told you how she is," Ben says, his voice cracking slightly on the last word. Red splotches of embarrassment, or maybe anger, bloom on his neck.

111

My body responds suddenly without any consultation with my mind, and I reach out over the central console and wrap my arms around his neck in an awkward embrace. A second later, I feel Ben reciprocate, his arms encircling my waist as he rests his head against my shoulder, his face buried under the curtain of my hair.

Somewhere in the back of my mind, I know this is dangerous. That we are too close in this moment, and not just physically. There's something else, too.

I don't know if it's friendship or romance or something in a third category that I don't have a word for yet, but Ben has, despite my meager efforts to dissuade him, woven himself into my life. The danger, of course, is not in this moment of togetherness but in the absences—both the brief hours spent apart and, more terrifyingly, the looming separation at summer's end. My heart will tear in two, I suppose, a ragged, bloody souvenir of my summer in Morgan Springs.

And I will have no one to blame but myself.

All of this takes a back seat to the warmth of his skin where it presses against me, a thousand new electrical connections now wiring themselves between us. The way the fingers of his right hand curl up into my hair. The feeling of each beat of his heart as it pulses out from his chest to mine. I count them as they pass, timing my breathing to their steady thrum to keep the delirium of his touch at bay.

Inhale. Beat. Beat. Beat. Exhale. Beat. Beat. Beat. Repeat.

It's a few minutes before Ben finally clears his throat and releases me. His face is red, and I can feel a damp circle soaking through the spot on my shirt where it had been in contact with it.

He gives me an uncertain look before he speaks.

"Amethyst, I'm sor—"

But before he can finish his apology, I stop him. "Don't. You don't need to apologize, and you don't need to take me to see your house or your mom. Not until you want to."

He gives me a watery smile and reaches out to hold my hands between his own.

"I do want to. You deserve to meet her, and she deserves to meet you."

The drive back to Morgan Springs is quiet. Whatever invisible line we crossed while parked on the side of Route 8 has rendered us both speechless.

On my part, I am fluctuating between the red-hot memories of the way Ben's arms felt around me and the stone-cold dread surrounding the short shelf life of our relationship. As soon as I get one side under control, the other flares up, like I'm trying to fight two raging infernos with only one worn-out garden hose.

I'm so distracted that I fail to notice Ben turning off the highway until the car is engulfed by thick trees on both sides. Instinctively, I brace myself for panic to wash over me at the sight of the forest, but nothing happens.

There's nothing for me to be afraid of out there anymore, I think, a brief image of purple flowers and dancing lights flashing across my mind's eye. He turns the car down a dirt driveway and parks, and then my stomach clenches with anxiety at the prospect of meeting Ben's mom.

Ah, there's the panic.

"I'm just going to go in first and see if she's up for company, okay?" Ben says, looking as nervous as I feel.

"Sure," I say back, trying to smile. I must be failing, though, because Ben's hand pauses on the door handle.

"She's going to love you, Amethyst. How could she not?" He squeezes my hand one more time before opening his door and walking up the slate path toward his house.

My eyes follow Ben until he disappears behind the front door, but once he's gone, I finally take the time to examine my surroundings. The front yard is small but well-kept, with recently mowed grass and small garden beds full of black-eyed Susans and some kind of blue flower that I can't identify. The lawn stretches around both sides of the house and, like Gran's yard, is ringed by deep forest. But unlike Gran's pristine side lawns, Ben's are peppered with clumps of long grass growing up around dozens, maybe even hundreds, of tree stumps.

He cut them all down, I realize, staring at the fifty additional feet cleared on either side of the house. A rush of admiration fused with pity surges through me. *He cut them down because she was afraid of the forest after what happened.*

But what did happen? I think of Ben's story, of my memories of strange lights in the woods, and finally, of everything I learned from Absynth last night. Was there a fairy that day on the trails outside of Morgan Springs? And if there was, was the creature friend or foe to the humans hiking through the forest?

Another memory passes through my mind, this time of a dream where a beautiful but monstrous Absynth stood below my bedroom window howling, fangs bared.

If I believe Absynth to be a monster, then aren't I one, too? I shake the thought from my head and shift my focus away from the yard to look at the house.

The Taylor home is a single-story cabin, very different from the large Victorian-style buildings that seem to occupy most of the rest of the town. It's smaller than Gran's house, maybe a quarter of its size at most, but what it lacks in space, it makes up for in what I can only describe as rustic charm.

The wood on the outside is a warm honey color, and there's a large front porch made from the same lumber. As I follow the lines of the house up to the peak of the roof, I expect to see the large plate-glass windows that are so often added to provide cabins with natural light and spectacular views. However, when my gaze reaches the place where the windows should be, all I see are large sections of discolored wood.

Plywood.

I search the rest of the house and see similar boards of varying sizes covering what I can only assume are other windows. Some of them even have additional two-by-fours nailed over them, forming large *X*s. Fleetingly, I wonder if they are there for structural reasons or as a warning to whoever— or whatever—might be lurking in the forest.

But before I can come to any kind of conclusion, the front door opens, and Ben reappears. I open my door and start to walk toward him, but he holds out his hand.

"She's, uh, she's not having one of her good days," he says, looking at me apologetically.

"Oh, okay," I say, and I can hear the relief in my voice that I hope Ben doesn't pick up on. "Another time, then."

"Yeah," Ben says, glancing over his shoulder at one of the plywood-covered windows.

"Do you need to stay with her? We can do this another day," I say, motioning vaguely at the car, where the gardening supplies are still sitting.

Ben shakes his head, and then he frowns at me.

"What?" I ask, trying to figure out what I said to elicit this reaction.

"We haven't even started yet," he says, "and you're already angling for a day off? I mean, I know you city folk aren't used to, you know, *hard work*, but I thought I'd get a week's worth of weeding out of you. A day, at the least." He's unable to suppress a grin from breaking across his face.

I'm still rolling my eyes when he joins me to walk back to the car.

Thirty minutes and three wheelbarrow trips through the wooded path behind Ben's house, and we're finally ready to get to work. Unfortunately, the sun must have missed the memo about our plans, because it's already low in the sky, casting long shadows across the overgrown flower beds. Just as I'm about to suggest beginning fresh in the morning, Ben asks, "Where do you want to start?" And his face is still shining with the same excitement from earlier, which renders me unable to do anything but lower myself to the closest flower bed and motion for him to join me.

"Good pick," he says, kneeling beside me at the edge of the weed-choked soil. "This one was rosebushes. I bet they're still in here somewhere, just aching for some sunlight!"

"There have to be at least twenty different beds in this section. How do you remember all of them?" I ask, shaking my head incredulously.

"I told you. I used to come here. *A lot*." He emphasizes the last words, and I wonder how many times he came here with his mother, and then how many times afterward alone.

We weed in silence for a few minutes, each of us working in opposite directions, searching for rosebushes I'm becoming increasingly more certain no longer exist.

"Oh! Oh! Ben!" I say, louder than I mean to in my excitement. "I think I found your roses!"

He hurries over as I work to liberate the plant from her weedy captors. It's a tiny thing: five white petals encircling a deep-red center dotted with gold. It's different from any other rose I've encountered; there's a delicate beauty to it that's unlike anything I've ever seen before.

"Where?" Ben says, sliding in next to me and scanning the area I've just cleared.

"There," I say, pointing to the flower. "The little white one."

Ben leans over me, taking a closer look at the blossom before shaking his head.

"Nah," he says, already moving back toward his section of the garden. "That's just rose mallow. It's a weed. Go ahead and pull it up with the rest."

"Oh," I say, looking down at the tiny flower. "Are you sure? It's so pretty."

Ben has already returned to weeding and doesn't look up when he answers. "Yeah. It might look like a rose, but it doesn't belong."

A strange and sudden sadness wells up inside me at his words.

It might look like a rose, but it doesn't belong.

She might look like a girl, but she doesn't belong.

A single hot tear slides down my cheek. I swipe it away angrily and reach out to rip the offending flower out of the ground. But before I can grab it, Ben's hand is around my wrist.

"Hang on," he says, leaning in again to examine the flower. "Yeah, you know, I think you might be onto something."

"No, I'm being stupid," I say, reaching for the blossom with my free hand.

Again, I find Ben's hand on my own.

"It's okay, Ben. You don't have to—"

"Do you know the other name for rose mallow, Amethyst?"

I shake my head, avoiding his eyes as he speaks. He seems to realize this and angles himself so that our faces are just inches apart. He has an earnest, almost emphatic look on his face as he continues.

"It's 'flower of the hour.' It's called that because it's only fully open for one, maybe two hours a day." He smiles slightly. "Roses—you can see those anytime in a million gardens around the world. But this … "

He looks back at the rose mallow blossom and releases one of my wrists to reach out and gently stroke one of its petals before looking back at me.

"This is special."

And before I can protest, Ben begins to uproot all of the plants surrounding the tiny flower, including a few of what I can tell are real rosebushes. When he is finished, the rose mallow sits alone in a small circle of cleared soil.

I'm not sure what to say, because I'm very certain that Ben was not entirely talking about horticulture just now, so I blurt out the first thing that crosses my mind. "But what about the roses? Won't people be upset?"

Ben turns back toward me and reaches up to touch my face, running his thumb down my cheek as gently as he did the flower.

"This garden is our place now, and if we want rose mallow instead of rosebushes, then that's what we'll grow."

116

It's full dusk by the time Ben pulls into Gran's driveway, and while I'm tempted to linger in the passenger seat a little while longer, darkness and the promise of another visit with Absynth is looming. So as soon as the car is parked, I unclick my seat belt and reach out for the handle of the car door in an attempt to escape before Ben's gravitational pull traps me in my seat.

"Amethyst?" As he speaks, I feel him place a hand delicately on my shoulder. The gesture acts like a stun beam, the electricity flowing between us rendering my limbs incapable of movement. I feel pressure on the spot where his hand rests and hear him shifting his weight in his seat. When he speaks again, his breath tickles the side of my face.

"I just … " He pauses, and I wish I could turn my neck to read his face, but all lines of communication from my brain are overloaded with disjointed observations of the sweet smell of spearmint on his breath and the way his hand is slowly moving along my shoulder. "Thanks for today."

A warm pressure caresses the apple of my cheek as his lips brush up against it.

In the fraction of a second that follows, adrenaline floods through my veins, and I feel my body break free from its paralysis. Every muscle, tendon, and nerve stands at attention, tensed and ready for me to give the command to reciprocate.

And that's when I feel the thorns, dozens of them, start to push through the surface of the skin of my legs, my arms, my face.

Instinctively, I jolt away from Ben, throw the passenger door open, and hurl myself out of the car. I don't dare look back at him as I rush toward Gran's house, too worried that the falling darkness won't be enough to conceal the thorns.

"Amethyst? Amethyst, are you all right? I'm sorry!" The concern in Ben's voice almost gives me pause, but I know that if he follows me, if he sees me like this, everything between us will fall apart. I make a beeline for one of the long shadows cast by the porch's railing and turn around, making sure my face is hidden in the darkness.

"I'm fine! I just need ... " I search for an excuse, *any excuse*, to get away, but my mind comes up blank, so I abandon all pretense of explanation. "Bye!"

"But—" Ben says, his body halfway out of the car.

"I'm fine, Ben!" I say again, now turning to rush up the steps. "I'll call you tomorrow!"

And before he can protest further, I run through the front door, up the stairs, and into the second-floor bathroom, where I slam the door behind me.

"Amethyst?" Now it's Gran's voice that is concerned.

"Give me a minute, please!" I shout back, my voice wavering as I struggle to keep control of myself.

But as soon as I turn the lock on the door, I feel the first hot tears start to run down my cheeks. I stifle the sob trying to push itself out of my chest and force myself forward to stand in front of the bathroom mirror.

I see a wild-eyed monster, with thorns raised like green hackles protruding from her face and the backs of her hands, staring back at me. I open my mouth and hiss, actually hiss, at her, bared teeth and all.

Suddenly, as if they sensed my anger, the green tips of the thorns start to recede, an action that would usually send relief flowing through me, but at this moment, it makes me rage.

Oh no, you don't! I think, frantically rummaging through the bathroom drawers for something to use to exact revenge. I pull out a pair of dainty tweezers and try to clamp down on the thorn protruding from the back of my left hand. It's enough to stop it from disappearing beneath my skin, but I can't get enough leverage to twist it free.

Frustrated, I throw the tweezers back into the drawer and bite down on the thorn. I can taste sap as my teeth puncture the thorn before ripping it from my hand with one quick jerk of my head.

The pain is immediate and so intense that I have to bite down on my fist to keep from screaming. At least the taste of blood helps to wash away the sweetness of the sap. While my eyes are streaming with fresh tears, I am almost comforted enough to be able to attribute them solely to the gaping hole in my hand—all thoughts of Ben, Gran, and my monstrous appearance muted by the white-hot pain radiating up my arm.

I close my eyes and focus on breathing. In the near-quiet, I hear footsteps coming up the stairs. I hastily reach into the shower and turn it on, trying to buy a little more time before I have to face Gran. I put my ear up against the door and listen as the steps stop and then slowly start going back down toward the first floor.

Sighing with relief, I undress and step into the shower.

It's nearly forty-five minutes later when I'm clean, bandaged, and finally back in my bedroom. I've just opened my window to watch for Absynth's signal when there's a soft knock at the door. I make sure to pull my sleeve down over my left hand before calling out, "Come in!"

I take the second it takes for Gran to open the door to hop back onto my bed and fix what I hope is an unassuming smile to my face.

"Amethyst, is everything all right, dear?" She stops to linger in the doorway, her eyes narrowed, scrutinizing me.

"Yeah," I say, looking away from her gaze. It's always easier for me to lie when I don't have to see someone's face. "It's just, you know, Ben."

Gran's face relaxes, and she crosses the room to sit next to me.

"Why? Did something happen?" she asks, reaching out to stroke my hair away from my face, but I flinch away, and she returns her hand to her lap.

"No, not exactly," I say, still not looking up at her. "I'm just not used to all the attention. It's a little much for me."

Gran gently takes my left hand between her own and squeezes it, sending a fresh flare of pain burning up my arm. I try to turn my head away quickly so Gran can't see me wince, but there's no need. She isn't looking at my face.

She's squinting down at my hand.

My breath catches in my chest as she runs one knobby finger along the place where my skin and the cuff of my shirt meet. Then her face snaps up to look at mine, and a thrill of terror runs through me as she scans every inch of my face with a steely glare.

She knows, I think, panic gripping me from the inside out. *She knows what I am.*

"It looks like you got some sun today," she finally says, and I am caught off guard by the comment.

"What?" I ask, my mind still trying to make the leap from thorn-covered fairy to sun goddess.

"Your skin," she says, gesturing to my face. "It's starting to freckle."

I look down at my pale hands, where little brown dots have indeed started to blossom. And if they're on my hands, there's no doubt that they're also cascading along my cheeks and over the bridge of my nose. It's the curse of my Irish heritage—I don't tan in the sun, just burn or freckle.

"Yeah," I say, still trying to understand her newfound interest in my skin.

"Hmpf," she says, and I hear a note of disbelief in her tone. "I guess I didn't realize the mall was so sunny."

Crap. She doesn't suspect I'm part plant; she thinks I've been in the Gardens.

"Ben and I walked around Greenport a little bit," I say, and when Gran still looks skeptical, I add, "It was all a ruse for him to try to take me out to a fancy restaurant. You know, like on a date."

Next to me, Gran relaxes.

"He does seem quite taken with you," she says, all hint of suspicion gone from her tone.

"He's being nice," I say, trying to downplay just how right she is. "He's probably just angling for a raise."

Gran shakes her head, smiling, and as she does, I see a tiny ball of light float in through the open window behind her.

"Well, you tell him that if he wants more money, he'd do better trimming my azaleas than romancing my granddaughter."

She laughs at her joke, while behind her the light revolves in place for a moment before drifting back out through the window.

"Right," I say, knowing how distracted I must sound but too excited to care. "I'll, uh, let him know."

Gran follows my gaze, turning to examine the empty air behind her.

"Amethyst?" she says, turning back to me. "Are you okay?"

"Yeah, just *tired*," I say, punctuating the word with a fake yawn. "Too much sun today, as you said."

Gran gives me another searching look before patting my knees and standing.

"Okay, well, you get some sleep, then," she says, scanning the room a final time before walking out and closing the door behind her.

I wait until I hear her footsteps fade away into the living room downstairs before jumping out of bed, locking my door, and rushing to the window, where Absynth's vine ladder is already waiting for me.

I slither down the vines and sprint across the dark grass, searching the black trees for any sign of Absynth, but it's not until I'm enveloped by the first row of enmeshed branches that I see her. She smiles in greeting but doesn't make any other movement toward me, so I close the distance between us.

"Is everything okay?" I ask.

"Yes," she says, squinting in the direction of the house. "I just wanted to make sure you weren't being followed."

"Gran thinks I'm sleeping," I say, but I can't help looking over my shoulder to make sure that no figure stands silhouetted against the backlit kitchen window.

"Good," Absynth says before finally turning her full attention to me and smiling in earnest. "How are you, Amethyst?"

"I'm—" But there are so many conflicting emotions churning inside me that I find myself unable to isolate even one to share with my aunt. "I'm honestly a little overwhelmed."

Absynth laughs and pulls me into a tight hug.

"I would be worried about you if you said any differently," she says, releasing me. "But let's walk and talk. I don't like being this close to the edge of the forest."

"Okay, but you'll have to be patient with me; I can't see anything out here," I say, imagining the twenty thousand tree roots and rotten logs that lie between myself and Absynth's forest home.

"Oh, that won't be a problem," she says, spinning me to face the dark woods behind us. Only it's not dark anymore. The path ahead of us is illuminated by dozens of white lights twinkling lazily between the trees.

I shake my head, unable to convince my mind of what my eyes are seeing.

"What?" Absynth asks as we start down the path.

"It's just surreal," I say, my head still swiveling in every direction to gaze at the lights as we pass. "I mean, weren't you shocked when you found out you were a … "

But I can't make myself say the word "fairy" out loud. It still sounds too ridiculous, even with Absynth and her magic walking right beside me.

"Well, I'd always known I was different. I just didn't know how," she explains, lovingly touching one of the lights floating beside her before smiling at me. "So I suppose that I was more … pleasantly surprised."

I want to ask her when she knew and who told her, but then another question skips to the front of the queue and out of my mouth. "And my mom? How did she react?"

Her smile falters, just for a moment.

"Annabell took it … poorly," she says, an answer that my brain finds woefully lacking in adequate detail.

"What happened to her? To my mom? I—"

Absynth stops walking and holds up her hand. Behind her outstretched palm, I can see a flash of annoyance or maybe anger cross her face.

"Tonight is not the night to talk about your past," she says, and the harshness in her voice takes me aback. She must notice, because she places her hand on my cheek, her expression softening. "Tonight, Amethyst, is about your future."

With her other hand, she reaches out to touch a thick knot of hanging vines, causing them to twist apart to reveal the glow of the hollow beyond. She motions for me to enter, but before I get more than one foot through the magical opening, I am nearly knocked back out again by a blur of dark-brown hair and olive skin, and I find myself ensnared in a bone-crushing hug.

"Easy now, Daphne, or else you'll kill the poor girl," Absynth trills behind me, the light tone of her voice not matching up with the warning in her words.

"Oh no!" the person holding me cries before gingerly disentangling her arms and backing away. "I didn't get you, did I?"

Worry clouds her beautifully inhuman face as she tugs anxiously at the top of one of her pointed ears.

"Get me?" I stammer, examining my baggy sweatshirt, not quite sure what I should be looking for.

122

"With my stings," the fairy called Daphne says, holding out her arms for me to see. Like Absynth, she has sharp protuberances growing out of her skin. Instead of green, however, Daphne's are a toxic shade of violet. "I turned out to be poisonous after my Changing. Of course, it took me accidentally pricking myself and winding up completely paralyzed for a few minutes before I realized it."

"Turned out to be what?" I stammer, but Absynth waves my question away, addressing Daphne instead.

"We'd know by now if you clipped her, Daph. *She'd* be catatonic."

Catatonic? But before I can register my complaint at almost becoming a personal pincushion for one of Absynth's fairy friends, she speaks.

"Amethyst," Absynth says, gesturing first to Daphne and then to another fairy I hadn't noticed in the excitement of my near-poisoning, "these are my sisters, Daphne and Naya."

"Sisters?" I say, my brows knitting together in confusion as I look at the women in front of me, all as different from each other as wildflowers in a meadow. Absynth with her pale skin, wild blond hair, and green-and-gold thorns. Daphne with her purple barbs, her sleek brown hair plaited smoothly down her bronze back. And finally, Naya, whose skin is ebony beneath burnt-orange thorns and whose black hair falls in tight curls around her thin face.

Absynth reaches out to take my hand and brings me closer to the other fairies.

"We may not be genetically related, but we've all got fairy blood, and that binds us closer than any biological family could hope to be." As she speaks, she beams at Daphne and Naya, who she calls her family, and I can't help but long for her, my actual aunt, to look at me with such affection.

"It's a pleasure to meet you, Amethyst," Naya says in a rich voice that seems too big for her willowy frame. "Absynth has told us so much about you, but we didn't want to make any decisions until we saw you in person."

"Decisions?" I echo, a warning shot of adrenaline spiking my system as the two fairies surround me, their eyes hungry and appraising.

"Hmm," Daphne says, reaching up and taking a lock of my hair in her hand before examining it as it slips down through her fingers.

"Yes, I see now," Naya mutters to herself. She pushes the sleeve of my sweatshirt up above my elbow and runs a long finger down the length of my forearm.

"Absynth?" My voice is tight with fear as I search for her between the bobbing and weaving bodies of Daphne and Naya. I find her about ten feet away from us, smiling as she leans up against a tree.

"Don't worry, Amethyst, they'll be gentle," she says, a mischievous glint in her eyes. "Normally I wouldn't have agreed to this sort of thing, but we've *got* to do something about those scars."

Without waiting for me to respond, Daphne and Naya push me down onto a mossy stump and start pulling the ratty sweatshirt over my head.

Then they unfurl their wings and begin their work in earnest.

Most of the next half hour is a blur. Daphne and Naya flit around me as fast as hummingbirds, first washing me with cold, clear water that leaves me shivering so violently that Absynth sends a few of her white lights over to warm me up. Next, they apply a thick, milky-white substance all over my body, rubbing it with extra vigor over the worst of my scars, which leaves them prickling uncomfortably.

When they finally finish applying the liquid, Daphne leans down so that her face is just a few inches from mine, alight with excitement.

"Do you mind closing your eyes for this last part, Amethyst?" she asks. "We want you to be surprised."

Yes, I think, but I shut them anyway.

Another twenty or thirty minutes of poking, painting, and hair pulling ensue, but it's somehow easier to endure now that I can't see what they're doing.

Eventually, the pulling and pinching subside, and despite my initial annoyance at having the fairy equivalent of a spa treatment forced upon me, I am cautiously excited to see the results.

"Go ahead and open your eyes, Amethyst," Daphne says from somewhere to my right.

So I do.

Standing before me is a pool of water so smooth that it acts as a mirror, and reflected in its shallow depths is the image of a girl that takes my breath away.

No, not a girl. A fairy.

My hair is pulled back, loose curls spilling out beneath a crown of flowers, and my sweatshirt and jeans have been replaced by a delicate-looking dress that appears to be made of hundreds of pale-pink petals—roses by the smell of them. Most notably, though, the scars that once crisscrossed up and down my arms and legs have all but disappeared, replaced by barely noticeable bumps. The thing is, even they don't look strange anymore when viewed amid the fairy features that Daphne and Naya have added.

"I'm so ... " I begin, raising a hand to my face and watching the otherworldly girl in the pool do the same.

"Beautiful," Absynth finishes, coming to stand next to me. Our reflection could be one of the oil paintings hanging in Gran's house.

A beautiful picture, I think, *but not reality*.

I turn away from the pool, away from Daphne and Naya, and away from Absynth and her magical world.

"It's beautiful, but it's not me. Not really."

"Girls," Absynth says behind me, "a moment, please." There's the faintest sound of fluttering wings and then silence.

"But it could be," Absynth says. "Once you have had your Changing, you would be a full fairy."

She moves to stand in front of me and reaches up with her finger to scoop a tear from my cheek.

"Amethyst, you wouldn't have to hide behind this *human* mask anymore."

Something about the way she says the word "human" makes it sound dirty, like something I should be ashamed of.

"But isn't that a part of me, too? Being human? Can't I be both?" I ask, maybe a little too defensively, because Absynth frowns.

"You can ... for a time," she says, her voice quiet and tinged with sadness I wasn't expecting. "But you won't ever be whole. Annabell tried, but she was never truly happy."

Her mention of my mother surprises me, and I jump on the moment in an attempt to draw more information about her out of Absynth.

"What do you mean she wasn't whole?" I ask.

Absynth doesn't look at me when she answers.

"She had the same fairy blood like you and me, but she chose to try to live a human life. Maybe she thought that ignoring her abilities would make them disappear, but that's not how it works," she says, sighing and shaking her head. "We can choose to become fully fairy, but there is no way for us to become fully human."

I think about my father then, and his reaction to my stories about the lights in the woods, about the therapists and the medications, and I have to ask.

"My dad. Did he know?"

Absynth shrugs. "It wouldn't surprise me if he didn't. Annabell knew how to conceal what she was."

She knew how to conceal it. Well enough for my father, for her husband, not to notice.

A surge of hope so strong that I feel as if I might fly off the ground, wings or no, courses through me. Because if there was a way for my mom to keep that part of herself hidden from my father, then there's a way for me to do the same with Ben.

"How?" I ask, longing in my voice.

In reply, Absynth holds out her arms, makes a slight inhaling sound, and the thorns retract into her arms, almost invisible except for a series of small ripples beneath her skin.

"It's like holding your breath," she explains. "Try it."

I nod and then close my eyes. I take one preliminary steadying breath and then inhale sharply, every muscle in my body clenching with effort.

I don't feel anything change, but when I open my eyes, my arms look as inconspicuous as Absynth's. The change is so immediate and so effortless that I can't stop the laughter that bursts out of me.

Absynth smiles but then looks at me seriously.

"This means no more … " She pauses, searching for the right word. "No more *pruning* yourself. Do you understand?"

I open my mouth to reply but end up yawning instead.

"Come on," Absynth says. "Time for the human to get some sleep." And before I can do more than stifle another yawn, Absynth has her arm around me, guiding me back down the dark forest path.

I practice concealing my thorns all the way back, and by the time we reach the tree line, I can do it almost as silently as Absynth.

"I think I've got the hang of this," I say as I pull my jeans and sweatshirt back on, the rose petals of my dress falling around me onto the forest floor.

"It's only a temporary solution, Amethyst," Absynth says as she causes the petals to wither away into brown leaves indistinguishable from the rest of the ground cover. "It only changes what you look like, not what you are. You can't hide forever."

"I know," I say, watching the last of the roses fade away. "And I don't want to. All of this is just a lot to take in, you know?"

"Of course. I understand," she says, her voice light, but I can see the disappointment in her eyes.

"Will I see you again tomorrow night?"

Absynth hesitates as she looks through the trees at Gran's dark house.

"No, I don't think so," she says, and my heart sinks.

"Did I do something wrong?" I ask, but Absynth shakes her head, smiling, the perfect picture of happiness.

"Not at all. I think every night would be too dangerous. I'll send a light like I did tonight the next time it's safe, okay?"

I nod, but I can't shake the feeling that I've upset Absynth and that her excuse of safety is just that—an excuse.

"We'll see each other again soon, I promise. We need to be careful. There are—"

"Dangerous people out there. I know," I finish for her.

As I turn to walk back to where the vine ladder waits for me, I hear Absynth's voice floating out at me from the darkness of the woods.

"No, Amethyst, you don't. And I hope you never will."

It takes me a long time to fall asleep. Even though my body is exhausted from a long day of illicit gardening and magical makeovers, my mind is working overtime trying to make all of the disparate pieces of my life here in Morgan Springs fit together. The longer I try, though, the more it feels like I've got parts of two completely different puzzles that will never create a single cohesive picture.

So I start to mentally sort my life into two different piles: human and fairy.

The Gardens—human
The forest—fairy
Daytime—human
Nighttime—fairy
Ben—human
Absynth—fairy

I continue like this until I reach Gran. My first instinct is to put her into the human column, but then there's the fact that her only two daughters were born with the latent ability to grow thorns and fly. As far as I can tell, she isn't some magical forest creature herself, but there's so much I don't know about her or her past.

I decide to put Gran aside, an outlier in the otherwise perfectly balanced dichotomy of my life.

One side is sunshine and rose mallow and the feel of Ben's kiss, warm on my cheek. The other is moonlight and flower crowns and Absynth's thorny embrace. The optimist in me wants to see complementary halves, each side strong where the other is weak. But my internal realist sees futures that are diametrically opposed. Conflicting, not congruent.

Two roads diverged in a yellow wood.

The line from the Frost poem pops into my mind, and I try to remember the rest. While the exact words remain elusive to my overtired mind, I can recall the general gist of the piece: two paths, equally desirable and equally mysterious, and a traveler who can choose only one. In the end, the guy winds up choosing "the road less traveled," lamenting all the while that he will never know what lay down the other path.

Mrs. Cannel said that the poem was a representation of the irreversibility of the choices we make in life, the permanent consequences of our decisions. But I had argued differently in my English final. I said that the traveler had let his future be dictated to him by resigning himself to choosing between the options presented to him. That instead of acquiescing to a fabricated dualistic choice, he should have blazed his own path, one that he could shape to encompass the best parts of both roads.

And there's my answer.

I won't choose between my human life and my fairy life, a division that only exists because I allow it to. No, I will make the same decision as my mother before me. I will make my future, one that includes both paths before me, as I said the traveler in the Frost poem should have done.

Of course, I did wind up getting a C- on that paper for "willfully ignoring the point."

But I'm sure that had more to do with Mrs. Cannel's limited perspective than the general premise of my argument. My eyes flutter closed, exhaustion finally winning out.

I sleep too long, and for the second day in a row, it's Gran's knocking that wakes me.

"Just a minute," I croak, groggily disentangling myself from the bed sheets. As soon as I'm free, I cross the room and open the door to my grandmother's face. Something in the way she looks at me says that this is more than a cursory wake-up call; this is a bed check.

Well, the inmate in bedroom two is accounted for.

"I'm sorry for waking you, dear," she says, peering over my shoulder at the room behind me. "But I just wanted to let you know that Benjamin called three times for you this morning, and—"

"Ughhhh," I groan, my awkward escape from the Camry replaying in high-definition on the inside of my skull. "Please say you told Ben that I'd call him back later."

I am nowhere near awake enough to figure out how to explain away last night's behavior. That will require a lot more time and an indecent amount of caffeine.

"I *did*," Gran says, the smallest hint of a smile pulling at the corners of her mouth. "But he insisted on coming over. He's downstairs in the parlor … seems very distressed, the poor boy."

Gran can no longer suppress her smile as she reaches out to pat me on the cheek.

"Don't make him wait too long," she says before retreating down the stairs while I frantically try to calculate how much is left in my bank account and whether it is enough to buy a one-way plane ticket to Siberia.

It takes me twenty minutes to shower and get dressed, and I use every second of that time to try and figure out what I'm going to say to Ben. In the end, I wind up with a plan to tell him a modified version of what I told Gran last night, which in itself was a heavily edited version of the truth: I was just freaked out.

As I tiptoe down the stairs in an effort at stealth, I hear the TV in the parlor, the breathy voice of some soap-opera actress lamenting the loss of her lover to his evil twin. It's loud enough to mask my footfalls, thankfully.

CREAK!

The fourth step from the bottom lets out a cry of woody pain underneath my weight, and I know the jig is up.

"There she is!" Gran's voice says from the parlor, and I sigh, giving up all pretense of quiet, and take the last few steps two at a time. But before I turn the corner into the parlor, I stop and take a deep breath. It's an action that serves two purposes: the first being to provide some measure of calm to my racing heart and the second being to secure any wayward thorns beneath the surface of my skin.

"Hey, Ben," I say, trying to make my voice sound light and casual but only succeeding in high-pitched.

"Hey," he replies, but he doesn't raise his eyes to meet mine. Guilt, a feeling as thick and scorching as magma, begins to flow through me as I look at him. There are dark circles under his eyes, and his clothes are disheveled as if he wore the first things he picked up off his floor this morning.

Making the entire situation exponentially worse is Gran's presence. Even though she is doing her best to make her sideways glances at Ben and me as inconspicuous as possible, I catch one of them and incline my head toward the doorway.

Gran gets the message.

"I'll be in the kitchen," she says. As she passes me, Gran squeezes my shoulder in a supportive way, and I wonder what she must think happened between Ben and me before almost immediately deciding that I don't want to know.

"So," I begin from where I stand, not brave enough to take the empty spot on the couch next to him. "About last night … "

"Amethyst," he says, finally looking up at me, "I am so, *so* sorry."

His apology catches me off guard, and I falter. I had prepared statements to counter confusion, sadness, and even righteous anger on his part. I should have realized that Ben would do something completely unexpected like apologize. That's his thing.

"Ben, come on," I say, floundering to adapt my mental scripts. "I'm the one who should apologize. I—"

"No, don't," he says, and I see red creeping up his neck. "You've been completely up-front with me about just wanting to be friends, and I know that I crossed that line last night, and I'm sorry. I promise it won't happen again."

Accepting his apology would solve a few of my problems. In the immediate, it would get me out of this conversation, and in the long term, it would probably prevent a lot more of these little chats from happening. I'm not sure what the whole timeline is on me turning into a mythical being. And who's to say that two weeks from now I won't sprout wings while Ben and I are bowling or something?

But even as I take a nanosecond to consider the possibility of forever sentencing Ben to languish in the vast wasteland known as the friend zone, my heart is already protesting. As much as keeping him at a distance would make my new "third road" strategy easier, I know that I won't and, more importantly, that I don't want to. Whatever strange energy flows between us when his skin touches mine is not something I want to live without. I'll learn to control myself around him, or at least the part of myself that is a fairy.

I make no promises as to what the human half will do the next time I feel his kiss on my skin.

"Ben, that's not what I want," I say, closing the distance between us and squatting down so that he has to look at me. "I'm just not used to this. Back home in Philly, well … "

I trail off, knowing that I'm entering dangerous territory, where saying the wrong thing could lead to questions about my past, which I've been so careful to hide. For a moment I'm tempted to tell him everything. Well, *almost* everything. But then my better judgment regains control of my mind, and I go with the thin sliver of truth I can provide to him.

"Let's say that this is all new for me, and I'm still figuring it out. So can we go back to being you and me, take our time, and not worry about labels or limitations?"

"Yeah," he says. "I think we can do that."

And his smile at that moment is bright enough to outshine the sun.

The next few days are some of the happiest of my life. Ben and I spend our days and most evenings together in the Gardens. By the end of our second day, we've culled the worst of the weeds in the entryway, and by the end of the fourth, we've successfully located and neutralized a large wasp nest Ben discovered hidden in the depths of one of the hedges.

But it's not all work.

Our many breaks for water or lunch—or because Ben finds a den of baby bunnies in one of the beds he's clearing out—are full of easy conversation where we trade information on the music we like and places we would visit if we had the money. There's even one very heated debate over the merits of the *Star Wars* prequels, which only ends when Ben concedes my point that Padmé Amidala was totally worth suffering through Jar Jar Binks for as long as I agree that the explanation of midichlorians was an abomination that robbed the universe of some of its overall mystique.

And even though the fifth night in a row passes without one of Absynth's messenger lights floating in through my bedroom window, my disappointment disappears as soon as I hear the rumble of the Camry in the driveway the next morning.

Our victory over the wasps means that we can finally get started on the hedges, which are so overgrown that many of the interior walkways are impassible. By "we," of course, I mean Ben. He says it's because there is only one stepladder and also because he has decided to limit my access to sharp tools, though I wonder if it's because of my legitimate if slightly overenthusiastic defense of Mace Windu's purple lightsaber.

So while he stands precariously balanced on top of a rickety ladder, hacking away at a bush with twelve-inch death scissors, I'm standing below, picking up the clippings as they fall.

"Hey!" Ben calls down. "Does this look level to you?"

I don't even bother to look up from the pile of branches I'm collecting. "It looks about the same as it did when you asked me about it five minutes ago."

"Thanks, Amethyst. Real helpful," Ben says. I don't need to see his face to know he's rolling his eyes, but I glance up anyway so that he can see me smiling at his annoyance. He sighs, and then his face shifts, jaw tightening and eyes squinting down at my upturned face.

"What do you have on your face there?" he asks, gesturing too vaguely for me to know what he's referring to.

"*What? Where?*" I ask, panic gripping me as I try to remember the last time I checked my thorns. My hand shoots up to my forehead, frantically feeling for any errant plant life.

"Relax there, Freckles," Ben says, and realizing his meaning, I do.

"Oh, these," I say, running my fingers over the bridge of my nose as Ben turns back to his hedge. "Yeah, they're a new development." Before I can continue, I'm forced to step away from the ladder as Ben works his clippers through a thick branch. It takes almost five minutes of hacking before the branch finally falls, which Ben fills with a near-constant stream of profanities that become so delightfully obscene that I don't want to interrupt.

"Gran noticed them, too, but I don't think she likes them very much," I say, picking up the conversation as soon as Ben finishes telling the hedge off.

"Doesn't like what?" he asks, wiping the sweat off his face with the bottom of his shirt.

I allow myself to enjoy the view of his bare chest before I answer. "Freckles."

"She doesn't like freckles?" he asks, dropping his shirt. I can see the confusion on his face.

"Oh, I'm not sure if it's all freckles, or just mine," I say, reaching down to pick up the big branch. "She didn't clarify."

"Well, I like them," he says as I start to drag the branch back to my pile.

"Freckles?" I ask.

"Oh, not all freckles," he says before winking at me and continuing. "Just yours."

I make a point of rolling my eyes, but when he turns back to the hedge, I can't keep from smiling.

"So I was thinking," Ben says to the bush in front of him. "Since we've gotten so much done this week, we should take tomorrow off and do something fun."

"Oh?" I say, keeping my voice noncommittal. Even though we've both agreed on not having labels, it makes it that much harder to divine the meanings behind these kinds of vague suggestions. "What did you have in mind?"

"Well, I've got a day shift at the diner, so I thought we could catch a movie. The drive-in usually does a double feature on Saturday nights ... "

He's still not looking at me, for which I am grateful, because I have no poker face.

"Yeah, I'd like that," I say, and I feel a swell of elation when Ben turns and beams at me.

"Okay!" he says, and I can hear my excitement mirrored in his voice. "Great! I'll pick you up around 8:30, then."

"I'll pencil you in," I say, pretending to write our date down in an invisible schedule.

"Pencil? Really?" he says, putting his hands on his hips. "I don't even merit ink in your pretend planner?"

"Well, it all depends on whether or not you finish your chores, Cinderella."

"At least she had magic mice to help," he grumbles as he raises his shears to work on another wayward branch. But before he can cut, the clippers drop from his hands, and he half jumps, half falls off the ladder.

"Ben! Are you okay?" I call as I rush to help him to his feet, but he's already scrambling up.

"Come on," he says, grabbing my hand and tugging me toward one of the overgrown pathways. "We've got to go!"

He pulls again, but I don't follow, still trying to figure out what could make Ben react this way.

"Why? Ben, what's going on?" I ask, looking back at the hedge, wishing that I, like Absynth, could will it to part.

"Your grandmother," he says, the color slowly draining out of his face. "She's here."

"Crap!" I say, my mind already scrambling to develop a plan, surveying the scene and weighing priorities. While there are a myriad of choices for escape, the only two I consider are those that protect my number one priority in this situation: Ben.

The first and more preferred option is to grab all of our tools and trash and haul them out the back. Pros: neither of us gets caught, and we both live to garden another day. Cons: there's a ton of stuff to move, and I have no idea where Gran is in relation to us.

As if in reply, the wrought-iron fence guarding the front entrance to the Gardens creaks open.

One option, then.

"Ben, did she see you?"

"I don't know!" he cries. "She might have!"

"Well," I say, pushing him in the opposite direction of the entrance, "we're going to hope that she didn't. Come on, out the back!"

Ben nods and takes a few steps toward the path that will take him to the damaged portion of the fence closest to the tree line, but he stops when he sees I'm not following.

"I'm not going without you!" he says, but my head is already shaking.

"It was my idea to do this, and I'm the only one she's going to see here." I pause to give him a reassuring smile, all the while mentally willing him to run. "Plus, she can't throw me in jail. I'm family, right?"

I can see the indecision in his eyes, but after a few more seconds of hesitation, he launches himself backward, disappearing behind one of the hedges we haven't had a chance to trim yet. I wait until the sound of his footsteps fades away before squaring my shoulders and walking in the opposite direction to face my grandmother's wrath alone.

Walking back toward the front of the garden where Ben and I have done the most work is like traveling back in time. Freshly trimmed hedges give way to an open space lined with garden beds brimming with bluebells, fuchsia, rose mallow, and dozens of other blossoms that Ben knows by heart. Although the benches are still vine-covered and the statues are coated in a decade's worth of moss, this part of the garden looks almost as it must have a hundred years ago.

Almost.

I round the corner into the entryway and find my grandmother standing statuesque near the iron gate. Her presence here feels wrong, a monument to modernity set in stark contrast to her Victorian surroundings. Her back is to me, and she doesn't move as I approach, leading me to believe that she doesn't hear my grass-muffled footfalls. I'm still a few feet away from her, readying myself for the anger I'm sure is coming, when she speaks.

"Hello, Amethyst," she says simply, not turning to look at me. Her voice is quieter than I expected as she brushes her fingertips across the tops of the coneflowers in the bed closest to her. "You and Ben got quite a bit done."

"Gran," I begin, wishing I could see her face to direct my words, "we were just—"

Gran's hand flies up next to her head, signaling for silence, and I brace myself for the deluge of anger and disappointment to begin.

But after a few heartbeats, Gran finally turns around, and I am shocked to see her eyes brimming with tears. My surprise must show on my face, because Gran sends me a peace offering in the guise of a watery smile.

"Did you know that this was where I first met your grandfather?" she asks, her voice wavering a little with emotion. "Just over there."

She points to the Garden's gates, and I can almost see her words come to life before me.

"I was twenty-two, fresh out of college." She pauses to smile at me. "I was only going to be here a few weeks. I had a job lined up in New York, but then ... "

Her words drift off, and even if I didn't already know her reason for staying in Morgan Springs, the wistful look on her face at this moment would have told me enough to guess. I follow her gaze to the iron gate, and I can envision him there, my grandfather, a young man, tall and blond, leaning against the post and smiling crookedly like Ben does when he teases me.

"You fell in love," I finish for her.

"I fell in love," she confirms, and even though the smile is still on her face, there is sadness in her eyes that I've seen all too often in my reflection. It's the look you get when your happiest memories are tinged with the bitter aftertaste of loss and grief.

"I'd dated some in high school and college, of course, but Arthur was like no man I'd ever met. He was the tornado that carried me out of Kansas and into the brilliant Technicolor of Oz." Gran sighs, plucking one of the pink flowers and raising it to her nose. "That summer, this became our place."

Our place.

It's an echo of the phrase Ben used to justify the rose mallow bed, a point of intersection between Gran's timeline and my own that makes me uncomfortable. It's not the same discomfort I felt when I first arrived here—a need to disavow myself from anything that resembled her. No, this feeling squirming through my insides is the direct result of knowing the trajectory of her life and hoping, perhaps rather foolishly, that mine could follow a similar path.

"It wasn't quite love at first sight, but it was close," Gran continues, sitting down on one of the old benches. She pats the seat next to her, and I cross the garden to join her. She takes one of my hands in both of hers, and there's a strength in them that surprises me. "We were married before the end of the year."

Before I can stop myself, my brain is hurtling forward at light speed, leaving me only glimpses of interlaced fingers, starry skies reflected on still water, white lace and a bouquet of rose mallow, and Ben in a gray suit beaming at me from the end of a long aisle.

I feel the heat rush into my cheeks, embarrassed by the fantasy playing out in my head. I've never been the kind of girl who daydreams about my wedding day. No, my dreams were always filled with too-green trees and clawed hands pulling my struggling body into the dark depths of the woods.

At least they used to be.

But perhaps now that I know the truth, those subconscious rumblings have finally been subdued, clearing my mind for more pleasant musings. Maybe my nights, when not plagued by exhaustion from gardening or late-night visits to the woods, will now be filled with the fluffy nonsense that has evaded me for a decade.

I am tempted to venture back into the fantasy, to let myself imagine the night that must follow that long walk down the aisle, but a soft sniffing sound next to me draws my attention.

When I look over at Gran, I see tears in her eyes now threaten to spill over, and when she speaks, her voice is tight with emotion.

"We came here almost every day for forty years—Arthur and I—and then with your mother. It was our family's place, more even than the house, and when I lost them, I just couldn't bear—"

Gran's voice breaks off sharply, and the tears lingering at the rims of her eyelids spill over. My reaction is as unconscious and quick as it was with Ben, and I throw my arms around my grandmother's neck.

"I'm sorry, Gran. I—" But before I can apologize further, Gran shakes her head against my neck. A moment later, she pulls away, wiping her eyes and clearing her throat in an effort to compose herself.

"No," she says, her voice still thick. "I'm the one who's sorry, Amethyst. Sorry for shutting down and sorry for shutting you out."

They're the words that I've waited years for her to say, but at this moment, the acknowledgment of her abandonment brings me no satisfaction, no sense of victory. There is no winner in this war of attrition we've both been waging for the better part of a decade. Instead, there are just two weary soldiers desperate for absolution and any measure of peace.

"It's … it's okay," I say, not sure how else to extend the proverbial olive branch.

"No, it's not," Gran says, firmly but not unkindly. "I've lost too many people in my life. I don't want to lose you, too."

I feel tears in my own eyes, not from embarrassment or pain but from relief as the weight of ten years of longing falls away in Gran's embrace.

"The Gardens are yours. And Ben's," she says into my hair before releasing me.

"Really?" I ask, searching her face for any sign of hesitation but coming up empty. "You're sure?"

"I think so," she says, looking around at the work Ben and I have already done. "It's too beautiful to keep hidden away, and … " Gran turns back to me, smiling in that knowing way of hers. "And it's a nice place for a couple of people to get to know each other," she finishes, and my ears redden.

"Ben and I are just friends," I say, not sounding remotely convincing, even to myself.

Gran's smile grows a little wider, and the blush creeps down into my cheeks.

"Of course you are," she says, unable to keep the satisfaction out of her voice, but thankfully she doesn't pry. Instead, she stands and offers a hand to me. "Now, come on. Let's get you home so you can call the poor boy and let him know the police aren't going to be breaking down his door anytime soon."

The excitement in Ben's voice when I tell him about Gran's change of heart is so intense that I'm grateful to be telling him over the phone. That much pure joy in a person might be enough to kill me. He does, however, almost put me into long-distance cardiac arrest by ending our conversation with:

"I can't wait to see you tomorrow night to celebrate."

The statement might, at face value, appear innocuous enough, but, when delivered via an uncharacteristically serious tone in Ben's voice, it becomes an infuriatingly vague promise. Exactly what is he promising, though? I spend all of dinner, and two reruns of *Everybody Loves Raymond*, trying to puzzle it out.

At eight, I say good night to Gran and head upstairs to begin my nightly vigil next to my open window. Ben's words are still buzzing through my mind, and the fried chicken in my stomach is starting to roil as I try to imagine every possible interpretation of the word "celebrate."

As the anxiety crescendos, I cast around desperately for something, *anything*, that will take my mind off tomorrow night, and that's when I see it, still where I kicked it, its gilded spine shining in the orange glow of the sunset: *Fairy Stories*.

I scan the sky one more time for any sign of lights before pulling the old book out from under the others and flopping down on my bed. I flip the cover open and see an inscription on the first page in handwriting I don't recognize:

To help you understand

I stare down at the words because although I am certain they weren't written for me, I cannot help but think they were written for someone *like* me. The realization grips me so suddenly and so completely that I can't believe I didn't see it before: Gran suspects that I am more than human, if she doesn't already know for sure.

The book was a message as clear as if she said it aloud: "You can trust me. I want to help you."

I'm on my feet, ready to rush downstairs to tell Gran everything, when another memory stops me: Absynth, Gran's own daughter, who has been stricken from existence in this house, warning me not to trust anyone with my secret. A shiver runs down my spine, and I feel goose bumps rise on my arms despite the oppressive July heat.

She wasn't just warning me about humans—she was warning me about Gran.

I turn away from my bedroom door and walk back over to the window. I drag the chair from the desk next to it and stare out into the darkness, trying to will one of Absynth's lights into existence.

I need to talk to her. I need to know how much danger I'm in.

It's after eleven when I finally give up. I return to bed and lie down, exhaustion pulling at my muscles and my bones, but I'm unable to find a handhold on my mind. Sleep won't come easy tonight.

Sighing, I bend down and pull Gran's book from under the bed.

The Great Schism

Ithir's veil maintained an uneasy peace between the Uaine and the Liathe, though neither side ever truly forgot their quarrel as they circled the earth, ever in pursuit of the other. As always, it was the humans who suffered, as bountiful harvests created by the Uaine withered away into years of famine when the Liathe instead roamed their lands.

Ithir would have wept at the state of the world she had left behind for her beloved children.

It was the Uaine who finally awoke to the chaos their feud had wreaked among the humans. Aible, an ancient fae who was old enough to have witnessed Ithir's sacrifice and remember the reason for it, was the first to suggest ending the feud. It did not take much for him to convince the other Uaine, tired from centuries of watching their creations destroyed, of the benefits of a peaceful existence—not just for the humans but for the fae as well. And so, a delegation, led by Aible himself, was dispatched to the Liathe to establish a truce.

While Ithir's veil was impenetrable, she had died with the hope of reconciliation between her children and in that hope had left secret doorways that could someday be used to reunite the fae folk. Aible remembered these doorways, but even so, they were so well hidden that it took many years of searching before he and his band found a pathway to the domain of the Liathe.

It is not known what transpired in there during their time with the Liathe, because old Aible was the only member of the group to return alive, too aggrieved to repeat the horrors that had befallen his companions. He explained that there could be no peace with the Liathe, that their long years of practicing such dark magics had left them feral and mad. They had only one choice: to seal the veil permanently and sever the Liathe from both the Uaine and the human worlds.

It was done using the very magic which the Liathe had used against Aible—though that magic is too dangerous to describe here. Nonetheless, the doorways were sealed, and the Liate were sealed off into the realm of the fae, where they remain to this day.

However, the Uaine's victory was short-lived, as not long after followed the rise of cities and their metal monsters. Men and their families left the countryside seeking new work, abandoning the Uaine, who had fought to protect them. And, as these new machines made of metal and steam needed no fae magic to function, slowly the fae's power began to wane and, many believed, was destined to be extinguished forever.

Not forever, I think, running a finger across the place on my wrist where a thorn lurks just below my skin—evidence enough for me that the fairies who remained behind had circumvented millennia of tradition and found a way to survive without humans. Curious, I flip the page once again and begin reading the fourth entry in the book: *The Fairy King.*

In the years following the Great Schism, the Uaine remaining in the human world struggled to find a solution to men's indifference to them. As time passed and their magic continued to drain away, it seemed as if all was lost. However, that all changed with the appearance of a fae who would become known as the Fairy King.

The true name of the Fairy King, along with his origins, is lost to history. What is known is that he was the first of his kind to discover a new source for his magic: fairy lights. The nature and creation of these lights is as mysterious as the Fairy King himself, a secret he shared with only those fae folk who pledged their lives and loyalty to him. As his prestige grew, so did his power, and although other fairies acquired as many or more of their own lights, none were able to rival their self-proclaimed king.

It is said that the Fairy King could raise an entire year's harvest in a moment and destroy it in a fraction of that time.

That he could draw the four winds to propel a ship across the sea or summon a storm powerful enough to sink a fleet of them. He has lived for centuries, growing more powerful with each passing year, and humans and fairies alike revere him—and fear him.

As I reach the bottom of the entry, I see that someone has inked a line through the last sentence. I hold the book closer to my face, squinting to make out the words.

And there is no power to match his, in this world or the next.

Before I can begin to contemplate just exactly who would cross that out and why, there's a knock at my bedroom door.

"Yeah?" I call out as the door swings open to reveal Gran in one of her flowery nightgowns.

"Amethyst, oh." She stops short as her eyes move down from my face to the book in my hands.

"What's up?" I ask, looking at the clock on my nightstand and wondering whether Gran needs something or if this is just another one of her random spot checks.

"Oh, nothing," she says, already trying to back out of my room. "I don't want to bother you."

Spot check it is.

I close the book and stare up at my grandmother's retreating frame. I'm not going to let her off the hook so easily.

"No big deal," I say casually. "I was just flipping through. What do you need?"

"No, really, it can wait. Go back to your book." She's just about to close the door when she adds: "Just let me know if … if you have any … questions."

I have lots of questions, I think, *but not for you.* I'm about to shake my head no when I realize there is something I want to ask Gran.

"I do, actually," I say, and Gran's face lights up in a way that makes me certain she suspects more about me than Absynth would like.

"Yes?"

"Was this my mom's? The inscription in the front … " But before I can finish, her face falls, and I know what the answer will be before she speaks.

"No, your mother wasn't very fond of fairy tales. Was that it?"

She gives me a long, appraising look, and I quickly turn my focus toward the wooden floorboards between us, worried that if I meet her gaze, my face will reveal everything I'm trying to hide.

"Yeah, that was all," I say, not looking up. "Night."

There are a few moments of silence, and I sneak a glance up at Gran. She isn't looking at me anymore but is instead staring at the chair sitting in front of my open window.

"Good night, Amethyst," she says, narrowing her eyes at the dark sky before closing the door behind her.

The sliver of white that is the moon casts just enough light on the entrance to the Gardens to show me that someone stands just beyond the open wrought-iron gates. I take a step forward, passing under the archway, my voice a hoarse whisper as I call out.

"Ben?" But even as I say his name, I know the shadowy figure is not him. His posture is too straight, the width of his stance too small.

A prickle of unease slides down my spine, leaving the hairs on the back of my neck standing at attention. My better judgment is telling me to leave, that I should not be here, but then I see the twinkling light dancing just ahead of the figure.

A fairy, I realize as I watch the tiny orb bob its way down to land on the man's shoulder.

"Hello?" I ask, my voice sounding weak as it cuts through the silence between us. I expect him to turn, to acknowledge me in some way, but instead the figure steps into the dark, hedge-lined path leading to the heart of the Gardens.

"Wait!" I call out, a sudden wave of panic washing over me. "Please!"

When there is no response, I take one last look at the iron gate behind me before hurtling into the hedges.

The boxwood presses in on all sides, its gnarled branches ripping at my hair and opening shallow scrapes along the exposed skin of my face and neck. Ahead, the fairy's light flashes in and out of my vision, guiding me through the otherwise impassible maze.

I burst out of the path into the large clearing surrounding Ben's reflecting pool and find the figure standing against the edge of the water, his back to me.

"Hello?" I ask again tentatively.

This time the figure responds by turning to face me, and I feel the breath catch in my throat. In the moonlight, his blond hair is silver, his pale skin smooth and shining as if it's been carved from mother of pearl. Behind him, translucent wings, like those of a dragonfly, unfurl, flit to life, and lift him effortlessly off the ground.

As if on cue, hundreds of lights emerge from the hedge line surrounding us, encircling him in their silent dance.

He looks down at me and smiles before raising both of his hands toward the sky.

Suddenly the ground around me erupts into life as dozens of coneflowers bloom in fast motion around me. I watch as the pink blossoms of the flowers weave their way up my legs and torso and fashion a crown around my head.

I turn to look back at the fairy, beaming up at him, and a thrill of terror rushes through me. His beautiful face is ringed with deep-red thorns, and his smile is a grimace of fangs. With a swift flick of his wrists, the stems of the flowers contract, pulling me back down into the ground with them.

Just as I open my mouth to scream, the vines tighten around my throat.

I jolt awake, the book of fairy stories flying off my chest and landing with a thud on the floor.

Just a dream, I think, taking a deep breath to slow my pounding heart. As I inhale, I feel the now familiar sensation of dozens of thorns retracting into my skin.

Damn it.

I look down at the ragged remains of my T-shirt and pajama bottoms, freshly peppered with enough holes to make a '90s grunge rocker jealous. Sighing, I throw the comforter aside and survey the damage I've done to the bed. The blanket seems to have escaped unscathed, but the sheets are completely ruined. Gingerly, I prod one of the holes in the flowery fabric and find that I've punctured all the way into the mattress itself.

Cursing under my breath, I begin to rip the sheets off my bed, wondering how long it will take me to order a new set online from one of the ancient computers in the library.

Gran is waiting for me at the dining room table when I come downstairs forty-five minutes later. She doesn't look up when I sit down across from her with my bowl of cereal, seemingly too engrossed in the morning paper to notice my presence. Her brow is furrowed in concern as she reads the article beneath the front page's headline:

Search Continues for Missing Branford Man

The story causes an image of eight-year-old Ben to float into my mind, followed by an echo of his mother's wordless shrieks, high-pitched and full of terror.

But not all of her screams had been incomprehensible, I remember, a twinge of unease knotting my stomach.

There had been lights in the woods the day Ben's parents had gone missing. Were they the same lights that haunted my nightmares for years—the same twinkling orbs that dance around Absynth's fairy hollow?

Could she have …

But before my mind can even finish formulating the question, it rejects the premise outright. I had been wrong to fear Absynth, who has never meant me harm, and I will not make that mistake again. If my time in Morgan Springs has taught me anything, it is that I need to open myself up, to trust people enough to let them in.

Absynth and Ben and even Gran are proof enough of that.

"Do you need a ride to the Gardens?" Gran's words cut across my thoughts, drawing me back into the present. "I have to go out to Greenport. I could drop you off on the way."

"Not today," I say, and when she arches one of her eyebrows in an unspoken question, I continue. "Ben's working a day shift down at the diner, so we're … Umm … "

Heat creeps up my neck and into my cheeks as I remember just exactly what we'll be doing instead.

"We're going to meet up later," I finish lamely, unable to bring myself to say the word "date" when Gran is already struggling to suppress a smile.

"Oh," she says, her voice thick with satisfaction. "What are you two doing?"

"Just going to see a movie," I say, focusing on my soggy Frosted Flakes in an effort to distract myself from Gran's curious gaze. Part of me is terrified that she is going to ask whether Ben is my boyfriend, while another deeper part is elated that I could probably answer her question with a yes.

But Gran surprises me.

"That sounds nice," she says, picking up her paper and purse and walking toward the front door.

"I'm sure you two will have a *great* time," she adds, unable to keep her grin in check this time as she waves and closes the door behind her.

After the sheet incident this morning, I'm more than a little concerned about how my body will react tonight when I'm sitting six inches away from Ben, so I spend most of the day stretched out on a lawn chair in Gran's sprawling backyard, running scenarios for the evening over in my head. I figure that by planning for every possible activity that could happen in a dark, semiprivate location, like the front of Ben's Camry, I can reduce the chances of turning his seats into my personal pincushion. If I can just plan my reaction for every lingering gaze, every touch, every kiss …

"Damn it!" I swear, pulling at my elbow, where an errant thorn is now lodged deep into the vinyl cushion of the chair. I close my eyes, take a deep breath, and feel the offender reluctantly retreat back beneath my skin.

"Okay," I say quietly, squaring my shoulders. "Let's run that one again."

I've killed time before in much less pleasurable ways.

I move inside at around five to start getting ready, and three and a half hours of prep time seems like more than enough. Until I open my drawers and realize that I have absolutely nothing date-worthy to wear. It takes nearly an hour and a half of arranging and rearranging my wardrobe in every possible permutation before I finally settle on a plain black V-neck (long sleeved, of course) and a pair of jeans. It's not much different from what I usually wear when we're together, save for the fact that it's not covered in dirt or hedge clippings.

Discouraged but not disheartened, I focus my efforts on making my face and hair marginally more alluring than my clothing.

I don't have much in the way of makeup, but the small bit of mascara and lip gloss that I do apply makes a noticeable difference. My hair is a different story. I use the memory of Daphne and Naya's makeover for inspiration and manage to, through the use of much heat and mousse, craft a poor replica of their delicate curls. I'm not sure how they managed the same effect in the woods without a curling iron or styling products, but I chalk it up to another benefit of fairy magic.

I'm just putting the finishing touch—a daisy plucked from the backyard earlier—behind my ear when Gran's voice calls up the stairs.

"Amethyst? Ben just pulled in!"

A jolt of adrenaline sparks through me, leaving my body tingling with anticipation in its wake. But just as I turn to pick my purse up from the dresser, I freeze.

A single white light is hovering in the space just beyond my open window.

"No," I moan, watching the orb revolve on the spot. "Not tonight."

I look from the light to the door and back again, my brain working furiously to find a way out of this dilemma that doesn't involve sitcom tropes or not-yet-invented cloning technology, but it's no use. I can't be in both places at once.

"*Amethyst!*" Gran's voice is accompanied by footsteps on the stairs.

I weigh my options as quickly as my panic will allow. In the end, my decision is based on sheer predictability: I know where to find Ben tomorrow, but I can't be sure when or even if I'll get another invitation to Absynth's hollow.

I come to my conclusion just as I hear Gran's gentle knock on my bedroom door. Sighing, I pull the blanket from my bed and wrap it around my head and body until only my face is visible.

"Amethyst, Ben's—" Gran's words cut off when I open the door, and she gets a good look at me. "What's wrong?"

"I don't think I'm going to go, Gran," I croak. "I'm not feeling very well."

Gran's eyes narrow for just a moment as she reaches out and places the back of her hand against my cheek.

"You don't feel warm; are you—"

But I cut her off, trying my best to look pained. "It's a stomach thing," I say, hoping that skipping dinner earlier will play to my advantage. "I've been nauseous all night."

To my surprise, Gran gives me a sympathetic look, all the suspicion in her face melting away. I must look more convincing than I feel.

"It's okay to feel nervous, dear," she says, placing her hand on my shoulder. "A first date can be a little scary."

Internally, I cringe at her inference. I was going for spontaneous gastrointestinal distress, not first-date jitters. But beggars can't be choosers, so I don't argue the point.

"Please, Gran. I can't," I say, guilt bringing real tears to my eyes as I try not to imagine Ben's reaction. "Tell him … tell him I can't, and I'm sorry."

She frowns back at me but nods after a few heartbeats.

"Do you want me to bring anything up for you? Some soup or maybe some tea?"

I shake my head, and the motion causes the brimming tears to spill down my cheeks.

"I just want to be alone," I say, and whether it's the crying or the way my voice catches in my throat when I speak, I can tell she believes me.

"I'll be downstairs if you need to talk," Gran says, patting my shoulder one more time before retreating back down the stairs.

I wait for the sound of the front door opening before closing my own. The crying starts in earnest as I turn the lock into place, and I allow myself a few minutes to mourn my lost evening with Ben before throwing the blanket over my chair and crossing the room to my open window.

I have a moment of panic when I notice that the fairy light has disappeared, but when I poke my head out of the window, I see Absynth's vine ladder waiting for me.

Her invitation must still stand.

I hoist myself over the windowsill and lower my feet until they find solid holds within the twists of ivy clinging magically to the side of Gran's house. I move as quickly as my hand-eye coordination allows, but I'm still at least six feet from the grass when the back-porch light clicks on and the vines holding me wither away to nothing.

I hit the ground hard, pain surging up through my spine as my back collides with the earth beneath my window. I gasp for the breath that has been knocked from my lungs, but before I can regain any sense of composure, I hear the back door to the house opening behind me.

I throw myself flat against the grass and army-crawl as quickly as I can to the edge of the porch. The sound of the screen door shutting is followed by a series of swift footsteps heading directly toward where I lie. All Gran has to do is look over the railing, and I don't even have Ben to use as an excuse if she finds me.

Desperation takes hold, and I pull myself through the small opening between the ground and the porch, refusing to dwell on what creepy-crawly creatures I will be sharing the space with.

I roll onto my back just as Gran stops above me, and I hold my breath and watch her through the gaps between the floorboards. She does what I feared she would and leans out over the railing, but instead of looking down, she gazes up toward my bedroom. I wonder what she expects to see. A rope ladder? Or maybe a comically long train of bedsheets hanging from my window?

Whatever it is, she must not find it, because, after a few heartbeats, Gran turns away from the house and gazes toward the dark tree line beyond. Although I can't see her eyes from my vantage point, I can tell she is scanning the woods, because her head slowly swivels back and forth. This time I worry I know what she's looking for, and I hope that Absynth has had enough time to conceal herself beyond the reach of the porch light's glow.

It's a long few minutes of ignoring the ominous rustling of some unseen creature while I wait below the porch for Gran to be satisfied, but she finally returns to the house. As soon as the light clicks off, I squeeze myself out from my hiding place—an action made all the quicker when I spot the reflective white eyes of a possum just to my right. I stay on the ground, waiting for a full count of one hundred before I dare to poke my head up to investigate whether Gran is still keeping vigil on the backyard.

I rise slowly, ready to retreat at any sign of her presence, but the door is shut, and the kitchen beyond is dark. Of course, she could still be there, concealed within the shadows, but there's no way for me to tell without pressing my nose against the back window and looking for myself.

I decide to throw caution to the wind and make a run for it.

It takes me less than a minute to sprint across the long stretch of lawn between the house and the woods, but each second I am out in the open feels like an eternity. Only when I enter the safety of the first line of trees at the forest's edge do I slow down and turn to make sure that my escape has gone unnoticed.

As I examine the still-dark outline of the porch, something hard and thorny closes around my wrist. Immediately I am six years old again, a scream rising in my throat instinctively as I struggle to pull away from the hand and its viselike grip.

But before a sound can pass my lips, a second hand is over my mouth, suppressing the shriek into a muffled moan.

"Have you spoken to your grandmother about me?" Absynth's voice is more a hiss than a whisper. Her hand is still tight over my mouth, so I shake my head as much as her hold will allow.

"Does she know what you are? Have you told her?"

Again, I shake my head, and after a moment of silence, Absynth releases me. I spin to face her, rubbing my wrist where a bruise is already forming from the strength of her grasp.

"What was that about?" I ask, pain and confusion making my words louder and more accusatory than I mean them.

Across from me, Absynth is wild-looking, her thorns raised and her usually beautiful face contorted by fear. It is her unease that finally triggers my sense of terror, because what could she possibly be afraid of?

"I'm sorry," Absynth says, her voice returning to its normal melodic tone, though I notice her body is still tense. "But that was too close."

I open my mouth to agree, but she holds up a hand for silence. When she speaks next, she doesn't address me but instead directs her words into the blackness behind her.

"Daph?"

She materializes seemingly out of nowhere and flits to Absynth's side. Daphne doesn't seem as tense as my aunt, but I notice that her eyes never stop scanning the area behind me as Absynth speaks.

"Go find Naya," she says, her words curt and authoritative. "Tell her it has to be tonight. I want Amethyst to be able to protect herself."

Daphne gives Absynth a quick nod and, in a flutter of wings, disappears back into the forest.

"What has to be tonight?" I ask, unable to keep the fear out of my voice. "Absynth, what's going on?"

"I told you, Amethyst, we have to be careful. Humans are dangerous."

"But what could Gran possibly do to hurt someone like you?" I ask, the question leaping to my lips before I can stop myself.

Absynth narrows her eyes as she looks past me to where Gran's house stands in the distance.

"Not here. It's not safe," she says, reaching out and taking me by the hand. "Walk with me, and I'll tell you everything."

I swallow back my questions and my unease and follow Absynth into the darkness. We don't speak again until the dense forest has surrounded us, obscuring both the moon and Gran's house.

"Look," she says, "I understand that you don't know much about our past, about fairy lore, but—"

"I do, though!" I say, excited that, for once, I have something to contribute to a conversation with Absynth. "Gran gave me a book about it."

Absynth stops short, giving me a wide-eyed look of incredulity.

"But she doesn't know anything about me, or you, I swear!" I add quickly, although it's a half truth at best. Sure, I haven't told Gran anything about my fairy exploits, but I have an innate certainty that she suspects as much. There have been too many pointed questions and suspicious looks between us as of late to pretend that she is blissfully ignorant to my condition.

"So what exactly did you read about in this book?" Absynth asks, her voice straining for normalcy as we continue our walk toward the hollow.

"Um ... " I hesitate, trying to make sure that I am not about to say anything that will upset her again. "A lot of history, mostly. A lot about Ithir and something about the schism that almost caused the fairies to die off."

I chance a glance at Absynth, and she nods that I am correct, so I continue.

"And then there's the Fairy King, who is the most powerful of all the fairies."

154

"Was," she corrects me. "He *was* the most powerful. At least until … "

I take a moment to remember the story, but I don't recall anything in there about him losing his powers except the one crossed-out line at the end. I'm just about to mention this when Absynth continues.

"*She* came," Absynth says, the icy tone of her voice sending a shiver through me. "A human woman who deceived him into revealing himself for what he was."

She stops just outside of the entrance to her hollow, and I see disgust etched across every inch of her face.

"She took *everything* from him, draining the power, the very *life* from him, until one day, there was nothing left."

I shake my head. It's not that I don't believe Absynth's words, more that I can't fathom how they can be true.

"But how do you—" But before I can finish, Absynth rounds on me.

"I saw the Fairy King ten years ago, just a few days before he died, Amethyst, and I wouldn't wish that on anyone." Absynth suppresses a shiver at the image the memory must be conjuring in her mind's eye.

"Why?" I ask, wondering what kind of horror would elicit this kind of reaction from someone as magical and powerful as my aunt. "What was he like?"

"Weak and pathetic," she says before pausing to give me a darkly significant look. "And loyal to my mother until the bitter end. So yes, Amethyst, I *do* think your grandmother is very dangerous."

My hands fly up to my open mouth in disbelief as the reality of Absynth's words washes over me.

"B-but," I stammer, "she loved him. She—"

Absynth clasps a hand over my shoulder, and it is only when her steady grip stabilizes me that I realize I am shaking. "Humanity is a disease for our kind, Amethyst." Her words are blunt, but her voice is soothing. "It took my father, and it took my sister, but I swore I wouldn't let it take you from me, too."

"Why didn't you tell me this before?" I ask, dread rising in my chest. "I've been living alone with her for weeks. I could have—"

But Absynth shushes me and pulls me into a hug; I bury my face in her tangle of blond hair. It smells like lavender, and it makes me wonder if Absynth is creating the scent herself to help soothe me.

155

"There was nothing for you to worry about—and there still isn't—as long as you keep our secret."

I want to argue with her, but the buzz of wings signifying the return of Daphne and Naya stops me. I pull away from Absynth and see the two fairies landing just a few feet beyond us.

"Good, you're here," she says, waving away the vines concealing her hiding place with a flick of her hand before leading me inside.

"This had better be important, Absynth." Naya's words are edged with annoyance, and as she steps into the hollow, I see that her elegant features are stony. "I was in the middle of—"

"It is, or I wouldn't have sent for you, Naya," Absynth says, irritation in her tone as well. "I think we need to see if Amethyst has an innate aptitude for your *specialty*."

"While she is still human?" Naya asks, looking at me appraisingly, seemingly unimpressed by what she sees. "Absynth, it's not possible."

"It is. I taught myself before my Changing, and Amethyst has the same magic in her blood." Absynth gives me a warm smile before inclining her head toward Naya. "And she has something even I did not—an excellent teacher."

Naya scoffs and rolls her eyes, but she doesn't offer any further protests.

"Thank you," Absynth says before turning her attention back to me. "Now listen, Amethyst, I'm going to take Daphne and inspect our defenses, to be safe. Listen to Naya, and I'll be back soon."

"Okay." It's a weak answer, but it's all I can muster as my brain bursts with a million questions I am unable to ask.

"That's a good girl," she says, gently touching my cheek before unfurling her wings and following Daphne back out into the woods. As the vines close behind them, I turn to face Naya, ready to learn whatever skill Absynth believes will help protect me from Gran, only to find that she, too, has disappeared.

"Naya?" I call out, tentatively looking up to see if maybe she is hovering in the canopy above.

The only response is Naya's laughter from somewhere behind me.

I spin around, but again, there is nothing to be seen but ivy-covered trees and a few fairy lights floating lazily just above the moss-covered ground.

"Naya?" I ask again to the empty air, my unease dissipating into irritation as another few seconds tick by without a response. "I know you don't want to do this, but Absynth said— Ow!"

My head jerks back suddenly as something yanks my hair from behind. My whole body bends backward as I struggle to keep my balance against the force pulling me down. But it's no use, and for the second time tonight, I find myself sprawled out on the ground, albeit this time after a much shorter fall.

The small circle of night sky peeking through the treetops is obscured as Naya materializes out of nowhere, laughing again.

"What just happened?" I ask, my mind scrambling to make sense of her sudden appearance. "Where did you come from?"

"Sometimes I forget how dull human senses are," Naya says, brushing a curly lock behind her ear as she reaches down to help me back to my feet. "I was barely even trying."

"Trying to do what?" I say, an edge of annoyance in my voice as I brush the dirt off my pants. "Embarrass me? Freak me out?"

"To conceal myself," she says, disappearing again right before my eyes.

Conceal herself? A rush of excitement surges through me when I realize that this must be what she is going to teach me to do.

"Absynth calls it our greatest defense," she continues, her voice sounding from off to my left now. "But I've always believed the best defense is a good offense, and it's incredibly useful always to have ... "

She stops, and for a few heartbeats, there is silence in the hollow.

"The element of surprise!" Naya's breath tickles the back of my neck as she finishes, causing me to jump about three feet, my thorns pushing out of my skin defensively.

Naya doubles over in a fresh gale of laughter. Obviously I've just given her the exact reaction she'd been hoping for. Annoyed, I pull my thorns back beneath my skin and try to cut her laughter off with a question.

"So, you can make yourself invisible?"

Her giggle fades away as Naya takes a moment to consider my question.

"Not *invisible*," she finally answers, emphasizing that while I'm not correct in my assessment, I am close. "You see, all fairies have the talent of concealment—one of our gifts from Mother Nature. Like our sister chameleons, we can melt seamlessly into the background. Watch, I'll do it slowly."

Naya nods down to her right hand, and I feel my eyes widen as her dark-brown skin begins to change. Green tendrils, the same color as the vines behind her, ink their way up her fingertips, the color morphing into the gray brown of bark as it passes her wrist. After only a few seconds, Naya's entire arm is indistinguishable from the trees beyond.

When I look back to her face, my own awash with amazement, she winks before disappearing once again.

"Now, Amethyst, tell me: What do you see?"

Is this a trick? I stare at the empty spot where Naya was just standing.

"Nothing," I say, not sure how else she wants me to respond.

"Wrong," Naya says, and I think I can hear a hint of frustration in her voice. "You know where I am. Look *harder*."

I furrow my brow in concentration, staring straight ahead at the place where Naya is concealed, and slowly I begin to see. Not Naya, exactly, more the absence of her—little anomalies that give away her position, like a tree trunk that appears to be breathing or a moth that disappears for a few seconds before reappearing a foot from where it vanished.

"I can see you!" I say, watching some dirt move as Naya shifts her weight. "Well, not exactly you, but I can see where you are!"

"Good. Very good," Naya says, rematerializing and giving me the briefest of smiles. "Now you try."

"*Try?*" I ask, incredulous. "What do you mean, 'try'? You haven't shown me—"

Naya interrupts me with a heavy sigh accented by much eye rolling.

"Show? How can I show you *how* to disappear?" she says, and there is no doubt now that she is frustrated. "It's not something that you learn; it's something that you *feel*."

"Well, what am I supposed to be *feeling*, then?" I say, shooting her own words back at her, but Naya rolls her eyes again at my inability to understand what she must believe to be simple-enough instructions.

"It would be easier if you had already made the Change," she complains, shaking her head. "You wouldn't be so blind!" Naya sighs loudly, pinching the bridge of her nose. "But if Absynth wants you to learn now … "

She turns back to me, staring as if the answer is written on my face.

"Try closing your eyes," she says finally, and I do, thankful for the clarity of her instructions.

"Okay, now what?"

"Just, um, listen with your skin," Naya responds.

What? I open one eye to make sure that this isn't another way for her to mess with me. However, when I catch her withering gaze, I shut my eyes tight again and try to do as she said.

It takes a minute, and I don't know if I'm listening or feeling, but I slowly begin to become aware of my surroundings. The colors behind me each give off different heat signatures, warm browns and reds and oranges and cool greens and blues, which prickle as they encounter my skin. With each connection, a piece of information travels to my brain, and I watch as an image appears, pixel by pixel, in my mind's eye: the rough brown trunk of a tree, a tuft of green grass at its base, a yellow-and-tan crisscross of vines.

"Yes!" Naya's voice is full of pleasure, and I don't have to open my eyes to know that camouflage is inking its way across my skin. "Now you are *feeling!*"

And I am. I can move my focus around my body and feel the colors surrounding it: a deep black break in the bark across my chest, a spring-green bud on my ear, and a cluster of tiny white flowers with red centers near my right foot.

Rose mallow, I realize, and suddenly my mind is racing in an entirely different direction as images of Ben begin flashing by: the electric shock of his hand in mine, the way his arms encircled my waist when I held him in his car, the warm pressure of his lips against my cheek …

"You're not concentrating!" Naya reprimands, and I open my eyes to see my noncamouflaged pale skin shining in the moonlight.

"Sorry, I-I got distracted," I stammer, a blush creeping into my cheeks as I wonder if my body gave any hint as to what had been on my mind. I decide that I don't want to know.

"Do it again," Naya says in a commanding voice. "And this time, *no distractions.*"

I nod and close my eyes, once again allowing the world around me to wash over my skin.

Hours later, I have almost mastered the art of concealing myself. I say "almost" because my ability to maintain my focus on my surroundings has gotten progressively worse as the night wears on and fatigue creeps in, resulting in a random earlobe or fingertip or elbow appearing to be floating in midair. Naya has taken great delight in pointing out these lapses by smacking the offending body part with a long stick she pulled from a nearby tree.

"Ouch!" I shout as Naya lashes out again. A sting of pain radiates from the back of my knee. I feel my concentration—and subsequently, my camouflage—slip away completely as I reach down to rub my leg. "Can you ease up a little on the stick, Naya? I'm tired."

"Lazy," Naya insists, but before she can chastise me further, Absynth and Daphne reenter the hollow. Absynth looks from where I am crouched down to the stick in Naya's hand and sighs.

"Really, Naya?" she asks, her question thick with disapproval.

"She needed some extra *motivation*," Naya responds, but I'm relieved when she throws the piece of wood off to one side.

"How did it go?" Absynth asks, this time turning her attention to me. "Were you able to do it?"

"Yeah," I say, standing up to meet her gaze before closing my eyes and allowing my body to blend into the background. Fatigue pulls at my mind, and I'm only able to hold the camouflage for a few seconds.

It must be enough, though, because when I open my eyes, Absynth is beaming at me, a certain savage pride radiating from her as she embraces me.

"I knew you could do it," she says softly into my ear, and I feel myself swell with satisfaction, something that hasn't happened in a very long time. Absynth releases me with a final squeeze and holds me at arm's length, examining my face. "But you must be exhausted."

I nod, but before I can reply, a wide yawn confirms her observation.

"Come on," she says, linking her arm with mine. "Let's get you to bed."

Absynth takes me as far as the edge of the forest before sending me to finish the final distance across the lawn on my own.

"Should I conceal myself?" I ask, weariness weighing every word down, and mercifully, Absynth shakes her head.

"There's no need. We've been watching the house all night. There hasn't been any movement in hours."

"Thanks," I say, stepping out from the tree line, but I'm not more than a few steps from the woods when Absynth calls out.

"Amethyst?" she says. "Don't forget to check the tags on your clothes before you wear them."

"What?" I ask, wondering why Absynth is suddenly giving me fashion advice.

"The concealment will only work as long as you're wearing natural fabrics—cotton or wool," she says, a grin playing on her face as she continues. "So, no polyester or spandex, okay?"

"You got it," I say, a weak smile playing on my face. "Night, Absynth."

"Good night," she says, fading back into the trees to watch as I make my way back to Gran's.

In what is quickly becoming routine, I am woken up a few hours later by knocking at my door.

"Amethyst?" Gran's voice is cautious, quiet. "How are you feeling, honey?"

I roll out of bed, kicking my dirt-covered clothes from the night before underneath before crossing to the door. I hesitate for a moment before opening it, wondering why I don't feel more scared of Gran after everything I learned from Absynth last night. The only answer I can come up with is the one she gave me: as long as the secret is safe, so am I.

"I'm okay," I say, sleep making the words come out thick and slow. "What time is it?"

"It's almost noon," she says, double-checking the time on her watch.

"*Noon?*" I say, a jolt of surprise ripping through me. I should have been at the Gardens three hours ago. "Why didn't you wake me when Ben came to pick me up?"

Gran's face falls, and she looks down at her hands when she answers.

"He didn't stop by, dear," she says. "He called to say they needed him at the diner."

My heart sinks down into my stomach, where it is basted in a vat of hot, roiling guilt.

"Did he say anything else?" I ask, hoping that I'm reading more into his change in work schedule than there is, but then Gran gives me a look of deep sympathy, and I know there's worse news to come.

"He wasn't sure when he'd be able to get back to the Gardens again," she says. "Apparently they're short-staffed down at the Biscuit."

This, of course, is patently false. There can't be more than a dozen tables in the diner, all of which are populated by regulars like Gran, who've ordered the same meal for the last twenty years—not exactly a scenario that calls for all hands on deck. No, I know as well as Gran does that this is an excuse, an extremely flimsy excuse, for Ben to get some distance from me after I bailed on him last night.

"Okay," I say weakly, trying to ignore the stinging in my eyes that precedes tears. Even though I know that I made the right choice in meeting Absynth last night and that it had to come at Ben's expense, I didn't imagine that he would take it like this. If the roles were reversed, and Ben had spontaneously canceled a date with me at the last minute ...

I would have reacted the same way.

Because it wasn't just a date, it was a threshold, an invisible border in our relationship, and we had committed to cross it together. Labels or no, we've been circling *something* since the day he left that flower for me on the front porch of Gran's house, and last night was our chance to explore that something. Right now, as far as Ben knows, I bailed because I wasn't interested. He put himself out there, and I rejected him.

No wonder he doesn't want to see me.

"I'm sure he'll come around, dear," Gran says, giving me a supportive sort of half smile.

"Yeah," I say, deflated because I don't know if he will. Because if I were him, I'd retreat into my defenses and find every reason in the universe to avoid the person who hurt me. Hadn't it been that way when I arrived here? Closing myself off to protect against the pain of rejection? It had taken Ben's patience, persistence, and a series of small and not-so-small gestures to coax me out.

And at that moment, I think I know what I have to do to repair the damage I've done.

"Can you give me a ride into town, Gran?" I ask, a plan beginning to take shape in my mind.

"Sure," she says, surprised. "I'll be downstairs whenever you're ready."

"Yeah, okay," I say, my thoughts already racing ahead to my *mea culpa* to Ben. As I try to imagine what he would do if our roles were reversed, I realize that it would be more than a simple apology. It would be something bold and a little risky—an action that could either result in incredible success or abject failure and humiliation.

"Gran?" I say, the idea now fully formed and ready for implementation. "Do you have the number for the diner?"

It's just after one when Gran pulls into the dusty parking lot of the Burnt Biscuit to drop me off.

"Do you want me to wait?" she asks, and I shake my head. If things go well, I won't need a ride, and if things go poorly … well, then, I'll probably throw myself into the deep fryer or something.

I push the screen door to the restaurant open, and it gives a pained shriek, drawing every eye in the small dining room toward me. Behind the counter, I see Ben look up at the sound, briefly meeting my eyes before turning his back toward me.

So much for an inconspicuous entrance.

"Amethyst, right?" It's the same ruddy-faced hostess who greeted Gran and me on my first night in Morgan Springs.

"Yeah," I say, momentarily pulling my attention away from where Ben is refilling the napkin dispensers. "I called earlier."

"Right this way, sugar," she says, winking at me as she leads me over to an open booth in the back of the diner. "I'll send Ben right over."

I give her a small nod, anxiety blossoming in my chest as I watch her cross the small dining room to where Ben stands, still pointedly not looking in my direction. There's a moment where I seriously consider trying to conceal myself and just let Ben and the hostess assume I left without them noticing, but I push the thought away.

I'm seeing this thing through. Ben deserves at least that much.

Across the room, the hostess has arrived at the counter, and although I can't hear their conversation over the din of the other patrons, it's apparent that Ben doesn't want to wait on me from the speed at which he is shaking his head. I don't know if it's her words or the way she is waving her index finger, her long ruby-red nails swinging dangerously close to his face, but eventually, the hostess wins out, and Ben reluctantly picks up one of the plastic menus

164

and walks over to my booth.

"Can I start you off with anything to drink?" he asks, not looking up from the pad of paper in his hand.

"You can start by sitting down, Ben," I say, gesturing to the seat across from me.

"Look," he says, flipping the tiny notebook closed in frustration, "I don't have time to mess around. I'm working."

He starts to turn away, and in desperation, I reach out and grab his hand. I don't know if he feels the same warm current that I feel coursing through the place where my skin touches his, but he stops regardless.

"Can you sit down for a minute? Please?" I ask as the tingling rushes its way up my arm into my heart, quickening my pulse. "I'm trying to apologize."

He looks back to where the hostess should be, but she's nowhere in sight. After a moment of hesitation, he pulls his hand from mine, and I'm sure he's going to leave, but then he crosses his arms and flops onto the opposite bench. When he looks up at me, his face is hard, completely different from his usual easy smile.

"You look like you're feeling better." His words carry bitterness that is so un-Ben that I'm momentarily rendered speechless, my rehearsed apology dissolving into a thousand disparate pieces.

"Yeah," I say, desperately trying to remember any part of my apology in the wake of his tone. "It was a weird stomach thing, I—"

"Save it, Amethyst. If you didn't want to go, you should have just told me. That's what *friends* do."

He emphasizes the word "friends" in a way that implies he's not certain that's what we are anymore.

"Ben," I say, reaching out across the table. But his hands are tucked away, inaccessible, so my palm lies there, open and waiting in a semipathetic sort of way. It's a pretty apt metaphor of my life. "I *did* want to go, really. Will you let me make it up to you?"

He looks from my open hand up to my face and sighs, shaking his head.

"It's fine," he says, and I'm relieved to hear that the bitterness has left his voice. "You don't have to."

"I know I don't have to," I say, squeezing out of the booth. "I *want* to. Come on."

I again stretch my hand out to him, but he doesn't move to take it.

"I'm in the middle of a shift. I—" But before he can finish, the hostess appears by my side, a to-go bag in her hands.

"No, you're not," she says, passing the bag to me with a wink. She turns to Ben, her hands on her hips, her face stern. "This young lady's seen to that, so I suggest you take the poor girl up on her offer and get out of here before I change my mind, Benjamin Taylor."

Ben looks from the hostess to me and back again, open-mouthed with incredulity.

"So," I say, allowing myself a tentative smile. "Are you coming?"

"Do I have a choice?" he asks, and relief pulses through me as I hear the slightest hint of playful exasperation in his voice.

"No," the waitress and I say in perfect unison, and that's all it takes for me to break through, finally. Ben's face is completely transformed by the smile that accompanies his laughter. Heartened by his response, I offer him my arm, which he enthusiastically takes as we leave the restaurant for the sunny afternoon.

"Where to?" Ben asks, pulling a fry from the grease-stained bag.

"Um … " I had only sketched out my plan as far as an apology and the offer of lunch. The rest was dependent on Ben's response, which I hadn't been able to anticipate with any kind of accuracy. I say the first thing that I think of. "The reflecting pool? We'll have a picnic."

An hour later, Ben and I are stretched out on a dirty comforter we salvaged from his trunk at the edge of the reflecting pool at the heart of our garden. Some foil wrappers and empty ketchup packets are all that remains of lunch. Well, those and the warm, contented feeling that follows a good meal.

"Thanks, Amethyst," Ben says, and I turn my head to find that he's already looking at me. "This is nice."

Before I can respond, he shifts his body so that we are sitting shoulder to shoulder, placing his right hand over my left in the process. We haven't been this close since the night I thorned out when he kissed my cheek in the car. And even though I've mentally prepared for this degree of proximity, I'm finding applying theory to practice increasingly difficult as the low-level current surges through me, growing in intensity each second our bodies touch.

Afraid that too much more of this will lead to another prickly outburst on my part, I lean away from Ben on the pretense of examining the reflecting pool.

My reflection stares back at me, but something about the way the water moves, slow waves emanating from some unknown source, or the pattern of the rocky bottom transposed beneath my pale skin, gives me an ethereal, inhuman appearance. I watch for a moment, transfixed by the way the light dances down through the depths as if it's traveling much deeper than a couple of feet.

"It's just like you said. Like looking into another world."

Ben's face appears next to mine as he joins me at the edge of the pool. It has the same otherworldly look as my own, but I realize with a surprising shock of sadness that his is an illusion, while my own is, well, not.

Humanity is a disease for our kind, Amethyst.

I'm not sure if it's his humanity or my fairy blood that is the cause for the diagnosis. I do know, however, as much as I have tried to pretend otherwise, that what we have is terminal. This friendship, relationship, whatever it is cannot indefinitely survive the secret hanging between us.

A tear unexpectedly rolls down my nose and drops into the pool, causing a hundred ripples to distort our reflections until they are no more than concentric swirls of discordant colors.

"Amethyst?" Ben's voice is full of concern. "Are you okay?"

"Yeah," I say, pulling myself away from the water's edge and dragging my shirt sleeve across the top of my face as if I was wiping my brow and not my eyes. "Just hot."

For a moment, Ben doesn't respond, and I'm worried that I'll have to come up with some excuse for crying, but then two bare feet plop into the water in front of me.

"Care for a swim?" he asks, taking a few steps out into the pool before turning to face me. "Or, I guess, a wade?"

"O-oh," I stammer, looking down at the long jeans that conceal my retracted thorns. Even with Absynth's technique, there is still a visible pattern of bumps crisscrossing my calves that Ben is sure to notice if I roll up my pants. But I'm also struggling to come up with an excuse for why I can't join Ben that doesn't involve spilling my secret or making up some disgusting disease. The first is a no-go for obvious reasons, and the second is not the kind of thing I want Ben associating with me, even if it's not true.

But maybe I don't need an excuse, I think, a third option blossoming. *Maybe I need an explanation.*

It's risky, and maybe that's why I'm willing to do it—to test my relationship with Ben to see if he can handle at least a little portion of my other life. I can't tell him what I am, but I can show him a glimpse of it with as much truth as I can give. It's like my apology at the diner earlier: I can offer up a limited version of what I am, and he can either take it or leave it.

"Yeah. Okay," I say, taking a deep breath and pulling my thorns in as far as I can before pulling my knee up to my chest. Slowly, I begin to roll up the material of my jeans, focusing on the movement of my hands while trying to monitor Ben's face for a reaction in my periphery. When the fold clears my calf, I hear him gasp as the largest of the bumps come into view.

"What happened to you?" he asks, sloshing his way back to me.

I wince away from the sting of his words, my fingers already moving to pull the jeans back down over my exposed leg. Before I can make any progress, though, Ben reaches out to stop me.

"I'm sorry," he says. "That came out wrong. You don't have to explain anything to me." He squats down in the water, his eyes drawing level to mine. "But you don't have to hide anything, either."

And for an instant, I believe him. Believe that I could tell him everything and that it wouldn't change the way he's looking at me at this moment. That he would simply smile and say some reductive comment like he's just grateful that I'm part fairy and not part troll.

But I can't tell him the truth, not because I'm worried about his reaction but because I promised Absynth I wouldn't. This is her secret as much as it is mine, and I won't break the trust she has placed in me to keep it.

"It's a skin condition," I say, hoping that this answer is close enough to the truth that the lie won't read on my face. "Genetic."

Ben moves to sit next to me, his hand never leaving its position over the top of my own.

"Does it hurt?" he asks, his face awash with concern.

"Not anymore," I say, shaking my head as images of pliers stained with blood and sap run through my mind. "I saw a … a specialist recently, and she helped a lot."

I smile slightly at this explanation, running my free hand over the ridges along my knee.

"Is it treatable?" Ben asks.

"It's manageable, but there's no way to make them go away completely.

And … " I slip my hand out from under his and grasp the hem of my shirt. "They're everywhere."

I pull the shirt over my head, revealing the camisole and my skin underneath. I watch as Ben's eyes roam over my bare arms and collarbone, his brow wrinkling in concern. He reaches up to brush the hair away from the side of my face, revealing the bumps along my temple and behind my jawline.

"Oh, Amethyst," he says, but I cut him off, my limit for exposure finally reached.

"I know," I say, looking away from him as I shove my arms through the inside-out sleeves of my shirt. "I don't like to look at them, either."

"Hey," he says, his hand moving to my chin, tipping my face up to meet his. "I don't care what you look like, just as long as I get to see you."

I shake my head, trying to look away from the intensity of his gaze, but his face follows mine. He is just an inch away from me, so close that I can feel the heat of his breath on my lips as he continues.

"And for the record, I happen to really, *really* like the way you look."

He leans in, and I draw a sharp breath, but for the first time, it's not to hide my thorns but to express surprise as his lips press gently against the small bump where my jaw meets my neck.

"Every part of you," he murmurs against my skin, shocking me so thoroughly that I fall sideways into the water, pulling Ben along with me.

My hair is still dripping when we pull into Gran's driveway a half hour later, though the ratty blanket Ben draped around my shoulders has saved the Camry's plush seat covering from the worst of the water damage.

"Are you sure you don't want to go out or something? I'll wait here while you change—or I can come back later," Ben says as I disentangle myself from the blanket and open my door.

"Tempting," I say, and I mean it. This afternoon has only increased my desire to spend time with Ben, but I don't want to disappoint him again should Absynth come calling. "But I think I've had enough excitement for one day."

"I excite you?" Ben asks, raising his eyebrows mockingly. The only response I give him is to toss the damp blanket at his face before exiting the car.

"Regular time tomorrow?" I ask, leaning my arms against the driver's side door so that I'm eye level with Ben. "Or are you still *super swamped* at the diner?"

He rolls his eyes.

"I'll be here at nine o'clock *sharp*," he says, punctuating the last word by tapping my nose playfully with his index finger. "That is unless you get some weird twelve-hour stomach bug again."

Now it's my turn to roll my eyes.

"I'll see you tomorrow, Ben," I say, pushing myself away from the car and turning to head toward the house.

"Amethyst?" Ben calls after me. When I look back at him, he's wearing my favorite half smile, indicating he's about to do or say something ridiculous.

He doesn't disappoint.

"You haven't seen excitement yet." When I raise my eyebrows, unable to remember enough English words to form a question, his only response is to wink before putting the Camry into reverse and backing down the driveway. He honks twice when he reaches the road, and I wave as he disappears behind the trees lining the street.

"It looks like Ben accepted your apology."

Gran's voice startles me, and I spin to find her sitting on the front porch, a glass of sweet tea in her hand. As her gaze sweeps over me, I am glad I decided to put my wet shirt back on over my camisole. As I make my way up to the house, I sweep my hair across my forehead, nonchalantly ensuring that the rest of the bumps are hidden away.

"Yeah," I say, climbing the steps. "I mean, a free lunch goes a long way."

"Have a seat, Amethyst," Gran says, gesturing to the wicker rocking chair next to her. She is smiling, but I notice that it doesn't quite reach her eyes. I don't particularly want to have a chat with Gran, but as my only useable excuse just drove away, I sit.

"Were you really sick last night?" Gran asks, and though her voice is friendly, I think I can hear an undertone of suspicion.

"Yes," I say flatly, not wanting to offer any more information than I need to.

"Look," she says, shifting uncomfortably in her chair. "I know that at your age … Well, things can be very confusing. That your body is going through a lot of changes, and—"

"Oh my God!" I moan, hiding my face behind my hands. If I didn't know that Gran was a potential fairy-cidal murderer, I would disappear myself right now and not stop running until I crossed the Canadian border. But with that option off the table, I move on to begging. "Please, Gran, you don't have to do this. I got this talk like five years ago in health class."

"No," Gran says, discomfort straining her voice, "I don't think you got this *particular* talk in school, dear."

My embarrassment fades into unease as her words take on new meaning, and I realize she's not concerned about my teenage hormones. She's talking about other, more magical body transformations.

"I brought you out here to help you, Amethyst," she continues. "I understand what you're going through. You can trust me."

Gran reaches out, her hand stretching to brush my hair back away from my face, and instinctively I recoil.

"I don't know what you're talking about," I say, pushing myself up off the chair. "There's nothing to understand, and I *don't* need your help!"

"Amethyst! I—"

But I don't wait to hear what else she has to say. I fling the front door open and run up the stairs, locking my bedroom door behind me. Breathing hard, I press my ear against the wood, listening for her footsteps on the stairs, but they don't come.

She knows, I think, the words playing on a loop as I try to figure out what to do, but no answer comes. The only thing that is close to being a solution, or at least a precursor to a solution, is seeing Absynth.

She will know what to do; she always does.

I talk myself into waiting until darkness falls before climbing out of my bedroom window. I don't trust myself to hold a concealment, not when I'm this keyed up.

It's just before nine when I decide it's safe to leave. Like the first night I met Ben, there is no vine ladder waiting for me, and I'm forced to hang from my window and drop onto the roof of the porch below. In my haste to get to Absynth, however, I land harder than I mean to, the ominous thud echoing off the walls of Gran's house.

Holding my breath, I wait for a full count of ten before I decide it's safe to continue. Taking a breath, I crawl to the edge of the roof and ease myself down, feeling blindly for the porch railing with my feet.

I am just crouching down to make my final leap onto the black lawn beyond me when the back-porch light clicks on.

There is no place to hide, and more pressingly, no time to do anything more than close my eyes and wait for Gran's wrath.

I listen as both doors open, and then I hear her footfalls drawing toward where I balance on the railing. It's unbelievable that she hasn't noticed me yet, but each step brings her closer and closer.

She walks right by me.

I open my eyes, staring at Gran's back as she leans out over the far railing, looking up at my window. Confused, I turn my attention to myself, but when I try to examine the place where I can feel my hands gripping the wooden rail, there is nothing there.

I've completely disappeared.

Behind me, Gran is moving again, back toward the center of the porch. I squeeze my eyes shut, focusing with every ounce of concentration I can muster on maintaining my concealment.

I don't move again until I hear her return indoors, followed by the click of the light turning off. As soon as I open my eyes to confirm that Gran is gone, I jump off the porch, landing awkwardly on the lawn as my legs give way beneath me, the pins-and-needles sensation stretching from my ankles to my knees. I rub them briskly, urging the blood back down into my deprived veins, before giving in to my anxiety and doing a shambling zombie shuffle across the grass.

Finding my way back to the hollow without Absynth's assistance takes almost an hour of stumbling through the black woods with only vague memories to guide me. It is only when I catch a snippet of Daphne's voice carrying through the trees that I am finally able to find the circle of vine-laced trees.

"Absynth?" I call, stopping just short of the hollow. "Absynth, please let me in!"

There's no response from inside, but just as I'm about to call out again, the vines in front of me untwist, granting me access to the fairies' forest home.

"Well, this is a surprise, Amethyst," Absynth says as I duck through the opening and enter the hollow.

"I need to—" I begin, stopping short when I take in the scene before me.

Absynth, Naya, and Daphne are sitting around a huge ... well, I'm not sure what the word is, or if there's even a word for it. It looks like a droplet of shimmering liquid, the way water looks when floating in space, except enlarged by a factor of ten. Whatever the liquid is, it's hot—bubbles roil through the substance, bursting with soft hisses of wispy golden steam, not just at the top but along the entire surface. There is no fire that I can see, just a swarm of dozens of fairy lights congregating at the bottom of the liquid, their combined energy enough to bring it to a boil.

"What's that?" I ask, transfixed by the slow undulation of the substance as it floats a foot above the ground.

"We're just doing a little *cooking*, sweet one," Naya answers, her tone indicating there's a joke in her words that I don't understand.

"Huh," I say, taking a step toward the liquid. "I've never seen you eat. I just figured you didn't have to."

"Oh, this isn't for eating, Amethyst. At least not directly!" Daphne says, giggling as if I've misunderstood something extremely obvious.

"It's a drink," Absynth says, cutting across Daphne, whose laughter abruptly stops. "Fairy wine. It helps us keep our powers strong."

"So you don't need to eat, then?" I ask, wondering if I'll have to give up Oreos and french fries once I become a full fairy.

"We eat," Absynth says simply before continuing. "We still need to fuel our bodies, but ... "

She reaches up into the air, her hand cupped, palm up, stopping about four inches below a barren tree branch. I watch, incredulous, as an apple blooms in fast motion, like the way they show plants growing using time-lapse photography in nature documentaries. Only this is happening in real time, right before my eyes.

When, after a few seconds, the apple hangs heavy and ruby red on the branch, Absynth lazily pulls it from the tree and takes a large bite.

I can smell the sweetness of the fruit from where I stand a few feet away.

"We don't make a big production out of meals," she says, tossing the apple to me. "We eat when we're hungry."

I turn the apple over in my hands, examining it for any flaw, any sign of its accelerated creation, but there's nothing.

It's perfect.

"Don't you ever get sick of apples?" I ask, thinking about the time when I was five and threw up in the middle of an orchard after eating a half dozen Granny Smiths.

This time Absynth joins Daphne in her laughter, and even Naya cracks a smile.

"Sometimes," Absynth says, her eyes sparkling mischievously. "And when I do ... "

She repeats the same motion, reaching up toward the branch, but this time the fruit that bursts from the tree is green and oblong. "I have a pear."

"Or a banana," Naya says, crossing to a second tree and conjuring a bloom of fresh, bright-yellow bananas that are so heavy they bend the branch until they rest on the ground.

"Or," Daphne says, pressing her palm flat against the ground, causing a coarse column of spiky green leaves to push up out of the dirt, "a pineapple." She tugs at the leaves, revealing a large brown fruit beneath the crown of green.

Absynth walks toward me, letting the pear fall, forgotten, at her side.

"Or maybe we're craving meat?" she says, making a summoning motion with her hands. There are a few moments of silence, and then I hear the soft crunch of something approaching from the forest beyond the hollow. With another flick of her hand, Absynth parts the vines to reveal a magnificent white-tailed buck as the source of the sound.

"I could have birds drop their eggs into my lap," she continues, stroking the deer's muzzle as he comes to stand beside her. "Bees bring me honey right from the comb."

While Absynth doesn't actually magically make the last two things happen, I have absolutely no doubt that she could.

"You can get *anything* you want?" I ask, the longing in my words surprising me.

"*Get* anything?" Absynth asks, her eyes alive with excitement. "Amethyst, we can *control* anything: plants, animals, the weather. I can make it feel like winter right now, in the middle of July."

The snow is falling even before she is finished speaking, fat, wet flakes that clump in my hair and eyelashes. An icy wind swirls down from the open canopy, causing goose bumps to rise on the exposed skin on my neck and an involuntary shiver to slide down my spine.

But Absynth isn't done yet.

"I can make everything from the ants to the trees bow down to me." She raises her arms above her head, and as she lowers them slowly, her brow wrinkled with effort, everything from the trees to the deer to every single blade of grass bends before her. Even I feel a weak pull, a voice whispering from the back of my mind to kneel down in the snow and bow my head before my aunt. It's an uncomfortable feeling compounded by the realization that I'm unsure whether I'm able to resist Absynth's command because I am immune to her powers or because she's not turning her full influence toward me.

Then, with a final wave of her hand, everything is over: The snow stops, melting away into slushy piles at our feet. The trees bounce back to their upright positions, and the deer bounds out of the hollow, leaping into the darkness without a backward glance.

"It's complete control over everything around us. No worries, no fear of the unknown, because for a fairy, *there is no unknown*," she says, crossing the distance between us in three quick steps to stand with her hands on my shoulders, her face inches from mine. "That's what you'll get, Amethyst. The power to shape the world into anything and everything you could ever want or need."

Absynth's gaze is so intense that I feel like I'm staring into the sun. I look down, rolling the apple between my hands, trying to envision what I would do with the kind of power Absynth has shown me, but the only thing that comes to mind is the one person I will lose: Ben.

"And for this power, I'll have to … to make the Change?" I use the term, even though I'm not entirely sure what it means beyond, well, changing.

"That's it," Absynth confirms.

I look back up at her, examining the wild beauty of her fairy form, still unconvinced that the same magic lives inside me, too.

"What happens at a Changing?" I ask, imagining some token ceremony, like graduation, where, instead of a diploma, I am awarded wings and unchecked power over nature.

Absynth considers my question for a moment before answering.

"You abandon your human shell, and you embrace your real self," she says, and I wonder if she could have possibly been vaguer if she tried.

"Okay," I say, attempting to make my words sound curious instead of frustrated. "But how exactly does that happen?"

Absynth takes one hand off my shoulder and holds it out until one of the lights heating the fairy wine comes to land in her open palm. She holds the light between us so that I can feel its warmth on my cheeks.

"This light is the source of a fairy's power—the difference between being human and being something *more*, something *divine*," she explains, looking at the light the way one might look at a favorite pet. "During the Changing, you offer up your humanity, and you gain your first light. It's as simple as that."

"That sounds … " I say, not wanting to sound afraid but unwilling to ignore the panicked beating of my heart in response to the idea of offering up my humanity. "Painful."

"It's not, though," Absynth says, her eyes filling with an ecstasy that can't be faked. "It will be the most incredible experience of your life."

My mind flashes to the feel of Ben's lips against my jaw, probably the most incredible experience of my life to date, which I can't imagine being outdone by many other things, all of which also involve Ben. But according to Absynth, all of that will come to an end the moment I leave my humanity behind.

"And if I don't make the Change?" I ask, not wanting to envision a life, even an immortal magical life, without Ben. "What would happen?"

Absynth's face falls, all the excitement fading away into a mask of sadness.

"Pain. Misery. Death," she says matter-of-factly, looking away from me when she speaks again. "Amethyst, your mother refused the Change. She thought she wanted mortality, wanted your father, wanted *you*."

Her voice breaks on the last word, and I'm shocked to see tears in her eyes as she turns back toward me.

"You've asked me before … how it happened," she says, clearing her throat of emotion before continuing. "The truth is that Annabell chose death rather than to continue living trapped as she was. She couldn't give up her ties to the mortal world, so she chose to give up her life instead."

My breath catches in my throat as the full meaning of her words overwhelms me, but it is guilt, not grief, that consumes me. I know despair, know how it feels to have to wall off a part of yourself against the world to be able to get through the day. But I was preserved from succumbing to the darkness by clinging to the knowledge that there was an escape in my future. My sentence was eighteen years, tethered to my father and Philly until I was a legal adult.

My mother, though, her sentence was life, not because she loved my dad but because she loved *me*. I had been the chain shackling her to a life incompatible with her nature—not only that, but I hadn't been enough to make that existence tolerable. She wouldn't leave me to become the fairy she was born to be, and she couldn't bear the pain of her half life as a human, so she chose a third path: the only way she could see to be free from the pain of her existence and the guilt of abandoning me.

She chose death. I look down at the apple in my hands, wondering whether I might be doing the same, trying to walk the line between my human and fairy lives just as she did. Wondering whether I'll be strong enough to break away from the human world. Wondering how I'm going to tell Ben that I can't see him anymore.

I lift the apple to my lips and bite down into its sweet flesh.

"You were right to come to me about Beatrice," Absynth says as we reach the edge of the lawn a few hours later. Her reaction to my conversation with Gran had been mixed, as she showed some of the fear I saw from her before. But there was also a strange frustration toward me for continuing to place myself in harm's way by remaining human. As if she can read my thoughts, she continues, "If she knows as much as you fear, I'm not sure it's wise for you to put off your Changing much longer."

"I know," I say, searching for the right words to explain my hesitation. "I just … I'm not ready to be done being human just yet."

"I don't understand," she says, frowning, "but it's your choice to make."

"Thank you," I reply, giving her a quick hug. "Really, Absynth, for everything."

She makes a sort of noncommittal sound, which I take to mean *you're welcome, but I still think you're making a dumb decision.* It's about the best reaction I can hope to get from her.

"Bye," I say with half a wave before leaving Absynth and the safety of the woods.

I'm only a few yards across the lawn before the light on the back porch switches on, bathing me in its harsh fluorescent glow. My grandmother stands at the edge of the porch, silhouetted against the house, her shadow cascading out across the grass ahead of me.

"Where have you been?" Gran says, striding down the steps to grab me by the arm. "Well?" she demands, pulling me back toward the house.

My brain's CPU is running at maximum capacity trying to complete several functions simultaneously, the most crucial being a believable alibi for my late-night escapades in the forest.

"Ben," I say, grasping onto the lie with the same desperation a drowning person has when they latch onto a floating piece of debris. It's not much, but at this moment it's all I have. "I was with Ben."

We reach the first steps of the porch, and Gran stops to glower down at me.

"In the woods?" she asks, her voice thick with skepticism.

"Yes," I say, trying to stay one step ahead of her questioning in my fabricated story. "I asked him to meet me there."

She narrows her eyes, looking past me to the dark tree line beyond.

"And where is he now?" The disbelief is still there, but her words are flavored with something else now. Concern. Or maybe fear.

"He's on his way home," I say, hoping she doesn't press me on it. While I'm sure Absynth is well concealed, the last thing I want is Gran marching out to the woods and poking around.

"You'd better hope he makes it there," she says, and it's the threat that pushes me from fear to anger.

"What's that supposed to mean?" I cry, jerking my arm out of her grip and backing away from her reach. "You *hope he makes it there?*"

"The forest is *dangerous*, Amethyst," she says, and when I roll my eyes, her face flushes red, enraged. "Maybe you don't understand that, but *Ben* certainly should!"

"I *understand* more than you could ever know!" I yell back, my anger making me careless with my words as I shove by Gran toward the back door. "I understand that there's nothing in there that would ever hurt me. *Or Ben.*"

Before Gran can respond, I rip the door open and run up to my room, locking myself away from her questions for the second time in a day.

I spend the rest of my night struggling to stay awake as I sit in my chair next to my open window, my head swiveling between the woods outside and my bedroom door, waiting for some sign from Absynth that she's okay, or some fresh attempt from Gran to interrogate me further. Nothing comes of either front, and by the time the sun begins to rise, I decide to forgo sleep entirely and commit to existing in a state of perpetual exhaustion.

I don't risk leaving my room to check where Gran is until just before Ben's arrival. So when, at 8:55, I creep out into the hallway, I am relieved to see her car is gone. I only have time to brush my teeth and run a comb through my hair before I hear the Camry's horn honking from the front of the house.

"Redecorating?" Ben asks as I slide into the passenger seat next to him.

"What?" I say, sure in my sleep-deprived state I've misunderstood, or at least misheard him.

Ben points back toward Gran's house, where I see what looks like a half dozen cast-iron frying pans hung at even intervals around the porch.

"I, uh ... " I'm not sure how to respond. "Well, you know, Gran's a bit eccentric."

"Yeah." Ben laughs, throwing the car into reverse, seeming to accept my nonexplanation without further question. I smile at him, but worry tugs at the back of my mind as I watch the heavy pans twirling slowly, because I'm sure they have nothing to do with Gran's design aesthetic and everything to do with our argument last night.

My task of the day at the Gardens is scrubbing a decade's worth of moss from the dozens of marble statues scattered throughout the path while Ben tames the last of the rogue hedges. It's not hard work, but the repetitive motion combined with the warmth of the day makes my battle against exhaustion all the more difficult. Finally, after forty minutes of drifting in and out of consciousness, I concede the fight and curl up on one of the low benches to catch a few minutes of sleep, a half hour, tops.

A few hours later, Ben's voice jolts me awake.

"You feeling all right?"

I sit up too fast, and dark spots cloud my vision as I struggle to stop my head from spinning.

"Yeah," I say, suppressing a yawn. "Sorry, I didn't sleep last night. Just got a lot on my mind, I guess."

"Anything I can help you with?" he asks, dropping his garden shears and sitting down next to me.

"No," I say, picking up my train of thought where I left it during my catnap. "You're, well, you're part of the problem."

Ben's smile falters, and he is suddenly serious. "Amethyst, if I did anything to—"

But I wave his apology away before he can complete it. "No, it's nothing you did," I start, not sure how to explain that it's not his behavior but his biology that is the issue. "It's *us*. It's what's going to happen when I have to … "

Change, I think.

"Leave," I say.

"Do you ever stop worrying and just let yourself be happy?" he asks,

180

dismissing my concern. "I mean, it's not like you're suddenly going to drop off the face of the earth. We've got phones and computers, and I can visit, and you can show me how you city slickers live."

"Ben," I say, allowing myself, just for a moment, to play this unattainable scenario out. "How long could we do that for?"

"Until next summer," he says automatically, as if he's thought all of this out already. His optimism is too much for me, especially when I know there is an expiration date on our relationship that is up the day of my Changing.

It's not fair—to me, to him, to the universal laws of karma—a fact that makes me sigh aloud in frustration.

"What?" he asks, concern knitting his brows together.

"You." I throw the word at him like an accusation. "You're making this so much harder."

"What am I making harder?" His voice is light and full of amusement, as is typically the case when he thinks I'm being overdramatic or particularly angsty.

"Ben," I say, looking away from him as I realize where this sentence, this conversation, this relationship has always been heading. "I'm trying to break up with you."

The silence hangs between us for a few long seconds as I wait for his response, trying to steel myself against his possible anger or sadness or pleading.

Instead, he bursts into laughter.

"What about this is funny?" I say, annoyed that, once again, he has managed to lay waste to my expectations.

"Well, one," he begins, ticking the number off on his finger as he speaks, "I must have missed the memo where we started labeling things again."

"I just—" An embarrassed flush fills my cheeks, and I struggle to find a way to walk back my words.

"Not that I'm complaining." Ben smiles, shrugging as he cuts me off. "And two, you seem to be breaking it off because you figure it might happen anyway at some unknown point in the future. And that's just being stupid."

"I'm not stupid!" I say, righteous anger flaring in my chest that he would think that I would throw what we have away arbitrarily. "I'm practical."

Ben snorts with laughter again, and I pick up one of the larger weeds I pulled and smack him with it, the dirt clod clinging to the roots, leaving a brown stain on the back of his shirt.

"I am!" I argue, pulling the weed back to ready myself for another swing, thinking that a mouthful of dirt would stop his laughing.

"No," he says, reaching up to catch my wrist in both of his hands. "You're not practical. You're scared."

"I'm not scared of you," I say, unable to see the logic in his point.

"You're scared of getting hurt," he says. "Well, so am I. So is everyone else. I'm sorry to break it to you, Amethyst, but that's just a part of being human."

It's this phrase that finally pushes me to tears because, at this moment, more than anything, I wish he was right. I wish I could be the human girl he believes I am, not this weird hybrid of mortal and myth that can't belong with him.

"Hey," Ben says, his voice soft as he puts his arm around me, pulling me close enough that I can bury my face against his shoulder. "Look, you at least have to give me the chance to be a proper boyfriend before you break up with me. One date—a *real* date. It's in the rules."

I pull away from him, wiping my eyes with the sleeve of my shirt.

"One date?" I ask, not sure if I'm doing it to appease him or myself.

"And then you can officially kick me to the curb," he says, holding his right hand in the air as if he's taking an oath.

I nod, and Ben's smile is blinding.

"I'll need some time to prep," he says, getting up to his feet. "Can you meet me back here later?"

"Prep?" I ask. "For what?"

"Oh no," Ben says, wagging a finger at me in mock reproach. "My date, my rules, and I say it's a surprise."

He extends his hand to me. "So, eight o'clock?"

I take his hand, unable to suppress my smile or my sense of excitement, even as the voice in the back of my head is warning me that this is just me kicking the can down the road. That now, when things have to end, it's going to be that much harder, that much more painful.

Stuff it, I tell the voice.

"Eight's perfect," I tell Ben.

The first thing I see when Ben turns into Gran's driveway is her lime-green Beetle, and my stomach turns over as I anticipate how uncomfortable the next few hours are going to be.

"I'll see you later," I say to Ben through his open window.

"It's a date," he replies with a wink that doesn't do much to counteract the innate lameness of his joke. But before I can properly ridicule him, he leans out and kisses me on the cheek, rendering me unable to do much more than watch him back down the driveway in stunned silence.

I may hate that he can still catch me by surprise so easily, but I can't say that I'm opposed to his methods.

I'm debating the best way to handle Gran as I pull myself up the front steps and decide to lean hard into the whole irrationality-of-teenage-love angle and hope she buys it. I'm just arranging my face into what I hope resembles "romantic bliss" when I hear Gran's voice carry out of the open window.

"Last night, I caught her trying to sneak back in the house at three in the morning."

I stop short, my hand falling from the doorknob. There are no other cars in the driveway, and no neighbors close enough to walk over for a visit, so I'm sure whoever she's speaking with is on the other end of the phone line, not sitting in the kitchen. I press myself against the front wall and creep as close to the window as I dare, listening hard.

"I know, Dave," she says after a few seconds of silence, and I feel my hands ball into angry fists as I realize she is talking to my dad. I wonder how long she's been giving him reports on me, her secrecy triggering flashbacks of every time Dr. Zahn or one of my half dozen other therapists filled him in on my daily activities. How could I have been so stupid, so naive, to believe that this wasn't happening? Why did I think that I would be allowed to exist as if I was normal and not some damaged, crazy girl?

"I was hoping this would work out, too," she continues, "but I don't think I can help her. She doesn't *want* me to help her."

Well, I think with savage satisfaction, *she's at least right about one thing.*

There's another long pause, punctuated by Gran sighing heavily.

"Does it have to be Hillbrooke, though? Couldn't she just—Ah, I see," she says, before adding, "no, I suppose tomorrow wouldn't be a problem."

*N*o. It's not a reaction of terror, a weak gasp of protest as my mind falters against the crushing realization of Gran's words; it's a declaration, firm and unwavering as steel. A month ago, the weight of Gran's words would have crashed down on me as heavily as if they were made of stone, encasing me in a crushing tomb of panic. Now, though, I find myself easily able to stand my ground, hand still poised on the doorknob, because I know that I have another option, another home, with Absynth.

It's that knowledge, combined with the burning anger flaring white hot in my chest, that compels me to pull the front door open.

While I've been angry before, even furious, I have never experienced this level of raw, wild energy.

Power, I think. Maybe it's not on Absynth's plane of elemental manipulation, but it is my human version of it. I feel it now, the center of myself, which I had always envisioned as a soft, fragile thing that needed to be walled off and protected, and I realize how wrong I was.

With all of my defenses dismantled, I see that my core is hard, an uncut diamond formed from a decade of pressure and pain, imbued with an energy that has been untapped, trapped behind the fortress I built to protect it. But now, freed from its internal prison, it sends a current running through me, hot and wild. It arcs and twists like lightning on a summer night as I cross the entryway, following the sound of Gran's voice.

"Goodbye, Dave," she says, and I hear the click of the phone on the receiver just as I reach the entrance to the kitchen.

"Hey, Gran," I say to her back, smiling with satisfaction when she jumps in surprise at the sound of my voice.

"Oh, Amethyst," she says, breathless from shock as she turns to face me. "You're home early."

She smiles, but it's a thin, anxious thing that disappears almost as quickly as it came.

"How's my dad?" I ask, taking a step toward her. My smile widens when she takes a step back.

"Fine," she says, swallowing before continuing. "We were just talking about—"

"Sending me to Hillbrooke," I finish for her, my voice calm even as another wave of outrage flares inside me. "I'm not going. You can't make me. I'm not afraid of him or you. Not anymore."

"Amethyst," Gran says, trying to take another step away from me but bumping into the counter instead, "I don't know what you think you heard, but—"

"Don't lie to me!" I shout, my fury finally coming to the surface, raising thorns along my body so violently that they rip through the thin material of my shirt.

Across the kitchen, Gran gasps, a flash of fear crossing her face.

"Please," she says, reaching a hand toward me in a pleading gesture, her eyes still greedily raking over my chest and arms. "Let me help you."

"I don't need your help," I growl, halving the distance between us. "I know what you are, what you did. What you want to do to me."

As I pass the place where the phone hangs, I reach out, ripping it from the wall with such force that a chunk of the plaster comes with it. With another jerk, I sever the wire connecting it to the jack along the baseboard before tossing the whole thing aside.

The act of destruction feels good against my skin.

"W-what are you—" she stammers, her eyes wide and full of fear.

"I'm done with him," I say, gesturing to the hole in the wall where the phone used to be. "And with you."

Before Gran can respond, I reach out with my senses, allowing the kitchen around me to ink into my skin, pull open the back door, and tear across the yard to the forest beyond.

Oh my God, I think, slowing once I can no longer see Gran's house through the trees behind me. *I can't believe I just did that.*

The sense of liberation is so complete, so overwhelming, that I laugh out loud—a short burst that echoes off the trees and sends a rabbit ahead of me running for the safety of the undergrowth. And although I do not yet have fairy wings, I feel light enough in this moment to take flight.

It doesn't take as long to find my way to Absynth's hollow in the waning daylight, although I still manage to get turned around once and have to spend a few minutes retracing my steps before I find the path again.

"Absynth!" I call out as soon as the outer ring of her hollow comes into view. My voice is still shaky with excitement and adrenaline.

The vines part just as I reach them, revealing Absynth, beautiful as an oil painting framed between the trees.

"Amethyst, what—" she begins, but then she stops short as she takes in my appearance, her gaze lingering on the dozens of holes in my shirt. "Are you okay? Have you been hurt?"

I shake my head as she rushes toward me, my throat contracting with emotion as I'm overwhelmed by her immediate concern for my well-being. As she embraces me, I am filled with a certainty, peace, that I have made the right decision.

"It's Gran," I say, and I feel Absynth stiffen against me. "She was talking to my dad on the phone. They … they wanted to send me away to some hospital, and—"

Absynth releases me, her face serious as she holds it close to mine.

"You don't have to go anywhere," she says, stroking my hair. "Not if you don't want to."

"I know," I say, and I can't help but beam up at her. "I know that I have a home here with you."

"Of course," she purrs, her hand moving from my hair to cup my cheek. "Just as soon as you make the Change."

"Wh-what?" I ask, my heart sinking. "But I can't go back to Gran's. She … "

I trail off when I realize that I'm about to tell Absynth that I've broken her only rule by confirming my fairy nature to Gran in the heat of my anger. "She wants to take me to that hospital *tomorrow*." Even though it's not a lie, it feels like one, and I have to look away from her as I say it.

"Then you'll have to make the Change tonight," she says, oblivious to my deception.

Tonight, I think, remembering my promise to Ben, any remaining elation I felt over breaking free from Gran and my father fading into oblivion.

"Why?" I ask, desperation creeping into my voice. "Can't I just stay like this for a—"

"Amethyst," Absynth says, softly but not without exasperation, "if you want to live with us, you have to be one of us. Being human would put us all at risk, especially if *she* is looking for you."

And she will be, I think, *now that she knows.*

Shame, thick and hot, slips into my stomach as I realize how it was my recklessness that has endangered not only myself but Daphne, Naya, and Absynth, too.

"I understand," I say, my words reduced to little more than a whisper as my throat closes around them, my human body seemingly protesting what I am about to say. I clear my throat before continuing, trying to summon some measure of the strength I felt earlier as I confronted Gran. "I'll do it. I'll make the Change. Tonight."

Absynth pulls me into an embrace so tight that for a few seconds I am unable to draw breath until she releases me again.

"We'll start the preparations right away," she says, taking my hand and pulling me toward the hollow. "I wasn't ready for you to change your mind so soon, but—"

"Absynth," I say, pulling my hand out of hers. As easy as it would be to follow her into my fairy future, I know that the moment I make the Change is also the moment I can never see Ben again, and after all he's done for me, all he means to me, I cannot just disappear without a trace. I owe him more than that. I owe him the chance to say goodbye. "Hold on."

"What's wrong?" she asks, frowning in confusion.

"I just need a couple of hours," I say, looking down at my watch. I have less than an hour to make my way to the Gardens. "I-I need to say goodbye to someone."

There's a long moment of silence before Absynth responds, her face an unreadable mask as she studies me. For a heartbeat, I am worried that she is going to stop me, but then she nods.

"Of course," she says, her smile returning. "We'll be ready when you come back."

I plan to allow myself to cry up until I reach the place where the forest meets the road. I expect huge racking sobs, but I find that my grief over saying my goodbye to Ben is beyond tears. Instead, there is just a sort of hollow sensation in my chest as if my heart has collapsed on itself like a dying star, the black hole left in its wake sucking all feeling into the void.

It's almost a quarter after eight when I finally make it to the gates of the Gardens, realizing only as I push them open how woefully underdressed I am for anything more than a '90s alt-rock concert. To at least give Ben the illusion that I want to be here, I abandon my hole-riddled long-sleeved shirt on one of the benches with the hope that the tank top underneath has fared a little better.

"Ben?" I call out, scanning the darkening entry for a sign of him, hoping that he hasn't left because of my lateness.

"Back here!" His voice is excited and comes from somewhere deeper in the garden.

I'm just about to ask where exactly "back here" is when soft music begins to play. I follow it, picking out the strum of a guitar mingled with the twang of a banjo underneath the soft voice of a male singer. It's a slow, folksy melody that somehow radiates Ben in every note.

The music draws me toward the center of the Gardens, and as I turn down the path that will take me to the reflecting pool, I realize that the area ahead of me, which should be pitch black now that the sun has set, is instead fully illuminated, though I can't yet see the source of the light. When I finally do reach the place where the hedge path meets the large grassy area surrounding the pool, I find that it has been completely transformed.

Hundreds of white lights have been wrapped around the hedges that enclose the pool, snaking their way up the dark-green branches and then reaching out across the clearing below, giving the impression that the stars have floated down to hover just above me. They remind me of the way Absynth's fairy lights float in the canopy of her hollow, and suddenly I remember why I've come here.

"Amethyst."

I look for Ben and find him standing at the edge of the reflecting pool. He's smiling, but it's a strange, nervous smile that I've never seen him wear before, and he shifts his weight from one foot to the other.

He crosses the distance between us, and as he draws close, I see that he's holding a single flower in one of his hands, tiny and white with a deep-red center—rose mallow.

"I was starting to get worried that you weren't coming," he says as he tucks the flower delicately behind my ear before extending his hand to me, an offer to dance. "May I?"

"Ben," I begin, not sure how to say all of the things I need to before I get to goodbye. "Wait, I—"

He presses a finger to my lips, silencing my protest as he shakes his head.

"One date," he reminds me. "You promised."

Reluctantly, I take his hand and allow him to pull me against him, his free hand wrapping around the small of my back as we begin to revolve slowly around the grass.

Everything about this moment should be perfect, and to an extent, it is, as long as I exist only in the now and ignore the pain looming just ahead for both of us.

"You didn't have to do all this for me," I say, resting my head against Ben's chest and watching the light spin around us as we turn.

"This?" he says, and I close my eyes contentedly against the rumble of his laughter against my cheek. "This is nothing. Just some lights and a little music."

"Well, I think it's amazing," I say. "I've never seen anything like this before, not in real life, anyway."

He stops suddenly, and when I look up to him, he lets out a long exhale before meeting my gaze.

"Amethyst," he says, a seriousness in his voice that makes my heart quicken, "you're not like anyone I've ever met before. You're so … different."

Even though I know he doesn't say it to hurt me, the truth of the word stings. I *am* different, more different than he can ever know, and that's why I need to end this now before either of us does something that will make it harder. I look away from him, gnawing my lip in preparation for the pain about to come, when Ben pulls my face back to his.

"I *like* different," he says. "I, well, I think I might love it."

My mind goes blank, unable to form a response in the aftermath of Ben's declaration. In those few nanoseconds of mental incapacitation, my body takes control, closing the gap between our faces until my lips press against his.

For a moment, I feel Ben's shock, but then his mouth softens against my own, and his arms curl around my back as my arms wrap around his neck. There is no thought, no past, no future, just this kiss and the feel of Ben against me.

The electricity that usually sparks between us pales in comparison to what surges through us now, the difference as stark as getting your energy from an AA battery and then a nuclear power plant. Every nerve in my body is attuned to him, sending messages of heat and pressure that only serve to pull him closer, even if the distance between us can now only be measured in nanometers.

We don't break apart until a dizzy light-headedness starts to pull at the edges of my consciousness, making me wonder how long it's been since I last took a breath.

"So," Ben says just as breathlessly, smiling as he leans his forehead against mine, "are we still breaking up?"

I know what I have to say as I pull away from him, the taste of him still lingering on my lips.

"Ben, I came here tonight to tell you goodbye," I say, my heart tearing as his face falls, the pain already so much more than I imagined. I am certain that continuing down this trajectory will cause me irreparable harm, but what other choice do I have?

Two roads diverged in a wood.

Swallowing back the fear rising in my throat, I take a moment to find Ben's eyes with my own before continuing.

"But instead I think I'm going to tell you the truth."

The music still plays, and somewhere beyond the reflecting pool, there is the buzz of an insect taking flight, but in the immediate space around Ben and me, there is a thick silence where my words hang between us.

"The truth?" Ben asks, his face twisting into a skeptical half smile. "What are you, some kind of spy? A secret double agent sent to seduce me?"

"Not quite," I say, not sure how to best explain the whole half-human, half-fairy thing in a way that won't cause him to have some kind of existential crisis.

"What, then?" he asks gently, drawing a thumb across my jawline and making my thoughts go fuzzy. "You can tell me anything."

"You're sure about that?" I say, catching his hand and holding it between my own. "Because I need you to promise that you'll keep this between us, even if, afterward, you never want to see me again. Can you do that?"

Real concern shadows Ben's face, and he seems to consider my words before nodding once.

"Your secret is safe with me," he says, pulling my hand up to his lips to kiss the backs of my fingers. "I promise."

"Okay," I say, pausing briefly to consider where to begin. If I tell him the whole story, we could be here for hours, but everything would be out there, good, bad, and magical. Then again, there is something to be said for simply ripping the Band-Aid off and filling in the backstory later. "You know, it might be easier just to show you."

I slip my hand away from Ben's and take a step back toward the hedge.

"Remember when I told you I had a skin condition?" I say, my eyes locked on Ben's, ready to abort mission at the first sign of a freak-out. "Well, I may have understated the severity a little bit."

With a deep breath, I relax my hold over the thorns, allowing them, all of them, to rise from beneath my skin. Ben's eyes widen as they move up my arms, across my collarbone, and finally to my face.

"Are those... " He's unable to finish the question, and I remember my initial reluctance to apply a name to something so unbelievable.

"Thorns?" I finish for him before answering my own question. "Yeah. Little freaky, right?"

Ben laughs, and I swear I have never heard a more beautiful sound in all my life.

"A little bit, yeah," he says, still chuckling as he shakes his head. "So, the secret is what? That you're part rosebush?"

"Sort of," I say, not ready to say the word "fairy" out loud just yet. "There's more, too."

"Super," Ben says, nodding vigorously, the way an athlete might hype himself up just before a big game. "Show me what else you've got."

"All right," I say, unable to hide my smile as I allow the evergreen of the hedges to ink into my skin, watching Ben's eyes slide out of focus as I become completely indistinguishable from the shrubs behind me.

"Invisible, cool," he says, feigning uninterest even though his eyebrows have disappeared beneath his hair. "So's that it?"

I let my camouflage drop so that Ben can see me nod.

"For now," I say, closing the distance between us again. As I reach the place where Ben stands, I retract my thorns, figuring that it's best not to press my luck with his reaction.

"You don't have to do that," he says, reaching out toward me. "You don't have to hide from me. Not ever."

His hand is just inches from my face when a loud hiss issues from the hedge tunnel behind me. Suddenly vines spring up around Ben, twisting their way around his chest and wrists before pulling him violently down to his knees.

20

"What are you doing?" Ben shouts, struggling against the thick green bonds.

"It's not me!" I yell back, dropping to my knees and trying to pry the vines away from his neck. "I don't—"

Another loud hiss drowns out my words, and I know immediately who has summoned the vines. I stand up, preparing to explain to Absynth that this isn't what it looks like, but as soon as I face my aunt, all thought of conversation flees from my mind, replaced instead by a fear I haven't felt in weeks.

Before me stand the creatures from my nightmares, wild and monstrous, all of their delicate beauty from our nights in the hollow twisted into fierce fangs and raised thorns. Daphne and Naya are crouched low to the ground, coiled as if ready to spring at a moment's notice, their eyes locked on Ben's struggling form. Absynth stands just before of them, her right arm extended as she controls the vines, her eyes on me.

"Absynth," I say, not bothering to conceal the fear in my voice. "I can explain. I—"

"How *dare* you." She doesn't shout, but the quiet accusation in her words is enough to silence me. As she continues, Naya and Daphne move in unison, circling me and Ben like lionesses surrounding their prey. "After everything I've done for you, this is how you repay me? With *betrayal?*"

She hurls the last word at me like a weapon, her disgust with me as palpable against my skin as the warm night air.

"Please—" I begin, but I'm once again cut off, this time by a gasp of pain from Ben.

"Such a handsome boy," Naya says, yanking Ben's head back to gain a better look at his face. "It's almost a pity that we have to kill him."

"No!" I shout, my body already in motion. I throw myself sideways into Naya. She lets out a growl as we crash against the ground, her thorns digging into my flesh as she pins me beneath her.

"Behave, now," she whispers, a ferocious smile on her face as she stares down at me. "You don't want to make things worse for your *friend.*"

I respond in the only way I can with my arms trapped under Naya's weight, by bringing my head up to collide with hers. I feel a satisfying crunch as my forehead makes contact with her nose. Quick as a snake strike, her clawed hand rakes across my cheek, leaving four long gashes in its wake and causing me to cry out in pain.

"*Amethyst!* Are you—" Ben's question turns into a loud gurgle, and cold dread floods through me as I hear him struggling for breath against the constriction of the vines.

"Absynth!" I scream, trying and failing to throw Naya off of me. "Absynth, please! *Please!* He won't tell anyone! I promise!"

"*Promise?*" Suddenly Naya is gone, and it is Absynth standing over me, an angel of death with her head ringed by the full moon above. "How can I trust a promise from you after this?"

She jerks her hand toward Ben, whose eyes are watering as his lips turn blue.

"I'm sorry!" I plead, not able to stop the tears from spilling over. "Please, Absynth, I'll do anything. Please, just don't hurt him."

"*Anything?*" she asks, cold calculation in her eyes. "What if I asked you to trade places with the boy? Your life for his?"

I look from Absynth to Ben, and I feel my heart rip in two as I take in the destruction I've wreaked on two people who have done nothing but care for me since I arrived here. It was my selfishness, my inability to sacrifice my happiness, that brought me to this point. I tried to have it all, to walk both paths, and I've wound up at the edge of a cliff with no one but myself to blame.

"Yes," I say, hoping that my life, as little as it's worth, will be enough to save Ben's.

Absynth stares at me for a long moment before waving her hand, causing the vines to wither away to brown husks.

"Ben!" I reach out as he falls forward, but Absynth beats me there, catching him under his chin as he gasps for air.

"One word to *anyone*, and I will not hesitate to end your life," she says, her claws digging into his cheeks. "Understand?"

Ben's jaw tightens, the smallest hint of a smirk pulling up the corner of his mouth. I have time to register that he is about to do something stupid before he jabs his fist upward, burying the edge of a jagged rock in Absynth's forearm.

"Amethyst, run!" he yells, but before he can do more than turn his head in my direction, Absynth recovers, catching his arm in her hand and twisting it.

Pop.

The sound is punctuated by Ben's anguished scream, the kind of high-pitched sound that only accompanies extreme pain. This time I'm fast enough to reach him as he falls, catching him against my chest. His breathing is shallow and hot against my neck, and I can feel the already swollen mass forming where his shoulder has been dislocated.

"You said you wouldn't hurt him!" I shout up at Absynth as Ben begins to tremble against me, a cold sweat spreading over his skin.

"I said I wouldn't kill him," she says. Daphne flits to her side, conjuring a fuzzy-leaved plant, and begins to treat her wounds. "I suggest you get rid of him before I change my mind."

I don't hesitate. Pulling Ben's uninjured arm over my shoulder, I help him to his feet. He's heavy against my side and unsteady as we walk toward the hedge path that will take us out of the Gardens. Just as we pass out of the open area surrounding the pool, I hear the soft buzz of fairy wings behind me. I glance back, and I can make out the edge of Naya's concealed form following us from a few feet away.

To make sure I come back, I think, wondering if Absynth will make my death quick or drag it out now as additional punishment for Ben's insurrection. I suppose in the end it won't matter anyway.

"Do you think you can make it from here?" I ask as we reach the mouth of the trail that leads back to Ben's house.

"What do you mean, make it alone?" Ben asks, wincing as he disentangles himself from me.

"I've got to go back," I say. "I can't go with you."

He shakes his head, reaching out for my hand, but I pull it away.

"Amethyst," he says, slowly, like he is explaining complex math to a toddler, "those things will *kill* you if you go back."

"They'll kill you if I don't!" I say, but it's no use. His sense of self-preservation is as woefully lacking as my own.

I can see only one option to keep Ben alive.

"It was a mistake, Ben," I say. "All of it. I never belonged with you. I belong with them—for better or for worse."

"Look," he says, anger in his voice, though I'm not sure who it's directed toward, "I don't know who they are or what they told you, but it's not right. They're monsters, Amethyst! You could never be like them!"

Next to me, I see the air shiver as Naya moves closer, and I know that her patience with me is wearing thin. I need to get Ben away from here now.

"*Monsters?*" I repeat his word, pain and anger contorting it into something that sounds more like a snarl. There's a stabbing sensation in my heart as Ben's face shows a shock of fright.

"You know I didn't mean that you—"

I cut him off with a hiss, using the ache radiating out from my chest to push myself further into my fairy form than I have ever done before. My thorns rise, but I also feel my fingernails push out into pointed claws, my canine teeth elongating into fangs as I lower myself into a crouch.

"Where do I belong now, Ben?" I growl at him, another knife lodging into my heart as he takes a step back from me.

"Amethyst," he says, pleading, "don't do this."

There are tears in his eyes, but I don't know if they're for me or from me.

"You have until three," I say, my words stunted as I struggle to take in a breath, my dying heart taking up too much room in my chest for my lungs to function properly. "*One.*"

"Amethyst … " His eyes search my face, and I wonder if he sees any part of the girl he loved in it.

"*Two.*" My heart rate accelerates, each beat a punching pain against my ribs.

"Please … " His voice is weak and watery. In the light of the moon, his tears run silver down his cheeks.

"*Three.*"

I lunge at him as soon as the word passes my lips, too afraid that any hesitation will cause me to lose my nerve. I collide with Ben's stomach, trying to angle my body so that I don't drive my thorns into him as we crash to the ground. He rolls away, coughing and clutching his already injured right arm, which must have taken the brunt of this latest fall.

"This isn't you!" he says, but finally, I can see doubt creeping into his eyes, and I know that my work is almost done.

I lunge again, and this time I feel my thorns embed themselves in his skin, and I drag deep cuts across the left side of his chest. It is this that finally pushes Ben over the edge.

He kicks out, his feet connecting with my stomach, throwing me off of him. I land on my back, bright-white lights bursting before my eyes as my head connects with something hard—a rock or maybe a tree stump.

The last thing I hear as the darkness takes hold of me is Ben's footsteps retreating into the woods.

I can't be sure if it's death or a dream as I push my way through the thick hedges of one of the garden paths. There is a dreamlike edge to my vision, as if I'm walking through a kaleidoscope as it twists rainbows around me, but I can't see them clearly from my position at its center. But there's also a sense of finality, a sense that, as I travel deeper into the hedge tunnel toward the bright-white light at its end, I'm leaving much more than the Gardens' entrance behind.

Whatever this is, it's not reality.

I finally step out into blinding sunlight, and it takes a few seconds for my eyes to adjust to the brightness after being so long in the green-tinged light of the garden path. Even before I can see, though, I know where I am, and I know who must be waiting for me.

"Ben," I say softly as his form comes into view, standing with his back to me by the edge of the reflecting pool.

His head perks up at the sound of my voice, and it's not until he turns to face me that I see that he's changed—not in the dramatic way of a fairy but in the ordinary human passage of time. He seems taller, his shoulders broader than I remember. His face is thinner and his jaw sharper, with the faintest shadow of stubble. But when he smiles with a brilliance that rivals the sun above, I know that he is the same Ben.

My Ben.

"Hey," he says, a slight constriction in his voice as if his throat is tight with emotion.

I open my mouth to speak, but another voice answers from behind me.

"Hey."

I turn just in time to see a woman, maybe a few years older than me, walk out of the hedges. She wears a long white gown of lace and pearls, her hair cascading down over one shoulder in a waterfall of chocolate curls. Somewhere, music begins to play, a single guitar picking out the notes of Pachelbel's Canon in D, and as I watch the woman pass me, I realize that we are not alone in the garden.

Rows and rows of white chairs fill the grassy space before me. I see Gran sitting a few seats from the front, and closer to the back, the hostess from the diner is blotting her eyes with a scrap of tissue. They all rise as the woman in white begins her slow walk down the aisle toward where Ben waits, beaming in a gray suit.

"Daddy!" The shriek of delight is so unexpected that I jump, once again turning to look behind me.

A girl, who can't be more than four or five, bursts out of the path. I recognize Ben's smile on her lips, his same shade of brown in her eyes as she sprints by me.

"There's my girl!" Ben cries, squatting down, alone now, in the autumn leaves to catch the child as she leaps into his arms. She hits him with such force that they both fall to the ground, his deep laugh mingling with her squeals of delight.

"Watch this, Daddy!" she shouts, pushing herself to her feet and taking off toward the opposite edge of the pool. As she runs, she transforms before my eyes, her body aging rapidly until a fully grown woman disappears down one of the other paths.

My eyes find my way back to Ben, and my breath catches in my throat. He is silver-haired and leaning heavily against a cane.

Suddenly something bright white floats out from behind me, bobbing its way slowly toward Ben. It takes a moment for him to notice the fairy light, but when he does, the color drains from his face.

His eyes meet mine just before he falls to his knees, a wrinkled hand clutching his chest.

"Ben!" I shout, running so fast to his side that I feel as if I'm flying, reaching him just in time to cradle him against my body as his eyes go dark.

I scream against his unmoving chest, a raw screech of agony, willing my very life to push its way into Ben's dead heart. As I bend over him, I catch a glimpse of myself in the reflection pool just beyond his body.

I am young and beautiful, and behind the translucent wings sprouting from my back, I am surrounded by dozens of twinkling fairy lights.

I gasp as pain flares across my bruised body. Blackness pulls at my vision as I struggle to maintain consciousness and take in my surroundings through the throbbing ache emanating from the back of my head.

"Nightmare?" Absynth's voice cuts through my haze, sharp and steely as a knife. As the world comes back into focus, I see her standing across the hollow from me, her face unreadable.

"We have a problem, Amethyst," she says, her voice calm and even, which is somehow more unnerving than her rage. And although she is in her human form, all I can see is the terrifying creature from the night before lurking just beneath her skin. "This boy ... "

A thousand images of Ben run across my mind in the span of an instant, but it is the final one that causes dread to rise like bile in the back of my throat: Ben's look of terror as he saw me for what I am.

A monster.

"Absynth," I begin, fear already grasping my words, choking the strength from my voice, "I can explain, please—"

"Enough," she says, raising her hand for quiet. She holds my gaze for a long moment before shaking her head and sighing.

"This *boy*," she continues. "You love him."

It is not a question, but it's not an accusation, either. It is a statement of fact, and I recognize its truth as clearly as I know the sky is blue and the grass is green. I am in love with Ben, as deeply as I have ever loved anyone, except for maybe my mother. And at this moment, as I stare at the beautiful face of my executioner, I am glad that I finally understand that. Glad that I will die having loved Ben.

"Yes," I say, holding my head high in a final act of courage. "And I will do whatever it takes to protect him."

It's another few heartbeats before she looks up, her eyes locking on my own with such intensity that I feel as if she can see straight through them, to my thoughts beyond. Whatever she reads in my face causes her to sigh again.

"It's as I thought. He's ensnared you," she says, her words heavy with what sounds like regret. "That leaves us no choice."

My bravado falters as fear, not for my own life but for Ben's, turns my insides to ice.

"*Please*," I say, the cold dread within me causing my voice to shake. But even though I sound small and weak, I know that I cannot stay silent, not when it's my fault, my selfishness, that has put Ben at risk. "*I* betrayed you, Absynth, not Ben. My life for his, remember? *You promised.* If you have to kill someone, it should be me, not him!"

"Amethyst," she says, and her voice is gentle, contrite, as she crosses the distance between us. "I'm not going to *kill* anyone. I ... " She pauses, kneeling down beside me. "I was wrong last night, and I'm sorry."

She reaches out to stroke my cheek, her warm fingers tracing the raised scars from Naya's claws, and I can see the tears forming around the edges of her deep-green eyes. I can see myself reflected in them, my face wan and unbelieving, the expression of someone who has just walked away from a horrific car crash with little more than scrapes and bruises, when by all rights she should be a red smear of gore against the asphalt.

"I know what you must be thinking," Absynth continues when I don't respond. "And I'm not sure I can explain last night in a way that could ever make you trust me again, but I need to try. I can't lose you, Amethyst, not the same way I lost Annabell."

"What does she have to do with this?" I ask, the mention of my mother spurring me from my stupor. Absynth drops her hand away from my face and begins to twist it into her wild hair, a nervous twitch that must be genetic.

"I made my Change almost as soon as I found out I was a fairy, but Annabell ... she was hesitant, reluctant to give up her humanity so quickly." She pauses to give me a pointed look, and I can't help but smile slightly at this connection linking me back to my mother. "I left for a time, partly to find others like myself and partly to get away from Beatrice, who even then looked at me with greedy, jealous eyes. When I returned, it was too late ... "

She breaks off, a tear trailing down one cheek.

"Too late?" I ask, trying to work out the timeline in my head but not able to line up her story with my own experience.

"She had … " Absynth begins, clearing the emotion from her throat before continuing. "Already met your father. I was too late to stop her from loving him. I was certain that she couldn't possibly feel as deeply for him as she did for me, for her sister, so I gave her an ultimatum. And she—"

Her voice breaks again, and she turns her face away, burying it behind her hands.

"And she chose him," I say, able to see her decision so clearly because it was the same one I made when faced with the same dilemma. Next to me, Absynth nods, wiping her face with the back of one hand.

"I left again, too hurt and angry at her betrayal to consider that maybe I was the one being unreasonable … that maybe there could be another way." She looks back at me, her face awash with grief and guilt. "Amethyst, I know which path you will pick if I give you a choice, and I don't want to drive you away, too. It was wrong of me to try to take that away from you."

"Absynth," I say slowly, unable to follow her line of thought. She has been very clear that the separation of the human and fairy worlds is vital for our safety. That people like Gran will hunt us and hurt us, and that people like me are a liability until the Change has been made. "I don't understand. You said there's no way for me to live like I am now."

"No," she says, the tiniest of smiles playing at the corners of her mouth. "You will need to Change, and so will the boy."

It takes another ten minutes of Absynth explaining her idea before I even begin to allow myself to entertain the idea of being able to have both Ben and my fairy birthright, but once the notion takes hold, I am unable to think of anything else. While Absynth launches into a detailed description of something called "Transference," I am distracted by imagining what Ben would look like under the ethereal hold of fae magic. It's harder than I thought to merge his earthy humanness with Absynth's otherworldly features, to try to picture the hue of his skin or the spread of thorns along his collarbone.

Then an image of Ben, red-eyed and fanged, floats into my mind's eye, and I am gripped by a sinking realization: Ben will never agree to the Change, not after what he saw last night, and certainly not after what I did to him.

"Absynth," I say, unable to lift my voice above a whisper, so heavy is the sadness in my chest. "He won't do it. I don't think I could even get him to talk to me after … "

My breath hitches in my throat as I am gripped by the overwhelming consequence of my actions. I've finally arrived at a place where I could have everything, and I've ruined it by pretending I was making decisions to benefit anyone but myself. For all the time I've spent congratulating myself on tearing down my walls, I've never bothered to really examine their reason for existence. Now, though, I think I built them not to protect myself from the world but to protect the world, and the people in it, from me.

"Amethyst!" Absynth is by my side just as the sobs overtake me, her arms encircling my shoulders and pulling my heaving chest against hers.

"He's not going to wa-want me anymore," I moan into her hair. "I've ru-ruined everything."

"Shhh," she breathes into my ear. "If he's half as enamored with you as you are with him, he will hear you out."

"And what if he won't?" I ask, pulling away from her so that I can see her face as she answers. I need to know if she's trying to spare my feelings.

"We won't let it get that far," Absynth says, running a hand through my hair. "He won't be able to refuse you, not when we're done with you."

Absynth sends two of her fairy lights out to recall Daphne and Naya, who I learn have been monitoring both Gran's and Ben's houses since our altercation the night before.

"The old woman hasn't left the house," Daphne reports, conjuring an oversized toadstool to sit on. "But she's got defenses in place—she's expecting an attack."

"What kind of defenses?" I ask Daphne, trying to remember if I'd ever seen a weapon in Gran's house and coming up empty.

"Iron," she replies, and immediately I recall the bizarre assortment of frying pans hanging over her porch. "It's a sort of fairy repellant, like trying to cross an electrified fence."

Absynth scoffs and rolls her eyes.

"As if any of it would protect her if I wanted to get inside," she says dismissively, placing a hand on my shoulder and smiling down at me. "She's lucky we've already got what we want from that house."

"Thank goodness," Naya says, entering the hollow from the opposite direction of Daphne. "The taste of metal was on my tongue for a full week the last time we broke through a barrier." She wrinkles her nose as she sticks her tongue out at the memory.

"How's Ben?" I ask, my insides twisting with guilt.

"The *boy*," she begins, turning her back to me as she addresses her answer to Absynth, "remains unprotected. We will have no problem disposing of—"

"Naya," Absynth says, giving me a reassuring look over the other fairy's shoulder. "There will be no need for that. Amethyst and I have decided to allow him the opportunity to join us."

"A human!" Naya growls. "What are you playing at, Absynth? We—"

"*Sister*," Absynth pleads, placing a calming hand on Naya's shaking shoulder. "Do you have such little trust in me? That I would bring such a danger into our midst?"

"Then I don't understand … " Naya trails off, and when she speaks again, there is a quiet understanding in her voice. "You're talking about Transference?"

"Yes," Absynth says, releasing her hold on Naya and turning her to face me. "That's why I've called you both back, to help prepare Amethyst, to make sure that he will be unable to refuse her."

"Then we have no time to waste," Naya says, a slow smile spreading over her face as she looks me up and down.

Behind her, Daphne's elated laughter rings out like birdsong.

My transformation begins with Absynth and Daphne removing my dirty, ripped clothes, revealing my bruised body underneath.

"What a mess," Naya says, sighing as she conjures a large bush covered in pink bell-shaped flowers out of the barren ground.

"Well," I say, unable to keep the sarcasm from my voice, "I didn't do this to myself, *Naya*."

She sniffs, ripping several leaves from the plant before shredding them and putting them into her mouth. I watch her chew for a moment but have to look away when green spittle begins to run over her lips and down her chin. It's enough to turn my already restless stomach.

"Naya, do you have to do that right he—*YUUCCHH*!" My statement turns into a cry of disgust as something warm and wet is pressed against the cuts along the side of my face. "What the—"

"Shhh," Absynth says, crouching down to put her face in front of mine. "A poultice of comfrey leaves is the fastest way to heal your skin."

I close my eyes as Naya applies more of the substance over my body, but I can't block out the mental image my brain has conjured of oozing green tendrils of saliva soaking into my open wounds and running in rivulets down my face and arms.

"Does she have to chew it?" I ask, trying to ignore the slurping sounds coming from beside me.

"It's the only way to imbue them with our magic," Absynth says, placing a cool hand against my other cheek. "Can't you feel it working?"

And once I force myself to move past the revulsion of it, I can.

The warmth that I assumed came from the poultice's origins in Naya's mouth has not only remained but grown hotter over the course of the last few seconds. In the places where the substance touches a cut, there is a tightening sensation in addition to the heat, and I can only imagine my skin is being drawn back together. The bruises on my arms and chest tingle as the blood vessels and muscle fibers are repaired.

"Okay, but it's still gross," I complain, causing Absynth and Daphne to laugh and Naya to grumble from somewhere behind me.

I have to sit for nearly an hour to allow the comfrey to finish its work, time that I spend trying to work out what I will say to Ben, but I'm finding it hard to get past the initial *Hey, so... sorry my aunt and her fairy friends tried to kill you last night.*

I'm pulled from my thoughts by a thunderclap so close that I feel the boom reverberate inside my chest, followed quickly by a deluge of warm summer rain. As I squint through the water pouring over my face, I see that the storm is relegated to a three-foot radius around me. Outside of that area, everything—including Absynth, Daphne, and Naya—is sunny and dry.

The rain passes as quickly as it comes, though, and when I look down at myself, I am clean and whole once more.

"Now," Daphne says, so close that I jump in surprise as her breath tickles my ear, "time for the fun to *really* begin."

I remember thinking that my first experience with Daphne and Naya's beauty regimen was overwhelming, but, now, after hours of allowing them to poke and polish every part of my body, I find myself looking much more fondly on that initial makeover. While I may not be a huge fan of their methods, it's impossible to argue with their results when I see my reflection in the pool Absynth conjures.

It is different from the first night. Daphne and Naya have taken care to draw attention to my human features, using their paints and pigments to conceal the ridges along my arms, legs, chest, and jawline. It reminds me of the way great makeup artists can change the shape of someone's face just by their placement of highlights and shadows. Half of my hair falls in waves down over my shoulders, while the rest is twisted into a dozen delicate braids winding their way into a delicate crown around my head.

I am more beautiful than I have ever been in my life, but it is not my face or hair but the dress they have created that causes my breath to catch in my lungs.

It's the kind of cut you might see on a Parisian runway, a form-fitting bodice that blossoms into a wide, flowing skirt at my hips. A hundred thousand white rose mallow petals blend into each other, forming a nearly seamless backdrop for the true stars: a rainbow of living butterflies cascading from my left shoulder and across my torso before scattering across the front of the gown.

"We thought the butterflies appropriate," Absynth says, joining me to gaze at my reflection. "Seeing as you're about to go through your own metamorphosis—your own Change."

"And Ben, too," I say, touching the spot on my cheek where he first kissed me. "As long as I can get him to listen to me."

I watch my reflection's face fall in concern.

"What if I could promise you that he would?" Absynth asks, turning away from the mirror to look at me.

"Absynth?" I start, remembering the fear in Ben's eyes when I lashed out at him. "You didn't see him last night. He's not going to forget that easily."

"But he can," she says, pulling a tiny glass vial from one of the leather cords around her neck. I recognize the faint golden glow of the liquid inside immediately.

"Fairy wine?" I ask as she places the bottle in my hand and pushes my fingers closed around it. "What do I need this for?"

"It will make you irresistible to him—not that you aren't already," Absynth says, smiling. "But a sip of this, and you won't have to worry about him walking away until you've said all you need to say."

I stare down at my hand, watching as the glow from the fairy wine illuminates it from inside out, casting my tendons and veins into sharp relief. It's an immediate reminder of what I'm about to give up—what I'm asking Ben to give up—humanity. I can't put my thumb on the scale on a decision this big, this irreversible.

"Thanks," I say, pushing the vial back toward Absynth. "But I don't think I could do that. It's not right."

"You don't have to make that decision now," she says, not allowing me to place the bottle back in her hand. "Just hang on to it—as insurance."

I shake my head but place the bottle inside my bodice, reminding myself that just because I'm taking it doesn't mean I have to use it.

"Absynth?" I ask, pulling her toward the edge of the hollow, as far from Naya and Daphne's listening ears as I can get. I don't want to give them anything to snigger about behind my back. "You're sure this will work?"

Absynth smiles, squeezing my hand in hers.

"Transference is old magic, Amethyst," she says reassuringly. "There is nothing more certain. You will be able to give the boy—"

"Ben," I interrupt, emphasizing his name. "If he's going to be one of us, you need to get used to saying it."

"Of course," Absynth says with an apologetic half smile. "You will be able to give Ben immortality in exchange for his humanity."

Immortal. The word makes my stomach lurch uncomfortably as the permanence of the Change, and the loss of the life before, moves to the forefront of my mind. All of this is happening so fast, too fast, and a few hours seems like far too short a time to be making decisions about forever— but what other choice do I have?

I shove the doubt back, instead trying to wrap my mind around the concept of eternity with a magical Ben. This summer he has been my touchstone to the human world that I can't imagine him any other way— even when the possibility is so tangibly near.

"Even if he's human?" I ask, needing to be sure not because I don't trust Absynth but because there's still a part of me that doesn't believe any of this—not Ben, not Absynth, not my fairy ancestry—can be true.

"It only works if he's human," she replies, shaking her head in mock exasperation. "As long as you say the incantation and kiss him, it will work. Trust me."

I nod, the butterflies in my stomach much rowdier than the ones fluttering lazily on my dress. Absynth reaches out, summoning a small white flower to bloom out of thin air: rose mallow. She tucks the blossom behind my ear before leaning in to place a gentle kiss on my forehead.

"You're ready," she says, her eyes reflecting the dozens of fairy lights floating above us. "Go get him."

Absynth lends me one of her lights to act as a guide through the darkening woods, but it still takes an hour for me to make the trek from the hollow to Ben's house. When I arrive, night has fallen completely, and the only light aside from Absynth's guide is the dim orange glow of the bare bulb hanging over Ben's front porch.

Even though I've spent every spare moment of my day crafting arguments to sway Ben, the best I can come up with is also the simplest, and the most honest: that I love him, and I know he loves me, too. It doesn't seem like much to go on until I place myself in Ben's shoes and realize that I wouldn't hesitate to say yes if our roles were reversed. I can only hope the same is true for him—especially after last night.

"Thanks," I whisper to the fairy light before leaving the trees and crossing the wide, overgrown lawn. Twice I almost trip over the stumps left behind from Ben's purge of the forest, each time whispering a hushed curse word so vulgar that I think he'd be secretly proud.

I stop when I reach the porch, taking a deep breath, not to conceal my thorns—there's no need for that anymore—but, instead, to try to slow the wild thumping of my heart. I feel like a runner, poised on the blocks, ready for the race although I cannot be sure whether I will be crowned the winner or face-plant into the asphalt at the sound of the starting gun.

All that's left for me to do now is run the race—for better or for worse. So, with a shaking hand, I reach out and knock twice on the front door.

I listen hard for any sign of movement and breathe a sigh of relief when I hear footsteps draw close on the other side of the door. There's a moment's pause followed by the sound of something heavy being moved aside, and I realize with a stab of guilt that Ben must have barricaded himself and his mother in the house to protect them both from, well, me.

The dead bolt slides out of place, and the door opens inward slowly, stopping when the chain lock reaches maximum extension. Through the narrow gap between door and frame, I get my first glimpse of Ben in nearly twenty-four hours, and it's enough to shatter my heart all over again.

Dark circles ring his eyes, and his jaw and cheeks are covered in stubble. Bruises ring his neck from where Absynth's vines strangled him into submission, and his right arm is cradled in a makeshift sling composed of what look like old bedsheets. Worst of all, though, is his expression as he looks at me. There is no hint of a smile on his face, no easy slouch against the doorjamb. No, instead I am greeted by a fear-filled animal: vigilant and tense, ready to run or fight at a moment's notice.

"Hey, Ben," I begin lamely, trying to make my voice sound gentle and soft. "I think we need to talk."

I watch him scan the darkness behind me, checking to see that I've come alone.

"I don't know if that's a good idea," he says, not quite able to reach my eyes.

"Okay," I say, feeling the tiny sliver of hope I've been grasping on to begin to slip away. "Do you mind if I talk, then? And you listen?"

"Amethyst." It sounds like even just saying my name is causing him pain. "Look, I can't—not right now."

He starts to close the door, every centimeter a move closer to the end of our relationship.

"Ben, I love you," I blurt out, throwing all caution to the wind. It's enough to stop the door and bring his eyes up to meet mine. "And, you said you loved me, too. Can you give me a minute, sixty seconds, to try to explain? Or at least to apologize?"

For a few seconds, I'm sure he's going to slam the door in my face, but then he sighs and nods. For a moment, I think I see the ghost of a smile, but it's gone before I can be sure.

"Give me a sec." Ben closes the door, and in the heartbeat that it takes for him to slide the chain lock free, I realize that one hour will not be enough to plead my case before him, let alone one minute. I don't even know where to start, and there's no way to ensure he'll listen even if I do find the right words.

My hand leaps to my chest, clutching the tiny vial from Absynth. I didn't want to use magic, but if I let this chance slip away, let Ben slip away, I will regret it for the rest of my life.

What other choice do I have?

I pull the bottle from my bodice and drink the golden liquid in one swallow just as the door opens, and Ben steps out onto the porch.

There's a strange warming sensation that seems to emanate out from my chest as the fairy wine makes its way into my stomach. I glance down to examine myself for any visible difference, but, aside from Daphne and Naya's handiwork, I appear the same to my eyes.

But then Ben looks up at me, and I know that it has worked.

All of the tension disappears from his body, and, although the smile doesn't return to his face, the hard, thin line of fear that had been his mouth has transformed into an awestruck "O" shape.

"Amethyst," he says with all the reverence of one standing in the heart of Saint Peter's Basilica or at the edge of the Grand Canyon. I feel the stir of guilt again, but I press it down, reminding myself that I've only claimed his attention. The choice will still be his.

"Ben," I say, and when I smile in relief, his face mirrors my own, and I feel the weight of last night lift off my shoulders. "I need to talk to you—to ask you some questions, and I need you to be honest with me. Can you do that?"

"Yes," he says, taking a step forward to run the back of his hand across my jawline. I grab it in my own and hold it between my hands, not wanting either of us to be distracted.

"Do you think that those creatures last night—that they're monsters? Because, what they are, that's a part of me, too." I bring his hand up to touch one of the bumps on my temple. "A part of me that I can't change. Can you accept that?"

"I've told you before," Ben says—his eyes have a strange faraway look as they trace over the ridges on my face—"I don't care what you look like."

"It's more than looks," I say. "Ben, I'm not human, not fully anyway, and I can't ignore that part of myself anymore. It's not safe for me, and, well, you saw last night, it's not safe for you."

"That's why you wanted to break up." It's not a question, but I answer it like it is anyway.

"Yes, but I- I couldn't give you up, Ben. Not even now when I knew it would be better for you if I did."

"It would be less painful; that's for sure." He laughs too loudly at his joke, and my stomach squirms uncomfortably.

Then Ben leans in, his eyes closed, his mouth so close to mine that I can smell the sweetness of his breath. It takes all the willpower I have to pull away.

"Wait," I say, holding a finger to his lips. I hold his gaze, trying to underscore the seriousness of what I am about to ask. I need him to understand there can be no going back—regardless of what he decides. "If there was a way for us to be together, would you want that? Even if it meant that you'd have to change, have to leave this place—your mom—forever? Because, Ben, the other option is that I can never see you again."

Again, Ben leans forward, but this time it's to rest his forehead against mine. There's an odd sort of out-of-focus look in his eyes, and I tell myself it's because we are so close.

"I want you, Amethyst," he says. "I don't care how."

"I was hoping you'd say that," I say, my voice quivering with a mixture of joy and excitement. I shift my head so that my lips are only millimeters from his as I whisper: *Mors tua, vita mea.*

I press my mouth against his, the current between us seemingly intensified by the heat already flowing through my body from the fairy wine. My arms circle his body, and my hands clutch his back, drawing him closer until I can feel the electric surge pulsing through every place where our bodies touch.

A warm wind picks up, swirling around us as it draws my hair, like a curtain, around the place where our faces meet. My mind is a rush of light and color, my skin drinking in every part of this moment, so that I can't tell if I'm seeing with my skin or just my imagination as images of flowers blooming in fast motion from every green surface in sight dance across my brain.

The hum of electricity between Ben and me reaches a white-hot level that I can almost feel burning through our chests, connecting us, heart to heart.

This is it, I think, holding on to Ben as the heat between us crackles and spits. This is the Changing.

Suddenly a bright-white light flashes as some kind of bomb detonates between us, blasting me backward off the porch. I sail like a cannonball across the yard, bracing myself for an impact that I realize is too long in coming.

When I open my eyes, I realize I am flying.

Laughter erupts from me as I watch my feet bob below me, a full twelve inches from the ground. A steady *whooshing* sound beats in my ears, different from the insect-like buzzing that accompanies Absynth's flight, and when I look behind me, I realize why. Stretching out from the place between my shoulder blades is a set of feathered wings, like those of a swan, snowy white against the black night beyond.

My gaze turns to my body, which sparkles in the moonlight. I lift one of my arms closer to my face and see that my skin has taken on a pearly white luminescence, subtler than the shocking hues of the other fairies. The thorns rising along my limbs and the elongated claws extending from my fingers are white, too, except for the tips, which are golden points shining like a hundred tiny constellations across my body.

But the most incredible transformation has happened inside of me, where a thousand new sensations bombard each of my senses—including a few new ones that seem to have developed in the last few minutes. My sight and hearing have improved exponentially, allowing me to locate the tiny creatures scurrying just beyond the tree line. But even if I couldn't hear or see them, a new part of me can feel them, the bioelectric beats of their hearts and the leaping transmissions across nerve synapses, building an image of them as clearly as seeing them with my own eyes.

Energy pulses from everything around me, from the tall oaks at the forest's edge to each blade of grass—each of them reaching out to me, waiting for me to call upon them. When I breathe, I am inundated by dozens of smells, each accompanied by its distinct taste. I am surprised by the sweetness that comes with pine and mildly disgusted by the bitter aftertaste that lingers on the back of my tongue from a nearby skunk.

I am just beginning to wonder what Ben's scent will taste like when something slides into place in my new brain. A thrill of worry ripples through me as I realize I can't see Ben anywhere, can't feel the electricity of his heart, can't smell the earthy musk of his skin.

But then another one of my strange new senses tingles to life, a sort of emotional telepathy that thrums with the warm, honey-sweet cadence of what can only be Ben's thoughts. And while I can't make out specific words, I can read his feelings as clearly as if he were standing beside me, whispering them into my ear.

He is close, and he is scared.

"Ben?" I shout, my new wings carrying me back to the porch in seconds. The explosion between us should have knocked him backward into the door, but when I look up and down the deck, there is no sign of him.

Maybe he went inside, I think, placing a hand on the doorknob. *That's what I would do if I were scared.*

Even as my mind creates the possibility, my new senses dismiss it. There is only one beating heart beyond the heavy door, and the electric taste of fear on my tongue makes me nearly positive that it is Ben's mother, not him. But I can still feel his presence, as undeniable as it is invisible and growing more panicked with each moment that passes.

It's okay, I think loudly, hoping that his new fairy mind can receive messages as easily as mine can send them. *I'm here, and I'm coming to find you.* I try to fill my thoughts with what I hope is reassurance so that even if the words don't translate, the sense of comfort will.

Somewhere, Ben mentally sighs in relief, closely followed by an urgency, a longing that I can only interpret as *hurry.*

I am, I think back, pulling the front door open and stepping into Ben's home for the first, and most likely only, time.

Although the house appears to be two stories from the outside, once I'm in, I see that it is a single-floor structure that stretches all the way up to the peaked roof. I'm standing in a large open space that serves as both living room and kitchen, the former denoted by a set of faded plaid furniture situated around an old wood-paneled television and the latter by a tiny section of whitewashed cabinets hanging over a sink and some ancient-looking appliances.

"Ben?" I whisper, taking a few steps toward the back of the house. "Ben, are you in here?"

There is no answer except for the nudge of Ben's mental affirmation I feel in my mind. The absence of a verbal response twists my stomach into an uncomfortable knot. Why won't Ben talk to me when I know he is near? Is it because he is unwilling to speak or is something, or someone, preventing him from drawing attention to himself?

An image of Ben's mother from an old news story floats into my mind's eye, and I think I know the reason for his silence.

Her room isn't hard to find in the small house—just a simple process of elimination after a quick peek behind the only other two doors. I pause just outside her door to take a breath, and my new body responds immediately to the silent command. The thorns retract beneath my skin, and my wings fold in on themselves, and in a half of a second, I am as close to human as I can make myself appear.

I knock gently, careful to make the sound as soft and nonthreatening as I can, and then I wait, my ear pressed up against the smooth wood of the bedroom door, for any sign of movement. When, after a full count of sixty, there is no response, I turn the doorknob and let myself into the bedroom.

The inside of the room is small and dim, the only light coming from a few small table lamps whose shades are covered with decorative scarves. The light that filters through is a strange reddish orange that casts the rest of the room in a fiery glow.

The opposite of green.

My understanding of color theory is rudimentary at best, but I can recall the red wedge sitting directly across from the green triangle on the color wheel in art class. However, as my other senses, new and old, begin to weigh in, I realize that the oppositeness goes far beyond color.

The room is austerely absent of any form of life outside of the beating heart of the tiny huddled mass curled beneath the quilt. There are no plants, not even cut flowers on the nightstand, and the air is warm and dry, devoid of any of the damp earthiness I've come to expect after a month of living in Morgan Springs and its ever-present forests.

Not just the opposite of green, I realize. *This room has been designed to be the opposite of the woods, of the outside world as a whole.*

A shiver of dread passes through Ben's thoughts as I take a hesitant step into the room. It is closely followed by a clear telepathic shout that I should not be in here, that here is a *very bad* place for me to be. The feeling is so all-consuming, so immediate, that it paralyzes me midstep, my right foot frozen in place just an inch above the wooden floor.

It hovers for a few seconds; then Ben must realize that I've heard his mental warning, and his fear begins to subside. Tentatively, I take a step backward. As my foot lands on the beam, a loud *creak* cuts through the silence, and I sense the sleepy rhythm of Ben's mother's heartbeat increase.

"Ben?" Although her voice is little more than a hoarse whisper, I can still hear a remnant of warmth as she speaks his name. Hot guilt twists inside me as I wonder how long that piece of her will survive without him.

In my mind, Ben's thoughts take on the tenor of a screeching siren as his mother begins to move under the blankets. I take another series of rushed backward steps but misjudge where the door is, and I run into a table and knock over one of the lamps. There is half a heartbeat after it shatters against the hardwood of the floor before the screaming begins.

The sound is one long, unbroken shriek that I've long relegated to the realm of horror films, not real life. It is so piercing that goose bumps rise along my arms as my hair stands on end, a shiver running down my back that is so violent it feels like I've shaken something loose.

And then nothing. Silence.

I look up, expecting to see Mrs. Taylor passed out from lack of oxygen, but instead, I find her kneeling stock-still atop her bed, her thin, pale face frozen in abject terror. Her chest is heaving erratically as she raises a trembling hand to point at me.

"*M-m-monster.*" Her word is barely audible, but my new ears have no trouble hearing her accusation. For a moment, I wonder what she means, and then I see the flutter of white from the corner of my eye.

No, I think, looking down at my body, where my thorns have risen in lieu of goose bumps. Behind me, my wings stretch out, almost touching the walls on either side of me, much too big for the small bedroom.

"*Monster!*" Mrs. Taylor shouts, her voice shaking along with the rest of her body. Then, with speed I didn't anticipate, she lunges sideways, grabs a thick book from her nightstand, and throws it at my head. My wings respond automatically, shooting in front of me to form a quasi-cocoon that protects my face from the worst of the impact.

"Please," I say, unfolding my wings too quickly and knocking a framed picture off the wall. "I'm not here to hurt you. I'm just looking for Ben!"

"*No!*" Mrs. Taylor shouts, the fear on her face dissolving into a rage. "You won't take him, too! Not like Adam!"

Although I don't know where Ben is, he must be close enough to hear his mother's words, because a pain that is not my own surges through me. My panic mingles with Ben's anguish as I realize, a millisecond behind him, that his mother has just confirmed something I've been trying to ignore since I first read about the Taylors' disappearance weeks ago: I am not the first fairy that Ben's family has encountered.

"Stay away from him!" Mrs. Taylor rasps, flinging what looks like the kind of clay dish an elementary child would make in art class at me. My shock renders me momentarily paralyzed, and the lopsided pot painfully connects with my left shoulder before smashing against the floor. When I don't move, Ben's mother, seemingly no longer capable of speech in her rage, lets out a primal scream as she pulls the lamp from her nightstand, brandishing it in front of her like a sword. But even as she takes the first shambling step toward me, I find myself unable to do more than watch her thin frame advance, ready to purge the danger from her home.

It is only a mental *shove* from Ben's psyche that finally jolts me into motion. I stumble backward until my wings catch on the doorframe, too big to fit through in their outstretched position, but unlike earlier, when they seemed to act instinctively, fear seems to have rendered them useless.

Come on, I urge them as I struggle to push them through the door. *Please.*

Mrs. Taylor is just a few feet away, her eyes alight with a decade's worth of anger and accusation. I throw myself backward, hoping the force of impact will be enough to get me through the door. Pain shoots through my wings as they collide with the wooden frame, but it does the trick, shocking them into limp submission and allowing me to half step and half fall out into the main room.

I don't look back as I cross the small living area in three long steps, throw myself through the front door, and race across the dark lawn, my eyes on the line of trees in the distance. I am so focused on the woods that I don't see the stump buried in the tall grass that sends me crashing into the ground.

I hit it hard, my momentum causing me to skid across the dirt until I hit a second stump, which stops me with a painful abruptness that knocks the breath from my lungs.

As I lay facedown against the cool earth, I listen for any sign of Mrs. Taylor, but it seems that her parental instincts are not strong enough to push her beyond the walls of the house.

"Amethyst?" Absynth's voice is accompanied by the buzzing of wings and the quick beating of her heart. When I roll over, she is standing over me, her face a mixture of concern and elation. "Are you all right?"

I shake my head. I am about the furthest from all right that it is possible to be right now, a sensation that is compounded by the waves of Ben's emotions that bombard my mind. Flashes of anger, confusion, sadness, and fear cloud my thinking so that I can't tell what my own feelings are beneath the deluge.

"Absynth," I say, more a cough than anything resembling speech, pushing myself into a sitting position. "Ben—"

"Incredible," she says, squatting down so that her face is level with mine. Her eyes have a greedy sort of look to them as she takes in my new body, her hands running gently across the downy feathers of my wings. "Congratulations on your Changing, Amethyst. You're more beautiful than I could have imagined."

"Absynth," I say, catching her hand on my shoulder as a rising sense of panic threatens to overwhelm me, "I can't find Ben. I think something's gone *wrong*." My voice breaks on the last word as the dread that I've been suppressing since my transformation finally breaks free.

"*Shhh*," she says, and there's a glint of mischief in her moss-green eyes. "Nothing went wrong, Amethyst. Everything is as it should be."

Foreboding, heavy and icy cold, settles deep in my stomach as Absynth's smile widens in a strange, manic way. I feel the shiver of thorns rising along my arms, my body reacting to a threat my mind is only beginning to comprehend.

"I-I don't understand," I say, leaning away from her unsettling gaze. "Ben ... "

She laughs, a gentle chuckle like someone might make when a young child says something incredibly naive, full of amusement and condescension.

"I told you Ben would join us, and he has," she says, laughter still dancing in her voice.

She pulls her hand from mine and makes a swirling gesture with her index finger. Immediately a warm breeze begins to blow, strong enough to pick up fallen leaves and carry them, tipping and spinning, through the night sky. I am just about to ask what she means when I see it, bright white against the blackness.

My first fairy light.

My first reaction is disbelief, an iron wall of doubt that shudders around my mind and heart to protect me from the abject falseness of Absynth's words. But as my eyes linger on the small white orb still twisting in the invisible wind, I feel Ben's muted confirmation push its way into my consciousness, forcing me to face the horrific consequences of my actions tonight.

No, I never wanted this, I think desperately, my mind already working to counteract the molten guilt churning inside me. I only did what Absynth told me to do, my only crime placing my trust in her. I feel the magma flare into a hot plume of anger as I turn my attention toward Absynth.

"You tricked me!" I hurl the accusation like a knife and watch with satisfaction as her smile fades into a grimace.

"Amethyst," Absynth says, her voice gentle, patient, "I couldn't stand idly by as you made the same deadly mistake as your mother. That boy had you confused, willing to give up everything, and for what? A miserable existence of pretending to be human?" She shakes her head at the thought. "Don't you see? I had to deceive you … to save your life."

But as I examine my ethereal reflection in her eyes, my face illuminated in the light coming from the orb that is Ben, I know this is just another of her lies. Her concern for me doesn't—and probably never did—extend beyond the fairy blood flowing green in my veins. All this time when I thought she was finally allowing me to be myself, I never noticed that she was manipulating me into what *she* thought I should be.

Her interest, just like the doctors before her, was not in my happiness but in my ability to conform. And just as I was never human enough to placate Dr. Zahn, apparently I have never been fairy enough for Absynth—both of them too eager to pull me into one sphere or the other. There has only ever been one person who has allowed me to exist in the gray place between the human and fairy worlds, and I am not about to let anyone take him away from me.

"I don't want this life," I snarl, pulling away from Absynth's grasp, my wings dragging painfully beneath me. "Change him back!"

The breeze between us stops abruptly, its warmth immediately replaced by the dewy chill of night, and when Absynth answers, her expression is almost remorseful.

"I can't," she says simply in a hollow voice that I don't recognize. "There's no way to reverse a Transference once it's taken place."

All of my senses, new and old, are telling me that she must be lying again, that of course she would tell me there is no changing back. But something about the tone of her voice and the haunted look in her mossy eyes makes me unsure.

"I don't believe you!" I say, trying to sound commanding, but the beginnings of panic cause my voice to crack awkwardly.

"Amethyst," she says with a desperation I've never heard before, "please—"

She reaches out for me again, and when her fingers are inches from my face, I slap them away.

"Don't!" I yell, and I don't know if it's anger or fear or betrayal that pushes tears in hot torrents down my face. "You don't touch me ever again, *monster*."

And before Absynth can respond or attack or call on Daphne and Naya, I stretch out my hand, gently close it around Ben's light, and take off running into the night.

For the first time in weeks, the forest feels too foreign, too *Absynth*, so I opt for the road, a silver-black river in the moonlight. Sharp pebbles dig into the soles of my bare feet, but a similar sense of unease keeps me from using my new wings. Wings which were bought and paid for at Ben's expense.

I'm so sorry, Ben, I think frantically at the spot of heat burning inside my cupped hands. *I'll make this right. I'll find a way.*

A mixture of hope and yearning pulses through my mind as Ben responds. I don't deserve it, his trust, and it causes another wave of tears to flow down my cheeks. If I'm honest with myself, Ben's trust is just one of many things I've never deserved to have, the topmost being his love. Because as righteous as my anger with Absynth is, she was not the one who did this to Ben—that was my choice, informed or not, and I chose myself, my happiness, without considering that Ben might want something different.

Two roads diverged in a yellow wood,
And sorry I could not travel both
And be one traveler...

But I never was just one traveler, at least not since I arrived in Morgan Springs and Ben worked his way into my heart. Although we journeyed together down this road, we were not obligated to arrive at the same destination. Ben and I had both been standing at the same crossroads, but I was the only one with a map, the only one who knew—or at least thought I knew—what lay at the end of each path.

But instead of allowing Ben to make an informed decision, I had forced him to follow me right into Absynth's trap.

I'm so preoccupied with the metaphorical roads in my mind that I'm not paying attention to where the actual one is leading me until I see the dark outline of Gran's house begin to take shape in the distance. Apprehension grips me, partially from the memory of my last encounter with my grandmother but more from my uncertainty about how much of Absynth's warnings about her was lies. If she was telling the truth, I could be gambling with my life, but then again, Gran is my last and only chance to help Ben, and my life is the least I owe him after what I've done.

It's another fifteen minutes before I finally reach the steps of Gran's front porch. I'm not sure what time it is, but it must be late, because there is no light coming from behind the drawn curtains, and even the porch's single bulb has been turned off for the night. It seems as if I'll have the element of surprise on my side, though I'm not certain that's a good thing.

I take a steadying breath and press Ben's light a little closer against my chest. Its warmth, or maybe Ben's thoughts, gives me the extra boost I need to push myself up the stairs. But just as I lift my foot from the last step to place it on the wide wooden porch, a surge of what feels like electricity pulses out from thin air, the shock sending me flying backward, my heart beating unevenly as it tries to reset its rhythm.

"What the hell was that?" I yell accusatorily at the house, an angry echo in the back of my mind telling me that whatever just happened, Ben felt it, too.

My skin still humming, I push myself up to my feet and scan the porch for some sign of newly installed electric fencing, but the only thing visible apart from the actual porch is Gran's strange garland of frying pans.

Iron, I think, suddenly remembering Daphne's explanation that the substance was a kind of fairy deterrent. And she wasn't joking, either: the pain, while it seems like not enough to hurt me permanently, would be enough to deter just about any fairy trying to get into the house.

But not me, not tonight.

I make my way back up the steps, Ben's light hovering just above my right shoulder, and take a moment to prepare us both mentally.

"Ready?" I ask him, and although his mental affirmation is mingled with a hesitation that mirrors my own, I know I must push forward for the both of us. I take the light in my right hand, balling a fist protectively around the orb with the hope of punching Ben through first and releasing him before he has to experience too much pain.

Okay. Here we go. I brace myself against the railing and slam my fist against the invisible barrier. The pain is instantaneous and radiates out from my knuckles, sparking from nerve to nerve until my whole body is burning from the inside out. Every logical part of my brain commands me to stop, but the white-hot heat coming from Ben's light, the only sensation more powerful than the electric current surging through me, urges me forward.

I push my fist harder against the barrier, straining against the invisible wall that seems not just to be blocking my path but actively resisting my passage. The marrow inside my bones sizzles, and my blood courses like lava through my veins as every cell of my body cooks in the electric storm. And then, when I think I can't take another second of the pain, my hand breaks through, cool night air acting as a salve against my burning flesh.

I release Ben's light so that I can grasp one of the wooden posts with my hand to help pull myself through. It takes nearly a full minute to drag my body, centimeter by excruciating centimeter, through the iron force field, and when my left foot finally clears the barrier, I collapse against the floor, gulping in large breaths of air to help quench the fire in my chest.

A wave of concern washes over my mind as Ben takes in my unmoving form. I roll over to look up at the light, bobbing silently just inches above my face, and give him my best approximation of a smile.

I'm fine. I think it instead of speaking, because I'm not sure my vocal cords are anything more than charred vestiges. Ben responds with something akin to a mental eye roll, which I ignore as I pull myself up to stand before Gran's front door. I raise my hand to knock, but an objection from Ben stops me. *Wait,* he seems to say, followed by an urging for me to listen.

"No, I understand." Gran's voice is barely audible through the heavy door, but my new ears have no problem hearing it, though I can't quite make out the crackle of the other voice coming from the phone. "Of course, you're right—no news is good news. I do appreciate you calling, Officer Ruiz. Please let me know if there's anything I can do to help."

She's looking for me. The realization reignites the fear that she may be just as Absynth portrayed her, that I am walking myself and Ben into another trap. The receiver clicks as she puts the phone down, and I barely have time to wonder when she replaced the one I tore from the wall when I hear it: a broken moan only softened by what I imagine is her hand pressed firmly over her mouth.

The sound pulls at my heart painfully as I realize that, once again, I've been fooled by Absynth. That Gran, like Ben, has been a victim not only of her lies but also of my naivete, and my stomach turns uncomfortably at the thought of my selfishness. They have both loved me in ways I am unworthy of.

"It's true," I say in response to Ben's mental protest to my train of thought. He replies with the equivalent of psychic muttering under his breath, which amounts to an unsatisfied hum of discontent radiating at a low frequency through my mind. "I can hear that, you know."

He knows.

I give up on arguing with him, as it appears that even when removed from his corporeal form, Ben's persistence is unstoppable. I turn my focus back to the door in front of me.

Part of me, undoubtedly the selfish part, wishes Gran were the murderer Absynth painted her to be, because, in many ways, that version of her would be easier to face than the brokenhearted woman inside. Easier to fight and run than to apologize and move forward, just as it has always been for me. But I don't have that luxury, not with Ben counting on me.

So before I can change my mind, I raise my hand and knock three times on the door.

I don't even dare to breathe as I wait, so I can hear every muffled step of her slippered feet as Gran approaches the door. I watch the peephole closely, and when the small circle of light is eclipsed by Gran's eye, I wonder if she will even recognize the girl standing before her.

The shadow disappears almost immediately, followed by the click of the dead bolt, and before I can even begin to formulate an explanation for my absence and return, Gran throws the door open and pulls me into a tight embrace.

"Amethyst," she sighs into my hair, relief and longing commingling in her voice, "I've been so—"

Her words cut off abruptly, and I feel her hands move shakily up and down the feathers of my new wings. Slowly, she releases me, and when I see her face again, it is taut with terror as she takes in my new body.

"Gran, I can explain. I—"

But Gran covers my mouth with a shaking hand, her eyes moving past me to scan the darkness beyond the porch. Then, without looking away from the trees, she pulls me into the house and slams the door behind us.

"Where is she?" Gran demands, her voice a harsh whisper. "Absynth. Is she here with you?"

"No," I say, unsure of how to proceed, of how to explain to her all the things that have transpired in the last few weeks. "Gran, I—"

"How much do you know?" she asks, catching me by the wrists and looking deep into my eyes. Her gaze is like something I've never felt before, or at least not in a very long time. It's full of concern, not for her own life but for mine. It catches me off guard, and suddenly the weight of everything— my years of isolation, Absynth's deceptions, and most crushingly, what I've done to Ben—comes crashing down on me.

"Ev-everything," I moan, a fresh torrent of tears streaming down my face. Gran moves to hug me again, but I pull away and turn toward the door instead. I open it just a crack, enough room to let the tiny light float into the house. When I look back at Gran, her face has fallen at the sight of the orb, anguish written in every crease of her brow.

Then she closes her eyes, shakes her head, and squares her shoulders the same way I do when I am steeling myself to do something dangerous. When she looks at me again, she is resolute.

"Get changed," she says, grabbing her coat from the rack in the entryway. "We're going to see your grandfather."

24

"My *what?*" I ask, certain that I have misunderstood Gran in my state of distress. Gramps has been dead for over a decade, so unless we are taking a late-night trip to the Morgan Springs cemetery or pulling out the old Ouija board, she must be talking about someone else.

"We're going to see your grandfather," she says again, picking up her purse and pulling out the keys to her car. "Now get changed. You can't go into town looking like that." She gestures toward the remains of my rose mallow gown, which I now see is wilted and tattered, with whole sections of petals missing in the areas where I fell against the ground.

My brain is struggling to process what she means. Maybe we are going to the cemetery after all, though I can't work out why that would be particularly helpful. "But—"

"Not now," Gran says, impatience fueled by anxiety clear in her voice, and I know it would be pointless to press the issue. Whatever she means, I guess I'll find out soon enough. I hope it doesn't involve grave robbing.

It takes longer to change my clothes than I anticipate; not many of my shirts seem to have been designed with wings in mind. Eventually, I dig out an old racerback tank top from the days before my body started breaking out in thorns and, after a few minutes of wrestling with the material, manage to get all of my appendages, new and old, through the right holes. The jeans go on much quicker thanks to the fact that my new fairy form doesn't include extra legs or a tail.

Gran is pacing in front of the door when I make it back downstairs, and as soon as my right foot comes in contact with the first floor, her hand is already turning the doorknob. She is across the porch and down the front steps before I even reach the door. I stop just before her invisible barrier. I'd rather avoid that experience again if I can help it.

In another corner of my mind, Ben echoes this desire.

"Um, Gran?" I call out, pointing to the nearest frying pan when she turns back toward me. "A little help here?"

"Oh, I didn't even think … " she says, hurrying back up the steps. She extends her right arm through the barrier, grasping my forearm with her hand. I mirror the action as she casually mutters: "*Te potest ad portam.*"

I expect to feel something magical or hear the crackle of electricity as the barrier powers down, but Gran releases my arm unceremoniously and continues on her way to the car. I use one finger to hesitantly prod the place where the invisible fence stretched across the entrance to the porch, sure that I am about to get shocked backward again, but my finger and then my hand slide through easily. I stare incredulously at it for a second, but then a short blast from the car horn sends me sprinting down the stairs to join Gran.

The car ride is uncomfortable, not just because my wings are folded awkwardly under my butt for the duration but also because Gran is uncharacteristically silent and driving like a maniac. We speed down the tree-lined road, taking corners so fast that I feel my body press back against the seat from the force of the turns. I try to scan the areas illuminated by the high beams for any sign of Absynth's pale face, but even my new eyes can't work fast enough to keep up with the quickness with which we pass.

She slows once we cross into town, probably not wanting to attract the attention of the single Morgan Springs police cruiser. Or perhaps she, like me, feels safer now that we're surrounded by decidedly nonmagical things like fire hydrants and park benches.

It takes less than a minute to travel down the single line of darkened storefronts that makes up downtown, after which we turn down a secondary street that brings us past an elementary school before ending in a dead end.

Gran puts the car in park and kills the engine, but before the headlights shut off, I catch a glimpse of the sign hanging over what looks like the main entrance of a glass-covered building. It reads Arthur Faye Memorial Gardens.

Gramps, I think, wondering if this place is what Gran meant by bringing me to see him. Still, I can't figure out how a visit in the middle of the night to a greenhouse will help me reverse whatever it is that I've done to Ben.

"Come on," Gran says, opening her door. "Quick, before anyone sees."

I follow suit, opening my door and pulling myself out of the car. Gran grabs my wrist and pulls me toward the door as if she's worried that someone will snatch me away if she doesn't maintain physical contact. With a shiver, I realize just how right she might be about that. Instinctively, I capture Ben's light with my free hand and hold it protectively against my chest.

Gran pulls another set of keys out of her purse and unlocks the front door. I follow her through, waiting just inside as she fumbles for a few seconds for the lights. When they finally come on, I am shocked to see that the greenhouse we are standing in is only one of five, all of which are linked by a circular central hub. We walk along the aisle, surrounded on both sides by plots of flowers and vegetables, each labeled with the name of the family who must tend to it.

When we reach the hub, Gran leads me past rows of trowels and watering cans to the very middle of the structure, the only part of the entire building whose walls are not made of glass. I watch curiously as she pushes aside a heavy stack of hoses and then gasp when I see the door that was concealed behind it.

Gran flips to the third key on the ring and inserts it into a tiny lock. There is the faintest of clicks as she turns it, and then the wall that is a door opens silently into the heart of the greenhouse complex.

The room is circular and small, no more than fifteen or twenty feet in diameter, but for what it lacks in size, it makes up for in beauty. Neat beds of flowers radiate from a central pond, each separated by small gravel pathways that make the floor into a natural sort of mandala. Moonlight shines in from the glass ceiling, perfectly mirrored in the smooth water directly below. Wild roses weave their way up delicate metal trellises, their fragrance commingling with the sweet scents of a dozen others.

It is, in so many ways that cannot be coincidence, like the gardens Ben and I have spent the summer restoring or, perhaps more accurately in this case, like the gardens where Gran fell in love so many years ago. Maybe that's what she meant by visiting Gramps, that she wanted to take me to this place that reminds her of him.

"Arthur?" Gran calls out softly with the kind of tone you use when you need to wake someone gently.

I follow her line of sight to the pool but see nothing but the circle of calm water and a single gnarled stump at its edge. Then one of my new senses registers a third heartbeat, weak and slow but definitely there, and I realize that Gran and I are not alone here after all.

Suddenly the stump begins to move, twisting until I realize that it is not a stump at all but a person. Or at least something that used to be a person.

Something that, according to Gran, used to be my grandfather.

Emaciated arms, like the withered branches of a dying tree, uncross from a sunken torso that ends in knobbed roots where legs should be. A head rises from where it has been resting, chin down against a lichen-covered chest. In the darkness, it is hard to make out his face aside from the grooves, which look more like tree bark than wrinkles, that fade back into hair white and stringy as Spanish moss.

"Bea?" His voice is like the crunch of gravel and full of an exhaustion that cannot be remedied with sleep. "Who have you brought with you?"

Gran crosses the distance to kneel beside my grandfather, and even her small body seems large in comparison to his slight frame. He turns to face her, and as the moonlight hits his eyes, they reflect the flat and milky-white sheen of blindness.

"It's Amethyst, Arthur," Gran says gently, kneeling down so that she is on a level with him. He looks in my direction, unseeing, but somehow I still get the sense that he is examining me. Gran turns her gaze on me as she continues. "Amethyst, this is your grandfather."

Now that I look at him, I can see remnants of the handsome man I remember from photographs in Gran's house: the cut of his jaw or the way his not-quite-skin crinkles at the corners of his eyes. Even his voice, rough as it is, rings with faint familiarity, with some long-forgotten memory I have. But there is one part of him that I cannot reconcile no matter how long I stare, openmouthed, at my grandfather: he's alive.

"But ... you're dead!" I say incredulously, unable to think of a more eloquent way to broach the topic. Then another piece of information, one more recent, floats into my mind, and I continue without thinking. "You're dead. And she—"

I stop myself before I accuse Gran of a murder she obviously did not commit, realizing, again too late, that I've stumbled upon yet another of my aunt's falsehoods. Across the small room, Gran winces anyway, my accusation apparent even without being spoken.

"Absynth's gotten to her already," Gran explains, and I can hear shame in her voice. Gramps must recognize it, too, because he shushes her softly, pulling her hand up to his misshapen lips and kissing it gently.

"As you can see, Amethyst," Gramps says, gesturing weakly to his body, "Absynth was wrong. I am not dead, though I cannot deny that I am dying."

Next to him, Gran whimpers softly, squeezing her eyes shut against the harsh truth of his words.

"And," he continues, his voice a little stronger, as if to underscore his point, "your grandmother is not responsible for my... well, my condition. There was no betrayal or theft, or whatever nonsense she came up with. Unless, of course"—his mouth twists into an unsettling approximation of a smile as he beams up at Gran—"you count her stealing my heart."

She doesn't return his smile, and I remember why we've come here.

"She's already been Changed, Arthur," she says quietly, her voice the morose tone you hear at funerals. Gramps's face falls as he sighs in disappointment.

"That is ... most unfortunate," he says, shaking his head slightly. "Who was it? Do we know them?"

The warmth of Ben's light pulses against my chest, and the guilt and terror at what I've done washes over me again. I screw up my face against the cry of anguish building inside me and watch as horrific realization begins to dawn on Gran's face.

"Amethyst," she begins before hesitating, not wanting to hear the answer to the question she is about to ask. "Who did you take for your light?"

"Ben," I say, my voice breaking. "It was Ben."

Gran's hands fly to her mouth as tears flood into her wide eyes before spilling over to run in rivulets down her cheeks. I feel my knees slam against the gravel, not realizing until pain jolts up my thighs that I've fallen, my legs giving way under the weight of Gran's grief, somehow heavier than my own.

"Please," I beg, turning my attention to my grandfather, the one person in the world who can help me to undo the damage I've caused. "I didn't want this! I didn't know. *Please*, change him back."

He sighs again, and the silence that follows stretches into what feels like hours as Gran and I both wait for his response.

"The Change is, as far as I know, permanent—for both of you. I'm so sorry, Amethyst, but there is no going back."

No going back, my mind echoes. It struggles to comprehend his meaning and, in its confusion, begins to call up every facet of Ben, cataloging that loss, piece by piece, so that my anguish will reflect the totality of my crime.

Never again will I see Ben's smile, wide and welcoming, or hear his easy laughter ringing in my ears long after I've left him. Nor will I marvel at the warm energy that travels up my arm when my hand is in his or feel the soft press of his lips against mine. All of those things, and a thousand others, are lost, not just to me but to the world, and it is all my fault.

A tidal wave of sadness, grief, and loss pours into my consciousness as Ben reacts to my grandfather's words. It flows down to mix with my rising tide of guilt and shame, creating a toxic flood that sweeps through me, leaving no part of my body unscathed in its wake.

I gasp for the air that has suddenly been sucked out of the room, my lungs convulsing as they struggle to function. My stomach roils, pushing hot, sour bile into the back of my throat as my vision blurs, though I don't know if it's from my tears or the suffocating lack of oxygen. And deep within my chest, my heart, the one so carefully walled off and protected, tears in two.

I gag, falling forward, the pain of gravel biting into my palms insignificant when compared to the agony in my chest. I heave, again and again, as if my body is trying to purge itself of emotion in the only way it knows how.

As I writhe on the ground of the secret room, a guttural wail punctuating the spaces between my retching and my sobs, my nose assaulted by the stench of blood and vomit and tears, some part of me notes what a feral creature I've become.

"So, I am a monster," I say aloud, unsure if it is because I want to be damned or comforted.

"We are what we choose to be." My grandfather's words cause anger to flare up inside me, a feeling I cling to as it burns almost hot enough to temporarily eclipse the pain. How dare he feed me some fortune cookie proverb, as if Ben's life was of no more consequence than a throwaway colloquialism.

"You have no idea what you're talking about!" I shout back, my rage allowing my body to return to some semblance of functioning. "What *choice* do I have?"

There's a loud creaking sound from the center of the room, and I look up to see that my grandfather has straightened his body, an action that only serves to accentuate the gnarled waste he has become. My eyes trace the rough skin, so much like the papery bark of an ancient tree, following the creases up to where they form the hard ridges of his face.

I meet his eyes and find that even in their blindness, they burn with a wild sort of pride.

"Don't you wonder why I am reduced to this?" he asks, slapping his withered chest with one long-fingered hand. "Why I am dying when by all rights I should live forever?"

He pauses, waiting for an answer, but I have none for him. There hasn't been enough time tonight for my mind to engage in idle speculation about his appearance. But now that the question has been posed, I feel the stirrings of curiosity, a desire for an explanation, or maybe even absolution, though I don't dare to think I come close to deserving either.

"It is by choice."

"I don't understand," I say, unable to look at his body and see anything worthy of such a sacrifice in its decay. And even if I could find something worthy of his physical decline hidden in the twisted waste he has become, I cannot reconcile his choice, which by his own admission amounts to a death sentence and means he will leave behind the crying woman next to him.

You just don't abandon someone you love.

"Come here, child," Gramps says, patting the empty space beside him. "There is so much you do not know about our world … about our family."

Reluctantly, I push myself to my feet with one hand, the other still cradling Ben's light against my chest. Although I can feel the heat radiating from it, the strange mental connection between us has gone silent, replaced by a wall of numbness that is somehow worse than his grief. I try to mentally prod at it as I cross the room, but my attempts to break through are either ineffective or unwanted, and I abandon the effort as I sit on the hard ground next to my grandfather.

"Bea," he says, turning his empty eyes up to Gran, "shears, if you please?"

"You're not strong enough," she says, but he waves away her concerns.

"She needs to see. She needs to understand," he says, and although Gran doesn't appear to agree, she leaves the small room for half a minute before returning with a sharp pair of clippers.

She grimaces as she places them in Gramps's outstretched hand and then turns away. I only have a nanosecond to wonder what she seems so upset about before my grandfather plunges the point of one blade into his palm, working it back and forth until liquid oozes slowly out of the wound. It's not like the blood that flowed freely from my foot so many weeks ago, more like a green-brown syrup, thick and gritty, like caramel that has cooked too long.

He clenches his hand into a fist over the pool, squeezing it until the slow-moving blood seeps through the bottom and drops, with a tiny splash, into the calm water. It disappears immediately beneath the ripples it creates as they undulate gently across the surface, distorting the image of the night sky above. I watch the moon dance in the water for a few heartbeats, until suddenly it disappears completely, replaced by a long dirt road surrounded on either side by miles of grassy fields.

I tear my eyes away from the silent scene to look at Gramps, who has pulled his hand back, cradling it against his chest. He inclines his head back toward the water, a silent request to focus on it, not him, and draws in a deep breath. His voice is tired when he speaks.

"Once I was called the Fairy King," he begins, and the still image in the water begins to move. I realize as the image of the road moves beneath my eyes, a distant farmhouse coming into view, that I must be seeing my grandfather's memories. As we draw closer to the house, a flash of movement draws my eye, and I see someone, a girl, by the shape of the skirt blowing in the light breeze, hanging clothes to dry on a line.

"For two hundred years, I roamed the world, using the lives of others to make myself strong."

To my surprise, I see the girl, who can't be much older than me, is wearing a long dress and white bonnet and that the clothes she hangs on the line appear to be equally archaic, belonging to the early 1700s, if I had to guess. She lifts a small piece of fabric, a handkerchief or scarf, out of the basket, but before she can pin it to the line, an unnaturally strong gust of wind pulls the linen from her hand.

"And while there were others who had lived longer or gathered more lights, I was stronger than them all."

The fabric twists in the wind, the girl chasing after it, her eyes locked on its progression through the air, too distracted to notice the strange man moving quickly toward her. I am not surprised when the wind carries the scarf directly into my grandfather's waiting palm, or at the look of surprise and sudden fear on the girl's face.

"Because I had discovered the secret to unlocking a light's full potential was not to simply change my victims … " I want to look away, certain that I am about to watch the girl's demise, but the hand that holds the scarf does not grab her. Instead it holds the fabric out delicately, giving a slight bow, before placing it in the girl's hand. I can tell by the way she smiles that her fear of this handsome stranger has disappeared as quickly as it came.

"But to make them fall in love with me," he finishes, and a second drop of his blood falls into the pool, the ripples erasing the first memory and replacing it with a new scene.

The same girl is reclined on a blanket, the remains of a picnic spread out between her and my grandfather. She giggles and claps as a robin swoops down to land on my grandfather's outstretched finger. He passes the bird to her, using the movement as an excuse to lean in close. The vision fills with her face, her closed eyes, the slight pucker of her lips, and this time I do look away as my grandfather transfers her life to his.

"You see," he says, allowing the image in the pool to momentarily fade back into the reflection of the sky, "I learned that their love remained even after their transformation, strengthening me in ways a thousand strangers' lives could not."

I feel my face wrinkle in revulsion, nausea threatening to overwhelm me again. Because while what I did to Ben is horrific and unforgivable, at least it was done in ignorance. My grandfather, on the other hand, had not only been aware of the consequences of his actions, he had refined them with such cold calculation that his victims were manipulated, body and soul.

At least Absynth comes by her duplicity honestly.

"By the time I came to Morgan Springs, I was, as you said, Amethyst, a monster," Gramps continues, and I can't bring myself to look at him as he speaks. "I was looking for my next victim, but of course, this time was different."

"What was different?" I ask, pointedly directing my question to the reflection of the moon.

"This time I fell in love, too." There's a warmth in his voice that draws my attention, and in spite of myself, I hazard a glance in his direction to find him staring up at Gran with a look I normally associate with religious devotion. "When I met Beatrice, I realized how wrong, *how selfish*, I had been. I swore from that moment that I would never claim another human life for my own."

For a third time, he squeezes a drop of blood into the water, and immediately I recognize that we are in my grandmother's parlor. Gran, or at least the young woman who would become my grandmother, sits next to my grandfather on one of the antique sofas.

"But I was ashamed of what I'd done, so my fairy life remained a secret, even from my new wife. However, a year into our marriage, I realized I couldn't conceal it any longer."

The young Gran takes my grandfather's hand between her own, kissing it before placing it on her round belly. For a moment, both she and my grandfather look down at their hands, but then he must say something, because she looks out at us, her head cocked in interest. Gramps raises his hand, and I watch my grandmother's eyes widen in wonder as it, and presumably the rest of his body, transforms beside her.

Then she silently cries out in pain, her face contorting as both of her hands wrap around her stomach.

"She took the news rather well, all things considered," Gramps finishes, the image of Gran's face fading away.

"What he means is that I didn't run out of the house screaming," Gran interrupts before pausing to smile to herself. "Well, I mean, I *did* run out of the house screaming, but only because I was in labor."

Gramps returns her smile, and I can't help but feel my own lips curving, just slightly, at the memory. But then I remember how Ben had been the same, minus the whole giving birth thing, when I showed him what I was: surprised and incredulous but not scared, and my brief foray into happiness ends abruptly.

"We decided the day your mother and Absynth were born that we would wait to tell them," he says, his attention turning back toward me. "You see, we did not know if either of them would manifest, and we wanted to make sure that, if they did, we were able to explain what was happening to them."

His thick blood seems to have congealed, and Gramps has to work for a moment to reopen the wound on his palm before he can once again show me a memory. When the ripples clear this time, I realize many years have passed.

Gran is middle-aged, the lines in her face just a little more pronounced, streaks of gray beginning to show in her hair. She sits next to Gramps at the long dining room table and smiles as she strikes a match to light the candles of a cake at its center.

"It was not until their sixteenth birthday that the signs began to show."

My heart skips a beat when my mother, young and smiling and beautiful, comes into view. Beside her is Absynth as I've never seen her: unmistakably human instead of the unearthly beauty I've come to expect. Both girls lean in together, closing their eyes in unison as they blow out the candles. There are a few seconds of darkness before someone turns the overhead light back on.

Gran picks up a knife and slices into the cake, placing the first piece on a plate she offers to my mother. My mom has to stretch across the table to reach the cake, and as she does, the long sleeve of her shirt rides up her arm, revealing a thorn poking out just above her wrist. My mom tries to hide it, ripping her sleeve back down, but it's too late—everyone has seen it.

Gran drops the cake, and the plate breaks in two as it hits the hard table. A weathered hand reaches out to snag my mom before she can run out of the room. Gramps pulls her back to the table, rolling her sleeve up to examine her arm. While only one thorn protrudes from the skin, a dozen pink and white scars crisscross up her forearm.

"It was that night that I explained everything to them," Gramps says, another drop of blood rolling slowly down his fist. He has to shake it to prompt the thick liquid to drop into the pool.

The room is the same, but outside the window, night has fallen. Gran is nowhere to be seen, but I guess she may not have had much to contribute to this particular conversation. Across the table, my mom and Absynth sit in the same chairs, but it is clear the celebration has long been over. Absynth leans in, her interest in the discussion palpable, while my mother seems scared, or possibly in shock.

"Well, almost everything," Gramps corrects as Absynth's face abruptly changes from attentive to angry. She slams her hands down, shouting words I can't hear. Beside her, my mom seems to be trying to calm her, placing a hand on her sister's arm, which Absynth slaps away. "I saw a spark in Absynth that was too eager, heard a longing in her voice that was too greedy. I didn't want her to make the same mistakes I did, and I thought that by keeping the secret of the Changing from her, she would be safe."

Absynth stands so quickly that she knocks the chair to the ground. She points a finger accusingly at us, her face flushed with rage, her eyes brimming with tears. Again, my mother reaches out for her, but Absynth turns on her heel and runs out of the room toward the stairs. I can almost hear her heavy footsteps as she stomps up to her bedroom.

"The next morning Absynth was gone," Gramps says, his voice once again weary with regret. "We didn't hear from her for nearly a decade."

He seems to give up on trying to force more blood out of the wound and instead rinses his hand in the pool. The back and forth motion of his hand in the water causes more agitation than the single droplets, and this time it takes almost a minute for the surface to calm enough for the scene to appear undistorted.

My mother is older, in her midtwenties, and sitting opposite a chessboard from Gramps on the wide front porch of Gran's house. As she picks up her bishop to take my grandfather's rook, I see that there is an engagement ring on her left hand, but not yet a wedding band. Gramps seems to have anticipated her move, because he responds with his own quickly, sliding his black queen toward my mom's white king for checkmate. He knocks her piece over with a little too much gusto, sending it spinning off the side of the board toward the wooden floor.

A pale white hand with a strange green hue catches it before it hits the ground.

"Absynth found others like us, others who told her how to harness her full potential. But even in the company of other fairies, she was lonely. She missed her family, and we, especially your mother, missed her, too."

My mom leaps out of her chair, almost knocking her sister over with the enthusiasm of her embrace. As they hug, I recognize Absynth's fairy form, hiding just beneath the human disguise she wears. After a few heartbeats, they break apart, and she turns to address my grandfather. As the vision-Absynth speaks silently, the real Gramps fills in her words.

"She had returned with a proposition. She said she wanted the Fairy King to live again, flanked by his two daughters, but really I think she just wanted to have her family back. Of course, I had already made my choice and told her as much."

Absynth's smile fades just a bit as she receives Gramps's no, but she quickly replaces it as she redirects her attention to my mother. I see her mouth the word "please," and I wonder if the desperation is as apparent in her voice as it is on her face. My mom reaches out to stroke Absynth's cheek, her fingers running gently across the bumps along her jawline, before shaking her head.

"I do not think she ever expected me to say yes, but when Annabell rejected her, well, it hurt Absynth more deeply than she wanted to admit."

Absynth transforms from mortal to monster in the span of a second, her thorns raised and teeth bared at her sister. But when I look into her eyes, I see the moisture threatening to spill over. My mother is crying, too, as she pleads, her arms outstretched toward Absynth, but it is no use. With a final *hiss*, Absynth unfurls her wings and flies off into the bloodred sunset.

"Things were quiet again until she showed up for you," Gramps continues sadly.

This time there is no need for his memories to swirl into motion in the water before me. I remember that incident all too well, having relived it almost every night for the last ten years. Who would have known then that I would one day become the thing I feared, and do so willingly, with the encouragement of the very monster who pulled me screaming into the woods.

"Your mother heard your yell, and when she saw your empty bed and open window, she feared the worst. By the time she caught up to Absynth, you'd been knocked unconscious. She begged her sister to let you go, tried to reason with her that she didn't know how to raise a human child. None of it worked. So your mother promised Absynth the one thing she wanted more than anything else in the world: herself.

"Annabell knew, of course, that even if she gave herself over to Absynth, you would still be in danger. That night, she called me from the hospital. She wanted to know how to destroy her sister. I told her to wait. Told her that she was no match for a fairy at the peak of her strength. I offered to do it for her, but she refused. She didn't want me to become a monster again."

Gramps pauses to sigh, and when he continues, his voice is heavy with grief.

"So I explained to her how to take a fairy's life, how to take her sister's life, and that was it. That was the last time I ever spoke to my Annabell."

The weight of this revelation is almost too much for me to bear: that my mother gave up her life to protect me from Absynth, and yet here I sit, a physical incarnation of everything she didn't want me to become.

I have wasted her sacrifice.

"Why didn't you tell me all of this?" I ask Gran, wanting to deflect the blame onto someone else.

"I tried to, Amethyst," she says, fresh tears streaming down her face. "I tried to see if you were manifesting. That's why I brought you here. I thought I could keep you safe, that I would know if Absynth came back, but ... "

Her voice breaks, and my grandfather picks up where she left off.

"But we've failed you, Amethyst," he continues, moisture further clouding his already milky eyes. "We failed you like we failed your mother. Absynth is very, very powerful ... "

I hear the defeat in his voice, and it triggers a surge of anger in me. He may be ready to surrender to Absynth, but I am not. Call it penance or vengeance, but I will use these abilities I have been cursed with to take her down once and for all or die trying, like my mother.

"Strong, but not invincible," I say, my voice steady and my mind calm for the first time in days. "You said she could be destroyed. I want to know how."

My grandfather turns his blind eyes toward me, and although their depths are obscured by a white film, I think I see a spark of something, a mixture of longing and sadness flashing in them at my words. Next to him, Gran's own eyes are squeezed tight, her lips a thin white line. This is not the ending they wanted for me or for Absynth, and for the briefest of seconds, I feel my resolve waver in response to their pain.

But then I remember my mother's smile and Ben's laughter, and I think that some things are simply unforgivable, some people irredeemable. It is a group in which I count both Absynth and myself as members.

"Please," I ask, placing my hand on his shoulder. It has the same texture as old leather, rough and cracked. "This needs to end."

I wait, watching the struggle play across his strange weathered face, until finally he sighs heavily in resignation.

"The key is the lights," Gramps says. "They are what give us our strength."

"Like our own little power plants," I say, thinking of how much heat and light Ben's single orb alone generates.

"No, not quite," he counters, before pausing briefly to consider the analogy. "They are more like batteries. They drain over time, and eventually they burn out altogether."

He makes a summoning gesture with his hand, and a tiny fairy light emerges slowly from its resting spot inside one of the red roses. Unlike Ben or any of Absynth's hundred lights, my grandfather's orb is a dull yellow, giving it the appearance of a dying lightbulb as it struggles to stay afloat in the space between us.

"This," he says, providing the light a resting place on the tip of one of his long fingers, "is why I've grown so weak, so inhuman. Out of my hundreds of lights, only this one remains. When it goes, I will go with it. That is how it is for all of our kind who remain in this world."

Absynth never explained this caveat to our immortality, nor the limitations of Ben's transformation. But then again, maybe she doesn't know, hasn't been a fairy long enough to watch her lights fade, one by one, into oblivion. Not that it matters, as long as she continues to make new lights to replace those she loses.

"There has to be another way," I say, unable to picture Absynth ever acquiescing to the path my grandfather has chosen. "I can't wait for her to suddenly develop a conscience."

Gramps wrinkles his already crinkled brow.

"There is only one other way I know of to destroy them," he says, shaking his head as he continues, "but I do not think it will work in this situation."

"What is it?" I ask, unwilling to give up so easily. "I'll do anything. Whatever it takes."

"You drown them," he says simply before adding, "completely submerge them underwater until they fizzle out."

"That doesn't sound too hard," I say, thinking how easy it would be to sneak away with one or two of Absynth's lights at a time, but Gramps is already shaking his head.

"In theory, yes, but each light lost physically changes a fairy." He inclines his head at his decaying stump of a body. "If you siphon them off a few at a time, Absynth will know."

"Oh," I say, realization of the enormity of the task rendering me momentarily speechless. How can I possibly hope to capture all of the lights at one time when I have never known them to be left unattended?

"Yes," Gramps agrees, weariness returning to his voice. "You understand the difficulty."

Difficulty is an understatement. Absynth alone with her hundreds of lights would be difficult, but she is not alone. She has Daphne and Naya, and their presence makes my task virtually impossible. If only I had come through my Changing with some kind of ability that could give me an edge—like Daphne and her poison.

Poison, I think. The memory of our first encounter, the one where she nearly killed me with her toxic thorns, suddenly comes rushing back to me. Daphne had explained then that she hadn't realized her own ability until she accidentally pricked herself. It had been enough to paralyze her, just for a few minutes.

And a few minutes is all I need.

"How quickly can you teach me to make plants grow?" I ask, the first traces of a plan taking shape in my mind.

It takes nearly three hours for me to generate my first scrawny seedling, which only sprouts for a few seconds before shriveling back into the soil.

"Come on!" I growl, kicking the ground and sending a clump of dirt flying into the wall.

"That was good," Gran says, but I can hear the false praise in her words, and I growl again, only wordlessly this time.

"I told you it would be more difficult this way," Gramps reminds me. "And frustration will only make it harder."

He's right. The anger fills my mind with a red fog, obscuring the image I'm trying to concentrate on so that I can will it into existence. It would be easier if I could actually touch the plant, feel the life inside it, instead of working from a tiny picture from one of Gran's old books. But still, a picture is better than nothing, so I squeeze my eyes shut and take a deep breath, silently cursing the townspeople of Morgan Springs for choosing to grow tomatoes and green beans in place of the belladonna I am so desperately trying to create.

I start with the roots, thick and brown, picturing them clearly as I move up to the stem, allowing each light-green offshoot to develop into its own branch. Leaves come next, darker than the stems, with a glossy sheen indicative of the poison within. Finally, I imagine the flowers, tiny purple bells, that wither away to reveal round black berries.

"*Oh*." Gran gasps, and I know I've done it. I can *feel* the new life in the room. The flowers of the belladonna may allow it to blend in with the other blooms in the greenhouse, but my fairy senses immediately note its more sinister presence. It knows it's dangerous and is more than willing to assist me.

The sky is just beginning to lighten, showing the faintest hint of purple at the line of the horizon, when Gran walks me to the front door of the greenhouses. She places a soft hand on my cheek; it reminds me of the way my mother once touched me a lifetime ago.

"You don't have to do this," she says, her voice almost pleading. The way her eyes search my face, like she's trying to commit it to memory, makes me think she has guessed at what I've left unsaid about my plan: no matter the outcome, I will not be returning.

"Gran, I ... " But I'm not sure how to finish my sentence, how to put all of the emotions swirling in my heart into words. So instead I wrap my arms around her, hoping this conveys at least some of the love and gratitude that I have for her.

We hold each other for a few silent moments, and when we break apart, there are tears in both of our eyes.

"Tell Dad ... " I hesitate again, trying to think of some last thing I want my father to know and coming up empty. "Tell him something he'll believe."

"I will," Gran says, and I know this is one thing I won't have to worry about. Whatever she tells him, it will be gentle enough for him to move on.

"And ... " My voice cracks, and I have to swallow back the guilt boiling in my throat. "Take care of Ben's mom."

This time, Gran just nods, not because I am asking too much of her but because she would have done this anyway.

"Be careful," she says, clearing the emotion from her own throat before continuing. "And remember, even though Absynth has quantity on her side, her lights were created without love."

I give her one last hug before I turn to face my future: the dark woods and Absynth beyond.

The forest is silent, unnaturally so, and I wonder if my aunt is suppressing its usual sounds to better listen for my approach. Not that it matters if she hears my footfalls crunching over the leaf-covered ground.

I want her to know I'm coming.

It's the other silence that bothers me, the one in my mind, the one where my connection to Ben's consciousness used to be. That he would no longer want me privy to his feelings in the wake of what I've done is more than warranted and, if I'm honest, not half as much punishment as I deserve for what I've done.

I can't keep myself from missing him, though, selfish as it may be.

The quiet gives me time to think, to try to flesh out the plan that is still only half-formed in my mind. The first part, getting back into the hollow, is almost fully developed. If I appeal to Absynth's loneliness, to her desire for family, I think she will welcome me back with open arms. The only details I'm lacking there are the exact words I will say to convince her, but they should be easy enough to improv when the time comes.

The second part, the delivery of the poison, is what's giving me trouble. I suppose I'll have to wait until they get hungry and implement some kind of distraction that will allow me to slip the poison unnoticed into their meal. There's a whole host of problems with this idea, though, and the closer I get to the fairy hollow, the more I doubt it will work.

I might have to improvise that, too.

The third part, where I escape from the hollow with a hundred fairy lights contained in an old mayonnaise jar Gran found in one of the storage closets, is the only one I'm one hundred percent sure on. If I make it that far, all I have to do is fly like hell to the closest water deep enough to drown them: the reflecting pool at the heart of the Gardens.

And after that …

I shake my head to clear the thought away. I can't allow anything to distract me, not now, when I can sense three magical hearts beating just ahead.

This means, of course, that they can sense me, too. I pause just long enough to conceal my jar at the base of a tree, not wanting to have to fabricate a reason for its presence, before closing the distance to the place where the vines conceal the fairies' hollow.

Before I can take more than a few steps toward where the fairies wait, the vines untwist and Absynth steps out, flanked on either side by Daphne and Naya. Her face is unreadable, a mask of indifference, as she closes the distance between us, but behind her, the other two fairies wear expressions of fear.

I wonder what Absynth told them about me.

"Where have you been, Amethyst?" It's an accusation more than a question. I'm sure at the very least she knows I've seen Gran, so it would be pointless to lie. Plus, I need her to trust me, at least for a little while longer.

"I went to see Gran," I say, watching her face carefully, but there is no change, which I take to mean I was right about her knowing. Time to pull out the big guns. "Then she took me to visit Gramps."

Absynth's composure cracks at this, just as I hoped it would. The news of my grandfather being alive is obviously a surprise to her, and hopefully, it's information that I can use to convince her of my intentions for returning.

"What do you mean?" She seems to have to force the words out.

"He's alive, Absynth," I say, watching her reaction carefully as it shifts from confusion to resentment or maybe revulsion.

It's the response I was hoping for.

"And how is *dear old Dad?*" she asks, and although her voice is dripping with sarcasm, I can see her desire for the answer burning in her eyes.

This, too, is good, I think, as I allow the memory of my grandfather's dying body, along with the real sadness and fear that accompany the image, to fill my mind until I feel the tears begin to prick at the corners of my eyes. When I speak, my voice is thick and shaking, the authenticity of my emotions unquestionable.

"Terrible," I say, blinking so that the tears spill down my cheeks. "I don't even know if what he is counts as alive. He's not a fairy … not even *human* anymore."

I throw my hands in front of my face so that Absynth can't see that my tears have already stopped flowing. I hope that they muffle my speech enough so that it still sounds thick and frightened.

"He told me exactly what you said, that there's no going back to human and that I should become like him!" I bite down on my lip until my eyes well with fresh tears so that, when I remove my hands, the pain on my face is real. "And I just *can't.*"

In a stroke of inspiration, I fall to my knees, gripping the ivy hem of Absynth's skirt.

"*Please,*" I say, bowing my head before her so that my tears drip down onto her bare feet. "I'll do whatever you want, Absynth, *anything.* Please just don't let me turn into *that.*"

Silence presses in on me again as I wait for Absynth's response. If she didn't buy my performance, then I may very well be awaiting my execution. My heart hammers against my ribs like a caged bird struggling for freedom. Perhaps it knows something I do not, can sense the end drawing near.

Then Absynth's arms are around my neck, and I stiffen, waiting for the snap that will end my life.

But it doesn't come.

Instead, she draws me into an embrace, and for the second time tonight, I am reminded of my mother.

"Oh, Amethyst," she says, pulling away after a few moments. Her eyes are moist, and her smile is genuine. "Welcome home, my niece. Welcome home, my sister."

The rest of my plan starts to come together as soon as I enter the hollow behind Absynth and see a fresh batch of fairy wine undulating slowly in midair. The golden liquid could be the perfect vessel for the belladonna, as long as I can give the others a reason to drink it, and what is more effective at compelling people to imbibe than a celebratory toast?

A thrill of fear runs through me as I realize that if my actions are quick and convincing, I could end this all tonight.

As soon as the vines close behind me, I lean back against them and allow myself to slide slowly down to the ground in exhaustion. I leave a small space between my lower back and the natural wall, just enough room to conceal the fresh growth of nightshade I coax from the soil.

"Amethyst?" Absynth's gaze is on me, her eyes narrowed in concern. "Are you all right?"

"Yeah," I say, allowing my very real fatigue to lend authenticity to my words. "It's been a long day."

Behind me, I can sense the first berries beginning to form on the plant. I raise my right hand to rest on my brow, remembering some half-forgotten TV special about how magicians use misdirection to do their tricks. I watch with satisfaction as three sets of eyes follow its progress while my left hand works at freeing a half dozen berries.

I don't dare wait for more to grow, too afraid that Absynth will sense the plant even through the cacophony of life in the forest. So when I push myself to my feet a few seconds later, all that remains of the belladonna is a withered pile of debris, indistinguishable from the rest of the forest floor.

"How do I get more?" I ask as I cross the hollow to stand beside the fairy wine.

"More?" Absynth asks, her head cocked to one side in confusion.

"Lights," I say, gesturing up to the canopy where the majority of the orbs dance against the now lavender sky.

The question does what I mean it to, and as Absynth, Daphne, and Naya follow the direction indicated by my right hand, I squeeze the berries in my left before shoving them through the thin membrane surrounding the fairy wine. The liquid within is hotter than I expect, and I gasp involuntarily at the pain that suddenly engulfs my fingers.

Thankfully, Absynth begins answering my question just as the sound escapes, and it goes unnoticed.

"The same way you made your first," she says, her hand waving to the spot where Ben's light hovers beside my right shoulder. "The incantation, the kiss, and of course, a little bit of fairy wine."

The last part catches me off guard because up until this point, I thought that part was optional, just an addition to make the seduction of our victims that much easier. If she's telling the truth, and I have no reason to think she is lying to me now, then it really was my selfishness that condemned Ben.

The decision to drink the wine had been mine and mine alone.

Nausea washes over me, and I have to fight to maintain my composure in its wake. There is nothing I can do to bring Ben back, and if I allow my guilt to give me away now, then I lose my one opportunity to avenge him. I swallow hard, the bile burning its way back down my throat, now thankful that Ben's mind has become silent. At least I don't have to feel his grief on top of my own.

"I don't want to wait," I say, hoping that the smile I've forced onto my face is convincing. "I want more."

Absynth's returning smile is radiant, so full of joy that it almost makes me feel bad about what I plan to do. Then I remember that her happiness is based on my feigned desire to rob more humans of their lives, and that feeling passes quickly.

"Of course you do," she says, pulling a hollow gourd from her side and magicking some of the fairy wine into it. I hold my breath as I realize that its color is darker, more amber than gold, but Absynth doesn't seem to be paying attention to it.

She is still grinning at me.

Absynth passes me the gourd, and I raise it to my lips, pressing them tight against the wine as I pretend to drink. Even the liquid just touching my lips leaves them with a strange tingling feeling, and I have to spend precious mental energy holding my tongue back from licking them.

Frantically, I worry that the poison may be too fast acting, but there is nothing to be done about it now since Daphne is already raising the gourd to her mouth. She drinks quickly, passing it to Naya, who does the same before giving it to Absynth.

My aunt pauses, holding the gourd up in the air in salute to me. My heart hammers in my chest as Daphne's eyes go wide, her mouth opening in a silent scream of warning.

"To your new life," Absynth says, inclining her head to me just as white foam begins to bubble out of the corner of Naya's mouth.

"To my new life," I echo, cold sweat dripping down the back of my neck as Absynth brings the gourd to her smiling lips.

She swallows just as Daphne's limp body hits the ground.

"What is this?" Absynth shouts, rounding on me as Naya falls next to Daphne, both of them twitching slightly, their eyes staring unblinkingly up at the canopy. "What's—"

Her question cuts off in a wet gurgle, the gourd cracking against the ground as it drops from her limp hand.

I take that as my signal and magically peel the vine wall apart with a single jerk of my head. It takes less than a second for me to retrieve the empty glass jar and return to the hollow, but even that was enough time for Daphne's tremors to begin to slow.

I place the jar on the ground and shift my focus up to where the lights dance in the tops of the trees. Absynth had once used the wind to trap Ben's light in a swirling vortex between us, and I think I can apply the same theory here, albeit on a larger scale. Using my best imitation of what my aunt did, I spin my index finger in a circle and wait.

Nothing happens.

Below me, Naya stops twitching, and her eyes roll to look at me.

There is fury in her gaze.

I close my eyes against her anger, focusing all my attention on the air around me. Unlike the plants and animals in the forest that each have their distinct feel, the air is different. It's a single web made up of a million invisible fibers that I can tighten or loosen according to my desire, like a giant net surrounding the earth.

I mentally gather the disparate strands that encompass the hollow and pull them taut. The tension seems to hum in the air, and now when I move my finger, I can feel it twisting the invisible strings of wind. It takes just seconds for the breeze to form a funnel of air that swirls from the tops of the trees down into the jar at my feet.

Once the lights begin to swirl down the vortex, it takes less than a minute for it to deliver all of them into the jar, where I trap them by twisting the metal lid into place. They buzz like angry bees inside the glass, slamming themselves against the jar in what I hope are futile attempts at escape.

I turn back to where Absynth lies on the ground. Although her body is paralyzed, her eyes are alert, and I don't have to guess at the emotion behind their red glare.

I am certain it is murderous.

"You are a monster," I say to her, my voice calm even as adrenaline surges through me. "And I will never, *ever* be like you."

Then I bend to pick up my jar before unfolding my wings and launching myself up and out of a hole in the trees above.

As I soar through the pale-pink sky, the breeze cool on my face and the miles of dense forest stretching out below me, I can't help but think about how, in another life, I would have enjoyed this. But that life can never be, not so long as my magic, my very existence, is conditional on the sacrifice of others.

It takes only a few minutes of silent flight for me to reach the Gardens, during which I sense no heartbeats following me. From my vantage point above, I can see the beautiful symmetry of the interplay between the multihued garden beds, gray stone paths, and deep-green hedges. Again, I think how beautiful this would be to me if I could share it with Ben, the real Ben, not this silent orb bobbing in my wake. He would have enjoyed this view, though it probably would have just made more work for me once he started envisioning ways we could improve upon the original design.

I land softly at the heart of the Gardens. The area is still decorated with the dozens of strands of Christmas lights Ben painstakingly hung for me. The gray light of dawn reduces them to dull echoes of their former allure, the sunlight making them look sad and pale in comparison.

But that is the way it is for all magic. What is enchanting and unbelievable in the flattering embrace of darkness can never survive long in the bright light of day.

I kneel in the soft grass next to the pool. Its glassy surface is still in shadow so that the gray water obscures the bottom. I could almost believe that it stretches deep into another world the way Ben said it did one night a lifetime ago.

My heart pounds as I lower the jar into the water, the ripples causing its light to refract in a thousand directions. The lights must sense what is to come, because they beat against the container with renewed agitation, their buzzing so frantic that it vibrates from my palms all the way up to my elbows.

I want to tell them not to be afraid, but I can't say that with any certainty. I do not know where they will go once I dismiss them from this place, whether I am taking away this strange existence only to send them into black nothingness. How can I, their executioner, hope to offer them any measure of comfort?

The cowardly part of me seizes control, and I close my eyes as I delicately twist the lid just enough to allow water to begin to flow into the jar. The vibrating grows stronger as the water flows in, and I imagine the lights scrambling away in terror from the invading force only to run again and again into the glass bottom of the jar.

I squeeze my eyes shut even tighter, trying not to imagine the faces of the hundred people I have sentenced to death for being victims of my aunt and her so-called sisters. I hope, for their sake, that there is a life after this one, so that they may experience some measure of the happiness that has been stolen from them.

Hot tears slide down my cheeks as the shaking slows, the jar growing heavy with water until, after what seems like an eternity, it stops completely.

I am so sorry, I think, though what good it does I do not know.

I open my eyes to make sure my work is complete, and for a moment tears obscure my vision so that I am only able to make out that the gray water below me is once again dark and opaque.

I use the back of my hand to wipe my tears away, and when the pool comes back into sharp focus, my breath catches in my throat as fear clutches my heart painfully.

Absynth's reflection glares back at me, wild and angrier than I have ever seen.

I barely have time for the shock to register before a thick green vine erupts out of the soil and wraps around my neck, cutting off the scream building in my throat. My hands fly up, trying to tear at the strangling plant, all thought of using magic gone in my desperate desire just to breathe again.

"Oh, Amethyst," Absynth says, her eyes sparkling maliciously, though her voice is sweet if slightly chiding. "You have *no* idea how *monstrous* I can be."

Black webs reach into my vision as I struggle against the choking pressure of the vines, and I search the sky around me for Ben's light, wanting to see it, see him, just one more time before I die. Then I remember that I can't die, at least not from suffocation, and I'm thankful that Ben seems to have had the good sense to conceal himself from Absynth's rage.

Just as I can feel myself succumbing to the darkness, there's a sound like the sharp crack of a whip, and suddenly the vines are gone, only to be replaced with the new realization that I am traveling, much too fast, through the air.

Before I can even attempt to right myself, I collide with one of the marble statues, taking off the wings of a cherub before crumpling to the ground at its base.

I gasp for breath, still trying to recover from the strangulation as a new set of pains radiates through my body. Their epicenter, however, seems to be the spot at the back of my head that made contact with the hard stone of the statue. When I touch it, my hand comes back streaked with red-and-green blood.

The ringing in my ears seems to echo the alarms sounding in my brain as I struggle to understand how Absynth is still alive, crossing the distance between us with quick steps, no sign of damage or decay on her terrible, beautiful face.

Something has gone wrong, I think as she summons a grove of rosebushes to sprout up around me, their thorny stems digging into my skin as they form a living cage.

"How could you?" she growls as the thorns begin to pierce the thin skin around my wrists and neck, my blood blooming in crimson unison with the roses. "I gave you *everything!* Acceptance, a home, a family, and *this* is how you repay my kindness?"

Her accusation cuts through the fear and pain, activating the part of my brain fueled by rage as images of her "kindness" flash through my mind's eye: a clawed hand on my young wrist, the last warm hug I received from my mother, the look of terror on Ben's face as she tortured him here, in our garden. It's that last one that combusts, setting a metaphorical fire in my chest that burns to the very tips of my fingers before leaping out into very real tongues of flame that reduce the bushes surrounding me to ash.

For a moment, I think I see a flash of fear cross Absynth's face, but it is replaced quickly by the bared teeth and set jaw of savage determination.

This is not a fight I can win, I realize as I see the flat red eyes of my aunt boring into me. I need to get out of here, to consult my grandfather. There must have been something I missed, or some magic she's learned of that can sustain her even after the loss of her lights.

I pick up one of the broken pieces of marble and throw it with all my strength at Absynth. It catches her on the left cheek, slicing a deep gash across her face. In the split second after its impact, while Absynth is still reeling in shock, I allow my skin to drink in the atmosphere around me, the greens and grays of the garden giving way to the pinks and blues of the sky as I make my escape by air.

"NO!" Absynth's cry is more of a roar, and with it comes a downdraft so strong that it sends me careening back down to the garden. I divert my body away from the concrete path at the last moment, pushing sideways so that I land in the reflecting pool instead. The two feet of water does little to slow me, and I hit the stone bottom face-first, hard enough to knock the air from my lungs.

I resurface, gasping for air as I scramble to get to my feet, but Absynth is already here. Her claws rake across my scalp as she grabs my hair, and her voice is a mixture of grief and rage.

"How does it feel?" she screams before forcing my head down below the water. My lungs react just a half second too slowly, allowing cold water to flood into my chest. I try to reach her hands, to loosen their grip on my hair, but Absynth slams my head against the rocky bottom before pulling me out again. "How does it feel to *drown*?"

I choke down as much air as I can, not sure how long I'll have to fill my lungs before she pushes me under again. In the reflection of the pool, I can see that her eyes are wet, the tears mingling with the blood as they run in pink rivers down her face.

"You're just like your mother!" she says, glaring down at my reflection, one of the pink drops hanging from the tip of her white nose. "She couldn't be trusted, either!"

The drop of blood and tears falls then, landing in the water before us. Its ripples obscure our images as a new picture begins to form.

As the water calms, I see my mother's face looking out at me.

The vantage point is strange, thick lines of color framing the top and bottom of my mother's face as she speaks on a cream-colored telephone. Then she moves, and I can see behind her to the hospital bed where I lie, six years old and unconscious, a large white bandage wrapped around my head.

We are looking through the shades of a window, I realize, watching my mom's last phone call with my grandfather, the phone call where she asked him how to kill Absynth. She speaks for only a few more seconds before she places the receiver back on the hook, her face twisted as she bends down to kiss my forehead lightly and whisper a goodbye I never heard.

A second drop falls, and when the scene resets, I see my mother once again, this time standing alone in the forest. She shuffles nervously from foot to foot, her hands twisting the hem of her shirt until it is stretched permanently out of shape. Our vantage point moves closer as Absynth draws nearer, and my mom gives a small smile of recognition.

Its falseness is apparent even through this silent memory.

She says something that I can't hear and waits for a response. Although I don't know what Absynth says, I can imagine it is sufficiently horrible, because my mother's face goes white, her eyes reflecting Absynth's monstrous face.

She takes a step backward, her body just beginning to make the turn that will allow her to run, but it's not enough. Absynth is too quick, and at the moment my mother turns her eyes toward the path that will lead her out of the forest, Absynth is in motion, pinning her to the ground. My mother's eyes fill with tears as she pleads silently for her life, but it will do her no good; I know how this story ends.

I want to look away, to shield my eyes from my mother's death, but some deep part of me needs to see it, if only to confirm, once and for all, that she is gone.

My mother doesn't stop her stream of pleas as I wait for the end, for the clawed hands to wrap around her throat or a vine to ensnare her and pull her deep below the earth, but it doesn't come. Instead, I watch my mother's face grow larger, as if Absynth's own is bending close, my eyes looking into hers. And then a bright-white light shines out from the memory, temporarily blinding me in its brilliance.

When the spots finally fade from my eyes, the scene is gone, and I'm once again staring at myself in the reflecting pool. Absynth looms behind me, bent over my shoulder to get a better view of the memories. One of the leather necklaces she wears has slipped out, and its charm hangs just beside my cheek.

It's a small glass bottle containing a single fairy light.

"Yes," Absynth says in an odd, detached voice as her hand travels up to hold the bottle. "I like to keep my sister close to my heart."

"No!" I say, reaching for the light that is my mother, but my hand stops just short of the vial as the water soaking every part of my body crystallizes into hard, unyielding ice.

My teeth begin to chatter as I strain against my frozen bonds, my immobile fingers only centimeters from the light. Tears turn to ice as soon as they spill over onto my cheeks, because this struggle is no longer only about destroying Absynth. This is now about freeing my mother from this existence she's been doomed to live, to spare her from a slow death as Absynth drains the life from her.

"Perhaps I'll keep you there as well," Absynth muses in that same detached voice, and a chill that has nothing to do with the ice encasing my body runs through me. "*Mors tua, vita mea.*"

Suddenly I feel a nudge of something in my mind, a fierce and protective kind of love that runs like a low current through my body.

Ben? I think, but there is no reply except for another surge of his love, this one more powerful than the last, a lightning strike of energy that begins to crack the ice around me. *Almost,* I urge, straining against the weakening ice as Absynth bends low, her lips drawing closer to mine with every beat of my heart.

A final blast of energy from Ben is all I need to break free, my hand grasping the bottle with my mother's light just as I feel Absynth's breath brush against my face. She gasps as I rip the necklace from her neck and slam it against the stone bottom of the pool.

I feel the crunch as the glass cracks in my fist, and although I know that Absynth may kiss me yet, I want to be certain that my mother will be free of her. So instead of using my last heartbeat to fight or flee, I throw the broken vial containing my mother to the other end of the pool and watch it bob once before sinking out of sight.

"Annabell!" Absynth's voice is high-pitched and frantic as she throws me aside, her wings already carrying her away. She does not slow as she approaches the place where my mother's light disappeared and plunges headfirst into the shallow pool.

She does not resurface.

I push myself up to my feet and cautiously slog slowly toward the spot Absynth went under, wary of another of her tricks. Aside from the single broken bottle, there is no sign of her or my mother.

I am once again alone.

Not alone.

The thought isn't mine, though it radiates from inside my mind.

Ben's light floats gently toward me, no longer the dazzling white of a sun, but a dim yellow orange. The very same shade as my grandfather's dying light.

"Oh," I say, holding my hand out to allow him a place to land. My skin is already brown and papery. "Oh, no, Ben."

That love, that protective strength, was him sending his energy to me so that I wouldn't become one of Absynth's prisoners. But it was more than that—he must have burned like a supernova to help me overpower her, and it has cost him almost all of whatever small life he had.

"I'm sorry," I whisper to his light. The words feel empty, even though I mean them with all of my heart. I wouldn't need to apologize at all if I had just left him alone.

Ben's weary thoughts chastise me weakly. He doesn't regret our time together, not even now as he lies dying in the palm of my hand.

And when he goes, so will I.

It should scare me, death, but the knowledge that it is a journey Ben and I will take together makes me brave.

"I love you," I say, cupping his dim orb to my chest to feel the warmth of his embrace one last time.

Love, he echoes as I lie back, allowing the cool water to overtake us both.

The water is black and deep, a crushing mass of darkness that pushes me down past where I think the bottom of the pool should be. I hold Ben's fading light tight against my chest as we sink, its flickering heat the only warmth in the ever-deepening chill of the water.

And soon he, too, will be gone, and I will be left alone to drift in this darkness until the icy fingers of death drag me down into whatever lies beyond this place.

I hope wherever Ben goes is filled with sunshine and long summer days that end with a hundred million stars strewn across an indigo sky. I hope he finds his dad and my mom, and I hope that he spends the rest of eternity surrounded by love and light and everything he should have had here in this life. I hope he has everything that I took away from him.

There is a weak nudge in my mind as Ben's thoughts intrude into my own. As ever, there are no words, just a feeling of tender concern wrapped around a note of contradiction—Ben's way of saying that it wasn't my fault.

I shake my head, even though there is no one in this cold, dark place to see it. I may have been duped by Absynth, may have been tricked into believing that I could have everything with no consequence, but in the end, it was my choice—and I chose myself over everything and everyone else.

And down, down, down I go.

I don't remember the last time I drew a breath, but my brain must be dying, because I can see the ghost of my mother fly by me in the darkness, a being of white light that burns my retinas. She turns when she sees me, her arms outstretched, longing in her eyes so intense that it causes me physical pain. I think I hear her say my name, but then she is gone, and the world is dark again.

She is dead because of me, too, another casualty of my existence. She hoped that I was like her, brave and selfless, but now, at the end of things, I know she was wrong. I am a creature of fear and brokenness and have far more in common with Absynth than the woman who chose death to give me life.

The remorse, like the darkness, closes in around me. My mind searching desperately for any form of contrition that could give me even the faintest glimmer of a hope for absolution. I feel death's cold fingers around my heart, and I know this is the end. With my last thought, I make a final request to whatever powers control life and death. It is the opposite of the incantation that Absynth and my grandfather had spoken to a countless number of mortals before me. The only apology I can make to Ben in this moment.

My life for his.

The sudden flash of light is accompanied by a searing pain that tears through me, as if every nerve, every cell in my body is being simultaneously pulled apart. I would scream if there were any air in my lungs, any air at all, but in its absence, all I can do is open my mouth in wordless agony as my body is torn apart.

Then, just as suddenly as it appeared, the light is gone, though the blackness does not return, and I find myself surrounded instead by a thick gray mist. This new place feels strange, neither here nor there. Like an in-between.

I wonder fleetingly if this is purgatory, and then I hear a sound that tells me it is not, because how could Ben wind up anywhere but Heaven?

"Amethyst?" His voice is not in my head. It is real, and it is close.

"Ben!" I shout back, turning in the direction of his voice.

Then I see him, whole and human, his arms outstretched to me, the water of the pool rippling above him, giving the sky beyond a strange painted feeling.

He is moving farther away, or maybe I am, because as hard as I push, he doesn't get any closer.

He mouths a word that looks like my name before the gray mists close between us, icy cold and thick as water.

No, I realize, as my head breaks through the surface, *it* is *water*.

The breeze is cold on my wet face, and the stars above twinkle against the inky black sky, and I take stock of the only two things I am certain of:

Somewhere, Ben is alive.

Elsewhere, I am alone.

Acknowledgements

There are so many people to thank, that I fear these acknowledgements could rival the actual word count of GARDEN. If you've enjoyed Amethyst's story, please stay a little longer to appreciate all of the folks who helped bring her tale to life.

To David, my real-world Ben: thank you for reading passages sent by facebook messenger, for endless words of support, and, possibly most importantly, for seemingly bottomless cups of coffee. I don't know why the universe blessed me with you as a companion, but I am so glad and grateful to be able to travel through this incredible journey with you.

To Mom and Dad, who surrounded me with books from the day I was born. Mom, thank you for showing me how to see the world through a creator's eyes. Dad, thank you for teaching me the value of hard work and perseverance. This book would not have been possible without those invaluable gifts.

To Sharon McKeown, Amy Crannell, John Dreimiller, and Deb Breitenbach, my English teachers: thank you for igniting my mind with stories and my spirit with poetry.

To John Lyde, who trusted me enough to shepherd his idea for a story about good and evil fairies. Amethyst and Absynth were born in his brilliant mind, and I have been lucky enough to have been their foster mother for the better part of seven years. I hope that this book's publication means they will soon be back in your capable care! For readers interested in some amazing filmmaking, check out John's work at: https://www.youtube.com/user/MainstayPro.

To Theresa Morgan, who was my first reader and founding member of the Ben fanclub: thank you for your feedback, your squees of joy, and your friendship.

To Miranda Beuerlein, Katrina Canallatos, and Shelby Hickey-Teaney, my beta readers who read multiple error-riddled drafts: thank you for your time, feedback, and enthusiasm about this story.

To Crystal Watanabe, my first editor: thank you for your laser-focused comments, kind-but-firm critiques, and for not running away screaming when you saw the number of semi-colons and hyphens in my roughest draft. Readers (and writers) interested in learning more about Crystal and how to work with her should visit: https://www.pikkoshouse.com/

To Ashley Sofia, whose music was a continuous presence during my writing, thank you for providing the unofficial soundtrack for life in Morgan Springs. Readers can learn more about Ashley Sofia's music at: http://www.ashleysofia.com

To Stacey Kondla, my amazing agent, and everyone at The Rights Factory: thank you for believing in this story and for finding the right home for both Amethyst and me. Readers can learn more about The Rights Factory at: https://www.therightsfactory.com/

To Georgia McBride, Emily Midkiff, Danielle Doolittle, Shara Zaval, Jackie Dever, and the rest of my Month9Book family: thank you for seeing the potential in Amethyst's story and walking with me through the process of preparing her to meet the world. Readers can find (lots!) more incredible fantasy and science fiction at: https://www.month9books.com/

Shylah Addante

Shylah Addante has an M.S.E. in Literacy Education and enjoys Netflix, crocheting, and just generally being awesome. She lives in Albany, New York, with her husband, David, her daughters, Hazel and Holly, and her dog, Andy.

CONNECT WITH US

Find more books like this at http://www.Month9Books.com

Facebook: www.Facebook.com/Month9Books
Instagram: https://instagram.com/month9books
Twitter: https://twitter.com/Month9Books
Tumblr: http://month9books.tumblr.com/
YouTube: www.youtube.com/user/Month9Books
Georgia McBride Media Group: www.georgiamcbride.com

OTHER MONTH9BOOKS TITLES YOU MIGHT LIKE

THE LADY ALCHEMIST
THE MATRIARCAS
THE BEST WEEK THAT NEVER HAPPENED
THE LOST PRINCESS OF AEVILEN